I0831850

MOTORISHI

BOOK II

THE CHURCH of MOTOR SCIENCE

A NOVEL BY

ROBERT D. GRECO JR & SHAUN M. SHELTON

FIRST EDITION: NOVEMBER 2008

ISBN 978-0-615-26485-1

Graphic design by Robert D. Greco Jr.

Greco Jr, Robert D.
Shelton, Shaun M.
Motorishi / Robert D. Greco Jr. and Shaun M. Shelton. – 1st ed.

1. Religion – Fiction.
2. Ancient wisdom – Fiction.
3. Automobile mechanics – Fiction.

10 9 8 7 6 5 4 3 2 1

DEDICATION

For Dave, who gave us the joke in the first place. May the god of your choice bless you, Dave, wherever you are, and may the Motorishi always smile on you and your ride.

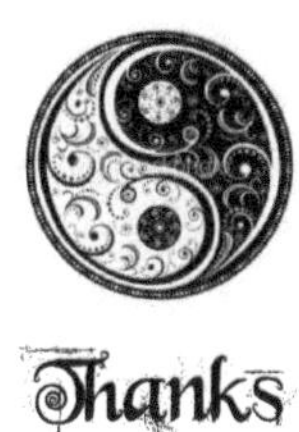

Thanks

Thanks to the family and friends who allowed us the freedom to pursue this dream to its intended conclusion. Thanks to our first draft readers: Nancy Villere, Mary Phillips, Barbara Greco and Bill Lindsey, who gave us invaluable feedback in the early stages of the project. Special thanks to David Jeffries, bass player extraordinaire, who coined the term "Motorishi", and who helped envision the initial concept during many hours of driving to and from band performances in a host of unpredictable cars, vans, and pickups.

Thanks to bandmates Steve, John, Andy, and Tris for putting up with our distraction.

Thanks to Stephen King, Christopher Moore, Woody Allen, Spinal Tap, Tim Burton, Peter Sellers and Monty Python's Flying Circus for their inspiration (although they don't know it, so you can't blame them for anything).

Thanks to the Internet, just for being there in so many ways.

Thanks to the Christians for such a great story to begin with. Thanks to the Sufis, the Zen Buddhists, Confucius, Laozi and especially G. I. Gurdjieff for their unintentional contributions to the philosophy of The Mode. The Mode, or something like it, is out there. Go find it for yourself.

"I guess I want to change the world... Is that a good thing?"

Dewey Pinkerton / The Motorishi.

Prologue

There are only two ways to be a Messiah. The first is to be born one, and the second is to become one. While four of the world's major religions: Buddhism, Christianity, Islam, and Judaism had prophets, two were predicted in their sacred texts, whereas others such as Mohammed and Siddhartha Gautama, the historical Buddha, found their divinity in mid-life.

Nevertheless, either of these methods of becoming a Messiah requires something more than divine birth or divine inspiration alone. They require a unique teaching. That a teaching is unique is to say it is uncommon or rare, not that it is contradictory or different.

While none of the world's great religions can claim to have all the answers to the questions of God's or man's place in the world, in order to become popular and widespread they each have to possess some truth, the original truth, a universal truth. Universal truths are just that, universal, and although different faiths have chosen to preach one piece of truth over another throughout the centuries, the underlying fundamental concepts are surprisingly similar in nature.

Even as the great religions of the world continue to fragment, the separation between scientific and religious ideas is relatively new compared to the amount of time man has spent pondering his existence in the universe.

The re-discovery of such a unifying teaching, a blueprint of the universe in terms that can bring together all aspects of science and religion would be the Holy Grail of universal truth.

Exploring the possibility that both scientific and religious doctrines were once united in an ancient codex identified as "The Mode", four young men, who were known as the "Seekers of Wisdom", left their homes in England and America in the early 1930s and went in search of the esoteric knowledge of ancient civilizations.

While in Abyssinia, they met a man who belonged to an ancient tradition of Gatekeepers. After passing a "wizards" test, the Seekers were shown a map, which would lead them on the trial of sacred hidden libraries, located from the sands of Egypt to islands in the south seas of China. The ultimate goal however was the "Great Library", residing high in the mountains of the Hindu Kush, which housed not only the ancient codex of The Mode, but also other knowledge and antiquities thought to be lost to the world.

Given little time to study the books of the Mode, with no copying of any kind allowed, the Seekers absorbed the texts at a fevered pace. It was while they were there that they received their true calling, becoming the teachers of the next coming Messiah, and were honored with the title, "The Lords of Libra."

However, their biggest adventure was yet to come, as the book of The Mode also predicted the coming of a Messiah.

Spending the next twenty-five years practicing the methods of The Mode and waiting, the Lords were ready when a young man who would come to posses a great understanding of universal mechanics was born.

CHAPTER I

A King is Born

Detroit, Michigan - Saturday, December 24th 1960

It was Christmas Eve and the snow that had been falling for hours drifted silently past the windows trimmed in tiny white lights. A small manger, lit by a single bright star that hung above it, was neatly tucked under a tree dressed in gold and purple. Father put only white lights on the tree that year, even though my sister Stephanie and two brothers, Joshua and Abe Jr. complained incessantly "unless the lights are colored *and* blinked, it didn't feel like Christmas." However, without a soul in the house, this silent night wasn't going to be like any other anyway.

A KING IS BORN

Mother had been in the hospital since noon and the doctors were certain if she were properly dilated by suppertime they could deliver me as early as seven o'clock that night. Father kept my brothers and sister occupied in the waiting room. Because in those days it was not socially acceptable for a man to actually witness the delivery of his own child, let alone participate in any way. Father had his coat pockets filled with Partagas, his favorite Cuban cigars, and was ready to hand them out at a moment's notice to everyone within fifty feet of him should the doctor announce my birth. Anyone who had ever tasted one of Abe Pinkerton's cigars was never more than ten steps away from him, and as the time grew later, the halls became filled with cigar aficionados.

By suppertime my siblings were growing more impatient and just as they were banding together to wish curses on me for ruining their chances of getting to open any presents that night, a nurse showed up with a plate of sugar cookies with sprinkles on top. Sugar, just what every anxious child needs.

I have always wondered why doctors give children candy lollypops after each visit when they know sugar is bad for them. They're doctors for Christ's sakes! Then, that's getting a little ahead of myself. I haven't even been born yet.

That evening seven o'clock came and went and by nine o' clock, my eight-year-old sister had fallen asleep on my father's lap from crying after he promised her a mouth full of soap when they got home for yelling at the doctor, "Why hasn't that little bastard been born yet?" Ah, sugar! By eleven o' clock, my Aunt Mary and Uncle Joseph had taken the kids to their house for the night, so at least *they* could get some sleep.

It was twelve-o-one when the doctor came running from the delivery room. Not because he was excited of course, he had delivered hundreds of babies, but because he wasn't about to have spent the last several hours delivering me and not get at least one if not two of my father's cigars.

Father left the hospital a little after two in the morning. Mother seemed to be resting comfortably and there was nothing more he could do. He pulled out a cigar he managed to save through all the commotion and excitement and lit it up as he drove though the snow and ice covered streets of downtown Detroit. "Happy Birthday, Dewey," he said to himself, while raising his cigar as a toast. "Welcome to *our* world."

The next morning, Father left early to pick up my sister and brothers at my aunt and uncle's house since they were committed to play the three wise men in the children's production of the birth of Christ at ten o'clock services.

When Christmas falls on a Sunday, there is more than the usual amount of religious fanfare. For kids, nothing is more nerve wracking than only getting a few seconds to play with your new toys before you are whisked away to Church, having to sit still with your hands in your lap and your mouth shut tight for over an hour. Of course, they know it's Jesus' Birthday. They just wonder why it always has to happen on Christmas.

Church services ran long and Father rushed to the hospital to see my mother and me. The nurses oooed and aaahed at my sibling's costumes as the three wise men, which had not been taken off yet due to Father being late, and promptly handed them more sugar cookies.

By the time my father entered the room, Mother was already sobbing. It would be another decade or two before they would recognize this condition as "postpartum depression." My father, who had seen it three times before named it, *"The feeling of sadness you get when that which was once on the inside of you is now on the outside."* He was quick to give her a hug and a promise to take her shopping as soon as she felt better.

My brothers, Abe Jr. and Joshua, were still clinging to my father's legs as he reached over and placed a vase of roses on mother's end table. He then hung a gold star ornament around the light above me in an effort to help decorate the room.

"Can we go home now, Daddy?" my sister requested. "My dolls must be very hungry by now."

"Don't you want to see your new little brother?" Mother asked.

"Oh, brother… not another…," Stephanie quipped. She was already not very happy with the male-to-female ratio in the house and this would really tip the scale.

"Well, O.K.," she said reluctantly. Hoping if she just did this quick it would help her get home sooner.

The three of them slowly poked their heads over the top of the bassinet. I could not see very well yet and the light directly overhead made things quite worse by only allowing me to make out the dark blurry outlines of their crowned and cloaked silhouettes.

Father handed each of them a gift he had purchased to give to me and chuckled as he snapped a picture. "I just couldn't resist," he said, "after all… he *was* born on Christmas." He gave Mother a kiss on the cheek. "Now get some rest. I'm going to take the kids home to play with their presents." They arrived home safely with plenty of daylight left to play in the snow on their shiny new sleds in bright colored mittens.

After a few days, Mother and I were brought home from the hospital. My father kept her comfortable with a continuous flow of tissues and liquids, and the occasional TV tray full of assorted sandwiches and snacks. This was long before the remote control and my poor father was up every ten seconds to accommodate her passion as an early adopter of channel surfing. The good news was that we only had three local network channels and two public access channels whose programming was so bad, it scared most of the local community, and no one ever watched anyway.

My first few times around the sun felt pretty much like any other youngest-of-four-children's lives might feel. A handful of kids later, the novelty of having another sibling to share everything with, who slobbers and pulls your hair, had long lost its charm and the only one that would play with me anymore besides my parents, was our family dog, Penny.

Penny was old by the time I was born, and had developed a serious problem controlling her bowels. Mother would put diapers on her too, and for a while, I was convinced I had a twin.

By the time I was four, I was more than two mitts full. Interested in taking apart every thing I could get my hands on, I couldn't get enough of what would later be known as my severely obsessive interest in all things mechanical, whether static, wind-up, or motorized.

Most of the toys in that day were of the static variety and did absolutely nothing on their own, and to make things worse they were made of sharp metal. If you've ever run as fast as you can while pushing a metal fire truck down the sidewalk and accidentally ran over a lizard, tripping on top of it, you know what I mean. One dead lizard and seven stitches later, I learned that even at the tender age of four, speed kills.

One afternoon, Mother was on the phone talking to our next-door neighbor, Helen, about the horror of her favorite television show being cancelled. She was very upset and making the usual commotion about nothing. Helen was known by most of the neighborhood kids as the "crazy lady," because she had one eye that never quite looked straight at you. She was also not very smart and because she hadn't a thought of her own in her head, she was quite content with being a good listener. She seldom disagreed with Mother and often looked up to her, as she too was a slave to these daytime television shows. When it came to the early days of "soaps," no one was more knowledgeable than Mother.

Father had just installed a fifty-foot phone cord in the house, which allowed Mother to move freely between the kitchen, dining room, and family room. He would regret this later as my mother would stay on the phone the whole day now that it reached most of the places she needed to be.

"We can put a capsule into space, and orbit it around the earth, for crying out loud, and we can't make a phone without a cord?" she would always say.

I was sitting on the floor watching her talk, fascinated by the swings in her facial expressions and emotions. When she was done talking, which for her was no small feat, she hung up the phone and set it on the table in the living room, returning to the kitchen to finish making supper before Father came home.

I watched her leave then turned to look at the phone. Standing up, I walked over to it and began to un-screw the mouthpiece. I was intrigued by this device and had to know more about it. It was a classic old pre-Princess phone; square-ish, bright blue, with a handset attached to the body by this new revolutionary "Mother approved" freedom cord.

She was whistling now as she wiped her hands on a towel, and turned back into the front room. Walking through the doorway, she saw me sitting in the center of a debris field made up of bits and pieces of the now disassembled phone. I was almost in a trance state, examining the very last bit that could be removed.

Mother yelped, running into the room shocked. Looking up at her, I realized that what I did was going to have grave consequences.

"Oh, Dewey H. Pinkerton, now look what you've done! That phone will never work again. Wait until your father gets home. You're in big trouble now, little mister!" She turned back to the kitchen, shaking her head and clucking words I had not yet heard, let alone understood later were the swear words all grown-ups use but are insistent their children never so much as even mutter. A timer rang and she ran back to her cooking, saving me, I am sure, from almost certain physical pain and suffering.

After a few minutes, I appeared behind her, "Mommy?" She turned to look at me standing in the doorway with the re-assembled phone in my hand.

"I'm sorry. I fixed it back the way it was," I said, looking down at my feet in shame and holding the phone out to her. She reached for it slowly, her eyes moving between the phone and me. When she picked up the handset and heard a dial tone, her mouth opened in astonishment. She placed the handset back in the cradle and putting the phone on the table, squatted down in front of me.

"That's wonderful, Dewey. I wouldn't have yelled at you if I knew you could fix it." My face brightened. "I'm still going to tell Daddy when he comes home." My face saddened, "But when he hears what you've done, he'll be as proud as I am." My face brightened once more. "Now go wash up for supper."

When my father came home, Mother filled him in on the day's activities; how her favorite soap had been cancelled, how the new phone cord he installed was the best thing ever, next to television of course, what my siblings had done and how I had taken apart and put back together the phone that day. Father was going to the great Detroit auto show for the next week and needed to be to bed early. He tucked in my sister and brothers, then came and kissed me on the forehead, "Get some rest now, Dewey. It seems you've been quite the busy boy."

As I approached eight years old, I had developed quite a hunger for mechanics, something my father was proud of since he had worked for auto manufacturers for many years. I would continue this habit of taking things apart and putting them back together, going from telephones and clocks to bicycles and lawnmowers. My parents no longer worried when I was knee deep in bolts and sprockets, and would even encourage me to be sure to have whatever device I had taken apart back together again before supper.

Working for the auto industry had its rewards, like being able to own the latest car models before anyone else. However, it also had its drawbacks, and part of the penance for working in that industry was manning the company display at the yearly auto convention. Father would be gone all week as he always was during the trade show, and Mother never liked being alone very much. She, of course, was thankful that he wasn't a traveling salesman or enlisted in the army and was glad to some degree that it would only be a week. Besides, this year she promised to take us to see the show.

Even though the show didn't officially start until Monday, Father had to spend the weekend there preparing. Mother would take us on Sunday, a day before it opened, because you couldn't so much as move through the aisles once it was in full swing. One time last year as she was pulling us through the crowds, my sister's hand slipped, and it took us the better part of an hour to find her again. Not to mention, in crowds that thick, perverts of all kinds dwell. Mother swore never to go back during the show again after several men that day had pinched her derrière.

On Sunday morning after church, Mother prepared us to go see Father. As much as I loved him, I was almost out of my skin knowing I was about to see the latest innovations in auto making and could barely contain myself. I sat in my room reading the latest car magazines when I heard the yell from out front.

"Hurry up, Dewey. My God son, you are the dilly-dallyest thing I ever did see," Mother yelled, while slamming the trunk. I quickly put the magazines away and hurried downstairs.

We got in the car and Mother cursed as she sat on her purse. Throwing it aside, she shifted into reverse and backed out of the driveway. Before coming to a complete stop, she shifted into drive and the car made a loud grinding noise as it screeched, smoked, and sputtered down the road.

"You should come to a full stop before changing gears you know," I said.

"I know," she replied, apologetically. "But, I'm in such a hurry. Maybe someday when you're working at the factory, *you* can fix what ever I break."

I sat quiet, staring out the window as we drove. As far as the eye could see, were rows of smoke-belching factories. I looked through the windows of other cars on the road and noticed that none of the drivers looked happy. They all had blank stares on their faces. Some were picking their noses, while others raised their fists, yelling at each other.

"The factory's for losers..." I murmured, under my breath.

Mothers not only have eyes on the back of their heads but ears as well. "You know, your father works very hard at that car factory," she blasted. "He worked his way up from the parts department to the head of east coast sales. He gives us the food on our table and the clothes on your back, little mister. So I won't have you talking bad about him again. Do you hear me, son? Do you hear me?" However, I didn't respond. I was focused on the sound of an irregular tire noise.

The convention was packed with the eccentric styles of the late 1960's, which were in full swing. There were female models dressed in psychedelic plastic clothes and car salesman in the latest large-collar lime green suits preparing their latest car model praises. When we arrived at Fred Motors display there were men in jumpsuits running around, and Father seemed preoccupied, obviously worried about something.

Mother approached him with the usual hug and kiss on the cheek. "Can't talk," he blurted. "We've got a truck full of cars stuck in the loading bay and I'm already a day behind at best. It's not a good time now. Take the kids and get them some popcorn or something. I'll be back as soon as I can get that truck in."

"Can I come?" I squeaked.

"Yes, son. Hurry up though; I'm already in deep..." He paused, realizing my mother was still standing there. This was the first time I realized that both my parents were quite unaware they swore when alone in front of the kids. However, they were always very careful never to do it in front of each other.

"Come on, follow me," he said.

At the loading bays, many huge semi-trucks were unloading the latest car models. "Damn new trucks!" he shouted. The trucking company delivering their cars had just purchased a new fleet, and these giants were six inches too tall to fit through the loading bay doors. A truck had gotten in a full ten feet before lodging under the doors, causing what would certainly become a job-demoting delay.

Men were frantically running around trying to look for a way to disassemble the bay doors, or unload the cars where they were and build a makeshift ramp to get them up to the loading dock. I looked up at the truck, whose top had bent the door slightly as it tried to squeeze through, and then down at the ground. Suddenly it hit me.

"Let some air out of the tires," I said. However, grown-ups tend to filter out all other "interference" when they are busy processing their own ideas. I pulled at my father's coat. He turned towards me briefly with that "not now, Son", look.

"Let some air out of the tires," I repeated.

Suddenly, a light went on and he ran to the tire closest to us, pulled out a pen from his pocket, and bent down to bleed out some air. Calling to the galvanized team of mechanics, they moved to circle the truck and began to let the air out of the other tires.

"Not too much," he warned. "We still want to be able to drive it."

After a few minutes of screeching, it slowly lowered to a passable height. Everyone let out a cheer as the truck was finally able pass through the doors. My father looked at me and smiled a smile that I will remember forever. He didn't need to say anything. The look said it all. He was proud of me and nothing could ever take that away.

As I watched him direct the unloading of the cars, a man standing by me who had been observing the whole drama turned to me and asked, "Is that your father?"

"Sure is," I said, proudly.

The man was a bit younger than my father was and wore a nicely pressed gray suit. "Well he's a pretty smart guy to figure out that tire thing," he said.

"I told him to do it," I replied, pumping up my boney chest.

"Did you, now? That's very interesting. You're a very smart boy!" He gazed up at my father. "A very smart boy." he said, again, almost to himself. He smiled and walked away. I didn't know it yet, but I'd just met Mitch Murphy, the man competing with my father for the same National Sales Manager promotion.

On the way back home, my siblings were engaged in the usual routine of fighting with each other. I did not take part in these exchanges and could never understand the reasoning nor the benefits of endless rounds of "nuh-unh, you are, but what am I?" or "I'm not touching you" as a way to settle any dispute. Not that I didn't have my bad habits. I was just more of a "are we there yet?" kind of kid. Everyone's emotions had reached a fevered pitch when all of a sudden we heard a loud bang and the car swerved almost out of control before being brought to a shuddering stop. "Oh, shit!" exclaimed Mother, "A flat tire."

At any other time, in any other neighborhood, this may have not been such a horrific event. However, it was getting dark and we still had a few miles to go before we were in a place you could even consider getting out of your car safely, let alone a woman in distress with children. My mother looked around and noticed as we all did that there were four or five thugs lurking less than a hundred feet away, who had also noticed that we weren't able to go anywhere, anytime soon.

"I can fix it," I said, still feeling the effects of my super powers over adversity from the earlier truck solution.

"You'll do no such thing! Think, think..." she said, nervously.

"I knew something was wrong. I heard it on the way to the convention. I can fix it. Dad showed me how!" I pleaded.

Before mother could respond, I jumped from the car. I opened the trunk, labored to pull out the spare, which weighed almost as much as I did, and quickly grabbed the tire iron and jack. I had never really changed a flat tire by myself and Father had only let me help once by allowing me to assist in the loosening and holding of the lug nuts. I looked over at the thugs and saw they were starting to move closer. Still feeling powerful, and perhaps as a fear reaction, I swung the tire iron around and around in my hand, something I had learned to do with my sister's baton. A skill my brothers laughed at, but for the moment had the thugs stopped in their tracks. I was just about to do one last fast toss in the air, when I dropped it on the pavement.

The thugs looked at each other; some chuckled while others just smiled. The biggest of the bunch, sporting massive tattoos and a bandana, put his hand up signaling the others to stop. He smiled, and giving me a heads up nod, moved back to the alley. I changed the tire and tightened the nuts as best I could, and leaving the flat by the side of the road, rose to my feet. Spinning the iron from hand to hand again, I did a perfect high toss and catch, opened the door, and jumped in telling Mother to get out of there fast.

She started the car and hit the gas, leaving a half a block of skid marks. My siblings had stopped fighting and were frightened beyond belief. Mother looked at me half-glad and half-mad.

"Don't you ever do that again!" she shouted, but didn't really have an answer for what she would have done if I hadn't.

This was to be a day I felt on par with Superman or Spiderman or Megaman, or any other superhero whose name ended in "man". I would be "D-man," pre-pubescent protector of automotive justice.

CHAPTER II

Learning to Fly

By the time I was sixteen, my room was littered in books and models from the greatest scientists and inventors in the world. The writings and drawings of Leonardo da Vinci and Einstein covered most of the spaces on my desk, walls and ceiling. I had become an avid reader of the great philosophers and poets as well, and over the years had taken more than my fair share of beatings for reciting bits of Plato or Shakespeare on the school playground. I had read everything I could get my hands on, staying up late at night with a flashlight under my covers, riveted like the wings of a plane to the fuselage of a good verse.

I had collected and read the better part of five hundred books and needed a way to organize them. I studied the way a library was laid out, but still wasn't satisfied, even though I share a name with the library's Dewey Decimal system.

Instead, I decided to arrange the books by subject matter according to their level of "vibratory density." Starting first with the sciences, I put subjects whose properties possessed the slowest level of molecular motion, i.e. base metal sciences, such as geology first, then moved upward through biology, chemistry, physics to the fastest vibratory subjects such as philosophy, psychology, and religion.

The arts, I arranged according to motion, starting with the static arts, such as painting, sculpture, and photography, and migrating to the moving arts, such as music, film, and dance. "The Dewey Vibratory System" I mused, while arranging the last of my books; a wonderful collection of Sufi parables in this most sensible order.

I was quite pleased with this arrangement and it wasn't until I read for the first time the fate of the Alexandria library, burned down at the hands of religious zealots that I realized the books themselves were useless and could be lost at any moment. However, knowledge itself could still be passed down in other ways, in other forms from generation to generation through stories, architecture, music, and dance.

That is, of course, as long as people with no understanding of anything at all, did not continue running around in mobs killing the rest of those that still held the keys to the universe. Nevertheless, I couldn't worry about that for now.

In two weeks time I would take my driving test. Father had taken me out to the suburbs many times and had shown me a few tricks for maneuvering in and out of tight parking spaces.

Living in the city gave you more than enough chances to see how accidents were caused and I wanted to be sure that I had mastered the art of avoiding them.

On the morning of my test, Mother drove me down to the local Detroit DMV. I took the written test first and scored high marks, but now it was time for the real test, driving itself. I pulled my mother's 1974 Grand Torino up to the official spot and waited for the instructor to arrive.

Soon a rather large man came into view. He had the back of his hair combed to the front of his head hoping that no one would notice he was missing some. Opening the passenger door, he proceeded to squeeze in.

"Dewey Pinkerton, huh? My name's Mr. Johnson and I'll be testing you today. Please back the car out of the parking space and drive down East Grand for a spell."

I started the car and looked in my rearview mirror, then over my shoulder before engaging it in reverse. I came to a complete stop then shifted into drive and accelerated slowly to the speed limit of forty-five miles per hour. After a short while, he asked me to parallel park. I was able to squeeze into almost any impossible spot, and had left exactly twelve inches in front and twelve inches in back to spare.

We were heading back to the DMV, when all of a sudden, a car tried to pass a bus on a two lane street and came at us with almost no warning at over fifty miles an hour. I jerked the wheel hard, sliding over to the right, then back again, perhaps exchanging just a few molecules with the oncoming car. The car beeped as it swerved past, as if, it was my fault. Mr. Johnson was white in the face and pulled loose the collar of his overstuffed shirt, looking over at me in amazement.

"I don't know how you did that, son. But what I do know, is even I couldn't have saved us from *that* certain death. If there was any doubt in my mind before, it's sure gone now. I don't think we need to question any more of your driving abilities today. In addition, just for the record… I'm gonna see if we can't extend the expiration date of your first license well into the next millennium. Take us home, son."

I was happy that day and while lying in bed at night a silly rhyme popped into my head. "Only the bird that prepares to fly learns the secret of how not to die."

Well, it didn't take long before I wanted to know how to tune up our family car. Before I started, I asked my father for the manual. He said he wasn't even sure if it had one, but I was free to check and see. I did find the manual, in its original case, in the glove box under the maps, and tissues, and band-aids, and gum, and six pairs of winter gloves. It had never been opened, and when I cracked the cover, as if suspended in time, the smell of fresh ink still rose from the paper.

Detroit, being the car capital of the world was loaded with information about cars, so it didn't take long for me to locate the Chilton manual for our Torino from a local dealer. Chilton was considered the mechanic's bible and if ever there was evidence of intelligent design, this was it. Before night had fallen, I had changed the oil and plugs and adjusted the timing belt.

Soon, I was tuning every car on the block. All the bikes, skateboards, toasters, and washing machines I had worked on in the past seemed like child's play now that I had my hands on some of the coolest cars in Detroit. My local reputation grew from a "gifted child" to a "superb mechanic," and before I knew it there were people lined up for a city block patiently waiting their turn to have me repair their crippled machines.

Now that I was sixteen years old, I thought it would be a good time to visit the Detroit Auto Convention again, because my father had recently lost another promotion to his company rival Mitch Murphy. This time, it was "the big one," Vice President of National Sales, and he might not be working at the factory much longer due to his dissatisfaction with the politics of the automotive industry in general.

It was 1976 and cars like the Camaro, Firebird, and Barracuda were the dreams of every testosterone-filled young man. This year, the "Muscle Car" was all the rage in America. The war in Vietnam was over, spirits in the country were high, and gas was cheap. Therefore, it was impossible to build engines too big for the power hungry demands of the drivers of the day.

Mother let me borrow her car and I arrived at the show on the first hour of its first day. I didn't have to fight the crowded public entrance because even though my father wasn't working the show that year, he could still get me in the back door. I wandered the packed aisles in amazement, and once had the hair actually stand up on my arms when gazing at the new cherry red Dodge Charger.

Disco's mark on fashion had engulfed the nation and the models at this show were dressed in flashy short dresses that sparkled when the lights hit them. The men wore polyester suits with large-collars and polyester shirts with patterns of all kinds on them. I was walking down an aisle of luxury family cars, when I happened upon a group of engineers from my father's company, Fred Motors. They were being interviewed by TV reporters, while spouting off the latest compression techniques as I walked past.

"Hey, it's Pinkerton's kid," one of the men said. "He's supposed to be some kind of mechanical wizard. Maybe he can tell us a few things we don't already know." The group laughed, as the press backed up a bit and turned towards me. When cameras are on, people do strange things and the ruckus they were creating had started to draw the attention of more than a few curious onlookers.

"Hey kid, what would you say is the most important tool a mechanic should own?" one engineer asked.

"The Manuals," I replied.

Everyone laughed and one of his friends punched him on the arm. "He got you on that one," he said. The engineer looked embarrassed and I could tell his blood was beginning to boil. I tried to defuse the situation a bit.

"Seriously, without the manuals we can only imagine how any machine works. We may recognize some of the parts, but we won't fully understand *all* that the machine is capable of."

"OK, let's try a harder one," another engineer said. "We've been struggling with ways to increase the power output of an engine without increasing its weight. What do you see as the best method of doing this?"

I had recently read about this and was certain he was just trying to trip me up. "I believe there's already great progress being made in this area," I replied. "By compressing the air that is let into the engine, you can squeeze more air into a cylinder. The more air in the cylinder, the more fuel can be added. Therefore, you get more power from each explosion in each cylinder. This compression of the air flowing into the engine can generate an additional 6 to 8 pounds per square inch of pressure. Since normal atmospheric pressure is 14.7 pounds per square inch at sea level, you can see that you would get about 50-percent more air into the engine. Therefore, you would expect to get 50-percent more power."

The crowd began to murmur and the press was now fully engaged. There were cameras and microphones pointing at me from all directions. Flash bulbs started to go off in my face, and the engineers desperately just wanted to find a way out of this nightmare.

"It's not perfectly efficient though," I continued. "There is a small overhead. These methods of compression will need to draw power from somewhere, either from the exhaust stream in the case of a turbo, or directly from the engine itself for a supercharger. Therefore, in reality you may only get a 30-percent to 40-percent improvement instead. Nevertheless, this is still substantial. All this by the way, without adding any significant weight."

The small crowd that had gathered went wild and cheered me, as photographers and local news reporters crowded in to find out who I was and where I had attained such knowledge. As everyone came closer, I knew I had to make an escape. I was never comfortable getting credit for taking the time to find out information that others much smarter than I had worked their knuckles to the bone to discover. I had done nothing that warranted such attention and was set to make a run for it the moment it was possible. I found a break in the crowd and started moving toward an exit.

As I did, a man appeared at my shoulder. "Hey Kid… Let me talk to you for a minute," he said a bit desperately.

"I've really got to go," I replied, continuing to scurry to the exit.

"Listen Kid, I heard what you said back there, and I can tell you that Fred Motors is looking for smart guys like you. Where are you going in such a hurry anyway?"

"I'm off to see the world," I said, a bit pompously.

"Well, Kid, the world's a big place, and I've seen my fair share of it. Let me tell you something, there are only two kinds of places in the world; places with malls, and places with open-air markets under ratty little tents. Besides, we can show you that world, if that's what you want. You'd get to travel if you came to work for me. Come by my office and we'll talk about it."

"I'm sorry Mister, I'm just not interested, and I've really got to be going now." By this time, I was rushing towards the door in haste to make a getaway. He was still trying to pitch me but stopped running as I reached my mother's car. His face seemed familiar but I couldn't place it. Still, I had the sense that I had met him before.

"The name's 'Murphy'!" he yelled, as I drove off, leaving him in a cloud of dust and dirt, "Mitch Murphy!"

When I approached the time one is said to be of legal age, as if all the years up until then I was somehow illegal, I thought it might be time for me to fly. Having worked on or tinkered with in some way or other more than half the mechanized products that existed in this part of Detroit, I wondered what else might await me out in the world. My parents were always very proud and supportive of me and though they were not very keen on this idea of leaving the nest, still wanted me to follow my dreams. My brothers and sister had long since been married and had moved off to adventures of their own, and they understood that perhaps it was time for their youngest to spread his wings and take the leap off that tree.

It was cool and windy the spring morning I left, and as the bus drove through the streets of downtown Detroit, the sights and sounds of the city seemed particularly vivid. Maybe it was because I wouldn't see or hear them again for a long, long time. Or maybe it was because I was starting to open my eyes and ears fully, for the first time in my life.

I rode the bus straight through to Chicago and bought a ticket on a classic steam train traveling west on the Great Northern Railroad. Once on the train, I wandered from car to car looking for that coveted seat near a window, in order to take in all I could of the wonderful sights and smells of places I had only heard of or read about in books. As I walked through the doors of one of the cars, I saw it, a seat by the window in a part of the train not too far back from the sounds and smell of the engine.

CHAPTER III

Ol' Mountain Monster

The morning air was cool and crisp and the early sunlight hadn't enough time to reclaim the dew from the ground or foliage. There was the smell of pine and sweet lavender that permeated the air, and in a place so unfamiliar, the rhythmic tempo of the wheels on the rails was as calming as a mother's heartbeat is to an infant. The sky was a deep blue gradient and with every bellow of steam that rose in the air, there was a loud "chug" that echoed off the mountain ridges around us. I signaled the conductor, who arrived without haste.

"May I help you, lad?"

"Would it be possible to take a look around this wonderful train and maybe meet the engineer?"

"You are free to travel about the train as you wish and when you are ready, I will take you to see Mr. MacGregor." I thanked him for his kindness and started to explore this most fantastic machine.

The train was old, but retained much of the original splendor and beauty of its heyday, obviously maintained by someone who cares about such relics. There were nine cars altogether; one tender, six passenger, and a bright red caboose. After my exploration was complete, I once again called on the conductor and asked to see the engineer.

"Mr. MacGregor has been the engineer of this train since I was a small boy. We don't normally let tourists into the engine," he insisted, "but since you have such a fine respect and appreciation of this old bucket of bolts, I think he would be happy to meet you and would be able to tell you much more about her than I." He led me to the first passenger car where we had to wait until the turns of the mountain passes gave way to the straights of the meadows before we could cross to the outside walkway of the coal car to the engine compartment.

The engine was huge and full of the kind of detail and adornments you don't see on modern passenger trains. "Excuse me sir," the conductor shouted over the sound of the raging furnace.

"No need to shout, Max. I knew yer were there," the engineer said, with a distinct Scottish brogue.

"Yes sir," the conductor replied, apologetically. "I have here a young man named Dewey, who wishes to know more about the ol' Mountain Monster."

"Fine, fine, Max. Thank you for escorting him." Max tipped his hat and disappeared behind the coal car.

The engineer was an elderly man in his sixties with a full head of gray hair and a face that the sun and wind had autographed, several times. He sat motionless, staring out the window and gestured with his hand for me to sit.

"She's a beauty inna she?" he said, sort of taking the words right out of my mouth. "She's a 'Mountain Monster', built by the Pennsylvania Railroad at Altoona in 1930 and considered by many, including meself, to be the best damn steam engine ever built. The tender holds over 32 tons of coal and carries 22,000 gallons of water," answering my next few questions in a row. His voice saddened. "They just don't make 'em like this anymore.... I've rebuilt 'er meself every time she's needed it since the day I found her abandoned in a Harlowton, Montana round house."

He was quiet for a few minutes and seemed to be concentrating. "Didja see that?" he said. I looked around as if to see something obvious. "There 'tis again."

I must admit I saw or heard nothing over the roar of the engine.

"Close yer eyes," he said, "and put yer fingers in yer ears."

"How could that possibly help me *see* anything? Are we in danger?" I asked.

"Just do as I say and ye'll understand."

I reluctantly closed my eyes and put my fingers in my ears. The loud sound of the engine was muffled to a dull rumble. I could hear my breathing and the sound of my heart pumping the blood through my head. At the same time, I became aware that the wheels passing over the track joints and the steady chug of the engine were in perfect rhythm. Chug, chug, clack, clack, chug, chug, clack, clack. There was also a faint clicking noise. It too had a pattern, but not in rhythm with the rest.

"I hear a clicking noise," I said, not really knowing what it was.

"Yes, yes, you *see* it," he said, "a piston is in need of repair."

"I *hear* it," I respectfully replied.

"You *SEE* it," he insisted. Just then, my attention was broken by the loud blast of a steam whistle. "Toooooooot, Toooooot." I jumped out of my seat and Mr. MacGregor laughed hard as he fell back in his chair. "I love ta do that," he said, grinning from ear to ear like a naughty child. "I still love ta blow that whistle."

He sat back and closed his eyes, leaning his head out the window, and seemed to be absorbing the sun and wind as if they were nourishing him.

"You can learn a lot from what you canna see with the eyes," he said. "We have become far too dependent on them. No one believes anything anymore if not verified with their own eyes. As if they were the *only* sense we have. However, the other senses can tell us just as much if not more about the world. Spoiled food for instance, may look fine, but the bacteria we canna see could kill us. It's our sense of smell and taste that tells us the food is bad."

"Thank God for our senses," I said, trying to get the image of eating rotten food out of my mind.

"A man's senses are connected to his essence," he continued. "What is taken in by one sense can sometimes be verified by another sense, but in some cases the senses can be fooled. In the dark, for example, yer eyes may play tricks on you, or you may pour yerself a glass of juice while reading the paper but in yer mind you think yer pouring milk. The first sip can taste a lot like milk before yer other senses tell you it's juice. What is needed is more 'awareness'."

"Awareness? Aren't we already aware just by being awake?"

"Not at all!" he said. "It depends on what ya mean by being awake. Being awake to most of the world is really just a walking sleep. Being awake in that sense doesn't necessarily mean we are aware of anything."

"I'm confused. I always thought being awake *was* being aware."

"That's the whole problem ya see. We believe we already are 'awake' *and* posses 'awareness,' but nothing could be further from the truth. The awareness that I speak of comes from a higher place in us than the senses, and can help to differentiate between what is true and what is false. What awareness we do posses is mostly instinctive, like the heightened alert we feel when we sense danger. Otherwise, we almost exclusively exist in a state of 'sleep walking personality,' a place where we are continuously reacting to whatever happens to us. We see food and we are hungry, so we eat. Someone yawns and we feel tired, so we sleep. We are glanced at by a pretty girl and the rest of the day we believe we are Casanova!

"No, what we posses is not higher awareness, but plain old personality, and personality may know and do lot of useless things. Higher awareness is not only able to observe our personality, but can also be quite free from it."

"How do we acquire this higher awareness?" I asked, puzzled by this distinction.

"Awareness takes years to acquire, but even decades or more to perfect. Perhaps even lifetimes," he continued. "Things are sometimes not as they seem, ya see. A rich man may not always dress in kings clothing, just as a poor man may spend all he owns on one suit. If you saw them both together, even with yer own eyes, you'd be wrong about their true nature."

"You're speaking in riddles," I sighed.

"Perhaps we are moving a bit too fast," he replied.

"No, it's not that!" I said. "What you say makes a lot of sense to me. I just never knew these differences existed."

"Everything we have ever known, we have learned through our senses, me boy," he said. "We could not live even one day without them, just as we could not live very long without food or water. Actually, impressions from our senses are a form of food, as is the air we breathe. However, awareness requires something more. All these things together: impressions, food, water, and air, consumed with 'higher awareness' give a man all he needs to properly understand the world around him."

I would not realize the full meaning of this until much later, but what he said rang true for me. I had often thought that the sad and angry faces on the drivers back in Detroit were reflected in the condition of their cars, and most of the bikes and skateboards I fixed came from the spoiled kids, who had no respect at all for their possessions.

He continued, "For true awareness to grow it must be properly watered with knowledge and observation until it becomes something useful, sort of an overseer of personality, and the senses."

"You mean by properly assimilating impressions together with awareness we can see their true meaning?" I asked, rather impressed with the sound of the question, but quite unsure of my conclusion.

He smiled at that. "Yes."

Our conversation was suddenly interrupted by the sound of animals moaning.

"What is that?" I asked.

"Goat mating call," he said, rising to his feet. I looked up ahead and saw a herd of goats collected on the tracks, but before I could speak, we hit them. They let out an awful yell as they splattered on both sides of the engine. Without so much as a flinch Mr. MacGregor said, "Damn, I just washed 'er this morning.

"It's a form of selection," he sighed, "not quite natural, but as effective just the same. The goats have over-bred this year and when they graze too close to the tracks, they eat all the newly grown shrubs. When they eat too much, they leave the ground void of moisture so nothing will grow there, which in turn causes flooding on the tracks when the next rain season comes." He paused for a second to reflect. "In the grand scheme of things it's better this way. I only wish I hadn't just washed 'er.

"Enough for now my young friend, as you can *see* we are approaching the station." But I could see nothing but forest and grasslands. As we rounded the next bend, a small station appeared off in the distance. Mr. MacGregor pulled steadily on the brake lever and the train slowed to a perfect stop right at the gate.

"Well, this is the end of our journey for today," he said, reaching behind his chair and pulling out a walking cane, a blind man's cane.

"*Blind*," I thought to myself, "*of course, it all makes sense now.*"

I found a room at the local inn but could not sleep much that night. I was mesmerized by the way Mr. MacGregor spoke about things. How much he seemed to know about life and how happy he was. Nevertheless, most amazingly, he was driving trainloads of passengers blind, and nobody knew it!

The next morning I was at the station as the sun's first light crossed the valley. Mr. MacGregor was just getting "Ol' Mountain Monster" ready for a long run to Washington State. I pleaded with him to let me help maintain the train, doing whatever he needed in exchange for the chance to travel and learn more from him.

"Hmm," he said, bringing his hand up and scratching his chin. "I probably could use another set of eyes."

"Another set?" I asked, quizzically.

"Yes," he shouted. "You keep forgetting that just because I can't see, doesn't mean that I can't *SEE*!"

"Yes sir," I replied, and with that, we were off to explore the Great Northwest.

One time, while traveling through the Absaroka Mountain Range, a sub-range on the eastern side of the Rocky Mountains stretching for about 150 miles across the Montana-Wyoming border, Mac let me drive the 'Ol Mountain Monster while he told me a story about the senses.

> *"Once a beast of mystery appeared in the land of the blind. The ruler sent his advisors out to investigate. Waiting until the mysterious beast was sleeping, they touched it. One blind man touching the beast's side said, 'It's like a wall.' Another man touching a horn reported, 'It's like a spear.' Another touching the ear said, 'It's like a fan.' Another feeling the leg said, 'It's like a tree.' One more touching the snout said, 'It's like a snake.' And the last man touching its tail said, 'It is like a rope.' The blind men all described parts of the same animal, a sleeping elephant."*

"So it is with everything," he continued, "that the same thing can appear differently, depending on our perspective, or more exactly, our level of 'awareness'. In some ways we all are like the blind men and the elephant, limited by our own perspectives of a given culture or geographical location, failing to see that a variety of viewpoints presented can represent the same thing."

"How can you tell when someone possesses this higher awareness?" I asked.

"Hard to tell, unless you know the signs," he quickly replied. "It may be easier to tell those who don't posses it. They view the world in black or white. Things are either *this* way or *that* way. They take great pride in arguing one side of any topic. With awareness, one begins to see the unity of things, that everything is innately connected. Things stop being only this way or that way, and become unified, contiguous, *harmonious*, and like the story of the sleeping elephant, that different views may actually not conflict."

I stared at him in wonder. "Can you give me another example?"

"Better than that," he said, "I can give you the biggest and best example in the world, 'science and religion'!"

"But everyone takes sides on that," I exclaimed. "Certainly the huge differences between the sciences and religions of today could never be fully resolved."

"They can, and they have my lad, in an ancient writing called 'The Mode'. It contained a complete cosmology that embodied a unified view of both science and religion that still holds true today. As a matter of fact, the split between science and religion is a rather current event, in 'cosmic' terms."

"I can't image how that's possible."

"Because you still see everything in black and white!" He tapped a gauge then pulled a lever and the engine let out a bellow of steam.

I sat there looking confused.

"Don't pop a corpuscle over it," he said, sensing my dismay. "For now just know that it *is* possible. In time, it will make more sense."

It was getting late and Mac and I were heading to the roundhouse for the evening.

"Slow down just a bit" he warned, as I pulled Ol' Mountain Monster across the track switch.

"How can you tell I'm going too fast?" I asked.

"I may have been talking to you, but another part of my awareness was focused on the echo of the stack chugs off the buildings. That and the rhythm of the track joints tell me you're going to fast for the balance of the distance.

"But how did you figure that out for the first time?" I asked, trying to slow the engine down.

He laughed aloud. "I couldn't, and as you can see *that* part of the roundhouse had to be replaced. Nevertheless, I was only wrong once. After that I could '*see*' the distance in my mind."

Even with the gift of sight, and fair warning, I too ran the engine through the roundhouse, and I'm embarrassed to say, more than once.

By the time I turned twenty I had mastered the art of train engineering. More importantly, I had budding interest in the teaching of the Mode. Knowing this, Mac told me late one afternoon that perhaps it was time I continued on my journey. I spent the next few days thanking him for his friendship and the knowledge he had bestowed on me.

"Just remember that sensing the 'earth' and being aware of it are two different things," he said. He opened a satchel he kept next to his chair and began digging in it for something.

"Here it is, take this," handing me an old crumpled business card. "He's a dear old friend of mine, Captain Sean

O'Connell. He's got a fine love of mechanics and if you ever get to the Alaskan seaboard, he'll surely wanna meet you." An obvious deep bonding memory forced him to smirk. "Oh yeah, be careful what you say to him though. He's quite the drunken ol' womanizing Irishman who takes offence to the drunken ol' womanizing Irishman stereotype." He winked. "And we all know that stereotypes survive the test of time because they are generally true."

After a short stop one day in eastern Washington he helped me off the train with my bags, and we said our good-byes. That was the last time I ever saw McQuay MacGregor. It was said by many who knew him that he died the way he lived, happily sitting in the engineer's seat of the train he loved. The strange thing was that when the train pulled into the station just as it had for over twenty-five years before, they found him stone cold. He must have died hours earlier but still managed to bring his passengers home safely.

CHAPTER IV

Angel Food

I decided I should go to see this friend of Mr. MacGregor's straight away, as I wouldn't get the chance every day to meet a real ship captain. Mapping out the next part of my journey by train as well, I traveled from Washington State up through Western Canada to the Alaska Seaboard. Once there, I would look for Captain Sean O'Connell in hopes of learning all I could about the great cargo ships.

The largest oil field in North America had just been discovered at Prudhoe Bay on the North Coast and the talk of a pipeline that would run all the way down to the lower forty-eight caused workers to come here by the truckloads with dreams of making their fortunes. The streets were lined with this new breed of oil warrior and I didn't feel so out of place as we merged together on the sidewalks, some totally unprepared for such freezing weather and in need of shelter.

It was cold and severely overcast the next morning as I rose from a boarding house bed and went in search of Captain O'Connell. I called the number on the business card Mac had given me, but no answer. The address on the card was a P.O. Box and no one there had seen him for quite some time. I patiently patrolled the harbor looking for any longshoreman who might know him.

One told he had died in the huge storm of '71 and another said he was sure he was lost in the great quake of '64 that measured 8.6 on the Richter scale. However, I was not convinced of either of these stories and continued to ask of his whereabouts until dusk had turned to a dull, gray, foggy night. I continued my search for days and just as I was about to give up something wonderful happened.

I was sitting in a local pub. You could drink as young as sixteen years old there as a reward for enduring the hell of freezing cold temperatures and sunlight for only five hours a day, and by now, I needed something more than water to wash down a loaf of bread and the local seafood. It was late, and a man came through the door with "Salty Seadog" written all over him.

He was a handsome, elderly man, who stood tall and proud, wearing long silver hair, a well-trimmed beard, and a trench coat that went all the way to the floor. He approached the bar and was welcomed by a busty barkeep with hugs and a single malt scotch poured from a bottle kept under the counter and opened in his honor. "Cheers Sean, you ol' sea bastard!" she said, with a short but seductive kiss on the lips as they crashed their glasses together. Then the old man settled down in a soft leather armchair near the fire.

By the time he had four or five shots under his belt, he was laughing with the locals and in quite the chipper mood. I thought that if I didn't approach him soon he would fall prey to the balance of the bottle, or to the bedroom with one or more of the finest looking women I had seen in this town in almost a week who were beginning to gather around him.

I made my way to my feet. This wasn't very easy, as I too had been a slave to a couple of shots or more, and tried not to stumble as I approached his table. "Excuse me, Slur… I mean, Sir, are you Captain Sean O'Connell?"

He looked up at me, not sure what to make of someone whose physique and manner did not fit in with the local lifestyle or decor.

"You must be that kid MacGregor told me about," he said grinning, "What's your name, son?"

"Dewey, Sir," I paused then added, "Pinkerton."

"Well, Dewey Sir Pinkerton, you couldn't have come at a better time. I set out to sea in a couple of days on a cargo run to Mexico. MacGregor told me you have a gift with machines. You're gonna need it if you want to go on this voyage. I don't let anyone ride for free."

"Oh, no, Sir," I pleaded, "I'll work as hard as anyone."

The room roared with laughter, as my shoulders and arms were sticks compared to the oak banister arms and backs of the sailors in this room. Even the girls laughed, which made me even more embarrassed.

"At least I will try my best, Sir."

"Very well, Sir Pinkerton. Her name's '*Sea Wise*', get plenty of rest the next few days, you're gonna need it. But before you go," he said, with a wink, and a pause to whisper something to one the girls sitting on the arm of his chair, "you're going to need this first. We may be gone for quite a while!" He laughed hard and began to sing as the jukebox started playing an old Irish drinking song, called 'Erin McGuire'.

"I met a girl named Erin McGuire,
One look in 'er eyes sets a man's soul on fire,
But is she the one? You'll wonder, as we sail away..."

The woman smiled at me as she got up, and introduced herself as Victoria. She led me back to my table for a nightcap and the room settled down to the gentle sounds of conversation and the roaring fire.

On Monday morning, I was up before dawn with a smile on my face. Filled with anxiety and wonder of what the next few months would hold, I packed my belongings, now up to a case and a half, and dragged them down the stairs to a taxi, which would take me to the docks. I gave Victoria a kiss and told her I would write. She laughed and started singing.

"He told 'er he'd write 'er, she said, she'll be fine.
This was a wonderful moment in time,
But is she the one? You'll wonder, as you sail away..."

"In this town a girl learns to not hold her breath," she said. "Take care, Sir Pinkerton."

The docks were frantic with activity. Cranes moved large cargo boxes onto ships while rows of pipes filled with oil and gases flowed into huge tankers.

I was greeted on the *Sea Wise* by First Mate Hudson who didn't look quite as intimidating as Captain O'Connell, and who showed me to my quarters. "Don't get too comfortable," he warned. "Capn' 'ill wanna see you by 0700 sharp." I thanked Mr. Hudson and threw my bags down on the bed.

I arrived at the bridge precisely on time, as the looks on the faces of the scurrying shipmates told me there would be hell to pay for being late. The Captain was busy looking over maps and using instruments to make some kind of measurements. He nodded to a few of his crew then gave the order to cast off.

"Well, Sir Pinkerton, I see you made it."

"Yes, Sir… I mean, YES, SIR!"

"That's better. Mr. Hudson, show Sir Pinkerton around the ship and when you're done give him some work to do."

"Yes, Captain," he replied.

The Captain shook my hand. "I'll meet up with you this evening for supper and we can spend some time talking then, but for now there is much work to be done."

First Mate Hudson took me down the stairs to the cargo deck. Row after row of huge containers, the kind that fit onto boxcars and big rigs were neatly stacked in straight lines; more than I had ever counted on any of the freight trains as a child in Detroit. They were green and brown and yellow, but mostly brown, with scratches that formed stripes on them from years of being lifted from train to ship to train again.

Soon we were off and the spray of the deep ocean waves hitting the hull occasionally showered us with a fine salt mist as we made our way down to the lower inside decks. We arrived in the engine room just in time to see the crew engage her at full speed.

"They're twin KAT P49 medium-speed diesel engines," Hudson yelled, over the deafening sounds of the huge motors at maximum throttle. "She can do a top speed of 18 knots and the engines can produce a total output of 12,000 bhp. For speed to turn around and maneuverability, she also has a controllable pitch bow thruster."

They were indeed beautiful. I asked if my work for the day could be in the engine compartment. He agreed and I began my tenure as an engine room assistant.

We were just north of the Queen Charlotte Islands when the last rays of sunlight fell across the starboard bow. I was exhausted from the day's activities and eager to have some time to talk to the Captain. The men were busy securing the decks for the night and preparing themselves for the evening's meal. We gathered in the galley, which was on the lower decks, and from the moment we started down the first flight of stairs you could smell sweet carrots, cabbage and beef stew.

I was seated next to the Captain and First Mate Hudson as kitchen help brought generous portions of bread and wine to get us started. Everyone dug in and the muffled sounds of talking with mouths full of food filled the cabin. Finally, Captain O'Connell turned to me and said, "A good meal for a good days work, huh?" I nodded politely not wanting to answer with a mouth full of bread as the others might have. "Have you a chance to see 'er engines?" he asked, with a boyish grin.

"Yes, sir. They're amazing," I replied.

"You could pull a twenty story building over with those beauties," he boasted. "Not that you would ever want to do such a thing." The men laughed and the Captain raised his glass of wine. The men followed suit. "To the young Sir Pinkerton, may the winds of change carry us safely to our destination. Long live the *Sea Wise.*"

"Hear, hear!" the men shouted, and everyone settled back into the evening meal.

After supper, the Captain invited me to sit with him in the lounge while we sipped warm cognac. He reached into his pocket and pulled out a Cuban cigar that he lit with a match from a pack with the words "The Donkey Bar, BC. Mexico" printed on the cover. He noticed that I was reading the matchbook and smiled as he took his first puffs. “There are many things in this world that sound worse than they are. But this place,” he said grinning, looking at the matches as he put them in his pocket, “is not one of them!

“Tell me, Dewey, why have you come? I take it you have traveled a bit to see me. What do you seek?”

“I am not exactly sure, Sir. Ever since I was little I have been fascinated by machines; motors in particular. I don’t know what drives this curiosity but I can’t seem to stop it. I left Detroit years ago and I don’t know if I have any more answers now then I did when I left, just more questions.”

“It’s good that you found MacGregor,” he said. “He’s a wise old goat. One of the best friends I’ve ever had. We served together during World War II. He was blinded by shrapnel while carrying a wounded Chief Petty Officer out of harm’s way. He has never regretted it, never complained about it, never let it slow him down. A wonderful man, with the knowledge of twenty men his peers.” He paused to reflect. “If the passengers only knew that train was being driven by a haggis-eating blind Scotsman they would be out of their minds with fear. Nevertheless, you and I both know *he* knows that piece of track better than the men who built it. He must have sent you to me for a reason, perhaps for me to help you with your quest.”

You could tell by the look on his face that he knew exactly why Mac sent me to him. He just loved to play the game.

“Follow me, lad,” he said, rising to his feet while re-kindling the flame under his cigar. He led me to the upper deck to watch the waves crashing against the bow. It was a full moon and the light sparkled like broken glass off the ocean surface. We stood quietly for quite some time before he spoke.

"A little river has to cross a desert, you see, and it runs into the sand and finds it's becoming a marsh. So the wind says to it, 'Come with me, and I will carry you over the desert.' But the little rivers says, 'No, no, I can't! I'll lose my identity! I refuse to be turned into water vapor!' So the wind says, 'Well, suit yourself, but look at you, you're becoming a marsh. You have to decide whether you wish to be a marsh or become water vapor.' So after a great deal of consideration the river finally yields up to the wind, which carries it high into the mountains and drops it again in the form of rain, where after it continued as a river."

"I take that to mean, even though I don't know where the road may lead, at some point I will find my destiny?" I was never very good at understanding the Sunday's sermon parables.

"Somewhat," he said. "It means that you must first give up what you think you are in order to find what you really are. Or more precisely, what you may become. We are so full of ourselves most of the time that we have no room to learn anything. It is only by emptying ourselves that we might have room to truly discover something new.

"This ship, as magnificent as she is," he continued, "can do nothing on her own. She needs an army of men and trucks full of fuel and oil to cause her to do even the simplest of motions. Yet the wind and moon have forces we cannot even see that move the surface of entire oceans with ease. We feed the ship's engines fuel and in turn, they feed electricity and compression necessary to turn her propellers and carry us over great distances of the most treacherous waters. These ships, and all machines for that matter, are a micro cosmos of the universe.

"The point is Dewey that everything *feeds* on everything else. The circle of life is not just limited to the plant and animal kingdoms. It applies to everything in the universe from the largest of galaxies to the smallest particles of atoms and is all guided by the laws of the Mode."

"Mac spoke about the Mode. Where did this teaching come from?" I asked.

"Quite some time ago, MacGregor and I were traveling together with a couple of other seekers on a great expedition. It was a search for knowledge of the great lost teachings of the world. We were lucky enough to have an idea of where such knowledge may be hidden and we pursued this vision through many dangers. What we found, was more than any of us expected. The teaching of the Mode, possibly written tens of thousands of years ago, told of the science of Universal Mechanics, the earliest known record of a complete unifying cosmology of the universe. A sort of blueprint of the science of God, long before most of modern mankind knew the universe was even out there."

"Who wrote it, and where is it?" I asked. "I would love to see it."

"No one knows who wrote it, I'm afraid. Folklore says it came from Atlantis. Others say it came from the Egyptians, while still others believe it came from a time before the last great annihilation, a time when a sister sun traveled through our solar system reeking havoc on any planetary life forms that that may have existed between orbits. As for where it is, I only wish I knew, and could see it again myself. In exchange for the knowledge of its location, we were only allowed to view, but not take this relic. There wasn't sufficient time for all of us to read it, so instead we divided the volumes between us, each one learning a piece of the complete cosmology."

"*My* studies dealt with the food chain," he continued, "that everything in the universe is connected, that everything feeds off of the higher vibrations or energies of everything else."

We were silent again for a while when suddenly I was struck with a disturbing question. "Who feeds on us?" I asked, in a sheepish tone.

"The angels of course," he said, with a grin. "So be sure to give them something good to eat." He chuckled and lit his cigar once more.

Again, I would not realize until much later that he was talking about our spirit or soul or whatever the spiritual movement of the day calls this energy. We are not born with it, like many world religions proclaim, and cannot acquire it by accident. It can only be produced by years of searching, years of learning, years of practicing universal truths over and over again until what is produced is pure, truthful, *nutritious.* I made up my mind that day that I would try to be the best food the angels had ever had. I looked down at my skinny arms and laughed; at least a tasty appetizer if nothing else.

Over the next few weeks, I practiced the idea of divided awareness that Mac had taught me while working in the engine room and thought much about the significance of the food chain. I tried as best I could to create in me a small but loyal observer that would watch my personality and movements in hopes of awakening my sleeping potential. The Captain taught me that all machines have a certain sound vibration or "mantra" that they make when running at optimum performance. A variance in this vibration usually means something is not right.

As we approached the Mexican town of Puerto Villarreal, I was pretty good at diagnosing the ship's engines and fuel systems by sensing the vibrations they made. The engines burned many quarts of oil a day and required numerous repairs, but they still got us where we were going, and all in one piece.

I had never been to Mexico, and growing up in Detroit was a far cry from such a wonderfully different culture. All I had ever seen of this land, besides what you learn in school, was a Donald Duck cartoon with Carmen Miranda where they fiesta the night away to a colorful rendition of the Mexican hat dance. However, this was nothing like that.

Everyone there was smiling and the food was the best I had ever tasted. I had the greatest time during those couple of days in a village where the only machine was an old VW bug that was used for everything from a taxi to the local hearse. Being the only form of transportation in town, everyone knew how to work on it, even the children. The place was so peaceful that I could die there. Which was not very far off if I drank even one more of the cactus drinks with the worm at the bottom.

Once, we were lucky enough to witness a very strange local custom. At dusk every evening the villagers would parade down the main street of town dressed in elaborate costumes celebrating the death of *this* person or *that* relative, dancing and singing as they followed the VW hearse. It appeared the townspeople there had taken it upon themselves to commemorate the right of passage into the next world almost anyone who died within a hundred miles, whether they knew them or not!

On the last day of our stay, many large trucks came from nearby cities to unload the cargo that would be driven to the nearest train station and taken to Mexico City. We said our good-byes to the friends we had made and set off to San Diego on our way back up the North American Pacific coast.

The months blurred and before I knew it I had spent more than two and a half years on the *Sea Wise* with Captain O'Connell. I was twenty-three and had grown considerably in both body and spirit. I now had some power in my handshake and wouldn't lose so easily, even while drinking Irish whiskey, the arm wrestling and rope climbing contests the men would have while enjoying our leisure time.

Our current voyage found us heading south, in route to Southern, California. Captain O'Connell had scheduled the *Sea Wise* for a major reconditioning, including an inspection, hull cleaning and shaft seal replacement. He would spend his time in the interim as Captain of a South Pacific freighter named "*Infinity*." He gave me the number of a close friend of his that lived in the San Fernando Valley and whom he thought might be able to use my mechanical services.

We arrived in Los Angeles before the sun and had to wait offshore for the port of San Pedro to open. Los Angeles, "*The Angels*" I thought, what an appropriate place to continue my journey. I went to the helm where the Captain was making his last minute preparations. When the sunlight broke over the bay, we pulled the *Sea Wise* into port and docked her.

The port was in full swing now and cranes were busy lifting cargo on and off the ships. I signaled to Captain O'Connell that I was ready to leave and he came and shook my hand with sadness in his eyes.

"I'll miss you," he said, with a crack in his voice.

"I will miss you too, Captain. Thanks again for all you have taught me."

"All I did was water a thirsty spirit, nothing more."

I waved again as I reached the dock, but he was busy now, busy with the kind of details that made him special, busy with the business of international shipping, but not too busy to wave back at me one more time.

CHAPTER V

The Flight of Icarus

In the city of Angels, I found an apartment in "The Valley" which lies just north of the Hollywood Hills and began my search for a new job. I was running low on funds and would need to work at least a year in order to replenish my travel purse. I looked amongst my belongings for the contact information of the friend Captain O'Connell had given me, but was unable to find it anywhere. While reading the paper that day I chanced upon an advertisement in the classified section looking for "a small- aircraft mechanical assistant, with knowledge of the twin engine Cessna a plus." I didn't know specifically about Cessna engines, but by now, I was pretty good with most engines and was sure I could do this work.

The name and phone number sounded familiar and when I arrived at the Burbank airport the next morning, I was surprised by my intuition to meet O'Connell's old friend Winger, an ex-air force pilot who owned and operated his own small fleet of business charter planes. He hired me at a fair wage after only thirty minutes. I must have shown him a sufficient amount of technical expertise or he knew that I was quick enough to learn what he wanted.

Starting my employment immediately, I was given the task of washing planes. It seems businessmen who have the kind of money to fly in private planes wouldn't be caught dead in a dirty one. Their limousines were clean. Their houses were clean. Their wives, children, and dogs were clean. Even their nails were neatly manicured and buffed to a light gloss; everything was clean except their mouths, which were full of unspeakable filth.

Winger looked young for a man who had flown Hellcats during World War II and Sabre Jet fighters during the Korean conflict, as no signs of the tragedies of war were etched on his face. He was very Zen in his actions and never wasted energy on any unnecessary movement or emotions. Not that he was void of them; he just conserved them until the time when they were most appropriate. He was much shorter than Captain O'Connell was and since he only came up to my brow, I found myself having to look down quite frequently to catch the subtle expressions of his face when he spoke.

Over the next few months, Winger taught me about the inner workings of plane engines, but most of the time my mind was filled with dreams of learning how to fly. Finally, after showing him hard work and the kind of attention to detail the likes of which he had never seen before, he promised to take me up and teach me.

We were flying at an altitude of three thousand feet with the wind out of the north at five knots when he said, "Ok, take 'er over." I cautiously put my hands on the controls. "Flying," he said, "is all about balance. More specifically," he continued, "there are four aerodynamic forces that act upon an airplane in flight: *lift*, the upward acting force, *weight* or *gravity*, the downward acting force, *thrust*, the forward acting force, and *drag*, the air resistance or backward acting force. These four forces are continuously battling each other while an airplane is in flight.

"Gravity opposes lift, thrust opposes drag. In order to take off, the aircraft's thrust and lift must be sufficient to overcome its weight and drag. In level flight at a constant speed, thrust exactly equals drag, and lift exactly equals the pull of gravity. To land, an aircraft's thrust must be reduced safely below its drag, as its lift is reduced to levels less than its weight."

After months of practice, Winger helped me get my pilot's license and I assisted him in flying planes back and forth between Southern California's private airports for various business reasons.

One day Winger came to me and asked if I wanted to go on a week's flight with him to look at a few new planes he was interested in buying, but were located in several states. In case he wanted to come back with one or two, he would need someone else to help fly them.

We left early one Saturday morning. Weekends were easier for him to get away and we had just hired enough help to cover the backlog of scheduled fights. After a few hours in the air, Winger told me a story about his time in the Korean War.

"My life was changed forever because of one event that happened just six days before I was to be discharged from my two year tour of duty as an Air Force fighter pilot in Korea," he said. "There were three of us flying F-86s back from a bombing mission in 'MiG Alley' deep over enemy territory, when we caught three supply trains at Sunchon, racing for the shelter of a tunnel. We blasted the tunnel mouth shut, trapping the trains in the open and then destroyed the boxcars and at least two locomotives, avenging the 'Sunchon Tunnel Massacre' where just two years earlier a group of American prisoners from Pyongyang were taken off the train in these tunnels and machine-gunned down.

"We were soon spotted and fired on by enemy air forces. One of our jets was struck hard in the cockpit before there was any chance of escape. I broke formation and was circling around to engage the enemy when I was hit in the tail. I brought my nose up just far enough to lock-on to the MiG-15 and fired on him; sending him spiraling downward. Ejecting just seconds before my plane hit the ground; I landed in a field on the edge of a thick forest and made a hasty retreat to the cover of the trees. I was spotted however, captured, then taken to a nearby village and kept in a bamboo cage to be transferred to Pyongyang prison camp a few days later.

"That night and every night for the next three days a beautiful young woman came to bring me food and water, and from the moment we saw each other we could tell there was something unexplainable between us. She was the enemy, but no amount of hate-training could have prepared me to resist the feelings I had for her. These feelings confused her and in very broken English, she told me she would need to visit her village matchmaker to ask if this forbidden attraction was valid.

"Later that night, she returned with an old woman who, after meeting me and asking many questions, confirmed to her that I was indeed a perfect match and meant by the wisdom of Buddha himself to be with her. They quickly cut me free and with the old woman's blessing, she handed me a flare and told us that we should flee immediately.

"Once out of the village we hid in the jungle that night and at morning's first light, I fired the flare at a rescue helicopter that was still searching for me and who picked us up and brought us to safety. Until this day I have never been without her," referring of course to his wife, Anna, who I knew was Korean, but I had never known the story of how they met.

"Tell me how you've come to know Captain O'Connell?" I asked. "Were you one of the group of Seekers?"

"Yes," he replied, "Sean and I go way back. Those were some pretty amazing times."

"What part of the teaching did you study?"

"I was given the 'science of types'. You've heard of the signs of the Zodiac, right?"

"Yes," I said. "My mother only kept three things on the end table next to her bed; a phone, a remote control, which she thought was the third best invention ever next to television and the fifty-foot phone cord, and a horoscope book that she would read during commercials."

"That type of 'horrorscope' is not the one I mean. I'm not talking about making a sorry attempt to predict when you should pay attention to your finances or beware of the mood swings of loved ones." He laughed aloud, something that I had not heard him do before.

"I am talking about the almost completely lost science of the twelve types of man, well eleven and a half really, because by now, this teaching has been altered due to the method in which we humans calculate our time.

"Long ago this original knowledge of the twelve types was once very well known," he continued. "When young people came of age, they would go to see a matchmaker, usually a woman, who was trained in this science. She would analyze which type the young person was and match them with another person of a compatible type. Because this science was based on a person's essence and not personality, they were seldom incorrect. And though at this time their life expectancy was only around thirty or forty years, they usually lived short but blissful existences, thus completely avoiding one of the plagues of modern man, 'divorce'.

"The demise of this ancient teaching has two origins. One is because the science of types is related to essence and not personality. It directly corresponds to the position of the stars and planets at the moment of one's conception. This was later misunderstood and wrongfully associated with the position of the stars and planets at the moment of one's birth, a belief that has been carried on to this very day."

"How many days in a year?" he asked, out of the blue.

"365," I replied, cautiously. Any time you are asked a simple question you are most certainly in store for a mind-blowing answer.

"365.6," he said. "Actually 365.2564 to be more precise, and because of this unfortunate event we decided to hack off the six odd hours and put them together creating a new day every four years. We then stuck that new day in the month shorted on days anyway, February. This is the second factor that has added to the problem of dilution for this ancient teaching and has caused the stars and planets to no longer be properly aligned with the signs of the zodiac, which represents the twelve types of man."

Winger then proceeded to tell me that the twelve types represent the root number of all the possible combinations of types of people in the world. Knowing these combinations made it easier to pass down truths through the ages by insuring all people would be able to receive knowledge directly relating to their type.

As usual, I could not sleep much that night. I didn't need to, and passed the night trying to figure out what type I was, and Captain O'Connell etc... All the way down the line of people I knew.

In the months to come with Winger's coaching, I practiced how to recognize which type a particular person was, knowing full well that calculating their type was more complicated than just taking the date of their birth minus nine months. There was the fact that the heavens don't line up exactly anymore to factor in, and cusp conceptions made it all quite tricky.

Once I could adequately tell a person's type, Winger deepened the scope of the teaching by introducing the possibility of "reading" a person. That is, the ability to sense information about someone by being in close proximity or direct contact with them. It's only possible when in the state of higher awareness that Mac had taught me, and Winger admitted he was not able to achieve this it to any great degree. With practice over time, there came moments when I began to be able to tell things about people, like where they had been that day, or what they were about to say, and occasionally even a moment when I could tell what was about to happen.

One beautiful summer afternoon, Winger was showing me how to do the elusive outside loop, a very tricky maneuver, which required exact timing as well as height and speed. He had done it four or five times that day and I had only managed to do it once, almost killing myself by not having enough height. He said that next he wanted to show me a vertical corkscrew. This is a maneuver that requires the plane to fly very low to the ground, and then pull up at almost a 90-degree angle spiraling upward, much like the maneuver a figure skater does when they grab one skate and then spin around and around. This creates a momentive force that drives them faster as they pull their foot towards them. However, I didn't feel good about it for some reason. Some inner awareness warned me of the impending danger and in that instant, I could see the future.

"Winger!" I radioed, "Don't do it..." but it was too late. He climbed higher and higher reaching a fevered pitch, then began to spin out of control, not able to level out.

There was nothing but static on the radio when I heard him say, "Tell Anna..." and then it was silent. I tried to follow him but he had gained so much speed that I wasn't able to climb as quickly and soon he disappeared out of view. Your eyes play tricks on you at those altitudes and these small planes were not made to travel at those heights. It would be days before rescue workers would find the wreckage of his plane miles away. Nevertheless, there was no sign of Winger.

Winger was very wise but also very practical. Too practical to do anything dangerous without having spent the time learning it well. Things had to make perfect sense to him, and one of the things, if nothing else, I had learned by now was that some things never make sense and can't be verified. Some things have to be taken as true because all of your being tells you they are. Some things have to be taken on faith.

I remembered a story I had read as a child that went like this:

A man was chased off a cliff by a tiger. He fell, and just managed to hold onto a branch. Six feet above him stood the tiger, snarling. A hundred feet below, a violent sea lashed fierce-looking rocks. To his horror, he noticed that the branch he was clutching was being gnawed at its very roots by two rats. Seeing he was doomed, he cried out, "O Lord, save me!"

He heard a voice reply, "Of course I will save you. But first, let go of the branch!"

When I first heard that fable I was eleven years old, and to this day, it still scares me. Could I, would I, have let go? Based on all my knowledge and experience would I have had total trust that if I let go I would not have fallen to my certain death. I want to believe that this is possible, that there is and can be a faith so pure that at that one special moment in time, a decision of that magnitude could be delivered, really acted upon. When Winger knew he was doomed, why didn't he eject? And if he did eject, where is he? Maybe Winger, like Icarus, flew too close to the sun and was punished for it. On the other hand, maybe he had already learned how to let go of the branch.

Winger's death was a shock to me. A shock whose force only helped to crystallize the lessons I had learned so far. He had opened my eyes to the natural and mechanical forces of nature, as well as the science of types, and I felt there was so much more I could have learned from him.

I thought long and hard about what I wanted to do next, and it was only after deep inner searching that I decided to leave L.A. and head east for a while. I traveled through Las Vegas; a place where you're reward for building in the middle of the Godforsaken desert is all the glittery lights, alcohol, and sex you can stand. Three things that everyone there is convinced go together well along with the scorching hot sun and endless sand. I did not stay there long as I could see there were many who did but could never leave; a sort of prison whose walls consist of an out in the open practice of all the sins of the world.

Just outside Las Vegas was Hoover Dam, a must-see stop for those of us with motors on the brain. It was one-hundred and ten degrees in the shade and the tour took just a little under an hour, so by the time we got down to the generator rooms filled with two story turbines that turned water into electrical power, I was exhausted. I leaned against one of the turbines and all of a sudden, something strange began to happen. I felt rejuvenated. I could feel the enormous power of the engines turning, and even though it was housed in fourteen inches of steel and concrete, the energy seemed to flow right out it. No one else on the tour seemed to be as amazed as I was, and the guide was getting a little suspicious of my preoccupation and asked me to please get back in line.

Hitchhiking, I traveled for a few hours in the passenger seat of an eighteen-wheeler. It was driven by a man who saw that I was never going to make it alive walking to the next city and had just enough mercy to pick me up and take me to his next stop.

"I'm only going as far as Mesquite," he said. "I've got a little lady waiting for me there and I don't want to be late." I could sense by the look in his eyes and the pale band on his finger where a rings usually sat that he was not meeting his wife. He dropped me off in a little shanty town that only had a gas station, a restaurant, and a trailer park to its name. Finding a room at the trailer park, I settled in for the night.

The night sky in the desert is incredible. City lights spoil everything. There were as many stars that night as I had seen while on the *Sea Wise*, and just as beautiful. While lying in bed I opened an envelope that Winger had told Anna to give me if anything were to happen to him. It contained the names of several people to contact. Mac had been gone for over a year now, and I had already sent word to Captain O'Connell. The next person on the list lived nearby, somewhere in the Nevada wilderness, but there was no phone number, just a map. Tucked behind the list of names was a small card with a single quote on it.

"Water is bound to its earthly lair, but as clouds for a moment it dances on 'air'."

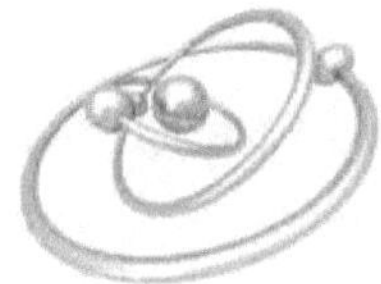

CHAPTER VI

In the World of Atoms, Everyone Can Dance

A rooster, whose sense of pitch was a bit skewed, announced the morning sun. Perhaps his painful crow was from years of living in the hot Nevada desert or perhaps it was because he had been run over a half a dozen times by local traffic. Everyone around there thought him to be the reincarnated ghost of an Indian that once lived on the land, because a lady who owned the gas station on the main highway was ran over just once and it killed her. I rose and went to the trailer offices and had some coffee, which by now in my mid-twenties I had grown to need like everyone else first thing in the morning before a good day was said to begin. I walked a few hundred feet more and then hitchhiked on the only road leading out of town.

This time, I was picked up by a skinny old man with long gray hair, which hung close to the sides of his face and almost touched his lap. He was driving a VW bus, the nightmare of any sports car enthusiast who happens to be behind one on a winding two-lane road with a double yellow line running down the middle of it. It traveled at a maximum speed of forty-five miles per hour while a growing string of impatient, weary travelers trailed behind. His name was Sir Isaac Swami, an odd name for someone who didn't even look Indian. I read it off the registration that was clipped to the visor. There was an Isaac on the list Winger had given me, but I shrugged it off as coincidence. He was very quiet and his face was calm and peaceful even as the angry mob behind him beeped their horns almost every moment. It made me uncomfortable, but he seemed to be enjoying it.

"They have no patience," he said, startling me. I wasn't sure he could even speak. "It is my role to do this, you know."

"It's his role to piss them off, or to speak in non-sequiturs?" I wondered.

"They expect this car to go slow, yet they are surprised when it does. They are machines, and can only react to outside stimuli. They have no actions of their own. Everything in them is dictated by something else. They will never be free from the machine."

I would have never thought of that, though somehow now at that moment it seemed quite obvious.

"To know the machine is to be free from being one," he said.

He pulled off the main highway and drove up a dirt road for a long time, and after a while, he reached down and flipped a lever mounted under the dash. The engine let out a backfire then revved up like a sports car. He looked over at me with a well sun-baked smile and hit the gas. The van lunged forward climbing to speeds of nearly one-hundred twenty miles an hour before he slowed back down. I was white with fear. Not only had I never been in a car going that fast; I couldn't believe we just did that in a 1965 VW bus.

"They expect me to go slow," he said, with a chuckle, "and so I do."

"Where did you get an old German car that can perform like that?" I asked.

"From an old German of course," he replied.

I had successfully resisted the temptation to ask several times "Are we there yet?" when we finally pulled up to his camp. There was an old rounded silver camper, an outhouse, and a car up on blocks, with some laundry over-drying on a clothesline in the hot Nevada sun. We hopped out of the van and he made his way over to a coffeepot that looked like it had been brewing all day.

"Hot, strong and sweet, that's how I like it." He poured in three packages of sugar and a good dose of honey as well. "Want some?"

"No thanks," I replied. "The last thing I need after a ride like that is another rush."

He sat down on a stone bench that had been crafted out of broken concrete. As the sun began to settle down, he lit a fire for us to sit by. That's when I noticed something moving in the shrubs just behind him. Several minutes later, a diamond back rattlesnake slowly made its way towards us.

"Don't move," I said. "There's a…"

"Rattlesnake behind me?" he interrupted.

"Yes," I replied.

"Don't worry, he's come for dinner."

"You feed rattlesnakes?"

"Nope."

Without taking his eyes off the fire, he reached down, picked the snake up from behind its jaw, in a quick fluid movement pulled a knife out of his pocket, and cut off its head.

"I prefer to eat 'em. The flames of the fire are hypnotizing. Bad for the snakes." With several more quick strokes, he skinned and gutted it. "Good for me." He then placed the snake in a pan and onto the fire.

"What are you doing living in the middle of the desert?" I asked.

"I'm a hermit; what better place?" he replied. "Perhaps the better question is what are you doing hitchhiking in the middle of the desert?"

"Touché... I am looking for a man named Isaac Newton."

"I'm sorry, lad. You're about three-hundred fifty years too late," he mumbled, taking a slow sip of his thick black coffee.

"I realize how crazy that must sound," I said. "Not *that* Isaac Newton, but a man with the same name. He lives around here somewhere."

He stuck his hand out to shake. "Well then, that's different. Seems you've found him. And who might you be?"

"I'm Dewey Pinkerton."

"It's a pleasure, Dewey."

"But I thought your name was Isaac Swami?" I asked, puzzled.

"It is now. You try going around in life as Isaac Newton!" He paused, perhaps remembering all the fallen apple jokes. "As soon as I was old enough, I starting telling people my last name *was* Swami, as kind of a joke, because I love spiritual learning so much. It just stuck. After a while, I made it official and had it legally changed. The Sir was added later by that sheep chasin', whiskey drinkin', womanizer O'Connell!"

"Hmm, I thought I was the only one. He used to call me 'Sir Pinkerton'."

"Well then... now you know! He must have thought quite a bit of you though. He doesn't bestow that honor on just anyone."

"How is it possible that I have found you all by accident?"

"Accidents can only happen when you are not looking. You on the other hand... were looking."

"You were one of them too," I realized, "the explorers?"

"Of course, the 'Seekers of Wisdom'," he paused and an expression of chivalry crossed his face. "That was a long time ago, and we were quite a bit younger then, my lad."

"What part of the teaching did you discover?"

"Who me?" he laughed. "Oh, I learned much more than the others that's for sure, because I could read faster. A skill they used to criticize me for if I remember correctly, sighting that the trade off for speed was less absorption. However, this teaching really spoke to my soul. I hauled ass through most of it!"

As the sky became dark and the moon was exposed from behind the horizon, the old hermit began to tell me more of what he had learned.

"What happens or may happen to us," he said, "depends on three causes; fate, accident or one's own free will, which by the way, is one's true destiny. If we are all machines and can do nothing then we will always fall under the law of accident. To be less of a machine allows us to fall under the law of fate. To be totally free from the machine is to be under one's own will. As we are now, we are very far from this. We 'are' as our cars 'are' driven by a madman! We are totally controlled by external events, as are all machines. The machine does not know itself, cannot maintain itself. It always needs something from above to take care of it. Nevertheless, a true 'man' may someday be able to be free himself from this external control.

He poked a stick in the fire sending red sparks rising into the night sky. "In the world of atoms, everyone can dance! Everything vibrates, everything radiates, nothing is standing still." He continued,

> *"Once two monks were arguing about the temple flag waving in the wind. One said, 'The flag moves.' The other said. 'The wind moves.' They argued back and forth but could not agree. Finally, the Master said, 'Gentlemen! It is not the flag that moves, nor the wind that moves. It is your mind that moves.'"*

"So while it may appear sometimes that we are standing still, in reality we are either moving towards or moving away from that which frees us from the machine.

"What appears harmonious on one level can be quite chaotic on another level. For instance, we sit here in the middle of the desert looking out at the peace and harmony of the night sky, because our solar system has had time to become a relatively peaceful place. Nevertheless, when it was new, stars violently collided as they worked their way into a functioning gravitational existence. The same thing is true when observing the molecular level. We again would witness extreme chaos, as trillions of atoms appear to randomly smash into each other, breaking apart and rejoining by their chemical and gravitational likeness or repulsion.

"Once we understand a little bit about this attraction and repulsion of electrons," he continued, "we can see how it applies to everything in the universe from the extremely large to the very, very small. Here let me show you something."

He rose and took me over to an old shed filled with all kinds of scientific test equipment. "Though we may not be able to affect the very large, we are not *totally* helpless, and every once in a while, we may even learn a trick or two to help with the very small."

The shed was old and dusty and bottles lined every shelf and table, some filled with ingredients that I had never heard of and others whose names I recognized from my studies in chemistry and biology.

He pulled from a stack an old book whose cover was threads away from falling off and read.

"*That which is iron will never be gold, true Alchemy lies in the birth of a soul,*" he said.

He went on to explain, that not only does everything vibrate, but the rate of vibration is closely linked to how many electrons a chemical has orbiting its nucleus. And that the ancient science of Alchemy was forever doomed to failure because its true purpose was the transformation of a man's spirit or soul, and not turning base metals into gold as it has since been misinterpreted. "But," he continued, "While we may never be able to make gold from iron we can, however, sometimes manipulate an electron here or there and produce more of the *same* substance or even turn a similar substance into something else."

Just then, I heard a phone ringing. Isaac rose and went to the trailer to answer it. "*That's strange; I didn't see a telephone line anywhere.*"

He emerged from the trailer and we took our place back on the bench. "I heard the phone ring," I said, "but I don't see a telephone pole anywhere around here."

He smiled compassionately, "Everything is material, even that which you cannot see. Air, radio waves, even thought is all made up of something. Though thought is finer than air, it is material nonetheless. Here, let me show you something else." He reached down and picked up an old spoon and set it on a rock so it balanced near the center. He concentrated on it for a few seconds and the spoon jumped off the rock.

"The old spoon trick," I thought.

"Not the old spoon trick," he said. My mouth dropped open, as I realized he was reading me the same way Winger had taught me. "I look like I'm concentrating because people believe that's what's necessary. But I can do it while reading the paper."

"Is it a trick?" I asked.

"No," he said, "I can do it because I understand that all things are material. I think of moving the spoon and direct the thought to it. The molecules that make up the thought bump against the air molecules, which in turn bump against the spoon. There is no trickery or magic at all. The reason most people can't do it is because they don't understand that thoughts are material, or, know how to direct them."

This made so much sense to me. I had often wondered how people were able to affect objects without touching them. He knelt down for a moment gathering a pile of sticks and leaves.

"How about this one," he said. Putting his hands together in a praying position, he rubbed them back and forth against each other. He kept moving them faster and faster until smoke began to rise. Then clapping them together, he pulled his hands away and a spark flew from them into the dry twigs. Soon a small fire was burning and just as quickly he ran a hand above it and it went out. "I've always liked that one the best," he said. "There's just something about fire. I wish I had perfected it earlier in my life. I could have used it many times in my life."

"Can you teach me this?" I asked, impatiently.

"Sure, it's easy once you know the secret. But let's try something harder." He walked over to an old Buick sitting up on blocks. The hood was opened, probably rusted that way, and the engine was thick with sand and grit. He grabbed a wrench and began to remove a spark plug. When he completed his operation, he handed me the plug and asked me to close my hand around it. He closed his eyes for a moment and without whispering a word began to raise his hand towards mine. "*More special effects,*" I thought. However, as his hand neared, my hand began to burn. I quickly dropped the plug to the ground. It was glowing red-hot and I had let go not a second too soon.

"Now for something really worthwhile," he whispered. Reaching in the engine, he pulled out the battery, put one hand on the positive cable and one hand on the block. His face became red and contorted and with a loud grunt, he started the car. Without a spark plug and a battery, the car started, and then just as quick, he released his hands and the engine came to a dead stop.

I was silent. I couldn't speak if I wanted to. I had never seen anything like that before and only after a moment of collecting my thoughts was I able to begin to see the light of its potential.

He spent a few moments next to me in silence with his eyes closed. I felt uneasy, as if he were easily searching through my thoughts like a chest of drawers, leaving no hidden weakness unnoticed and coming to some kind of conclusion of my worthiness.

"Come," he said, "and I'll show you how to do it. But before I do, I must tell you one more story whose moral is 'be careful what you wish for'." He proceeded.

"A beggar was walking in the desert with a Sage. The beggar pleaded with the Sage to tell him the 'Secret Name' by which he could restore the dead to life.

'If I tell you, you will abuse it,' the Sage said.

'I am ready and fitted for such knowledge,' the beggar replied, "and besides, it will reinforce my faith.'

'You do not know what you ask,' The Sage said, but he told him the Word anyway. Soon afterwards, the beggar was walking in a deserted place when he saw a heap of whitened bones.

'Let me make a trial of the Word,' he thought, and he did. No sooner had the Word been pronounced than the bones became clothed with flesh and retransformed into a ravening wild beast, which tore him to shreds."

With the moral of that story firmly embedded in my psyche, I spent the next few months almost without sleep or food learning the wonders of this gift. It all came together for me as Isaac was trying to teach me how to push thoughts into the material world. As I tried to push the spoon off a rock, I suddenly began to see the chain of molecules that connected me to everything else in the universe. I could see the higher "feeding" off everything beneath it and in that moment there was great clarity. It seemed like these events were a bit more focused than everything else around them and after a while making my thoughts affect molecules was a simple exercise of cause and effect. The results may have been the small jump of the spoon off the rock, or the lighting of a few leaves, but I knew that it would just be a matter of time before I could master that effect on a bigger scale.

I practiced these techniques almost non-stop and then one afternoon in a moment of prolonged clarity it finally happened; I started the old Buick. It was only for a second or two, but that was all I needed. I knew what energy was necessary to make the connection and before long, I was starting and stopping it repeatedly.

"You are truly the gifted one," Isaac said, smiling as he sat down to rest his old bones. "We have been waiting a long time for you. You have learned in a few short years what has taken us a lifetime to perfect. We can teach you no more."

"We?" I asked.

"Yes 'we', the Seekers of Wisdom! We hoped someday we would meet a gifted student who could understand the pieces that each of us had labored to learn, someone capable of putting the whole thing together. We have passed you along to each other and you have shown us that you are the chosen one."

"I'm not sure I am all that!" I exclaimed.

"The rest will come in time, my lad. Be patient, you will see. What will you do now that you have learned the secrets of the oldest teaching known to man? What will become of this knowledge?"

"Are there more of you? I asked. "The Seekers, I mean, the Lords of Libra?"

"I am the last of *these* Seekers and the last of the teachers that I know of who can bestow the wisdom of the Mode on you. However, if you wish for more, then know that you are not the first student."

"I'm not?"

"There was one before you who wished with all his might to grasp the full meaning of the teaching but did not possess the natural gifts that you have. I will give you his contact information and if you are ever in Detroit you can look him up."

"Detroit," I gasped. "I grew up there. My parents are still there. I was thinking of returning soon."

Isaac rose and went into the trailer and after a few minutes returned with a piece of paper. "Here, take this," he said. "But beware. Though he tried his best to understand and practice these teachings the result of his efforts make him appear to be one sandwich short of a picnic. He's the one that created my VW van and if nothing else you may be able to get a good used car from him." Professing that he could teach me nothing else, Isaac set me on the road one spring morning.

While passing through Zion, Utah, I came upon an old abandoned car lying half-buried in the sand at a rest stop. There weren't many people around and I could not help but be tempted to try to start it. I looked over my shoulder and saw everyone going about their business. I moved closer to the car. Just as I raised my hand to meditate on it, the story Isaac had told me about testing the faith rushed through my head. *"It's not as if it's going to turn into a ravenous beast,"* I thought to myself. I raised my hand again and started it. The sudden noise caused several people to turn their heads my way. I quickly dropped my hand, severing my focus and the car came to a stop. I could tell that this actually caused more of a stir than starting the car, since it was obvious that I was controlling it.

"Hey, fella, how'd ya do that?" the man closest to me called.

"Do what?" I answered in my most innocent tone of voice. I noticed a bus loading up to leave and made my way towards it.

"That was some kind of magic, wasn't it!" the man continued as he followed me.

"No, your eyes must have been playing tricks on you," I said as I reached the bus. Soon the driver closed the doors behind me and I made my way to a seat by the window.

As we began moving out of the rest area, I looked out to see the curious bystander talking to another man who was holding a video camera. They looked up as the bus passed and saw me. The bystander pointed and said something, then the other man lifted the video camera triumphantly, nodding and smiling while he pointed to the camera and gave the "thumbs-up".

"Great," I thought to myself. *"I hope they just show it to their wives, otherwise it could turn into a 'ravening beast', just like Isaac said."*

Of course, they didn't, as I would find out later.

I enjoyed the secluded cover of the bus for the balance of my journey and bought a ticket east traveling through Colorado, Nebraska, and Iowa, ending in Wisconsin. I took the ferry across Lake Michigan from Port Washington to Grand Haven Holland finally arriving back in Detroit.

Once home, my parents who I had not seen in nearly a decade looked much older and more fragile than I would have expected. It's funny how once you have a memory of something stuck in your mind it often does not age even though you know great amounts of time have passed. This impression of my parents as retired senior citizens was new and unfamiliar to me.

Having my father around all the time was driving my mother nuts, since she was not accustomed to having to share the house, let alone the TV or the phone. Father loved being retired and would putter around the garage tinkering with this or that grandchild's broken toy that he had already had for months and would someday get around to actually fixing.

However, most of all he liked doing nothing but asking my mother to wait on him, hand and foot.

Strange, that a man when he retires is expected to do nothing, while his wife, if she is a "housewife" not only never gets to retire, but is expected to continue doing what she has already been doing for most of her life until she drops dead.

My stay with my parents was short but sweet, and I finally met the nieces and nephews who were born while I was away, and whose knowledge of me was beginning to reach that of urban myth proportions. I assured every one of them I was indeed human and even got around to secretly repairing and returning many of their imprisoned toys from my father's workshop.

CHAPTER VII

The Demon Crusher

With my bags in hand and a mind to get back on the road, I was just leaving the house when I saw my mother talking with our next-door neighbor Helen. Helen's car sat in her driveway, crushed on the passenger side and banged up all the way around, with one bumper gone and the other only attached to one side of the car from an episode where she entered the expressway via the exit ramp.

Helen had very bad vision and probably shouldn't have even had a license. However, in Detroit, as long as you had one eye that could focus on the first row of letters on the DMV eye chart and at least one leg and arm to steer and press the gas and brake pedals, you were good to go.

One of the cars she struck was a police car, and barely escaped being arrested. They called a tow truck, which brought the car back to her house. She was telling my mother that the insurance man had said they were declaring the car totaled, and that a tow truck was on its way to take her vehicle to the junkyard. When the tow truck arrived, the driver hooked up Helen's car.

"What do you do with a car that ends up like this?" I asked him.

"I take 'em to the Demon Crusher!" he said with a laugh.

"Who?" I asked.

"The Demon Crusher. He runs the local junkyard and he's a real character. An absolutely crack mechanic, specializing in German cars, and as crazy as they come. 'Mad' actually is almost the perfect description. He's on some kind of crusade and his customers can't buy a simple part without getting an ear-full from old Johann."

"Johann? Johann Wagner?" I blurted out.

"Yeah, Johann Wagner, that's him," he replied.

"That's amazing! He's just the person I need to see. Can you take me there?"

"Most folks aren't that anxious to meet him," he said, scratching his head, "But sure, hop in." I jumped in the passenger seat and we pulled out of my old neighborhood.

After a while, we pulled into a dirt parking area, from which the rest of the wrecking yard radiated, stretching away in all directions and disappearing in a haze as it backed up to the Interstate in the distance. A variety of mongrel dogs came from all directions to check the tow truck out. Beneath an awning that stretched to one side of a rusted aluminum building, sat a roughly made counter, and behind that stood the man who must surely be "the Demon Crusher" himself, Johann Wagner.

He was a large man, over six feet, and powerfully built, as if he could lift a car with his bare hands. He had wild white "Einstein" hair, a beard liberally peppered with gray, and wore blue-jean bib overalls. He was fairly old, probably in his sixties from the look of him, but he certainly wasn't visibly frail in any way. Instead, he looked like a rather tough old man.

Three customers were standing in front of the counter, and Johann broke off his conversation with them to look at the wreck entering the yard. He cocked his head for a moment, as if listening to something, before he yelled out to the tow truck driver, "There's a fair-sized demon in that one! Send him to the crusher. I'll deal with him later." I jumped out and walked towards them as the tow truck driver began to negotiate his way down a twisting pathway to unload Helen's car.

Just as Johann was about to continue with his customer, he stopped and looked back at Helen's retreating junk car with anger in his face.

"I heard that, you little demon bastard! You'll get yours!"

He returned to taking money from the customer, an older man in a business suit, while the others waited behind him. As I got closer, I could hear Johann speaking.

"For the third time now you come to me for parts you know only I have and argue with me about the price I ask. Your honor satisfied, you then pay my price and take your goods and yet you are completely oblivious to the real value of what I give you."

He shook the fist-full of money at the man. "Do you not hear the words I say to you? Do you not see the things I show you? Have I not told you these failings in your machine are just manifestations of failings in yourself?" Johann lifted an old beaten part off the counter and thrust it at the man.

"This replacement brake shoe tells me that you are an impatient man. You are the cause, this is the effect!" He dropped the part on the table and put the money in a drawer.

He counted out change to the customer who was now prepared to bolt as soon as the transaction was complete. Before he could, Johann dipped his finger in a small bowl of oil sitting on the counter and quickly marked the man's forehead with a single spot. The man backed up, stunned, and started rubbing the oil off. Johann leaned over the counter, slapping the man's hand away.

"Why do I continue to tell you these things each time you come, when it is clear that your ways have changed little? It's because there is hope, even for one such as you. Sometimes a gentle nudge is all it takes to get someone to change, and sometimes it takes several hard slaps."

The man hurried to his car with the dogs yapping excitedly after him. "But change, you will!" Johann yelled. "And if not because of what I tell you, then know that someday one will come who will have the ability to make you truly see yourself."

The next customer, a kid in his late teens or early twenties, was wide-eyed as he watched the first man's retreat, and nervously turned to Johann, holding out a part. He began to speak but Johann held up his hand, stopping him. He turned to me and looked me over intently. You've heard the phrase "the force of a person's gaze". Well that's exactly what it was, a force. I got an intense feeling that he wasn't just looking at me; he was *seeing* into me.

"What is it that you want?" he said.

I looked at the kid, just as confused as him, then stepped up to the counter in front of Johann. "Isaac recommended you to me. He said to look you up when I was in town."

"Isaac recommended me, you say? Humph! I can just imagine. You will wait?"

I nodded. "Would it be all right with you if I just looked around? I love cars and it looks like you've got quite a collection."

"From me, you don't need a blessing," he said.

I looked at the kid, then back to Johann, "A blessing?"

Johann leaned down into my face, "I see no demons in you. Are you willing to accept a true blessing?"

I didn't know exactly what to expect, but I sensed the importance of the question. "Yes," I said, and lowered my head. He dipped his finger in the bowl of oil and daubed my forehead with a spot.

"Seek until you find." I raised my head and smiled.

"Do you do this to everyone?"

"No, just the ones who need it." He turned to the kid and beckoned him back up to the counter's edge. "Now, what can I do for you?"

"Um, I was wondering if you might have a fuel pump for a 1970 Karmann Ghia?" the intimidated kid asked. "I'm getting this, um, rotten egg smell inside the car."

Johann took the fuel pump and after scrutinizing the part and the young man, asked, "Does it smell all the time you drive?"

"Um, no, it comes and goes."

Johann lifted the fuel pump to his face and breathed in deeply, his eyes closing as he concentrated on the smell. He opened his eyes and shoved the part at me. "Quickly, what do you smell?"

I took the pump and held it up to my nose. "Just gas," I said.

He looked at me with exasperation. "What kind?" he asked, with a bit of a bite in his tone.

I smelled the pump again, this time closing my eyes and drawing the air in slowly. After a moment, I opened my eyes. "At least three common types, mostly 87 octane."

He smiled and took the part back from me, then held it up in front of the young man. "Look boy, I could sell you one of these. Gott im Himmel, I could sell you a hundred! However, this pump? It is not your problem. The problem is your gas." He handed the pump back to the kid. "Cars can be a lot like people, boy. This smell you smell, sometimes you make a smell like this, with your body, yes?"

The kid's eyes widened. "Um, yeah."

"And what do you do that causes this smell to happen?" Johann asked loudly. "You put something inside you that does not agree with you! The same thing is happening in your car. Not all fuels are the same. Different companies make their gas in different ways. One of these fuels is not agreeing with your car. Stick with one type for a while and if it still smells, change to another type, maybe a higher octane rating."

He handed the pump back to the kid, who looked completely bewildered by the way this transaction hadn't gone.

"Can I offer you a little advice, my young friend?" Johann said, a bit more gently.

"Uh, sure."

"Your car is a reflection of you. What have *you* had to eat today? If your last meal came in a greasy bag, handed to you through a window, then my advice is, go have a nice soup dinner, and maybe a piece of fish!" Johann paused, leaned in closer to the mesmerized kid, and continued in a conversational, almost jolly tone of voice, "What else are you putting inside, hmmm? Are you watching the junk TV? Are you listening to what 'they' say when you make decisions about what to buy?" Johann's face became stern and his voice began to rise. "Beware! Beware of what you feed any machine, especially your mind!"

He stood up straight. "Pay attention to what your car tells you!" he thundered. "Pay attention to what your body tells you! Pay attention to what life is telling you!" He suddenly leaned back down into the kid's face. "Are you paying attention to what I am telling you?"

"Um, yes," the kid answered.

"Are you willing to listen harder to life?" Johann asked him.

"Yes."

"What is your name, young man?"

"Anson Safford."

"Close your eyes, young Anson Safford."

Johann dipped his finger in the bowl of oil and daubed the kid's forehead tenderly. "I stand in the sacred presence of Anson Safford, a human with the potential for awakening. Go forth young Anson and listen. May your ears learn to hear."

The kid opened his eyes, looked around, and turned to walk back to his car a bit dazed

Johann watched him walk away, and with a smile on his lips turned to the third customer who had been watching the exchange in amazement. His smile disappeared.

"And what may I do for you?"

"I'm looking for a 1966 Alfa Romeo Duetto that I can restore to show condition," the man said. "Someone told me that you might have a line on a car like that."

Johann leaned closer to the man, examining him up and down. "I'm afraid you've been misled. I have from time to time come across leads for this car you seek, but the last time was many years ago and I've heard nothing since."

He leaned in a little closer. "You know that even if you found such a car, it would break your heart in the end, don't you? Such a car requires a commitment that you do not want to make. Take my advice and put this dream on the shelf until a much later time." He stood straight again, "You are welcome, good bye." The customer looked bewildered as he retreated to his vehicle, a mini-van, then drove out of the lot.

"Why did you turn him down?"

"Sometimes, what people want is not what they need," he answered. "I didn't want to see him make a big mistake. Did you notice the wedding ring was new? And the car, a baby-mobile-in-waiting! He had that young, scared look a man gets when maturity is forced upon him and he doesn't think he's ready for it. Unconsciously, he's listening to a part of himself, a tiny little demon that is trying to hold on to his carefree past. That little demon blocked common sense and left him with desire. I did him a favor and didn't give him what the demon wanted. He's going to need the money and he'll know it was the right thing to do once he gets some more miles on him. However, for now, tell me why you have come."

"I'm Dewey Pinkerton," I said holding out my hand.

"Johann Wagner," he reached out and we shook. "I know who you are. Come with me to the crusher and we'll talk."

Johann pulled on a rusted gate that closed the driveway into the yard, locked it, and turned over a sign that read, "IF THE DEVIL'S LOOKING FOR ME, HELL CAN WAIT. I'M CLOSED!" He gestured me to follow as he began walking down the rows of stacked hulks of wrecked cars. Occasionally, he would stop and yell insulting non-sequiters at an empty car, then continue on as if nothing had happened. The dogs followed us, occasionally barking at whomever Johann was yelling at as if they too could see or hear whatever he did.

He spoke over his shoulder as he walked. "I have heard stories about you. I expected you to come to me one day, Mister Dewey Pinkerton."

"But how do you know about me?"

He looked at me as if I was an idiot. "I have seen the way you came to me! The way you dress! The way you respond to things around you! The knowledge you display!" He shrugged and added, "Besides, I've heard of you from the Seekers, of course. I have kept in contact with them. I recently received a phone call from that cricket-loving English monarchist Isaac, who told me you may be paying me a visit."

"But Isaac doesn't have a phone!"

"Isaac doesn't have a phone *'line'*," he corrected. "He didn't tell you about everything being material, hmmm?"

"Of course he did, I've been studying the Mode for years. I just didn't know he could get long distance service in the middle of the desert."

"He can't," Johann replied. "There's a Telco box about a quarter of a mile away. He can push his thoughts just about that far, and from there it's all Ma Bell. Nevertheless, this is all beside the point. I know you to be a very promising student of the Mode. Your teachers have made that very clear. Let me tell you a story.

"When I was young, my love of mechanics was not limited to just automobiles, but also, the universe itself. I read in a science magazine that a group of seekers had seen a piece of map of pre-sand Egypt, a map that also told of the possibility of unseen treasure hidden away in secret places. It was then that I dreamed of someday I would try to find and join them in their journeys.

However, I had no way to discover where they were. Then, I caught wind that Hitler himself also wanted this map, and by chance, I was asked to go along on an expedition to Abyssinia with the German S.S. to steal this relic. It was there we became aware that the Seekers had already left and had in their possession the map. From then on, I dedicated my life to the opportunity of finding and joining the Seekers.

"Unfortunately, after getting a brief chance to meet them while under pursuit, I was accidentally left lost in the Syrian Desert alone. It was many days before I emerged from the wilderness. As I thirsted, crawled, and baked in that hellish place, I began to hear the voices of demons. I've heard them ever since. This affliction put an end to my dreams of being a student of the Mode.

"Now you come along. A great student, with the potential to be a great teacher, perhaps the one in the prophecy, although I think that is for you to decide, yes? I look at you and can see instantly that you are not mad, yet. This is very promising to me."

As he talked, I thought about all the teaching that had brought me to this point. "I don't know how I feel about being in a prophecy," I said. "However, it does make a kind of sense. I mean, I've always had this way with mechanical things. I understand the idea being a 'machine', but I also see a much bigger picture than just engines, motorcycles, cars and all that. Life is so much bigger than cars!"

"Yes" Johann replied, "But cars are what you know best! See the car as your own personal metaphor."

He stopped in front of a wrecked sedan long enough to shout at it, "Oh yes, Mr. Potty Mouth? Let's see how rude you are after I give you a good crushing!"

He began walking again. We could hear the dogs scampering off to our left somewhere. Up ahead there was an area where a section of junk had been cleared, and in the middle sat a 1966 Alfa Romeo Duetto in gleaming, perfect shape.

"Hey, that's the car your customer wanted! You had one right here the whole time."

Johann shook his head. "I see that your teachers have taught you well about the ways of the machine, and you have learned things about people as well, but you haven't seen how the two things are connected."

"What two things?"

"People and their machines!" he shouted. "One is the reflection of the other!"

He brought his voice down to a gentler level. "Look, you say you've been taught something of the Mode? Well then, show me something special that you have learned. Impress me, Mister Motor Guru."

I looked around at the endless vista of cars in various states of decay and wondered what Johann expected of me. I noticed an old Mustang off to one side that didn't appear to be too beat up, except for the nasty crushed look of the driver's side door. I stepped up to the car, suddenly unsure and a bit shy.

"It runs," he said, "just barely."

I put my hands on the car, closed my eyes, and concentrated on the old hulk. After a few moments, the car let out a loud backfire and turned over once, belching blue smoke into the sky before it died. After a few moments more, I meditated on the totality of the car, and this time it started more softly and began to idle in the gentlest manner.

"That's a good one. I don't know that one yet," Johann said quietly.

He paused a moment. "What can you tell about the owner of this vehicle?"

I looked at the car, trying to be aware of more than just the obvious mangled body, but nothing came to me. "He was in an accident?" I finally said.

The look on his face showed disappointment. He lowered his head for a moment, as if coming to a decision, then waved me away. He walked around the car slowly, studying it. He pulled open the passenger door, which groaned and clanked. Putting his head in the car, he looked around, sniffed, and stood back up.

"This car belonged to a man who was in his mid-forties," he began. "He was just less than six feet tall. He was right-handed. He didn't smoke. He was not married. He had a job... I'm thinking a clerk of some kind, maybe."

Johann sat in the passenger seat and looked at the crumpled driver's side. He seemed to envision the man who used to sit there as he said, almost to himself, "A cautious driver. A cautious man! With a cautious job… accountant or insurance adjuster is my best guess."

He stepped out and walked around to the driver's side of the car, which was violently bent from an impact. He put his hands on the crushed driver's door, moving them around slowly as he felt every curve and angle. He was quiet for a minute as he pulled his hands away.

"This man was too careful for his own good. He was sure to take risks whose odds were severely stacked in his favor. He never did anything important, he never got the girl he wanted, and he never took chances. He was stopped somewhere. A stop sign maybe? No, probably a railroad crossing. Something had his attention. Perhaps he saw a car stuck on the tracks! Yes, a family, stuck and trying to get to safety as an oncoming train grew closer. He could have helped them! They could probably see him stopped just yards away. Maybe they signaled to him or called out! Nevertheless, he could not; he *would* not attempt to help, even if others would suffer. He was a careful man, you see."

Johann stood back and looked at the crushed door, then leaned close and examined it from just inches away.

"The train struck the car just as the family jumped to safety. Because their vehicle was more than half way across the tracks when hit, it shot at an incredible speed into the car of the patient man, killing him on impact."

"Too careful was this man, as it cost him his own life. If he had tried to help, he would have been out of harm's way when the train's damage was done."

Johann went back around to the passenger side of the car and opened the glove box, pulling out all of the random stuff inside. He sorted through it briefly and handed a few items to me. One was a business card for a CPA. The other was a driver's license that listed the man's height and weight. His status was unmarried. Finally, there was a receipt for the car from the NTSB, the agency that investigates train accidents.

I was stunned, "That's a good one. I don't know that one yet either."

"Come on," he said, and we walked further down the meandering rows of junk, with Johann yelling, "Rot in Hell!", "I hope your soul burns a long time!" and "So's your mother!" at various cars. He seemed to know exactly where he was going, but I had to admit that I was thoroughly lost.

"This is a big place," I said.

Johann smiled, "It's even bigger than I think it is."

"What do you mean?"

"Well, I've been running this place for almost twenty years now," he continued, "and I've never run out of room yet. It was full when I bought the place from the owner before me, and it's full now, but somehow there's always room for one more car."

"Can you really read people just from their cars?" I asked.

"What? You think you were the only one who learned something from the Seekers?" he smiled and pointed randomly to cars that were stacked on both sides of us as we wandered down the aisles. "A man who drank too much. A woman who was not faithful to her husband. A man who told many lies. A man with no job. A woman with a long degenerative disease." He shrugged as we turned the corner to the area where the crusher sat. It was a huge metal box with a conveyor belt coming out of one side of it. There was a large crane arm hanging over it with a huge metal claw at the end.

"Reading the details takes longer," he continued, "and occasionally one generalizes too much only to find that they are dealing with a true individual. However, by and large, it's easy once you put your mind to it.

"You've reached a higher level of awareness than what only your senses tell can you. This is just an extension of that. A tall man leaves behind one kind of impression on his car. A short man leaves a different impression. A single man, a married man, a cautious man, a careless man, each leaves a kind of mark. When I look at a car, I perceive small details that point to the kind of person who drove the care. Slowly but surely, I begin to see the person. It's like looking at the negative of a photograph. I see the shape of the person as they sit in their car, the empty space that they would fill if they were there. As the details become clearer, the negative turns to a positive and the owner of the car is revealed. You could do this yourself with the skills you have, if you practice."

He shrugged, "Besides, I hear demons. You don't hear them?" He looked at me expectantly. I shook my head. He shrugged and continued up a small set of stairs, which lead into the control booth situated just above and behind the crusher. At the end of the conveyor belt sat an empty flatbed trailer.

Johann settled into the operator's seat and guided the control arm to select a car from the yard, then deposited it into the crusher and pulled a lever. A loud grinding noise filled the air.

"I hear the voices of demons in the cars," he continued, shouting over the crusher. "Not in all the cars. Some cars are demon-free, although they are in the minority, and some cars have demons so small or weak that I can barely hear them."

The noise stopped and he maneuvered the claw to pick up the crushed car, now a solid rectangular block, and load it onto the flatbed trailer.

"Where do the demons come from?" I asked.

"They come from the owners, of course, who have demons of their own they carry around with them. Cars take on the characteristics of their owners, and when they leave their imprint on a car, their demon is imprinted too. Most of them are mouthy little bastards, too. They yap on and on… I hear them chattering in the background all day long. They give me no peace!"

A smile lit his face, and he straightened up as he came out of his reverie, "And so, the crusher!" He maneuvered the claw to pick up a mid-70's Chevy truck that had been mangled in some sort of horrible accident. "There's a good-sized demon in this one. The owner was a pathological liar. Listen carefully. See if you can hear him."

I strained to hear as the claw picked up the truck and swung it over the opening of the crusher. The rusted hulk groaned evocatively as it swayed in the claw's grip, but I had to shake my head and admit, "I don't hear it."

Johann nodded, and then tipped his head as if he had heard the car speaking to him. "Oh, Yeah? You'll burn in hell for that!" he yelled back as he positioned the truck over the huge hopper at the top of the crusher and pulled the lever that released the claw's grasp. The truck fell into the hopper and he pulled another lever that began the crushing mechanism. "See if you can hear him now. He's starting to scream like a wounded animal."

I listened as the crusher slowly pressed the truck into the shape of a large brick. The noise was deafening, and in the midst of the shriek and snap of crushing metal, I thought I heard an almost primal howl. It reached a peak then stopped abruptly when the crusher had completed its cycle and a large metal brick was ejected onto the conveyor belt.

"Maybe, there just for a second… I'm not really sure…" I trailed off.

"OK. So, maybe not hearing demons is a good thing," Johann said, brushing my failure off. "Come and tell me about your adventures with the Seekers. I want to hear all about what Mac and Isaac and the rest of those esoteric misfits have told you."

Johann shut down the crusher, giving the controls a loving pat as he got up to leave. We went back to the office where he began setting up a small barbeque under the awning, preparing for an evening meal. All the while, I talked of my adventures, pouring out every detail of the things I had seen and learned traveling with Captain O'Connell and Winger and the rest. Johann responded to me at polite moments; "They had to replace the roundhouse wall? Really!" "Twin KAT P49s? You don't say!" "Ah, the outside loop! I've seen him do that!" 'They expect me to go slow, and so I do,' ah, that's rich! I like that."

As I finished telling my story of the events that led me to the junkyard, Johann had finished the cooking. He piled up a plate then motioned me to help myself. He sat by a small fire he had built at the edge of the awning and the dogs came to sit in front of him in a rough half-circle, like an audience, as he fed them scraps off of his plate. They were gentle and goofy; smiling, tongues hanging out, occasionally rolling around on their backs like puppies.

I sat next to him and ate, and after a bit, when the edge had been taken off everyone's hunger, Johann looked at me and asked, "And so, now, you've learned much, but what will you do with this knowledge? What will you make of your future?"

"I don't know for sure," I responded, "there's still so much more to learn that I could spend a lifetime as a student, but I also want to share this knowledge with people, somehow. Their lives could be so much better if someone could help them."

Johann set his plate down for the dogs to lick. "Look son, it was obvious to me, and to your teachers as well, that someone with your gifts would one day appear. I imagine that Sean and the rest were quite excited at the prospect of adding to the influences of the one before them. Except for MacGregor of course, he took a gamble on you. However, we all do that sometimes.

"You see someone who is ready for the message, and you toss them a bone," he said, quickly throwing a piece of meat up in the air as the dogs scrambled to their legs. "You tell them the truth as you know it and see if they bite, that's all preaching is, really. If you're lucky, you've touched someone and because of it, they are changed. Sometimes it's a big change, sometimes a small change. Any change is good."

"I do want to help people change!" I said, "But I'm not really sure what to say or how to say it. You were a student of the Mode and you tell people the truth, why do they run away?"

He looked at me and thundered, "Because I'm crazy, you fool! Look at me through their eyes. Oh yes, I know how I appear. That's one of the reasons we've waited for someone like you to come along. Can you imagine any of the Seekers interacting 'normally' with society?"

I thought briefly of Mac's passing and Winger's untimely end. Winger would have hated the spotlight and Mac would have scared everyone as a preacher. Sean was too big a ham and Isaac was just too bizarre. "No, they certainly were an odd bunch," I conceded.

Johann laughed. "An odd bunch? That's the company I keep? Well, I could do worse, I suppose. Still, I say again, you've learned much, but what will you do with it? Thought is admirable, but action is needed and must be consistent with thought. Let me tell you a short Zen story about your dilemma. I love those Zen masters. They have a sly sense of humor.

> *"Anyone walking about Chinatowns in America will observe statues of a stout fellow carrying a linen sack. Chinese merchants call him Happy Chinaman or Laughing Buddha. This Hotei (one of the seven lucky gods of Japan) lived in the T'ang Dynasty. He had no desire to call himself a Zen master or to gather many disciples about him. Instead he walked the streets with a big sack into which he would put gifts of candy, fruit, or doughnuts. These he would give to children who gathered around him in play. He established a kindergarten of the streets*
>
> *Whenever he met a Zen devotee he would extend his hand and say, 'Give me one penny.' And if anyone asked him to*

return to a temple to teach others, again we would reply, 'Give me one penny.'

Once as he was about his play-work another Zen master happened along and inquired, 'What is the significance of Zen?'

Hotei immediately plopped his sack down on the ground in silent answer.

'Then,' asked the other, 'what is the actualization of Zen?'

At once, the Happy Chinaman swung the sack over his shoulder and continued on his way.

"So, no matter what you decide to do, do something you must. I feel that it is time for you to swing your sack over your shoulder and get on with it. You Americans, who have the knack for putting high concept into low language, would say, 'Shit or get off the pot.' So, what will you do?"

"Well, I do feel like I'm in a special position," I answered slowly, "I've had amazing teachers and I've learned incredible things. I have this dream... What if everybody knew what I know?"

Johann laughed, "'Everybody' is a lot of people, and 'what you know' is a lot to know. How big do you want this to be? Do you want to change Detroit? America? The World? You? The world is a sleeping giant. Do you wish to wake it?"

I was getting excited now and beginning to rant, "Yes, I want to wake up everyone!" I howled into the night, "Everyone, wake up!" The dogs howled along with me. "There's no excuse for sleeping in these times. We can help people with this teaching if we could get them to understand. People can learn and they can change, and I want to help that along. I want to change the way people think, the way they live. I mean... I guess I want to change the world!" I paused to consider what I'd just said. "Is that a good thing?"

Johann laughed and grinned, happy in my revelation, "You ask a German this?" Then his face sobered. "What, exactly, do you think you want to accomplish? It is very important at the beginning of any venture to understand what the goal is, regardless of whether you reach it. How do you want to share this? At what level? With whom? For how long? At what cost?"

"Well, I hadn't thought about how much money it would take."

"I'm not talking about the money cost! I'm talking about the cost in balance, what some people think of as Karma," Johann corrected me. "Changing the world will cost you. How much are you willing to pay? Your love life? Your privacy? Your fortunes? Your life?"

"You're not painting a very pretty picture."

"Listen," he said softly, "you say you want to change the world, yes? Well, many people have tried and failed to conquer the world, but few have tried to change it, and the last person that did was nailed to a cross. Whatever path you take will have severe difficulties and the possibility of failure is a very real one. For every action, there is an equal and opposite reaction. However, in the case of trying to change the world the reaction is not proportional. Many forces will act against you. You want to change the world? Are you willing to accept the world changing you?"

I sat and thought about it for a while, envisioning a world where man was free from the law of accident, truly under his own will and in tune with the mechanics of nature. "If I could change enough people, I would pay any price. It would be worth it."

"Well then, if you would change the world, I would tell you to keep this in mind: Cars reflect people. Make the people more consciously aware of their relationship with their cars, and you will be making them unconsciously more aware of themselves. You *can* read a book by its cover, to some extent, and this is useful when trying to change the way a person thinks. The demons in the cars are just little demons. The big demons are in the people. So, teach them about their cars, help them with their lives."

He stood up and spoke as he cleaned up and put out the fire, "So, you have a message you want to give people. You must practice this, or your message will not be heard. In addition, you must make a plan on how to spread this message. This also will take time. Hmmm," he mused, "let me think on it tonight. I may have a way to help you get started. In the meantime, it is late and talking is over. Let me show you where to sleep."

He led me down one of the aisles of junk to an area that had been cleared. In the middle of it sat a dumpy looking school bus, which was leaning at an angle because all of the tires on the driver's side were flat. Johann opened the door and gestured, "Go in, I've started to fix this up as a mobile living space. There's a bed, a sink, and a toilet that works, not much else because I haven't had time for this project. Nevertheless, you can close the doors and it's fairly warm. You'll get a good night's sleep."

I looked around and for all of its apparent dinginess, the bus was actually warm and clean. Johann lit a small gas lamp then walked down the steps of the door. "Gute Nacht!" he said.

"Danke Hund," I answered with the only German I knew, and which I think means 'thanks, dog' in translation, then settled in for the night.

The next morning, I awoke refreshed and relaxed. The cozy atmosphere of the bus had worked its charms and my sleep had been deep and dreamless. I walked over to the awning and saw Johann by the fire, drinking fresh coffee and dressed in amazing contrast to his attire from the day before. He was wearing white cotton shirt and pants, with a straw boater on his head. "Are you in a barbershop quartet?" I asked, accepting a steaming mug of coffee from him.

He laughed, "No, this is my vacation suit. Today I leave on vacation. Until then, the yard is yours. Use it to practice your message. When I come back, we will see if you still want to change the world."

I stared for a moment as the weight of what Johann had said hit me. "You want me to run the yard? By myself?"

Johann nodded, "Yes, but not by yourself. I'm giving you two gifts and one task before I leave. First, the bus you slept in last night? It is yours. It's guaranteed demon-free and I think it's the right ride for your immediate future. Second, I'd like to introduce you to Jesus Lopez. He's been helping me here at the yard for years." He paused for a moment. "Well, more like following me around like a puppy, but he knows a lot about the yard and he'll be a great help to you while I'm gone. I've been giving him some of the deep teaching of the Mode, and while he has trouble with things like patience and focus, he has enthusiasm and a desire to please that makes him quite endearing. Of course, I don't tell him that."

He called into the office, "Jesus, come out here." I heard quick steps and saw a small Hispanic man in jeans and a work shirt hurrying out the door towards us. He stopped in front of Johann and waited expectantly.

"What is it I do every year at this time?" Johann barked at him.

"Vacation," Jesus answered instantly in his accented voice.

"And for how long do I go?" Johann continued.

"40 days and 40 nights," answered Jesus.

"And where do I always go on this vacation?" Johann grilled him.

"Puerto Vallarta," Jesus said, and here his accent made him fluent. He smiled.

Johann frowned, "And what do I do in this town?"

"You go sailing."

Johann smiled a predatory smile. "And why do I go sailing?"

Jesus, looking bewildered and slightly angry, answered, "I don't know, Señor. I know you do this always, but do not understand it. A boat in the ocean… this is not the place for a smart person."

Johann shook his head. "You see that he means well but still has far to go." He looked briefly at Jesus, then back at me, "I go because there's a different kind of learning to be had there. All the time we work with engines, mechanical power. Out there, you work with wind power and water power, and neither one is at your command. It's the other way around; you are at its command. Yes, a great many things to learn on a sailboat on the ocean."

He turned to Jesus, "Jesus, let me introduce you to Dewey Pinkerton, a great student of the Mode and soon to be a great teacher himself. I want you to help him here in the yard while I'm gone. Don't let him break anything and don't let him hurt himself, otherwise he can do things however he wants. Got it?"

"Si!" said Jesus.

"Dewey, meet Jesus Lopez, a bus driver by trade, a great natural mechanic and my best pupil. He doesn't say much but when he does, listen."

"And now for your task; practice your message here, Dewey. This is a good place for it. Your successes will be almost instantaneous and your failures will go by mostly unnoticed. People are expecting the crazy German, they'll be pleasantly surprised to find you here running the show."

A cab pulled into the driveway. Johann loaded his bags, climbed in, and waved saying, "Make sure I'm still in business when I get back!"

I turned and looked at Jesus, a little stunned at how fast all of this had happened. "What do I do now?"

"No scheduled deliveries today, no pickups, so just open the gate and see what comes," and with that he smiled and shrugged, then walked towards the gate to open it. I sat down on a stool behind the counter under the awning… and waited.

CHAPTER VIII

40 Days in the Yard

My first day as a teacher was unexceptional. People came in, off and on, and I tried Johann's approach of baptizing them when I thought they needed it. However, most were confused or hostile. I tried to recall some of the Swami's better sayings, but they didn't go over that well either. I knew I wasn't getting across to them. It was hard to put the Mode out there.

At the end of the day, as Jesus and I closed up the yard and counted the receipts, I told him how I felt.

"It's OK, jefe. You just getting started. It don't all come on the first day," he said, and went back to finishing the paperwork. He looked up again and smiled, "And even if they no hear you, I am! You got one convert!"

"You mean I'm making sense to you?" I asked.

He nodded. "I see why Johann thinks you are good teacher. It's how you treat people. You are being polite, fair, kind... you are interested in them. Even if they don't get it, at least they get you." After he left, I thought about what he said and decided he was right; it was too early to get discouraged.

As I lay down in the bus that night, I realized that I hadn't really tried to imagine the kind of effect I was trying to create. The more I thought about it, the more I wanted to gather a network of people who could understand at least a little of the Mode, and could expand what they knew and pass it on; a self-sustaining reaction; a grass roots campaign. Nevertheless, to change the world, I was going to have to take it much further than that. The teaching needed to be on everyone's lips, part of the everyday culture. It needed to make an impact. I knew that an approach like that would focus a lot of attention on me, and suddenly became aware of exactly what Johann had meant about paying the price my dream might ask.

As the days wore on, I got better at running the yard. I found out how to tell who would let me baptize them, and those that did were truly touched by it. I amazed more than one customer with a fairly accurate impromptu reading of them via their rides. This piqued their curiosity and helped to hook them. I had to laugh at the image of me as a fisherman... or was that a fisher of men?

I also found that many of my customers had a real need to confess their automotive sins, and that once they got even the slightest encouragement to do so, the dam burst and they spilled their guts. I think this has a lot to do with the fact that the car is so much a part of people's daily lives. It's part of the family, and so we grieve when we treat it badly. We want to apologize. We want it to forgive us, and seeking forgiveness is a good start towards becoming a bit more aware of ourselves. The confession became a popular pastime with many of the regulars and many of the first-time customers seemed to catch the spirit. Some people saw it as a bit of play-acting fun, but it still gave them an opportunity to touch something deep and true within them. Those that truly unburdened themselves were so amazed at the change that they were also hooked for good. Jesus was right. They weren't all completely getting it, but they were getting something. It was a good start.

Jesus and I fell into a pattern of sorts over those forty days. Mornings would find him just finishing making coffee under the awning as I woke up and stumbled out of the bus. Somehow, he did this regardless of what time I woke up. We usually opened the gates by 9:30 each morning, and there was always either one customer waiting for us to open or one that drove up just as we did. I did the initial "meet and greet" with the customers, getting a read on them, and turned them over to Jesus who would help them with the parts they needed, and then bring them back to me to handle the money. Sometimes there would be slow periods, and Jesus and I would use this time to work on restoring the bus. Other times a small crowd would accumulate. I took these opportunities to do a little old-fashioned oration, Johann-style, but with a bit less of his "fire and brimstone" and a little more humor and compassion.

After each day was done, Jesus and I would take a break for coffee, then work on the bus for another hour or two. Over time, Jesus and I got into a good working rhythm at the yard and on the bus. He had no problem watching me do something that was new to him and then executing the exact same thing, and had no problem telling me when I was missing something obvious, like a customer that hadn't paid me yet. We made a good team. While we worked on the bus, I told Jesus of my journeys and used him as a sounding board for some of the parables I was thinking of telling when I began to teach the Mode to the world.

I was actually starting to get the hang of putting the Mode out in the world.

CHAPTER IX

Tempted by the Loot of Another

One day a man entered the yard and scanned the place. He was older, well groomed, and well dressed. I remembered two things immediately; I'd seen him before, and it wasn't a good thing. He walked towards me as I was just lifting my head from the bus engine.

"I'm looking for Dewey Pinkerton."

"He's not here right now, but I'd be happy to take a message for him," I replied.

The man's eyes narrowed just the tiniest fraction. "Well, when he gets back, tell him that I'd like to help him make some money," he said.

"Really, how much money?"

"More than he could make repairing buses and running junkyards," he replied, gesturing to the bus.

I paused for a moment. "Alright, you've found Dewey Pinkerton. Now what can I do for you?"

"My name is Mitch Murphy and I'm the Vice President of Sales at Fred Motors. I knew your Dad, back in the day, and I've met you a couple of times at the auto show. I've kept an interest in you, kid. You have a real different angle on cars. I'd like to hire you to come and work for me... in marketing."

His mention of the car show placed him for me. Now I knew why he looked familiar. "I've already got a job," I replied, putting my head under the bus hood again.

He smiled and glanced around the yard. "Yeah, some job. Look, you've got some real talent and I figure with the exposure I can give you, this would be something that you'd be interested in."

I smiled. "And I could just say what I wanted? Say what's true?"

Mitch held his hands up. "Whoa there boy, let's not get ahead of ourselves! We'd start out with some carefully scripted press releases. At first, we'd just want you to help us reach a new audience with our message." He stopped to see if I would respond. When it became clear that I wouldn't, he continued, "Listen, there's some good perks involved in this job."

"Like what?"

"Well, I can tell that you're planning to get this old bus back on the road, and if you're serious, then you must know that just the gas alone for this beast is going to cost you a fortune. So one of the perks I'm offering is free gas for as long as you work for me."

I looked at the bus, then back at Mitch. "Man does not drive by fuel alone."

"Hmm, OK, so I throw in oil changes, brake fluid, gear oil…" I shook my head. "OK, OK, so maybe that doesn't do it for you. How about this?" he continued. "You'll have access to a professional test track where you can put this big old beast through its paces. How's that sound?"

"I believe that someone once said 'Thou shalt not test the limits of thy machine.'" I said smiling again.

"OK, OK. That may not be the right thing for you either. Listen; think of all the stuff you could get as part of the promotional deals we could work out… cars, clothes, endorsements, TV, almost anything could be yours! As long as you show the Fred logo, flash the Fred colors, you know?"

For just a moment, I could see how easy that way would be. My needs handled, my whims catered to, all for a little show to be put on for the public. There certainly would be none of the hardship I fully expected to find in the future that I was currently creating for myself. However, I shook my head again.

"Thou shalt honor the car, thy transportation, no matter what brand it is."

"Look, I can see that I'm not getting through to you just how important to me… uh, us… this could be," Mitch said, trying not to get too exasperated.

I stood silent for a moment, just looking at the man, before I answered. "I think I do know how important this is. Don't you think that I know what's in your heart? Do you know what I've done for the last forty days? I've been in this junkyard studying every person who came in here like my life depended on it! And I think I've just found out that it does depend on it. I look at you and see you're not listening to what your real self is telling you. You really would sell your mother, for the right price."

Mitch looked shocked. Then, just as suddenly, shock turned to rage. "Hey, I'm just trying to do you and me both a favor!"

"You think that getting me to work for Fred Motors will make you happy, but it won't. I've learned the difference between what people want and what they need. What they want seldom makes them happy. I'm going to make you really happy, and tell you 'no'."

Mitch began to speak, but I cut him off. "You don't like this right now, because it means you don't reach your short-term goal of 'recruiting' me. However, you'll go away with something to focus your energies on. I'm going to stand against everything you represent. Every time you think you're going to pull one over on people, I'm going to be there to tell them how things really are. The thing you're going to want, more than anything, is to get rid of me. Because I am going to tell the truth, as I see it, and that's going to hurt you more than anything."

Mitch looked at me in anger and frustration and finally pulled himself up straight. "Well, I can see that you're a fraud, or you wouldn't have to resort to insults. I wouldn't have you work at Fred Motors now if your crippled old grandmother begged me on her knees. Don't cross me, Pinkerton! I'm not just anybody! I can make things happen and I can get people to listen to me! So just stay out of my way!"

He turned and left in a rush. I let out a slow breath and closed my eyes in relief, and muttered to myself, "Too late now."

On the forty-first day, as I opened the gates, a cab pulled up and out stepped Johann in the exact same outfit he'd left in. His hair was wilder and sun-streaked and he had a deep tan, but he also looked calmer and quite happy.

"So, Mister Motorman, I see I am still in business," he said cheerily. "This is a good thing, and I see no obvious scars, wounds, or missing limbs so you must have survived also. Come, let us have some coffee and you can tell me what I have missed."

We sat under the awning and drank coffee while I told Johann about my experiences trying to get people to hear the message of the Mode. Jesus and I also showed him the bus, which was now almost completely restored and even had a few "extras" installed. I couldn't wait to take it out on the road. As the morning wore on, customers wandered in and out. Johann watched carefully as I handled them with ease, and even got to hear one of the parables that I told to a small crowd of customers that had backed up at the counter. All day, Johann just hung around in the background and watched, seemingly pleased to be back and to let us do the work.

Later that day, after we closed the gates, Johann, Jesus, and I sat down to rest. Johann looked at me and smiled, "You've done well here," he said. "The people respond well to you. They like you. This is important. Now you must go and begin another journey. Your time here is done. There is nothing else I can teach you. Now you must let life teach you."

"What kind of journey?" I asked.

"Any journey, something will come up. You just need to be out on the road, preaching your message everywhere that you go. You will take the bus and Jesus as your driver, if he is agreeable, and go where you are called."

Johann looked at Jesus, who nodded his agreement and smiled. "Yes, that will be good. Who else is better to have as a second set of hands when the old bus begins to feel its age again, no? I will go with you."

"I am proud of you, and I have great hopes for what you may accomplish in your life," Johann said. "I am also worried about the reaction you will generate. Nevertheless, I'm an old man now, and worries come much more easily and are dispelled with more difficulty. When this trip begins, and I believe that you will begin tomorrow, go with my blessing and with all of my good wishes. Be careful, but don't be afraid to accept help from unlikely sources. You may find that these are the best people to gather around you for your cause." He rose and gripped my hand in a firm shake.

"Never stop asking questions, and of all the questions you ask, ask this; Where does your awareness stop? When you find a place where your awareness stops, then examine that place and push your awareness forward. There is always more to learn. See that you do not forget this." Johann rose and headed off to bed. I was touched by his concern and his benediction. I lay awake late into the night asking myself many questions.

The next day when Johann opened the gates, he picked up the mail and brought it back inside, where he held out a letter addressed to me. In it, I received word that Anna, the wife of my dear friend, Winger, was in need of some assistance selling the airplane business. She was never very good at managing the family business and was anxious just to be rid of it. She didn't trust anyone else and would be grateful if I could assist her in its sale. I told Johann, and he smiled at me, "Here is the journey I knew was coming," he said.

CHAPTER X

Fisher of Men

The autumn leaves had yet to turn yellow and red and the trees that lined the roads and hills of Lenawee County, Michigan were just beginning to hint at the inevitable surrender that awaited them. There were children playing in the parks without jackets, perhaps as an unconscious sign of protest that soon they would have to trade in their swings and slides for schoolbooks and homework.

Having my own wheels and a driver, I finally wasn't so dependent on the kindness of strangers anymore and decided to explore that classic American travel path affectionately known as "Route 66," while making my way out west to help Anna; the wife of my dear deceased friend and teacher Winger. Jesus drove us southwest through the northern tip of Indiana, then

Northern Illinois into Chicago where we would pick up the starting point of this route at the Northbound Terminus near Lake Michigan.

After driving for some time, it became obvious that we were getting closer to St. Louis when the famous arch became visible up ahead. As we passed through the city, the bus, which I had nicknamed "Angel Food," stood out like a sore thumb amongst the mid-sized American made family cars that lined every street and thoroughfare.

Several hours later, we pulled over to rest in a little town in Missouri called Devil's Elbow. The town got its name from a sharp hairpin turn that a river tributary made there as boats often got stuck trying to navigate the narrow, twisted bend. I was getting quite thirsty and decided to stop and relieve both the pressure in my bladder and the dryness in my throat. Jesus stayed on the bus to get some sleep while I, being interested in the human psyche, decided to go to one of the biker watering holes in town called the "Devil's Elbow Saloon."

Bikers have always been misunderstood. There was a time when I was a child that a gang of them pulled into Detroit and caused quite a scene at some of the local bars there. However, they wore leather jackets with "Hell's Angels" embroidered on them, a group that already had quite a reputation for stirring things up. During the early nineteen seventies, most of the rambunctious bikers ended up in jail while the more conservative among them traded their riding gloves in for golf gloves and a job that supported the families they had strewn throughout the country.

Over time the new riders of these wonderful machines, came to be made up of a variety of people as diverse as the styles and paintjobs on the bikes themselves. Of course, there are those who still ride because of the freedom it represents, but they have become mostly responsible, even respectable, patriotic citizens; a far cry from the bar fighting, troublemaking riders of the free-wheeling sixties. Whenever you see a Harley today you would have to agree that perhaps with the exception of fire trucks, nowhere in America is any other vehicle kept so clean.

As I walked up the to saloon door, I passed a guy who was looking at his bike's temperature gauge, which was in the red. He stepped off his bike and onto the curb and we arrived at the door at the same time, bumping shoulders on the way in.

"Hey, bud. Watch where the hell you're going," he said, rather pissed off.

"Sorry," I replied. However, something strange had just happened. While bumping shoulders with him, I saw a flash of the problem he was having with his chopper. "Your oil case has a crack in it."

"What? You talkin' to me?" He said, inhaling deeply. It broadened his massive chest and shoulders. He was already quite a big guy, around six-feet-two and weighing about two-hundred-seventy pounds. He had tattoos across both arms and a red bandana worn tightly across his forehead.

"That's, why you've been running so hot," I continued, a little more cautiously.

"Look, buddy, I don't know who you are, but if I was leaking oil, don't you think I'd know it?"

"You can't tell," I said, "because you park your bike in the same place most of the time, over wood slats on a bridge or a pier of some kind. The oil leaks through the cracks in the wood down to the water below. You never see it."

He stood there for a second, all tensed up, before slowly relaxing his "ready to strike" coiled physique. "I *have* been running kinda hot," he said, in a slightly gentler tone. "Come on in, I'll buy you a drink and you can tell me how the hell you know where I live!"

After having only spent a few seconds in this joint, I could tell that everything I just told you about Harley riders being nice did not apply to this place. Someone selected a disco song from the jukebox and was immediately grabbed, beaten to a bloody mess, and thrown outside. All of a sudden, I felt as though eyes were on me as we approached the bar.

"What'll ya have mister?" the bartender asked.

"We'll have J.D. shots," the biker replied, for both of us. "Rocco's my name," he said, and raised his shot glass in the air.

I stumbled for a suitable name for myself. "Ah… D-man," I finally replied, knowing that if anyone heard me answer "Dewey" another fight would have broken out.

"Cheers, D-man," he replied, and we drank our shots. Just as fast, he slammed his glass down on the counter. "Are you done yet?"

"Yeah… why?"

"Cause now I'm gonna have to kill ya!"

"What?" I said, scanning the room for the nearest exit. "What have I done?"

He laughed. "I'm just kiddin' ya man, relax. But I do wanna find out how you knew about my bike, *and* where I live."

"It's this gift I have. It allows me to sense things about a person by touching them," I answered.

"Sounds kinda queer to me!" he retorted.

"It's nothing like that, really. Its part ancient teaching and part hard work. It took me many years to learn how to do it, and I still can't make it happen every time."

"Prove it!" he said, puffing his chest up again. "Tell me more about… *me.*"

I had forgotten we were in the "Show Me" state, and felt this was neither the time nor the place to exercise what would surely be perceived as mysticism. "Really, it's nothing…"

"Show me something or I am gonna kick your ass, then I'm gonna kill you, then I'm gonna kick your ass some more."

I tried to relax, and focus my attention on the ominous task at hand. *"What else did I sense about him?"* I wasn't getting very much. It's not as if I could ask to touch him again. That would mean certain death. It had to be subtler. "*Perhaps if we did another shot we could toast glasses and accidentally bump hands, that should be enough,"* I thought.

"How about another shot first, on me?"

"Sure, but your not gonna be able to drink your way out of this. I'm a *serious* drinking man!"

"*I can hold my own,"* I thought. "*I spent a few years with a bunch of crazy drunken Irish sailors.*" The bartender poured us another round of shots and I positioned my hand in the air in front of his.

"Cheers," I said, and brought my hand forward into his. Our knuckles touched and just as quickly, he pulled his hand back and took his shot. I took mine too, knowing that at least I would feel a little less pain should he follow through on his physical threats.

Impressions from him started pouring in. I fought to sort through them, piecing together what I could about him, searching for the ones that were least likely to get me killed. He had a past of constant disappointment and loneliness. He had lost several people near to him and was living with the guilt that he was still alive and they were gone. That would explain some of his anger. I decided to start with a line of questioning, starting with the obvious.

"So, you served in the military?" I asked.

"If you were a blind man, then I'd be impressed, 'cause I'd know you didn't just read that on my arms. But seeing as how you walked in this joint without cracking your skull open on anything, and the fact that I have military tats all over me, I'm guessin' you can tell me what branch too?" He flexed his biceps, which expanded the "Army Ranger" insignia there. "You've gotta be able to do better than that, son!"

"Ok, ok," I said, abandoning my initial approach. "You lost some loved ones at war; one of them was your brother in Vietnam. You spent some time in captivity, and are angry about something… your mother… you're angry with your mother. She didn't love you as much as your broth…

"STOP!" he bellowed. "That's enough! Are you with the V.A. or the police?" He glanced around the room a bit nervous. "Look kid, I'm still taking my meds. I'm still unable to hold a steady job, but I'm staying out of trouble… mostly! I did *my* part for America, why don't you go pick on some illegal immigrants?"

"No, I'm not with anybody, really. I'm sorry. I didn't mean to bring up any bad memories. I apologize."

"Good, you scared me for a minute. I don't want to go back to the ward, man. I don't ever want to go back. I've had some rough times in my life, D-man. For the last twenty years, I've been living off the wounded Vet assistance I receive for some psycho shit I did in Nam when I was just a kid. Anger is a defense mechanism for me, but my bark's not quite as bad as my bite," he said.

"You mean, you're 'bark is worse than your bite'?"

"No, my bark is nothin'! My bite's some really mean shit. You don't want to go there, believe me! Anyway, the point is, Nam messed me up pretty bad."

"You're a decorated veteran, and you were wounded. You must have been very brave."

"Stupid, is the word I would use… Hey, you can tell all that just from touching me?" he asked, concerned that I could see his darkest secrets.

"Well, not really. There are two Purple Hearts and a Bronze Star tattooed under your Ranger insignia."

He looked at his arm and laughed then punched me on the shoulder, "You little bastard!"

"That's gonna leave a mark," I thought. With some of the pressure off, I told him my real name was Dewey.

"Well, I can see why you'd want to be called 'D-Man' instead," he chuckled. He held out his hand. "Rocco," he said, Rocco Scarbino."

"Dewey Pinkerton," I replied, as we shook.

He called to the bartender for more shots and we spent the next few hours talking and drinking. It turns out that three of the men in his family were killed during military service: his grandfather in World War II, his father in Korea, and his brother in Vietnam. While his mother was proud of both his father and his grandfather, she had the highest hopes for his brother, who had received a scholarship for football at Notre Dame before he was drafted. When he died in Vietnam, she became a withdrawn caricature of the woman she once was. Rocco felt both the need to avenge his brother's death and to win the love and respect of his mother by enlisting in the Army. What he didn't tell her was he intended to die in a more heroic way than his brother or father or grandfather did, which he believed would secure a place of pride for him in his mother's heart.

"And so, I joined the Army and within a few years had become an elite Special Ranger in the 151st Infantry Division," he said, showing me that tattoo on his other shoulder. "We were Indiana Rangers, assigned to reconnaissance and intelligence-gathering missions. We operated deep in enemy territory, conducting raids, ambushes, and surveillance missions. The problem was no matter what I did I couldn't get myself killed. I tried a bunch of times, jumping right out in front of the enemy and not a one of those little gook bastards could put a fatal bullet through me. I just kept gettin' wounded and received Purple Heart after Purple Heart. My unit started calling me 'Bulletproof Rocco'. It was embarrassing. Shrapnel would miss me; mortars would land next to me and not go off. Everyone started following me around like I had some kind of divine shield around me.

"So, one day I had finally had it. We had just encountered an enemy convoy comin' out of Quang Tri. I was determined to attack them alone and meet my maker. Without telling anyone, I jumped in my jeep filled with explosives, planning to strike at the center of the convoy to cause the most damage. I said my goodbyes to God and Jesus and hit the accelerator. The jeep shook like a mutha as it bumped its way down the hillside full of thick brush, and then just before I stuck them, the truck slowed down and came to a stop. I ran out of gas! Do you believe that? Am I cursed or what?" Rocco slugged back another shot and wiped the excess off his chin. "I couldn't even commit suicide. What the hell?" He sat quiet for a moment, still be in disbelief.

"So, what happened after that?" I asked.

"What do you think happened? No, I couldn't be shot on the spot like any other self-respecting soldier. I had to be captured, right there in front of all my buddies who had smarts enough to stay quiet in the brush. What an idiot I am! After that, I was thrown in a Vietcong holding tank and eventually did a couple more years in a POW camp. That is, until the damn war ended and I was released. By then my mother had already died! It's better that way, I guess… saved her the embarrassment and all!" He signaled the bartender for another drink.

Just then, one of the other bikers yelled out from across the room. "Hey, I know him. He's that motor guru dude we saw on TV raising a car from the dead!" he said, referring to the video of my indiscretion at the rest stop. He lifted his fingers in the air and waving them, made ghost sounds. "He's supposed to have, woooooo… magic powers! Hey boy, you ever rode a hog?"

"No," I replied.

"Then I suppose because you think you're some kinda gifted motor freak, you can just walk in here and stir things up! Don't forget, you're a stranger here, boy!"

I realized that my speech about how misunderstood bikers were, on the decency of most of them these days, and the pride and history of the ride, was not flying well here. There was a long pause when everyone was still, and I could feel a nervous pressure building up in me; and then it happened.

"I don't need to ride a hog to know when I've seen one!" I blurted. "*Oh, no,*" I thought to myself, "*That was the dreaded 'nanny, nanny, naa, naa…' It's finally happened, all those years of suppressing the urge to fight with my siblings had erupted into one stupid, childish verbal blurt.*" Somehow, I knew I wasn't going to hear, "I know you are, but what am I?"

The biker stood up and lunged towards me. "Yeah, on what planet you little shit?" Rocco and everyone else laughed at him, and just when I thought I was out of the woods, someone else shouted, "OK, boys, it's time we showed him the love." Rocco tried to stop them, but they grabbed me and threw me out the front door into the dirt. The laughing mob quickly dispersed, getting on their bikes and almost running me over as

I lay face down in a cloud of dirt and dust. After the smoke cleared, only Rocco was still there, smiling and sitting on his bike.

"You gotta lotta balls, D-man. I'll give you that. You could've gotten yourself killed." I rose and dusted myself off. "'Don't need to ride one to know one…' that's just the best," he said, still laughing. "Well, what are you going to do now that your drinkin' days in this town are over?"

"I'm traveling west on Route 66 to visit a friend in California," I said.

"Well, I don't know where you're from, but now that I know where you're going, it's obvious to me you're gonna need someone around to make sure you don't get yourself killed. I don't know if even I can stop that from happening. But if you like, I'll ride with you for a while. God knows, your gonna need someone like me out there."

I smiled at his offer remembering that Johann had said that help might come from unlikely places. "You'd be more than welcome as a traveling companion."

Jesus, who had just woken up from his nap, stepped outside to stretch and yawn.

"Who's the wet?" Rocco asked.

I didn't want to act as if I understood his question and launched into an introduction. "Jesus Lopez, meet Rocco Scarbino. Rocco, Jesus."

"Havin' a little *siesta* there, Pancho?" Rocco said, with a big grin as he shook Jesus' hand.

"My name's not 'Pancho'; and yes, I was sleeping. I have driven for many hours."

"Hey don't get touchy there, *Jesus*," which he pronounced correctly as "haysoos".

I quickly explained to Jesus that Rocco was going to join us for a while on the road, and then turned to Rocco to ask if he wanted to ride with us. "In that thing?" he protested, pointing at the bus. "That's OK, I'll ride my bike."

We pulled out of the parking lot and onto the road that led back to the main highway.

"I'd rather be one, than to never have ridden one," I heard Rocco shout out in the night to no one in particular.

CHAPTER XI

The Chief Diner

We traveled for close to two hours when Rocco gestured with his hand that he wanted to pull over. Possibly to eat something or perhaps to use the bathroom, as never had I met someone who could drink so much and not have to release any of it. Route 66 was lined with classic car and truck stops and Rocco had pulled up to one of the coolest roadside diners I had ever seen.

It was called "The Chief Diner" and had the head of an American Indian Chief, Cherokee, I believe, lit up on a big neon sign that rested atop an art deco style silver and white trailer. There was a long chrome running board serving as a step up to the front door and a flowerbed planted with mums and daisies around the base to help disguise the eight wheels, taillights, and hitch. A power and telephone line ran down from a nearby pole. There was quite a crowd gathered inside and even though it was small, it appeared to be a favorite stop for many a weary, hungry traveler. Jesus pulled the bus into the parking lot and looked for the ever-illusive end-to-end parking spot required to park a twenty-eight foot bus. Because no one seems to question Rocco, he found a spot right up front, even if a wheel or two did come to rest in the so-called "Handicapped" parking space.

We walked in and following the sign, sat ourselves in the 50's style, brightly upholstered red plastic seats. The walls of the diner were covered in pictures; photos of customers and other people and places I had never seen before. I had already read the menu from cover to cover and back again and even had time to spot a typo in the "Specails of the day" insert when the waitress finally came around.

Her tag said, "Hello, my name is Marian," only the "Hello" part had been crossed out in black marker. She plopped three waters down, accidentally spilling one on the table, which then ran down on my leg. Without even the slightest smile, she put pen to paper and asked us, "What'll we be havin?"

The menu read like a who's who of American Indian history. Running Bear Club Sandwich, Little Creek Side Salad, Pocahontas Pancakes. I ordered the Geronimo Ham Sandwich and fries. Jesus had the Tomahawk Turkey Sandwich, while Rocco ordered the Sitting Bull Beef Dip and a couple of cold beers.

"That's it?" she asked, surprised, "No, appetizers?"

"That's it for now," I replied, still amazed that she spilled water on me and didn't even apologize.

She put both hands down on the table in front of me and got right in my face. "Sorry about the water, Darlin'," she said, gently dabbing the wet spot on my leg with her towel, and winked at me as she spun around to turn our order to the cook.

She returned to the table a few minutes latter with a tray full of beers. She set one down in front of Rocco and Jesus, and pretended as if she was going to spill mine on me. I flinched and everyone laughed. "Just kidding, mind if I take your picture? It's a hobby of mine."

"Ah, no, I mean yes… I guess that's OK," I said.

She snapped a few shots and returned to the kitchen.

"Wow, I think she likes you," Rocco replied taking a huge swig off his beer.

"There's one thin' you can count on in the American mid-west," Jesus said, interrupting the awkward moment. "Not only are all the cars mass-produced and made in America but the cervesa is too. Even if that means you can't taste it, no one will care because it's 'Made in America,' and that's all that matters! You should try the local beers of Mexico. You would find them to be 'Cerveza muy buena,' possessing a thick body, choice grains and hops, but more importantly, 'Sabor,' or as you gringos say, taste."

"Look here, you little shit, there ain't nothin' wrong with American beers," Rocco rebutted, "at least our water is clean!"

"What, you don't think we get the shits at first from your water? Jesus countered, "usted pedazo de los pompass de crap!"

"Jesus, Rocco, Stop!" I said, "Beer is beer, it doesn't really matter whose is better, just as long as we have some, huh?"

I took a sip. It was warm and flat. Jesus took one too and gave me the 'see, I told you so' look, and set it down on the table waiting for Rocco to taste his. Rocco drank his straight down, savoring the last drops without even making a face.

"Mmmm, now that's a beer," he said.

"The worst part," Jesus continued, "is the thinking of these so called 'makers of beer'. If they bottle it up and rush it to every local mercado and restaurante quick enough, before people can try anything else, they not only get to call themselves a 'classico Americano' premium beverage, but also proclaim themselves, 'El Rey de Cervezas' or "The King of Beers."

Jesus may have been right about this one, but because there was no good alternative, we drank this weak concoction of water mixed with a few molecules of wheat and hops anyway. Because they're mostly made of water, these beers go down easy, and by the time we had finished our meals, Rocco, Jesus and I had consumed a few six packs of them. Rocco insisted we have one more for the road, but I was the strong one and drew the limit there and respectfully requested that our waitress total our damages and present us a check.

She approached the table with our bill, looking tired, as if she needed a break. I asked her to sit for a minute because everyone but Rocco, Jesus, and I were long gone and it looked like she had been working the room for hours without a second to rest. She sat down and let out a big sigh. She was much prettier than she let on and wore her hair tied up tight in a bun. The large glasses and waitress outfit only added to the typical greasy spoon look.

"So what's your story, honey," Rocco asked, with all the charm and finesse of a pimp. "Where're you from, I mean?"

"I'm originally from Oklahoma City. But I did a few spells in other places," she said.

"Like where?" I prodded her, "I've traveled a bit myself."

"Oh, I ain't never traveled much; Illinois, Kansas once. Mostly I spent time in New York, that's all." Her smile quickly turned into a frown.

"What happened there?" I pushed further.

"Well, I left Oklahoma City five years ago and moved to New York City," she said. "I wasn't there very long before I became disenchanted with my dreams of becoming a famous chef. You know, always under the constant pressure of living with supermodels and fashion designers and their need to be 'thin to be in' mentality, I mean. Like them, I eventually became a victim of the disease 'Bulimia.' It hurts to throw up," she confessed, "and after spending years fighting it, I finally won back my ability to keep things down. I decided from that day forward to help ease the suffering of others with this horrible disease by opening a chain of restaurants called 'Déjà vu;' serving only the finest Bulimian cuisine.

Rocco laughed aloud, "You're kiddin' me, right?"

"What kind of foods do you feed Bulimics?" Jesus asked, looking genuinely interested in food that may also 'come up' well with Tequila.

"Why, food like 'Twiggy Noodle Soup' and the 'Karen Carpenter Boneless Buffalo Drumsticks' which not only tasted great but were chocked full of fast absorbing vitamins. They were specially prepared to be as easy coming up as they were going down. Investors however, didn't see things the same way I did, and promptly turned me down one by one. After that, I realized I couldn't stay in New York City any longer, and eventually I ended up taking a job at this halfway hash house. Now I can't find the will or the way out of it."

"Can't you just pack up and leave?" I asked.

"Oh, I can pack up all right. I keep a suitcase in my car just in case someday I've had enough, which has happened several times already, due to my anger towards my boss, and all. You see, he shares in my tips and occasionally gropes my breasts, but worst of all, takes credit for most of the dishes, which even though he prepares are my recipes, and after years of cooking them himself considers them his own. I've left a bunch of times, but I've always come back, cause… I really don't have any other place to go."

"Don't you have any family?" Jesus asked.

"Not anymore," she said, "My Mama died when I was just a baby. I was raised by my Daddy, who I loved very much. Daddy never remarried after Mama died. He always said that she was his one and only true love. I didn't have any brothers or sisters, so I stayed with him, cooking and cleaning until the cancer finally took him when I was eighteen."

"That's pretty sad," I said. "So besides New York, you've never traveled anywhere else?"

"I've been to Illinois once, and also to Kansas, but I've never seen California. That's where I really want to be."

I explained to her I had spent the last decade or so searching for the so-called "meaning of life" and had come to meet many wise men that had helped solidify what I had learned. They pointed me in the direction of gathering a group of individuals who could help me further my aim, perhaps teaching others who were disenchanted with their lives how to live more in harmony with the mechanics of the universe. I talked about how we are all machines and the ways in which we might someday be able to be somewhat free from this control.

"So what's holding you back from leaving right now," I asked.

"Why, everything, and nothing, I'm just afraid to fail again."

"Failing is an important step in learning how to change," I said. "Without failure, there would be nothing to measure success. What keeps you here is the belief that someday something will be different, something will change that will allow you to leave. That kind of thinking will never lead to true happiness and leaves you open to forces that are forever outside your control. You must take the first step, and everything else will follow."

She listened like a flower that needed water and by the time I finished speaking, even though only fifteen minutes had passed, was begging us to take her with us, trailer and all. She offered her services as cook, told us the trailer was still on wheels and that she had agreed a long time ago to pay half the lease on it, and by now was sure she had paid her boss twice what the trailer was worth.

Rocco and I looked at each other and before I could say another word, he smiled and signaled Jesus to get the bus and pull it up to the diner. Jesus backed slowly up to the trailer hitch. Rocco hooked it up and with Marian safely in the bus with us, gave us the sign to pull forward.

The trailer resisted movement at first since it had been sitting there for many years. Once the flowerbeds and white picket fence had been sufficiently crushed, it began to tug at the power and phone lines. A few pops and sparks later we were free of the foundation. With Rocco leading the way, the trailer successfully in tow, and only having left a few bits of white picket fence and flowers littered on the highway, we continued west on "The Mother Road."

Marian smirked, "The only thing I'll regret is not being there to see the look on Sam's face when he comes to work tomorrow' morning. He is just gonna die."

She asked Jesus not to look as she changed from the confines of her waitress outfit into some more casual clothes. With her hair down, she looked much more beautiful and relaxed and I thought as she fell asleep in the seat next to me that I even saw her smile.

We drove late into the night since Jesus was not only a school bus driver back in Mexico, but had also ridden a lot of Greyhound buses here in the states, and he not only knew most of the roads we were about to travel, but was able to stay awake while driving for longs stretches of time.

We slept on the bus that night, because we didn't have the bankroll to spend on hotels or even motels every night. We did stay whenever possible at a Motel 3, which was half the price of a Motel 6 but also half the amenities. You got a single bed, but only one sheet, no TV, and a toilet, a shower, and a sink. Nevertheless, it would save us plenty, especially when our numbers began to grow.

The night air was hot and thick and even though the bus had air conditioning, it would always overheat the engine. We were forced to use it only when the heat of day became so cruel we could stand it no longer, and then for only a few moments at a time. Sometimes it was better not to turn it on at all because once you felt its coolness you would suffer even more when it had to be turned off.

Rocco, who was lying next to the bus on his back atop a sleeping bag, laughed as he noticed my inability to get comfortable.

"You should try sleeping under the stars," he cackled. "You wouldn't feel so trapped!"

I leaned my head out the window as much as I could of course, because it was a school bus and the windows did not go all the way down for fear a child might accidentally fall out.

"Maybe I should!" I replied, rising to my feet and walking off the bus to visit with him. "I can't sleep either anyway."

"Windows don't go all the way down, huh?" he said, still smiling as I sat down.

"For a child to fall out those windows they would have to stand up and jump another two feet or so. Of course, if they were carrying a backpack full of schoolbooks, which have now become the size of encyclopedias, they would not fit out the window, nor be capable of being able to stand up high enough to be at risk of even falling out!

"Why have school books gotten so large anyway?" I asked, maneuvering the dirt on the ground around with my hand to be more compatible with the shape of my behind.

"Influx Syndrome!" Rocco said.

"What's that?" I asked.

"It's what happens when we take sides," he continued.

"On what?"

"On a number of things, geography, economics… but these days, it's mostly about oil!" he replied. "Oh, the government's always quick to tell you politics, ethics, or even terrorism, but it always boils down to natural resources. I mean, how the hell were we to know, when them damn Arabs settled in the middle of the frickin' desert there was tons of oil under that sand. Go figure! However, the answer to your question about why schoolbooks have gotten so big is Influx Syndrome! It's what happens when we go to fight someone else's war because we have a strategic interest in either the physical location of a country or a resource we need. I joined the Army to keep those Commie foreign bastards out, then we turn around and let every weary, persecuted or repressed Tom, Dick or Harry, come to America the free by the boatloads, and we give 'em benefits, too!

"Recently, everybody's coming from Asia, due to our regret for having gotten into the affairs of their civil wars. After living here on our fertile intellectual soil for a while, they discover that they learn a hell of a lot faster than people born here do. I've been over there many times, you know, they have a strict upbringing and make their kids work extra hard to earn a living. Anyway, because they learn so quickly, it makes our own children look stupid!"

Rocco was right; Influx Syndrome has forced into action all kinds of new laws and standards. Those that were born here would now have to be burdened to step up the rate at which various facts and histories would need to be learned in order to stay competitive, let alone not fall too far behind the immigrants.

This pressure of having to learn in the 5th grade that which was previously learned in the 7th grade and so on up the ladder has caused the children of today, and the parents who have to help them with their homework, much wider and earlier developed neurosis and other inflictions, which manifest themselves in the form of migraine headaches and pimples.

"But immigrating to America is how our country was started. There are always going to be people fleeing repression!" I said.

"Yeah, well then there will always be Influx Syndrome!"

Rocco took less than two seconds to finish that sentence before he was in a deep snoring sleep. I too had grown weary and returned to the bus to close my eyes… at least for a while.

The next day, the morning sun beat hot and heavy through the windows of the bus when Marian came to announce she had breakfast ready back in the Chief Diner. I smiled, thinking this might be quite nice to have a traveling kitchen just a few feet away. I stepped out of the bus and made a mental note that as soon as possible we should tint the windows on the bus to not only give us more privacy, but also help cut down on the amount of photons that would find themselves there at morning's first light.

I stepped up into the diner and saw that both Jesus and Rocco were deep into a breakfast that could only be described as "Made in heaven itself by an Angel of the Lord." The eggs, hash browns, and toast, done well as I like them, were the best I had ever tasted. Maybe it was because it was made from the loving hands of someone who truly appreciated being saved from the dragon-guarded castle, or maybe, I was just really hungry.

CHAPTER XII

Route 666

The rain in Spain may fall mainly on the plains, but it does the same thing in Western Missouri too. It had been pouring since earlier that morning and hadn't let up by mid-day. Indian summer storms as they are called, even though they did not happen until late autumn, were humid and sticky in this region of the country, and just because you were wet didn't mean you were cool. One thing is certain in the flatter parts of America; "water can't run down hill!" That means for every inch of rain that falls, there is nowhere for it to go, and it ends up flooding everything quite frequently.

To make matters worse the bus had developed a slow leak in a rear tire from a bit of debris we had picked up on the road. With no signs of a temporary suspension in the onslaught of H^2O, or of the laws of gravity as they relate to pressure, the tire had gone completely flat. To make matters worse, the bus was giving us false fuel level readings and the truth was there may be some question as to whether or not we would make it to a gas station before the engine was starved of its primary energy source.

Now, I could have easily gotten out of the bus, in the rain, and performed a little "molecular magic" Isaac had taught me, solving at least two out of three issues. However, I decided instead to see how the others might solve these problems and perhaps to illustrate something from the teaching of the Mode.

Jesus pulled the bus over to the side of the road to wait for a lull in the storm to fix the tire. "They should add another 'seis' or 'six' to the name of this road and call it Route 666," he complained.

It appeared that unless forced by the elements, Rocco would never hang out on the bus with us and was quite content to be sitting on his bike, or if stopped, lying under a tree. However, since it was raining so hard, he had come inside and was sitting on the bench seat right behind Jesus, berating him on his lack of foresight about the gas gauge and about what he might do to him if we didn't make it to the next gas station.

"You should have known the gas gauge wasn't working. I thought you were a mechanic!" Rocco said.

"You mean like you knew the oil in your bike was running hot, because you had a crack in your case?" Jesus replied. "Well, I thin' you have a crack in your head!"

"Jesus, do you know what the difference is between an 'illegal' and an 'illiterate' alien? Nothin', cause they both make me 'ill'."

"Look, Senior Chopper…" Jesus countered, "nobody asked you what you thin'!"

"Stop, both of you!" Marian said, surprising everyone. "You're looking at this situation all wrong. When I was a little girl, my Daddy used to say, 'To be content, you need to be able to spot the rainbow through the storm'. So until either one of you can do that, while we're just sitting here, please be quiet"

I saw this as a good time to intervene with Jesus and Rocco and launched into a Sufi parable I had learned from Captain O'Connell.

"A group of frogs were traveling through the woods, when two of them fell into a deep pit. All the other frogs gathered around the pit. When they saw how deep it was, they told the unfortunate frogs they would never get out. The two frogs ignored the comments and tried to jump up out of the pit.

"The other frogs kept telling them to stop, that they were as good as dead. Finally, one of the frogs took heed to what the other frogs were saying and simply gave up and fell down dead.

"The other frog continued to jump as hard as he could. Once again, the crowd of frogs yelled at him to stop the pain and suffering and just die. He jumped even harder and finally made it out. When he got out, the other frogs asked him, 'Why did you continue jumping? Didn't you hear us?'

"The frog explained to them that he was deaf. He thought they were encouraging him the entire time."

"I don't get it," Rocco confessed. "If he couldn't hear them, then how did he know what they were asking him?"

"Maybe he could read their lips once he was close enough," Marian offered as a logical explanation.

"Have you ever seen frog lips?" Rocco questioned. "I don't think they even have lips! Well, now that I think about it, I might have seen frogs with lips in the jungles of Vietnam, but I'm not sure they weren't just Cong."

"I don't thin' that's what Senior Dewey means by telling us this story," Jesus interrupted. "I thin' he means we shouldn't be so bummed out about being stuck here."

"Very good, Jesus," I said, "you are right! It doesn't matter how the frog knew what they where saying as long as he didn't give up hope, and that just believing the others were cheering him on, led to his ability to overcome the obstacle."

"I like that one," Jesus said. Do you have another?"

"Sure," I said. "I will try to relay the message with a different story that illustrates a similar lesson."

"Representatives of all the various kinds of birds decided to find out which species was able to fly highest. They formed a council to judge, and experiments were started. One by one, they dropped out, until only the Eagle was left. He continued his upward flight higher and higher until, when he was at his maximum, he exclaimed, 'See, I have reached the highest point, leaving everyone else behind!'

"At that moment, a tiny Sparrow that had been riding on his back leapt off his wing and flew even higher, because he had conserved his strength.

"The Council met to decide the winner. 'The Sparrow,' they declared, 'gets a prize for being the cleverest, but the recognition for attainment must still go to the Eagle. And in addition, he gets a prize for endurance, for he outdid all the other competitors with the Sparrow on his back!'"

"See," Jesus, said. "It's about banding together to help the 'Kami-Kazi'."

"You mean, 'common cause', don't you, Jesus?" Marian asked.

"Yeah, that's what I said… the Kami-Kazi'!"

"I want to know what kind of prizes they got," Rocco interrupted.

"Rocco!" Marian chastised.

"I'm kidding. Geez, Marian. I'm just kiddin'." He laughed hard and then hit Jesus on the arm as a gesture of affection. "Alright man, I get it. I'll give you a ride on the back of my bike to the nearest service station if we run out of gas and you can fly off' to the pump and fill up the gas can. Just remember, Jesus, I get the prize for flying the farthest and the one for endurance for traveling all that way with an illegal wet on my bike!"

"Ah yes… well, that's close enough to the message," I said.

Marian prodded me on. "Tell us another one… please. There is still so much we don't know about you or your quest."

I didn't have another wise story that I thought would be useful in this situation anyway, so I just began to tell them about how the teaching I had learned was discovered and about the most interesting of all yogis, Sir Isaac Newton Swami.

"Once, while Isaac was teaching me to meditate on a single flame of the fire at a time, which is very hard to do as flames not only move and morph very fast, the lot of them together can get quite distracting; he gave me more insight into the sources of his knowledge. Long before he began his hermitship in the Nevada desert, he and his fellow explorers, who called themselves, 'The Seekers of Wisdom,' traveled quite a bit into Eastern Africa between World War I and World War II, and it was there that he found the most amazing things.

"Abyssinia or 'I'll be seein' ya' as it is affectionately referred to by foreigners who have traveled through its sun-baked terrain, is perhaps better known these days as Ethiopia, and had been played like a tennis ball between the English and the Italians for several centuries. During this time, the Italians held the upper hand to this 'beach front vacation spot' and using the occasional safeguarding of Italian trade routes as justification, had once again claimed the eastern part for themselves. Even though a culture thousands of years earlier still lived on its soil and who, I am sure, had claims to it first.

"That thought never seemed to bother any of the 'hooked on conquering' countries, and Italy, a boot shaped peninsula, much like England, a peninsula shaped island, were two countries in the last few millennia that learned to carry a very big stick and bully most of the known world into submission.

"Anyway, while in Abyssinia, Isaac met a man who was the great, great grandson of Aden Abdullah Gelayadh, a fellow seeker of truth who had handmade a copy of the long lost 'Book of Enoch.'

"Enoch, as you may know, was the grandfather of Noah. This copy of the book, containing many parables and other teachings never seen before, was written so long ago, it was making quite the 'to do' in both European and American countries upon its discovery. An explorer found it in the late seventeen hundreds, and returned from six years in Abyssinia with not only one, but also three Ethiopic copies. However, because he was so hell bent in his obsession with this one book, he completely missed discovering a map that showed the exact location of thousands of scrolls in the upper northwest shore of the Dead Sea that contained the mother lode of ancient writings and teachings ever found in that part of the world.

"Aden Abdullah Gelayadh's great, great, grandson, Uden Abdullah Gelayadh took a liking to my wise friend Isaac and his Seekers, and after passing a sort of 'Wizards test, recognizing their pure desire for all things wise and mystical, not only let them see copies of other undiscovered ancient works of teaching and literature, but also showed him this map. Upon closer inspection, Isaac realized that the document in his hands listed much more than the location of the Dead Sea scrolls, but that of several thousand other ancient teachings and works as well.

"Uden explained to the Seekers that he was one of a very old tradition of 'Gatekeepers', a secret society having already existed for millennia, whose job it was to spot the wisest among men and to pass along the whereabouts of the this library of the world's most ancient treasures. Uden warned Isaac that if he and his band of seekers were compelled to follow the map, that could not remove anything from its eternal hiding place. My friend agreed and thanked him for his wisdom and guidance.

"By the day's end, Isaac and his small but capable team of knowledgeable researchers made up of my other teachers, MacQuay MacGregor, Sean O'Connell, and a very young Winger left the next day in search of what was on the maps.

“The first destination was the desert cliffs of what was then Roman Palestine. The sun did not give them any help either, but tried its best to cook them well done and would have left their weathered bones to be picked by vultures if they didn't have the stamina to live to see the glory of this first Library branch.

“Their adventures lasted for many more years, and after visiting many different Library staging areas, they earned the right to visit the Great Library itself.

“Access to this last hidden library was not for a weak man, let alone one with a fear of heights, since complex hung off the cliffs of some of the highest mountains in the world.

“There, they met the Council of Twelve, the Council of Seven, and the Council of Three. They were given a group of books that made up the teaching of the Mode, the teaching of universal mechanics, the teaching that I was handed down by each of them over the last ten years.

“The library's secret location, which had been honored for a millennium, was almost broken a few decades later, as a local shepherd looking for a lost sheep, stumbled onto one of the caves, immediately prompting a discovery party. Realizing they had little time, the Librarians called on the Lords of Libra and hastily moved the bulk of the library in the dead of night. Unable to remove every document in time, they had to leave some scrolls behind, which were found by the search party.

“The first collection of these “Dead Sea Scrolls” discovered ended up in the hands of the Jews, but the Christians, not wanting to be outdone or be left out of a finding of this magnitude and also not having any substantial additions to their library of gospels in almost two-thousand years, sought out the rest.

"However, by then the bulk of the library was safely re-established somewhere else, high in the mountains of the Hindu-Kush.

"Therefore, it has become my destiny to carry on the truth and tradition of this ancient teaching of the Mode. It teaches us that everything in the universe is connected, and that everything, mechanical or otherwise, affects everything else. Our goal is to be free from the machine, which controls everything we say and do. If we can become even a little bit less under its influence than we may be able to accomplish great things."

"Like what?" Rocco asked, like a true Missourian.

I walked to the front of the bus and put the palm of my hand gently on the gas gauge. I could sense that something was stopping the indicator from giving a proper reading. Once done with my vibratory observation, I flicked my finger hard against the quarter tank marker and a small cloud of rust fell from under the dashboard. The gauge then settled back to the quarter full mark.

"Wow," Jesus said, amazed.

"OK," Rocco murmured. "I guess that answers that!"

Jesus rolled down his window and looked up at the sky. "Look, Senior Dewey, the rain has stopped."

"Don't tell me... you did that too?" Rocco asked.

"Of course he did!" Jesus rebutted. "He is the most amazing, Senior Dewey."

Marian smiled like a child, who looking up at the heavens, realized for the first time they were standing on a world that is revolving around a universe that orbits the eye of God. Even though not by my doing, the rain had finally stopped and Jesus and Rocco went outside to see if the wheels of the bus were sufficiently above water. At least for a brief moment everyone worked as a team to change the tire. Marian gave a quick run of her fingernail across my arm as I walked back to my seat.

"A girl could get used to a guy with brains *and* a magic finger," she said, kidding, and snapped a photo.

"What I miss?" Jesus asked, looking at the expression on Marian's face as he entered the bus.

"Nothing, Jesus darlin'," she said, as he sat in his seat and closed the bus doors, "Nothin' at all."

Rocco wiped the water off the seat of his Harley and led the way back on the highway. Before we had gone ten miles, a gas station loomed in the distance. It could have been quite embarrassing you know, preaching about knowledge of the machine and all then run out of gas. Spared this cruel punishment and with lessons learned we arrived at the service station and filled up the gas tank, picked up an extra spare tire and replaced the gas gauge at the same time.

CHAPTER XIII

New York Wizard

While taking our quick break to fill up the bus's tanks and repair the gas gauge, I took the opportunity to call my parents, something I'd promised to do from time to time as I made my way out west. My Mom was obviously proud of having seen me on TV, but it was also clear that she had no idea what I had done. She was telling me how she used my newfound fame to lord it over Helen, her best friend, when I heard my Dad's voice interrupt her in the background. She paused and listened for a moment and went on to say, that a man from New York, named Bruno Goldblum had been calling regularly trying to get in touch with me. He was in the entertainment industry and had obviously charmed my Mother into thinking that he was just the man to help her "famous son" really get launched in life. She'd told him she would be sure to pass along the message. I could tell that it would make her happy if I called this guy, and reluctantly told her that I would. After we finished talking, I placed a call to Johann, who confirmed that this Bruno Goldblum had also tracked him down and left messages for me to contact him as soon as possible. He had apparently done his homework and probably found out about my stint with Johann from my Mom, tracking him down from there.

I called the number. It rang and rang and as I was about to hang up, suddenly someone answered.

"Yo, speak to me..."

"Mr. Goldblum? This is Dewey Pinkerton, from Detroit. You've left messages that you were trying to get in touch with me?

"Dewey Pinkerton! Yes! I've been huntin' yo ass… I mean looking to find you for days now. Your mother finally clued me in that you were on some kind of road trip. I'm glad you called. Where's your hood?"

"My what?"

"Your position… Your location… Where are you now?"

"I'm just outside of Oklahoma City."

"Do they have an airport there?"

I was a bit unsure of the direction this question was going in. "Uh, it's the state capitol. I'm sure they have an airport."

"State capitol, huh? For what state?"

"Uh, Oklahoma!"

"Oh, right, of course. Geography wasn't my best subject. I majored in graffiti."

"What?"

"Listen… could you stay there for another day? I'd like to fly in and talk to you."

"Talk to me? About what?"

"About putting you on TV. I'm an agent here in New York and one of my clients is Simon Jones. We have an idea for a TV show that involves you and Simon, and we think it has the potential to be a groundbreaking hit."

"But, I'm not sure I want to be on TV."

"Oh please! Everybody wants to be on TV."

"But, that's not what I'm interested in doing."

"Ah, that's the beauty of it. You don't have to change a thing about what you're doing. Look, can I arrange for us to get together and have dinner tomorrow night in whatever passes for a nice restaurant in the state capitol of… oh yeah, Oklahoma?"

"Can't we just talk this out over the phone?"

"Nope, won't work. This needs to be in person. Listen, let me introduce you to Simon and we can explain our idea in detail. I'll find somewhere nice and pick up the tab. All you have to do is listen. Whaddya say?"

I could see why my Mom and Johann had talked to Bruno. He really was a charmer. We'd only lose a day in our travels west, and could actually use the time for some mundane chores like laundry. The fact that he was willing to fly in meant that he was serious.

"Could I bring my traveling companions along to dinner as well?"

"Traveling companions? How many?"

"Three besides me."

"Of course, bring them along, by all means. Old friends of yours?"

"No, new friends, actually."

"Sounds very interesting, can't wait to meet you."

Almost twenty-four hours later to the minute, we entered the lobby of the Marriott Waterford downtown. There, two men sitting in large leather chairs stood up to greet us. Bruno was a thin, handsome black man who displayed a gold tooth that shined every time light hit it at just the right angle. Simon was a smiling white man with a clean cut, vaguely Nordic look to him. Introductions were made and we made our way to a large table in the corner of a hotel restaurant, making small talk along the way. Bruno asked what we were traveling in and I told him the story of the bus and its new appendage, the diner. Bruno encouraged everyone to start with a drink and ordered some appetizers to get the ball rolling.

He went on to explain that he and Simon had been exploring a concept that they were calling "reality TV," where real-life people were filmed doing interesting things. They had the ear of some executives at MTV, and had already tried unsuccessfully to sell a show called "Simon Says." MTV hadn't bought it, but said they'd be willing to look at other ideas. He and Simon had agreed that a show based around me had a chance to be a big hit.

"But, why me?"

"Because you're a real person and you're doing something interesting," Simon answered, "I'm not even sure what it is exactly that you're doing and I can tell you that I'm already fascinated.

"Television is a powerful medium. That's where people saw the way you handled those mechanics at the Detroit Auto show all those years ago. They also saw the story of the car you started in the desert at that truck stop in Utah," Bruno added. "There's some built-in interest in you, already. Now I find you're on a road trip out west for reasons unknown and that you're traveling in an old bus with a group of newly minted friends. I'm even more interested in whatever your story is than I was before, you see?"

He paused for a moment and scratched his curly black soul patch. "So, what *is* your story?"

I looked at the others for a moment, not sure what to say. Then told Bruno and Simon about "The Mode," about how I was beginning a mission to expose people's lives to it so that they could see the benefits of this new kind of thinking. I briefly told them how I'd met Jesus, Rocco, and Marian and explained that each of them had agreed to come along on the ride out west for their own reasons. I also explained my motivation for the road trip to California was to take care of Winger's estate. It all sounded a bit ridiculous and random to me as I heard myself tell the story, but I could see Bruno and Simon occasionally share a look at odd moments in my recitation. When I was done, Bruno leaned back in his seat and smiled, showing off his gold tooth to great advantage.

"To me, this sounds like a match made in heaven. You're traveling to California for a noble and sympathetic purpose. You're traveling with an interesting group of people, each of whom has their own story to tell. And, you're going by an interesting route in an unusual vehicle. That's a good combination for TV."

I stopped him. "But, I'm not sure that we have any interest in being on a TV show. While our stories might be interesting, I don't know if everyone wants theirs made public. Besides, I'm still in the process of working out how best to spread the Mode."

"That's just it," Simon interrupted. "You have a larger message that you want to spread but you're still working out the details! This kind of a show could help you do just that. What could be a better test market for your teaching than the exposure a television show could give you?"

That kind of exposure could be a benefit to teaching the Mode, but there was sure to be a cost. I stalled to think.

"How would you actually do the filming?"

Bruno answered, "We'd put Simon and one cameraman with you and your group. They'd travel with you and just film the events of your days. Simon would introduce the bits, telling the viewer where you were and things like that, and he'd interact with you and your friends, asking questions if he didn't know what was going on, or if he didn't understand some reference. They wouldn't be any more intrusive than two more friends joining you on your trip would. If we were doing the show right now, there'd just be some other guy sitting where I am, holding a camera.

Simon added, "And while I admit that having a camera on you all the time is at first a great distraction, it only takes a couple of hours before the novelty wears off and you begin to behave as if it's not even there."

I was starting to get a feel for these two men and their proposal and could tell that they felt like there was a lot riding on this. They were gambling.

"What about payment?" I asked.

Simon looked quickly at Bruno who coughed, "Well, we can't sell the show until we have enough footage in the bag to make a good pilot episode. Once that happens, the floodgate of corporate money opens up and we all get the rewards. Until then, I can only offer you four thousand dollars to let us ride with you for two months, beginning as soon as possible. We'd also cover the day-to-day expenses for Simon and his crewman of course. I know it's not a fortune, but it's respectable and it's really just to get us to the point where we can sell this for the big money."

I suddenly realized what it was about these guys that I was sensing: desperation. These guys were desperate. Bruno and Simon were at the end of some kind of rope and their hope for this show was the only thing keeping them in the game. I was willing to bet that the four thousand dollars plus expenses Bruno was offering, along with the bill for this meal and their travel and trip accommodations represented the very last of there combined assets. I also realized that this gave me the advantage in any deal I could cut with them. I wanted to think about this, and I knew how I was going to play this game.

"You brought a contract, didn't you?" I asked them.

They looked at each other before Simon said "A contract?" in the same tone of voice one uses to say, "It wasn't me", when it really was.

"Yes," I answered, "a contract. You've come to me with a fully developed plan in mind, obviously in haste to begin, and you have the appearance of being reasonably professional."

"Yeah," Bruno said, "You're right. We didn't anticipate moving to this stage of the negotiations so quickly."

"Give it to me and I'll look it over this evening. We'll meet again tomorrow morning and I'll give you my answer then." I held out my hand to Bruno, who placed a large manila envelope in it.

"It's a very standard agreement."

"It won't be when I get done with it," I replied.

Bruno and Simon were still standing there in shock when we left the room and returned to the Motel 3 where we could discuss their offer in private.

"Do you think those clowns could actually get us on TV?" Rocco asked. "They seemed a little ragged around the edges to me. I'm not sure they could get us local access, much less MTV."

"They've already talked to the network once. They can probably do it again," I countered. "I think I've actually seen Simon on TV before, doing some kind of animal reporting if I remember correctly. They have some credentials. Not a lot, but some."

"But what if they make us look like a buncha idiots?" Marian asked.

"In all honesty, Marian, I thing nothing would make those guys happier than to be able to show you as a gang of kooks, and me as a big fraud. Nevertheless, they don't know us. We're none of those things. Besides, no one except some TV executives may see any of this, you know. Just because they shoot video doesn't mean it will ever get to TV."

"Well, I thin' that big dreamers can sometimes pull off their dreams," Jesus said. "I thin' you can't make the Mode look bad anywhere, TV or anywhere else. And I also thin', Jefe, that we could use the money."

"We are a little short in the funds department, Jesus," I replied laughing. "That's only an extra bonus here. Look, this opportunity has just dropped out of the sky and I don't know if I see a downside to it… yet. If nothing comes of the footage, then we still were paid. If Bruno and Simon can sell it to MTV, then we get the chance to put the Mode on TV."

Rocco said, "I'm not sure I've ever seen a message like yours shown on TV that didn't get cheapened somehow."

"Maybe that's because there's never been a message like this on TV before," I said.

I looked at everyone else. "Do we do it?" Everyone nodded. "Alright then, let's get some sleep."

The next morning we walked into the lobby of the hotel and joined Bruno and Simon for coffee. I handed him the contract, which to my surprise was in fact rather fair and standard, as he had said. "I haven't signed it. However, I will sign it if you'll write in my three special conditions." Everyone looked at me in surprise. "First, I want it stipulated that Simon and the cameraman will participate in our journey just like everyone else. If we're all doing something, they have to do it too."

Bruno nodded and said, "No problem."

"Second, we start today. We're taking off this afternoon and if you want to be part of the journey, you'll be on the bus."

"I'm not sure we can get a cameraman in time to have him leave with you this afternoon," Bruno said.

"That brings me to number three. Bruno acts as Simon's cameraman."

"Now wait a minute! I'm just an agent. I'm not actually part of the shows."

"You're part of this one. You and Simon are the ones who came to us. You and he are the ones who had the vision. You and he can get on the bus, no one else." I looked right at Bruno. "I want you close to us, if we're going to put ourselves in your hands."

"But I'm not a professional! I mean, I know a little about cameras, but…"

"But nothing. This is a deal-breaker. You can learn while you go."

"But what about my other clients? My commitments?"

"Have someone else handle them, reschedule, whatever it takes. What do you say? Are you in or out?"

He and Simon looked at each other again, in that mutual way they had of talking without saying anything. However, their eyes said plenty. "All right, I guess. If that's what it takes to make this deal then that's what you get."

I smiled and gestured to the contract in Bruno's hand. He wrote in my conditions and we all signed and shook each other's hands. "I don't know any more than you do about what we've all just gotten ourselves into, but from here on out, we're all in it together. Welcome to the team! You've got a couple of hours to get your affairs in order and we'll pick you up out front in the bus."

Bruno and Simon went back to their rooms to make phone calls to arrange for their traveling with us. Two hours later, when we pulled the bus up to the hotel, they came out the front door with their luggage in hand and a couple of cases on a dolly, which contained a camera and sound gear. We got everything stowed and then just as Bruno was about to step on the bus, Rocco put his arm across the bus doorway almost stopping him by the neck.

"We're not friends and I've got no reason to trust you, so I just wanna make sure that you understand something up front. If you cause us one little bit of trouble, you're gonna have to spend all your remaining time looking over your shoulder for me. I'm keeping an eye on you!" Rocco lowered his arm and smiled a big grin as he straightened Bruno's collar and brushed some non-existent lint from his jacket. Then he mock bowed to Bruno and Simon and gestured to the bus door, "All aboard!"

And with that, we were six.

CHAPTER XIV

Tornado with a Twist

On our way back to Route 66, we heard a tornado warning on the radio. A category F3 twister was moving east on highway 40 towards Oklahoma City. Jesus suggested we head North on Highway 44 and pick up Route 66 heading west in order to miss the tornado should it touch down there. I agreed and signaled Rocco who led us north in haste.

As Highway 44 approached Highway 66, the sky was dark and troublesome. The wind had picked up considerably and we would have to find cover soon since not only was the diner at risk of being blown over, but Rocco was in danger of being killed by flying debris. Just then, the radio announced the bad news. The twister had veered north and was on a collision course with us at the Highway 44 and 66 junctions. We looked for a place to park and ride it out as everyone, including myself, was getting quite worried. Up ahead and across a small field was an old barn. It appeared abandoned and weathered to the point of having no doors, let alone a fully covered top, but was our only chance.

"Help us, Jesus," Jesus said, which somehow just sounded funny, and told everyone to hold on. We ran the fence and came to a skidding stop inside the barn just as the tornado crested the hill a few hundred yards away. Everyone began to duck for cover in the bus. Bruno and Simon, who were both born and raised in New York, had never seen a real tornado and were too shaken up to get anything more than some amateur footage of the twister before jumping for cover.

I, on the other hand, was more worried about the safety of the group than my own life. I had already learned that in the worst situation, fear would have no home in me. Fear could not solve anything. It would only allow the laws of accident to play themselves out, and more often than not on your head. I had to do something, but what I did not know, since I had never encountered a force of nature with this much fury. I tried to think quickly, what would Mac do, or Sean or Winger? What would the old hermit do? Then it hit me.

Once, Isaac and I were sitting as we usually did in front of the fire when the wind picked up. It was blowing at such a high rate that it seemed within a few hours his camp would be covered over by the sand. He showed me that even though the wind was a very strong force it nonetheless obeyed laws like everything else and by knowing these laws one could create a field around oneself that with practice could be extended outwards to include quite a large area.

Isaac was very clear that though our energy was far too weak to stop the forces of a severe wind entirely, we could still affect the air that was directly in contact or near to us. With that knowledge, he was able to divert the winds around the camp for a sufficient period of time and save it from almost certain ruin.

I had never been taught this skill and having only seen Isaac perform this act once, was hell bent on trying it anyway to save the group. I climbed to the top of the bus against the wishes of everyone and looked out at the pasture through the missing boards on the side of the barn loft and began to meditate on the high and low pressure points of the storm. All of a sudden, I could feel the positive ions in the air thicken and the electricity generated from this mobile turbine had all of the hair on my arms and head standing straight up. I meditated even harder as the twister grew closer, picking up a large oak tree by its very roots and hurling it aside as if it were a twig.

I could still hear the others yelling for me to get down, and just as the tornado crossed the field in front of me I felt it happen. I was pushing my thoughts as hard as I could, outward towards the air around me, and could feel as a spiral moving away from me an area of calmness that was not affected by the oncoming disaster. As the tornado moved closer, I continued to push out the area of stillness until it engulfed the bus. All of the debris that up to that moment had been flying through the air near us came crashing downward at the very same time with a large thud, and for a moment all you could hear was the tornado's deafening roar as it crossed near the barn. By the time it had passed and I began to tune back in to my immediate surroundings, I noticed Marian's voice. "Are you all right?" I heard faintly. “Are you all right?” the voice said louder. I looked down at her from my perch on the roof of the bus and smiled.

“How long have you been there?” I asked.

“Long enough to see that. You were amazing!” Rocco and Jesus had the same look of amazement on their faces as Marian. Simon and Bruno didn’t know what had happened because they were crouched down between the seats of the bus away from the epicenter of activity.

“The Mode teaches you more than just the mechanics of machines. It teaches you about the mechanics of the universe. That’s the principle I used to shield us.”

I heard later that day that fourteen people were killed in that twister, perhaps one of the worst this county had seen in decades. It made me feel sorry and drove home even more the importance of the teaching in helping humanity.

Marian never doubted me or the Mode again from that day forward. Jesus was now also a firm believer in my abilities, mentioning that Johann had talked about this phenomenon but had claimed not to understand it. Rocco was completely blown away and at first wanted to rehash the event over and over, almost as if he were ashamed to believe in something “impossible”. Simon knew that I was the cause of whatever had happened but didn’t understand completely, and Bruno was just sorry that he didn’t get anything good on tape.

CHAPTER XV

E TE TEYO

Recovering a bit from the tornado, we made our way back to "Route 666" and continued west towards Amarillo, Texas in hopes of getting there by early the next morning. In the meantime, Bruno and Simon started shooting introductory footage of the bus and its occupants. As late afternoon became night, we stopped at a turnout to eat and settled in for the evening. After the excitement of the day, it didn't take long for everyone to fall into a deep and restful sleep. Marian slept in the diner. Rocco in his sleeping bag next to his bike under a tree, and Jesus, Bruno, and Simon slept in the bus on bench seats that converted into small beds.

I on the other hand, could now get by on as little as three or four hours of sleep per night. Sean O'Connell was the one who taught me this trick. I've passed his lesson on to many people over the years, and yet everyone who tries it finds they can come no closer to living this lesson than two positive magnetic poles can come to rest together. What is the lesson in a nutshell? "Sleep little, without regret." The "sleeping little" is easy, compared to the "without regret" part.

Early next morning, as Marian made breakfast in the trailer, Rocco rode off and returned with a local newspaper. As we sat down to a meal of "Buffalo Bill Biscuits", "Sioux Scrambled Eggs," and "Six Gun Sausage", the paper got divided up between us. Simon took the entertainment section. Bruno took the financial section. Marian grabbed the lifestyle. Rocco took the headlines to see what kind of a mess the world was turning into and Jesus took the sports section to see how Mexico was doing in the soccer finals.

All that was left for me was the local news and advertising. As I paged through the stories of farming and ranching issues and exposés of bureaucratic incompetence that can be found in almost any city, I noticed that we would arrive in Amarillo on the same day as a big race. They event was located at some sand dunes, found just a bit west of the city towards the border with New Mexico.

"I'd like to go check out this local race," I said. "This would be a good place to show some of what the Mode can offer."

"What kind of race?" Rocco asked.

"Sand drags, motocross, mud bogs, all kinds of stuff." I passed the article around for everyone to look at. Once everyone agreed, we cleaned up the breakfast mess and headed back out on the road.

As we passed through Amarillo on our way to the racecourse, Jesus took the opportunity to clear up any misunderstandings about the name of the city, lest anyone continue the rest of their lives saying the name of this poor bastard town incorrectly.

"Amarillo means 'yellow' in Spanish," he lectured as he drove, "and in Spanish, the 'L' sound is said like a 'Y'. Therefore, the name of this city is 'Amarillo', like 'EYO'. Now, ignorant Texans living here will tell you it is said 'AmariLLo' accenting the 'Ls' in all their double glory. So the lesson that can be learned from all of this is that here in the U.S.A., 'English is English, *especially* if it's Spanish'." He laughed at his own joke.

Jesus took some personal satisfaction from then on emphasizing the correct pronunciations of every Spanish word on every sign and building we saw. Delighting too much, I believe, in the sounds that are not produced in any English words such as the trill a Spanish double "R" makes when rolled off the tongue correctly, like in "BuRRRRRito".

Amarillo was indeed "yellow" and the color of the landscape varied by only a few degrees, as did the topography for that matter. It was "flat as a pancake just off the griddle" and equally as hot.

When we arrived at the races, Bruno and Simon used their New York charm and showbiz credentials to wrangle us pit passes to the event. Once seated, Marian, Bruno and Simon wandered off to the concession stands to peruse the goods, while Rocco, Jesus, and I wandered our way through the pit.

We saw endless rows of sand rails preparing for drags, customized trucks getting ready for the mud bog, and dirt bikes of all kinds revving up for the extreme motocross. As we passed each team with their drivers and mechanics and support crews, I occasionally could identify a specific failing of a machine and would stop to alert the team. One sand rail that was revving its engine as we passed had a spark plug that I could hear was fouling faster than the others did. I told the crew chief, who thought at first that I was crazy, but in an attempt to prove it, he found that I was right.

One of the mud bog contenders was having trouble with their clutch, which was an important part of navigating a mud bog. I asked them to perform a series of tests, by engaging and freeing the clutch in a variety of situations. I determined that the clutch was being hampered by a small piece of metal that was somehow stuck to the face of the clutch plate. The lead mechanic pulled the entire assembly within twenty minutes and sure enough, there was a small shaving of metal embedded in the face of the clutch plate.

Rocco and Jesus watched all of this silently but with growing interest. Finally, Rocco had to speak up.

"You can really do all this stuff, can't you? I don't know how you do it, 'cause it looks like voodoo to me. But I'll be damned if you aren't right every time."

"Mr. Dewey is a great man," Jesus added. "I was the student of a great man, and he told me to follow Mr. Dewey. That is how good he is."

Rocco looked at me. "O.K. it's going to bug me until I figure out how you do it."

"I'll be happy to show you, Rocco," I answered. "That's the whole point; to share what I've learned so that people like you can benefit from it. It's like anything else. You can learn it if you really want to and make efforts. It doesn't come by magic."

Jesus chimed in, "Is true. Not magic. I have started to learn some of these things in a very slow way." He stopped and smiled broadly, "I am good with spark plugs! And now, with Mr.

Dewey's help, I will learn even more, and be good with everything. You can do this to," he urged Rocco, "I will help."

Rocco seemed surprised by this sudden pledge, but I could see that he wanted to learn more about the Mode, and that Jesus' offer had touched the part of him that was open to new things. "Well sure, Jesus. I'll likely need all the help I can get. You really know how to do some of this?"

Jesus said proudly, "I can make a spark plug spark all by itself, but it takes hours of concentration to do it just once."

Rocco was duly impressed. "That's a trick you'll have to teach me."

We moved to a section of the pits that held the motocross riders. They had finished their trials and elimination races and were preparing for the finals in that category. I asked one of the onlookers what the standings were, and he pointed to a pair of teams working across the pathway from us.

"Well, you see these two local boys? That's Rusty Owens and Buzz Johnson, and they're two-time winners here, going for a state record by winning three in a row; something they're calling a 'three-peat'. But, they've been having bike troubles all day. Now the team next to them with the girl rider, that's Brenda Malone, and she's had a real good day, making it to the finals for the first time. She's the only rider so far that's good enough to give Buzz a run for his money. He's usually so good that it's never a contest when it gets to the end of the race, but that girl is mighty determined. They're coming up to the final race in about twenty minutes."

I thanked him for the recap and Rocco, Jesus and I went to check out these two teams.

Rusty and Buzz, the local boys, were in the middle of a very heated discussion. Buzz was the rider; a young, brown-haired country boy with enough looks to catch the eyes of the ladies. Rusty was his mechanic; a thin-haired young man with deep brown eyes and a tattoo covered muscular body that must have also appealed to the feminine contingent, which would explain why both of them had a large number of female fans standing a respectful distance away as their favorites prepared for the next race.

Buzz was sitting on his bike, looking down at Rusty, who was prying into the engine. "I don't know why this is happening now. We've never had a problem that we couldn't put our finger on. It's like we're cursed all of a sudden."

"Look, Buzz, it's not a curse… That's stupid," Rusty said, tying to keep his attention on the engine. "There's *some* kind of problem… we just haven't figured it out yet, that's all. We're gonna have to face the possibility that we won't be able to figure it out in time for the next race. But, that doesn't mean we're cursed; just screwed. I'll keep at it."

Just then, Brenda, the rider for the team next door came over and stood next to them. Without her helmet, her long brown hair hung down past her shoulders and a yellow and black leather jumpsuit fit tightly around her healthy feminine body.

"Hiya, Buzz," she said, smiling. "Hi Rusty, how's it goin' guys?"

"Uh, just OK at the moment," he replied. "We're having some technical troubles."

She pouted at him. "Oh no… I'm so sorry to hear that."

"But don't worry, we'll be ready in time for the race," Buzz assured her.

"I wouldn't want it any other way, Buzz," she said, and blew him a kiss. "If anybody can figure out a tough problem, it's Rusty. Besides, when you lose, it won't be because of your bike!" Leaning down she took both of Rusty's rather smudged hands in hers and studied them, turning them over once, and looked at him straight in the eye. “He’s got mechanics hands. They’re magic.”

She stood up and starting walking back to her team. “See you at the starting line boys,” she said, over her shoulder. “And remember, it’s not about whether you win or lose…” She waved as she walked away.

Rusty watched her go in rapt fascination. “Hey, I know she’s hot, but we’ve got a sick bike,” Buzz said, trying to draw his mind back to the task. “She likes you though. You should try to hook up with her after the race. I’ve heard she’s a wild ride even when she’s out of those leathers.”

Rusty slowly turned back to Buzz, awakening to the here and now. “Yeah, hook up after the race, you bet,” he muttered.

I took a few steps forward and introduced myself. “Gentleman, my name is Dewey and this is Jesus and Rocco. We noticed you’re having trouble with your bike. Being students of mechanics perhaps we can help.”

“Howdy, I’m Buzz and this is Rusty. Rusty’s the best there is, if he can’t figure it out, no one can.”

“Try us,” I said. “Can you explain your problem?”

Buzz looked at Rusty and then back at me “Why not, nothing else has worked.”

He went on to say the bike was running smoothly, but that he wasn’t getting the power he was used to and noticed the tone of the engine had changed slightly. Rusty explained that they had replaced the plugs, checked the valves and pistons, examined the exhaust system, and that nothing had turned up as being out of whack.

“Chain tension?” Rocco asked, from what obviously was personal experience.

“Yeah, that’s fine,” Buzz answered.

"Fuel filter or line?" Jesus questioned; homing in closer to what I suspected was the problem.

"Replaced 'em both. No difference," responded Rusty.

"Buzz, tell me about how it sounds different now," I asked.

"The pitch is higher. You know how you get used to the sound of an engine at certain times; well the tone or pitch is just a little higher than usual," he replied, shrugging his shoulders at his own explanation.

"And while I'm sure that's true, it doesn't give me anything to go on," Rusty said, who had clearly heard Buzz's impressions before and discounting them as meaningless.

"But that clue gives us everything to go on," I countered. "With what you've already replaced and re-tested, Buzz's sound is pointing to the one thing you haven't considered; the fuel itself. The engine appears to behave perfectly, taking in what you feed it, setting it on fire to create an explosion, using the resulting force to turn a metal shaft, expelling the remains of the explosion. However, if the gas is weak, the force of the explosion is lessened, and the result is that power is reduced. Therefore, the pitch created by the explosions will be just a little bit higher. The gas you're using is either a lower octane than you usually use or it's got something in it, like a little bit of water."

Buzz looked at Rusty. "You brought all the gas. What do you think?"

"The gas is fine. It's the same stuff we always use," Rusty said angrily. "I picked it up just yesterday."

Buzz persisted, "Do you have any other suggestions? I mean, we've been knocking our heads together since the day began, and nothing's worked. I say we try some other gas."

With that, Buzz jumped off the bike and made his way to a team across the walkway, who having not made the final, was packing up their gear. Within minutes, Buzz returned with two large gas cans. Rusty, who continued to mutter that it wouldn't make a bit of difference, drained the gas tank of the bike and poured in the new stuff. They started the bike and revved it a few times. Just a few seconds later the track officials asked for all of the finalists to approach the starting line. Buzz put on his helmet and waved before riding the short distance to where all the riders were lining up. Moments later, the starter pistol was fired and the riders were off in a cloud of dust. Bruno, Simon and Marian joined us as we caught them up on the drama and watched the riders battle it out.

Halfway through the race, Buzz began to extend a large lead out over the other riders, although Brenda could be seen tearing along half a lap behind. It was a marvel to watch these racers slide, jump, dip, and dive over the bumpy course. Buzz was amazing to watch. It was clear that he enjoyed every bit of it, in a way that made it more of a performance than a race. His jumps were spectacular and the audience cheered him wildly when he pulled off one of these amazing feats.

The race finished with Buzz winning and Brenda coming in second, and some other guy coming in third to round out the prizes. Brenda looked mad as Buzz was handed the winning trophy and check, and shook her head in disgust as they made their way from winner's circle.

After the ceremony, the group headed back to the bus, while I joined Buzz and Rusty on their way back to the pits.

"Hey, Dewey, you were right!" said an enthused Buzz when he saw me. "The bike was singin' like a bird this time around." He turned to Rusty. "You gotta admit, Rusty, this is one time that your 'magic mechanic hands' failed you; and it turned out to be such a simple answer, too. If I didn't know any better, I'd say you set me up."

Rusty looked back and forth between me and Buzz. "Set up for what?" he said, angrily.

"Why, set up to lose! Set up so Brenda could win! Set up so you could get into her pants. The more I think about it, the more sense it makes. Tell me, Romeo, were you going to play up on her winning high, or did you just cut a deal with her?"

He looked over at where Brenda and her team were loading their gear into trucks. We could see her slamming things around in frustration.

"She knew, didn't she?" Buzz asked Rusty. Rusty looked like a schoolboy who'd been caught with a wet spot on his pants.

"Well?" Buzz pressed.

"Yeah, I made a deal with her. I'd make sure she had an edge on you and she'd let me do whatever I wanted for a night. You saw her Buzz! Can you blame me? She's hot!"

Buzz shook his head. "You'd throw the race for that? What about the 'three-peat'?"

Rusty answered, "Aw, you know that don't really mean nothin'. We've been state champions two years in a row. One more don't mean that much. Around here, you're the best there is on wheels, and until now, I thought I was the best there is on engines. We're just two schmucks stuck in a small town pond and you know it. This race don't mean nothin'."

Buzz shook his head at Rusty as they watched Brenda getting into the truck and burst into laughter. "She really is pretty hot," he said, in a low voice.

Rusty laughed in relief. "I would have told you about it later. Now I'll never get the chance."

"You bastard!" Buzz said, and threw a rag half-heartedly at Rusty. "You haven't changed a bit since the day I met you in grade-school. I tell people how smart and sneaky you can be, but no one believes me. 'Not Rusty. He's so quiet and nice'. Bullshit."

Rusty extended his hand out to Buzz. "For what it's worth, I'm glad you won the race. The 'three-peat' feels good."

The two of them shook hands, and Buzz responded, "*We* won the race. You know, when you aren't sabotaging me you're the best mechanic I have ever seen."

Rusty turned and pointed a finger at me. "You're good. Dewey, did you say? Man, you busted me somethin' fierce. I was sure Buzz wouldn't stumble onto the gas being a lower octane; and he wouldn't have, if you hadn't come along. It's such a subtle thing. Most people would never have noticed. Where did you learn it?"

"The laws of mechanics open your senses and abilities if you focus your mind. Here, I'll show you. Where's the can with the gas you were using before I came along?" Buzz looked around, pulled a can from the pile of gear, and handed it to me. I opened it and looked at Rusty. "What octane do you usually run in the bike?"

"Ninety-five. It's the hottest the rules will allow," answered Buzz.

I took a deep sniff. "This is eighty-nine. This is what you get from commercial pumps for cars; and the cheap stuff at that."

"You can tell that from the smell?" Rusty asked.

"Sure, and plenty more. That's what this new method of learning mechanics is all about. It's called the Mode and can teach you more than you ever thought possible."

Rusty and Buzz looked at each other and then back at me. "What are you doing for the next few hours?"

Turns out, they were hungry and would always go out to eat after a race, win or lose. We met them at a steakhouse just a few miles from the race site. As Buzz and Rusty drank a few beers, we learned that they were mini-celebrities: high-school stars in baseball and football, drummer and guitar player in a band, extreme adventurers, and now a famous racing team. Two of the most popular guys around and here they were, chafing at the bit to get out of town and try their luck in the wider world.

Rusty asked more about the Mode and was impressed that there was a deeper meaning to the workings of machines, something he'd suspected but never heard anyone else voice. Being "in tune" with an engine was not a problem for Rusty who'd been employed as a mechanic in local shops since his junior-high days.

Buzz was fascinated with our trip out west and wanted to know about the route we were taking. They turned out to be funny, good-hearted people and everyone responded well to their antics, which were the product of a combination of brotherly affection and fierce competition. They kept mentioning how stifled they were starting to feel, and how going somewhere new seemed to be the logical next step. I asked them if they'd be interested in traveling along with us to California.

"The desert races in California are supposed to be some of the toughest," Buzz said to Rusty. "It would be fun to see what that kind of terrain is like. Whad'ya say, man? Are you ready to look for a bigger pond?"

Rusty smiled. "Long past ready. Let's do it."

A few hours later, they'd collected their things and made arrangements for their absence which, since they were young and single, didn't amount to much more than them quitting their jobs to which they weren't attached and saying goodbye to their parents, who were used to them running off on one adventure or another.

We pulled onto the road with Rusty sitting in the front seat of the bus, behind Jesus who was driving, when Buzz startled everyone by suddenly appearing on his bike, leaping across the road just in front of us and performing a mid-air turn before coming down to the right of Rocco. We would soon become quite accustomed to Buzz's sudden appearances and disappearances. That boy loves to jump.

CHAPTER XVI

Indian Soup

They don't call the Southern Plain States "plain" for nothing and for miles around all one could see was the flat horizon and melting sun as we headed for the Texas-New Mexico border. The bus had enough of its primary energy source left to get us to Albuquerque, but we weren't in all that much of a hurry and had decided to stop in Santa Fe along the way as a rest spot.

After a while, Rocco waved us over at a roadside landmark called, "The Dust Bowl Museum", apparently dedicated to the regional disaster. The Dust Bowl was the result of a series of severe droughts in the early nineteen-thirties that hit the plains, which were deeply plowed and planted with wheat. As the droughts deepened, the farmers kept plowing and planting but nothing would grow. The ground cover that held the soil in place was all gone. The Plains winds whipped across the fields raising billowing clouds of dust to the skies. In some places, the dust would drift like snow, covering farmsteads. So how, with such an important piece of history just knocking on our door, could we not stop and get a look at this "Dust Bowl Museum." Besides, Buzz and Rocco needed a bathroom break.

We each paid five dollars to get in, which we were told goes towards the upkeep of the establishment. Once inside, we found it was nothing more than a large piece of dirt about the size of half a football field containing an old barn, a car, a fence post, a wagon, and a mailbox that were all covered within inches of their tops with a fine dusty dirt. As the guide explained the significance of the disaster and the representation of it that we were viewing, I could see each of us looking at the other in amazement. This was it? No one wanted to make light of the real tragedy that did befall this region, so instead we listened seriously to the guide, picked up some souvenirs, tiny bottles filled with dust, and got back onto the bus to continue west until our next stop was in full view.

The sun was now surrendering its huge orange glow to the rising horizon, which *is* the way it happens, by the way. It's funny, even to this day we still say "the sun is going down" or "the sun is coming up" as some vestige of when we truly believed the world to be flat and the rest of the universe revolved around us. In reality as the world turns, the horizon *is* moving up.

Santa Fe i.e. "Holy Faith" doesn't really sit on the direct path of Route 66. However, at some point in its history it must have lobbied hard enough for people to draw a little line up to there and back, so that it shows as an official part of Route 66 on most maps instead of the small side detour it really is. We had been climbing slowly over the past four or five hours and you could feel that the air was getting thinner. Santa Fe sits at just less than seven-thousand feet above sea level and you could tell by the pace of the locals nobody moved very fast. In order to give Marian a cooking break, we decided to eat at a place called "The Billy the Kid Inn."

The food was decent and had names not unlike The Chief Diner but whose themes were local outlaws instead of Indians. Like The "Black Jack Ketchum Burger," the "Butch Cassidy Cashew Chicken," and of course "The Slippery Sundance Kid Sandwich." They even had "Eggs Benedict with Doc Holliday Sauce". As we filled both our stomachs and our curiosities with outlaw delights, Jesus decided to lecture us once again on language.

"The word 'Albuquerque' comes to us again from the early claimers of this land, the Spanish. Our friends the Spaniards named Albuquerque after a city in their beloved Western Spain, which was later misspelled by some Englishman (obviously not an Oxford man). It comes from the words 'albus' and 'quercus'."

"What and what?" asked Rusty.

"'Albus' and quercus'." Jesus added helpfully, "Like 'Albus and Costello', or 'Albus Presley' or 'God please albus'." Laughs abounded around the table. "'Albus' means 'white' and 'quercus' means 'oak'."

Marian said to me, "Sounds like the Spanish pulled the same thing that you told us happened in Abyssinia; waltzed in and claimed the place without noticin' that folks were already livin' there."

"Yes, the Spanish were the conquering nation of the day in this region, and like most, paid no regard whatsoever to the indigenous people who had lived here for millennia before, promptly claiming it as a great discovery. To the rest of the world, they presented the Indians as 'villains and savages of the most hideous kind'."

Rocco chimed in, "I remember, when I was a little kid, seeing pictures in my schoolbooks of Indians holding the scalps of white men who had been killed while protecting wagons full of women and children."

"But now they say that the Indians learned that scalping trick from the white men," Bruno interrupted.

"Yes, that's right. History is a lot easier to assess from a distance of some time, compared to when it's actually happening," I replied. "That's why our perception of the American Indian is so different now compared to what it was back then."

"Once the American public got a dose of 'the guilts', it did what it's always done; reversed its view one hundred and eighty degrees," said Rocco, getting a little heated up.

"And isn't that the correct view?" I asked, "That the Indians were horribly mistreated?"

"Of course it is, but have you seen the school books kids get exposed to these days? They're apologetic to the point of making me sick. 'We are so sorry for the actions of our ancestors. We shall study and praise the 'Native American'. They were a great culture living in totally harmony with nature, bullshit. It sounds better than saying 'they're savages', but it's not any more true. I'm telling you, anytime humans lean real far in one direction, they swing equally as far back the other way. And it's not good, even if it seems like it is. It's just creating another warped view, only in the opposite direction."

"You're right," I said.

He looked at me with astonishment, as did several others at the table. "I am? I mean, of course I am! But why would you agree?"

"Because unfortunately it's true. Humanity has a hard time finding the middle ground. It tends to swing back and forth from one extreme to another. It's both the light and dark side of thinking I can bring some of the Mode to people. I want the world to swing one way; it may just swing the other."

Albuquerque had some great pieces of American engineering and I wanted to see some of them before we blew through town too fast. There were some classic trains here and since I had developed quite a love and respect for these machines, I wanted to get a look and maybe even ride on them if any were still functional. One was the Atchison, Topeka, Santa Fe Locomotive 2926, built in nineteen-forty four. It represented one of the last steam locomotives used by the Santa Fe Railway. She had a 2900 class steam locomotive engine and a beautiful, long black body. Ah, the good old days, I sighed.

As we drove around town, stopping here and there to see the sights, Bruno filmed Simon as he brought "the audience" up to date on our trip so far. Over the last couple of days, Simon had conducted short interviews with each of us to establish "the cast". He and Bruno were at a bit of a loss when I insisted that they also take a turn in front of the camera as interviewees instead of interviewers. Nevertheless, they held up well as Marian conducted the interviews with virtually the same questions they had asked us. I think she got a kick out of turning the tables on them.

I also noticed that Bruno was becoming more comfortable as a camera operator. At first, he was always tangled up in wires or missing some piece of gear or other, but now he knew where everything was and could whip out the camera at a moment's notice. He was also getting good at being unobtrusive. I mean, it was a good-sized professional quality camera, so there was no way to hide it, but Bruno had learned how to make it seem like it wasn't right in your face.

Occasionally, during a moment of downtime, I'd see Bruno scribbling away in a small pocket-sized notebook. When I asked what he was writing, he just smiled and said, "Ideas, dreams, names, numbers, you know, just stuff," and went back to writing.

As we left Albuquerque, I thought about "us". There were now eight of us, two on motorcycles up ahead, and six in the bus, which pulled the trailer. We were turning into quite a caravan.

A social dynamic was developing between us all that reminded me of the twelve types Winger had told me about and the way in which different aspects of a person's type attracted and repelled other aspects of other types. Jesus and Rocco, despite their antagonism, were both drawn to the open road and were matured by the ways of the traveling man. Rusty and Buzz shared a love of competition, but Rusty was cautious at heart while Buzz was radical. Bruno and Simon shared the dynamic of fame; Simon thought being in front of the camera would do it, Bruno sensed more power in controlling those in front of the camera from the background. Marian, who had just wiped the entire slate of her life clean, was embarked on what was turning out to be a real adventure and was in turn working her charm and magic on all of us.

Something had attracted me to these people and them to me, and now those lines were converging and multiplying. Everyone but Bruno had gotten a little taste of the Mode, and at least he'd heard them talk about it. *What do I do with them?* I asked myself. Could these people help me bring the Mode to the world? I wasn't sure of the answers yet, but decided to give it some serious thought between now and the end of the ride in California.

We all agreed that we wanted to complete the full length of our Route 66 adventure at the famous Santa Monica Pier, spending some time there. I still had the obligation to my dear friend Anna to take care of, and selling Winger's planes would perhaps take more than a few weeks.

We decided we could squeeze in a couple of side trips and one place that I held firm on as a must-stop cosmic attraction was the Grand Canyon. Everyone else voted for Las Vegas, a place that I found to be quite meaningless. However, the die was cast. The Grand Canyon and Las Vegas were next on the agenda.

CHAPTER XVII

Molecular Magic Beans

An hour outside of Lake Mead is nothing but desolate wilderness. Up ahead, a hot and tired looking young mother with two small children clutching her legs stood by the side of the road. An old Chevy with the hood open rested at an angle off the pavement.

"That doesn't look good," Jesus said.

Rocco signaled he was going to pull over.

"That figures!" Jesus snapped. "Had she been Indian, Mexican, Asian, Black, or a dude, he would have never slowed down, let alone stopped. But a young, thin, brunette… he's all about helping. He's gonna scare them to death!"

Jesus pulled the bus off the main highway and before the wheels had come to rest, Rusty flew out the door. Marian and I followed him to see if we too could be of any assistance, while Simon and Bruno grabbed their equipment and took up a position from the window. Jesus stayed on the bus and Buzz, as usual, disappeared into the barren horizon to find out if a sand dune about a hundred yards away could be jumped from more than one side without landing in cactus.

"Hello Ma'am, what seems to be the trouble?" Rocco asked.

"Can we help you miss?" Rusty added, reaching them a bit out of breath.

"That's OK. I've got it, Rusty."

"No, I think I can handle it, Rocco."

The children buried their faces deeper into their mother's legs.

"Look, you're scaring the little ones, Rocco!" Rusty scolded.

"It looks as if at least one or more of us can help you miss. My name's Dewey," I said, reaching out my hand. "You've just met Rocco and Rusty, and this is Marian."

"I'm Angela."

"What happened to your car?" Marian asked.

"It was running hot when the 'check engine' light came on. Smoke started coming from the tail pipe so I immediately pulled over. I don't know much about cars, but my ex-husband told me that it leaked oil and that I should check it every so often."

"Mind if I take a look?" Rusty asked.

"Mind if *we* take a look?" Rocco said, following him.

"Of course, please do," replied Angela.

They opened the hood and the two of them stuck their heads in to investigate.

"Look Rusty," Rocco whispered, "I saw her before you did!"

"Why don't we just see what's wrong with her car first. In case you didn't notice she's got kids."

"Yeah, I know that probably scares a young punk like you, but a guy like me's not afraid of baggage, at least she's not married. I heard her say 'ex-husband'."

"When's the last time you checked your oil, Angela?" Rusty yelled.

"I don't really know, my husband, I mean, my ex-husband usually handles that sort of thing."

Rusty pulled his head out from under the hood with the dipstick in hand. "The radiator coolant is all but gone and she's at least three quarts low on oil. She may have warped a head a bit, but other than that, it doesn't look like the block is cracked. With some fluids, she should be good to go."

"There might be some oil in the trunk," Angela replied. "You can check if you like. It's open."

Marian reached over and took Angela by the hand. "Why don't I take you and little darlins' back to the diner and replenish *your* fluids."

Rocco went to check the trunk for oil. A couple of minutes later he emerged from behind the car. "Only one quart back there," he said, handing it to Rusty.

"We're going to need some water for the radiator. Rocco, can you go back to the diner and get some?" I asked.

"Sure… and while I'm at it, I'll check and see how the little lady is doing." He smirked at Rusty. "Besides, it looks like you mechanical dudes got things under control out here."

I joined Rusty at the front of the car.

"One quart's not enough," he said, holding out the can of oil. "What are we gonna do now?"

"Trust me on this one. One quart will be plenty."

I had Rusty start the car as I laid my hands on top of the fender. Closing my eyes, I meditated to see if I could sense anything else wrong.

"Can you tell me what you're doing?" Rusty asked. "I want to try to understand this stuff."

"I'm sensing vibrations. Everything in the universe is in motion; nothing is standing still. Therefore, everything must possess an optimum state of vibration, which in Buddhism is called Nirvana. In the Mode it is called, 'Samavana', from the Sanskrit word Samadhi, meaning harmony or balance. When something is not right, a vibration will expose irregularities in its pulse. The hardest part is deciphering what they mean. I find it easier to concentrate with my eyes closed, but one of my teachers, Isaac, could do it while reading the paper. Anyway, the point is that vibrations can tell us a lot. One of the easiest forms to decipher is the *sound* a car makes."

"You're right, now that I think about it. As a trained mechanic, I can pretty much just listen to a car and tell you what the problem is. Can you teach me some of that, 'feelin' the vibe' thing, like you did back at the races?" Rusty asked.

"Sure, but let's start our diagnosis here, with simple deductions of noticeable physical clues." I scanned the engine with my eyes. "There's a lot to be told just by looking at this engine, huh?"

"Yeah, I can tell at least five things that are about to go wrong with this car."

"Follow me," I said, and led Rusty to the cabin of the car. "Here is where it all starts. This is where the machine behind the machine lives."

"What do you mean?"

"I mean the psychology of the driver. Look around the cabin. It says everything. Rocco may be back at the diner with Angela right now, but in a few minutes, you're going to know more about her than he will. Start by telling me what you see."

"I see some pretty shredded seats. You know, if she'd a kept ArmorAll on those they wouldn't have cracked like that. And the carpet is pretty soiled."

"What else. I'm looking for you to derive something less obvious from things that are very obvious."

"Well, I don't know. There sure is a lot of stuff packed into this thing!"

"Precisely! She is leaving home, and my guess is it's because of an abusive and controlling husband."

"How can you tell that?"

"Look at the angle of the car. The trunk is lower than it should be. Either she's finally killed the bastard and stuffed him in there, however, Rocco probably would have noticed that, or it's loaded with belongings. My guess is the latter. She wore her wedding ring on her right hand, but her left-hand ring finger was white as a ghost where the ring had been for years, and the kids had bruises on them. She might have had a couple herself.

"Look at this. The drawings on that map lying on the front passenger seat are in different colored pens. She's been planning this for a while."

"That's amazing. I didn't notice any of that. But how does that explain the car breaking down?" asked Rusty.

"Her husband either took the oil out, or let it run low. He knew she wouldn't get far. His behavior is compulsive and, being asleep psychologically, he will come looking for her soon. He probably had abusive parents himself. He's merely acting out the sleep scenario taught to him by them."

"Can't we do anything?" Rusted asked.

"We can get her on her way." I grabbed the map from the passenger seat. "Let's see… the map says she's headed towards Washington State. Maybe she's going to her parent's house. We need to get her back on the road."

"Is everyone 'sleeping'?" Rusty questioned, suddenly hit by the revelation that this concept may be bigger than he originally thought.

"There are people who were once asleep and are now free, but we can't concern ourselves with them. The question is do we want to wake up? Do we want to be free from the affects of genetics? Do we want be free from the control of the universal machine? Most people are quite content where they are. Waking up means becoming responsible."

"Can't people be told they're sleeping? Look what you've showed us already. It makes *me* want to wake up!"

"People don't know they're asleep, Rusty. If they did, they would be horrified. If they knew that every action they think they make is only a pre-determined re-action to something else, they would truly see the paradox of the situation. But that seldom happens."

"How does sleep start?"

"It starts in childhood, around the age of five or six. It starts the day you stop thinking for yourself and start taking on the thoughts and opinions of others. Many things influence this; technology, teachers, siblings, friends, parents, before you know it, you have no more actions of your own, only re-actions."

"What about heredity?" Rusty asked. "Some people are born with a disposition to be a certain way, right?"

"There is nothing we can do about what race we are. Beyond that, the changes I speak of happen in the psychology of a person, not in the body."

With everyone still gathered back at the diner, I asked Rusty to grab a funnel from the bus's storage bins. He returned a moment later with both the funnel and the water for the radiator.

"I thought Rocco was getting the water?" I asked.

"Yeah, well Rocco's so busy showing Angela his military tattoos, he didn't even remember you asking him."

Rusty filled the radiator with water while I opened the can of oil and spread a little on the fingers of my right hand. I rubbed the oil around, in a circular motion, so that the layer was evenly distributed. I began to meditate.

"Oil is made from other life forms," I said. "It comes from the plants and animals that inhabited the earth millions of years ago. Being under pressure all that time had compressed it, so that even when it is refined it releases that pressure back, giving us a form of concentrated energy. Nevertheless, oil, like everything else, is made up of elements, as we are, and in that sense, is no different from a rock or water.

"Elements are made up of atoms, and these atoms all have three types of orbiting forces."

"I did pretty well in chemistry; you mean protons, electrons, and neutrons. I'm still with ya, go on."

"One force has a positive charge, one has a negative charge, and one is neutral. This law of three is essential to the understanding of everything in the universe, and is common across all elements. The only difference between 'basic elements' is the number of each of these forces."

"Can we see the law of three in everything?"

"There is one problem," I said. "While it is fairly easy to determine a positive and a negative force, it's quite another thing to recognize the neutralizing force. This is because of the limitation of our sleep. Our sleep limits us from seeing the neutralizing force. Let me give you some examples; religion and science, good and evil, light and darkness. The list goes on forever. Everything we can think of has an opposite, but without the neutralizing force, nothing would be possible. Everything would forever be polarized. There would be no progression or resolution in anything.

"The Father, Son, and Holy Ghost," Rusty said. "Is the neutralizing force… God?"

"Some may call it God, others plain old science. What is important is that we learn to see the law in action. This will allow us do things we never thought possible before. Watch…"

I grabbed the can with my left hand and held my right hand about two inches away from the top. After rubbing my lubed fingers together for a few seconds, a small amount of oil began to pour off them and into the can.

"How are you doing that?" Rusty gasped.

"I'm borrowing protons, electrons, and neutrons, from the air and linking them together, creating more oil molecules."

"But that's impossible!"

"What is not possible with duality *is* possible with triality."

I handed the can to Rusty and he began pouring it in the block. Because the oil inside was multiplying, it made the can bulge slightly with pressure.

"Thanks, Dewey. Thanks for coming along when you did. If you hadn't I'd be living in Albuquerque forever, with the highlight of my life racing in mud bogs. I've learned more about machines in the last couple of days than I have my whole life."

"The Mode may be a bit easier to understand for us mechanics. We're already familiar with seeing things as interconnected processes."

Just then, Angela and her children who had just finished their hydration stepped outside the diner with Marian and the others and made their way back to the front of the car.

Rusty looked over at me a bit unsure what to do.

"Be careful," I said, as the others approached. "That can's been exposed to the desert sun too long and is full of pressure."

"Damn," Rusty replied, "I'm already spilling what little we have."

At first, no one noticed the can kept pouring and pouring oil, but one by one everyone stopped talking and eventually saw that Rusty's arm had been in the engine for a long time. Finally, the can ran out and he set it on the ground and inserted the dipstick for a measurement. When he pulled it out, it read "Full" as he shook his head with amazement. Everyone knew something had just happened but no one was sure what.

Rocco picked up the can from the ground and looked into it. It was still three-quarters full.

"What the hell kinda oil is this?" he asked. "Magic bean oil? I just saw Rusty empty that can into the engine."

"Simon scurried out of the bus with the camera on his shoulder. "What's going on?" he asked, as he approached us. "Did something just happen I should have gotten on tape?"

Bruno, who had left to relieve his bladder at the diner, came back just in time to see the faces of everyone and to ask the mother of all questions, "What'd I miss?"

"That's the third time you've missed something, Bruno," Simon said. "Dewey's doing some kind of 'magic' and you keep missing it."

"That's cuz it's probably some voodoo magic slight of hand trick," Bruno replied. "He can't hide the truth forever. Eventually we'll get it on tape. I'm gettin' out of this blazing sun. See ya'll on the bus."

"I'm not convinced it's voodoo or slight of hand," Simon yelled, to Bruno as he walked away. "I'm not sure what it is… yet."

"They're miracles," Marian teased. "He has a magic finger, you know."

"What are miracles?" I asked, "I have only learned to manipulate a few laws of the universe and, just like everyone else, I am not able to break them.

"Well, then again, maybe that's what miracles are, Darlin'," she continued. "Maybe the great religious teachers of the world rose to such a level of understanding about the laws of nature that what seemed impossible… becomes possible."

"You are correct, Marian. That which seems impossible on one level *is* possible on another level, and the lower level will always see that which happens on the level above it as miraculous."

Sensing that Angela was unsure what we were talking about, Rusty announced, "Your car should be good to go, Angela."

"Yeah, if there's anything else we can do to help you…" Rocco said, and surprised all of us by opening the door for her.

"Get going, girl," Rusty whispered. "He'll be coming after you soon. Be careful out there."

"Thanks so much, all of you," Angela said. "Especially you Rusty," and winked at him.

We assured Angela she was safe to go now, but that as soon as she could she should look into the problem of her engine leaking oil, and with a wave from the kids, she took off into the desert.

As we were returning to the bus, a car slowly approached through a heat wave on the horizon, rolled up to us, and stopped. A large bearded man rolled down the window.

"Any of ya seen a broken down Chevy around here anywhere?" he asked.

Before any of the others could speak, I asked Marian to escort everyone but Rusty back to the bus and that I would handle it. I laid my hand on the hood of the man's car and bent over as if to quietly speak to him. Touching the car was just enough for me to sense that this was indeed Angela's husband, and as I leaned in, I noticed a shotgun lying across the passenger seat.

"It's best you leave her alone, Mister."

He started to reach for the gun. "Yeah, then you have seen her. What are you gonna do, stop me?"

"I wouldn't do that if I were you," Rocco said, surprising everyone and pulling open the passenger door, grabbing the rifle.

"Look, I don't want any trouble. I just want my kids back, that's all," the man said.

"By the look of those kids, they don't want to come back! I think its best you go back the way you came."

"I'll find her," he shouted, rolling up his window. "And when I do..."

He hit the gas and left a skid mark down the road as he fled.

"He won't find her," Rusty snickered.

"What makes you so sure of that?" I asked.

"Because I'm betting you just did a little voodoo on his car just now, I saw the little slight of hand thing you did."

"Well, I did convince his fuel pump to act up a bit."

"And in case you couldn't get the job done," Rocco added, standing up from the pavement with a Swiss army knife extracted. "I gave his gas tank a little prick. A prick for a prick, huh, Dewey?"

Rocco's protective sensibilities were beginning to show.

"Good job, Rocco. Now let's get out of here."

Rocco climbed on his Harley and waved us back on to the road. "What happened back there, Jefe?" Jesus asked.

"That was Angela's husband, and what you guys didn't know is that she was running away from him," Rusty said.

"Why?"

"Because he was abusing her and the kids. If we hadn't come along when we did, there's no telling what he might have done."

"What if he's going after her right now? She only left a few minutes before he arrived." Marian said.

"You don't have to worry about that. Dewey fixed him, and Rocco helped."

"Rocco helped?" Jesus asked.

"Yeah, he put a hole in his gas tank."

"Wow, there may be hope for him after all," Marian said.

As we traveled down the desert highway, my mind was filled with thoughts of how quickly things were coming together, and how some of the group had already embraced the Mode with an open mind. If nothing else, the others knew *something* different was happening, even if they weren't sure what it was.

We had already learned by now not to wait for Buzz before leaving, because when he was done climbing or jumping things he would eventually catch up with us. Rocco was quite the opposite and conserved what little energy he had. Buzz would tempt Rocco to "give it a try sometime, you might like it," but Rocco seldom took his bike off-road, if for nothing else other than he knew he would have to spend time cleaning it again.

CHAPTER XVIII

Buzz vs. the Primary Energy Source

The Navajo Indians believe that the highest peak of the San Francisco Mountains, lying just outside of Flagstaff Arizona, marks the tribe's rightful western boundary of the Navajo Nation. And who were we to argue that point to the three quarters of a million Native Americans that inhabit that area?

Rocco came close to several encounters of violence with the locals that day, insisting that Indians didn't really have a claim to North American soil because the white man's weapons were superior to theirs. That's not something you think, let alone say in these parts, and we were lucky enough to have gotten out of town unscathed, let alone at all. I guess that kind of behavior is to be expected from a decorated Veteran who still believes the spoils of war should always go to the guys with the biggest guns. More importantly, I learned from the almost-ceaseless scuffles that afternoon that he felt that the problem all stemmed from the early days of our trading with the Indians, in that something as mundane as corn was not a fair cultural exchange for something as wonderful as whiskey.

Rocco dropped his speed down a bit and pulled up beside the bus, still pissed off from his previous encounters with the natives. "You know, I was just thinkin'!" he yelled from his bike through the open windows.

"What?" Bruno asked, quickly pulling his camera up and rolling tape in case Rocco did something crazy.

"Why couldn't the 'Injuns' have traded us something good, you know, something that messes you up, like whiskey does?"

"Why don't you just let this Indian thing go, Rocco?" Jesus said.

Rocco ignored him and continued. "I mean, at least you Mexicans gave us Peyote and Mushrooms, huh, Jesus? That's not so bad, but corn? You've never heard anyone say, Wow man, I was so messed up last night on corn! I'll bet if you go far enough back in Indian history, you'd find that Injuns evolved from mutant buffalo!"

"Why you such a racist, Rocco?" Bruno yelled back at him. "If you go back far enough in yo' family tree, you wouldn't find immigrants, you'd find inbreeds! 'Hi, my name's Rocco and this is my other brother Rocco…'"

"Yeah, well I'm sure we don't have to go that far back in *your* family history to find monkeys!" Rocco gave Bruno the finger and pulled his bike ahead of the bus again.

"He's an angry man," Marian said, shaking her head at him as he passed by her window. Bruno smirked and pointed his camera at her. "And you, Mr. Goldblum," she scolded, "are no better!"

Loud voices drew Bruno's attention to the other side of the bus. He turned to find his camera on Buzz and Rusty, arguing over which sport was more extreme, "Bouncing" or "Racing". Buzz argued that bouncing, that is, the art of balancing a motorcycle on one wheel along rock cliffs was more extreme. Rusty felt that strapping yourself to a rocket with wheels and hurling through the desert salt flats at speeds exceeding seven hundred miles per hour, was more extreme.

Bruno kept the camera rolling with a look of joy on his face. "One thing's for sure," he said, "there's never a shortage of conflict around here."

"Is that all you see, Bruno, conflict?" I asked.

"What else is there?" He moved to a seat closer to Rusty. "Conflict makes good television!"

"There is harmony as well," I said, "and harmony makes good living. One cannot exist without the other."

"Yeah, well, I'm about to get some of that *harmony* on tape right now."

"Dude, look," Buzz yelled from outside the opposite side of bus while riding on the wrong side of the road, barreling down the highway. "Don't you think that bouncing on the edges of rocks, hanging off cliffs hundreds of feet above the ground with only a plastic helmet is more extreme than going real fast across the flat desert sand, close to the ground, with a parachute, fire suit, and a ton of safety gear?"

"Crazier, yes," Rusty explained, "but not more extreme. I'd be traveling faster than the speed of sound. One small mistake and I would be turned into salt dust."

"Yeah, but what are the chances of something going wrong, especially in a sport where everything is planned and calculated? Where's the fun in that?" Buzz argued. "All I would have to do is miscalculate a three inch tire against the angle of a rock, and I'd be splattered all over the landscape on my way down."

"You mean, like the car coming at you right now?" Rusty warned him. Buzz swerved his bike left and off the road. He traveled along a small drainage ditch for a few seconds before using the angle of it to hurl his motorcycle into a spectacular jump back on the highway as the car passed by him.

"You see," he said. "It only takes one mistake, but I'll never make one!" He pulled his bike up on its back wheel and sped up to join Rocco at the front of the bus.

"Yeah, I see the harmony, all right," Bruno teased. "He'll need 'our money' to get him out of the hospital or to pay his funeral bills. I just hope I get it all on tape!"

"Buzz seems strange, Darlin', for sure," Marian said. "I think he just lives in the moment, that's all. Something I wish I could do more often!"

Rusty laughed, "Buzz *is* crazy. But that's what I like about him. He's not afraid to take the chances I would never take and as long as he survives them, I get to live the experience through him." He stopped speaking and looked at everyone as if he had just let out a secret weakness. "But I would never tell him that, of course."

"Buzz *is* guided by impulse." I said. "Though he can't help being this way, he enjoys the energy created by living on the edge. I'm sure he's well aware that at any moment it could all be over, and of the dangers that go along with that. Nevertheless, because he lives every moment as if were his last, he also lives every moment to its fullest, something the rest of us cannot claim. Realizing the inevitability of death on a daily basis helps make one more compassionate towards others. It forces us to come to understand that no one is around forever."

Marian gave me an 'Amen' and supporting nod and gave Bruno an, "I told you so", glance.

Bruno put his camera down, discontented with my logical explanation, and for getting it all on tape.

"Reason doesn't make good television," Simon said. Bruno laughed, "Yeah, thank God for editing."

"You should thank God, for *everything*!" I replied.

Even though Bruno and perhaps Simon didn't get it yet, the look on Jesus' and Marian's face, told me a lot. Perhaps now they would be able to tolerate Buzz's odd behavior a little more than they would have. *"Harmony,"* I thought to myself.

We passed through Grand Canyon National Park early that evening. I was lucky enough to have witnessed the beauty of this place once before on the way home from the travels with my teachers. What has happened here demonstrates more than anywhere else that most sacred law of mechanics known as Galileo's principle of Inertia, which states that a body in motion generally stays in motion, unless something stops it. Water, being that staunch obeyer of gravity, travels in the easiest direction forever, unless acted upon by a resisting force, and has created this most beautiful piece of natural art along the way.

Hoover Dam, one of the world's greatest examples of man's ability to harness nature to generate power, lies on Highway 93 between the Nevada and Arizona borders. We arrived there in the afternoon and because it was late in the year, Hell had taken a holiday and it was a charming eighty five degrees with the wind out of the west.

"I thought we were going to Vegas?" Rocco asked, as Jesus pulled the bus into the parking lot. "Why the hell are we stopping here?"

"I want to show everyone something incredible," I said. "That is, if you open your minds up enough to experience it."

"What's so special about Hoover Dam?" Buzz asked. "Other than someday I would love to ride my bike along the edge of it."

"You mean, *try* to ride the edge, don't you, Buzz?" Rusty said.

"I mean ride it. Maybe even on one wheel! There's no trying in anything I do. You know that, Rusty. When I want to do something, I see myself already doing it. I visualize success. Trying implies the potential for failure. That's the day I'll die."

"You're a cocky little punk!" Rocco scolded. "You'd be dead in ten minutes in the military."

"No I wouldn't, Rocco. I'd be a hero. I can visualize it!"

"You wouldn't be sayin' that if you had to visualize a few of your friends dead right next to you!"

"Sometimes fear can save your life," Bruno said, "In New York, if you're hangin' with your homeys and a car comes barreling down the ally with guns hanging out the window, you better run for cover or your ass is toast."

"Yeah, Buzz," Simon added, "a little fear is healthy. You're not immortal you know."

"Fear is weakness," Buzz continued, "I may be skinny, but I'm not weak!"

"Perhaps we are confusing fear with the ability to sense danger," I interrupted. "We have built into our being the ability to sense when we or others may be in harm's way. This is not fear but a natural higher sense of protection."

"Intuition, us ladies call it," Marian added. "We've got it and you men don't. That's why ya'll are able to do stupid stuff like war, gettin' yourselves and a lot of other innocent people killed."

"We die in war to save your sweet little asses!" Rocco replied. "Faced with a crisis, you girls would run for the hills."

"We would not! We would work things out. Which is the sensible thing to do."

"But, without war there would be no freedom!" Rocco continued, rather loudly, drawing the attention of nearby tourists.

"War to protect freedom is not freedom from war, Rocco." Marian added. "Dewey, can you help us out on this one? We seem to be deadlocked."

"You are all right in a sense. Protecting freedom may mean going to war, but it is also true that man will never be free from war itself. Wars are fought by sleeping people for sleeping governments who are fully engulfed in the power of the machine. Freedom from the machine... freedom from sleep... this is the freedom we should concern ourselves with. That's one of the reasons I brought you all here."

"What did you want to show us, Jefe?" Jesus asked.

"The primary energy source," I said.

"You mean food?" Buzz asked, "'Cause I'm getting screamin' hungry."

"That is not what senior Dewey means, Buzz. He means... What do you mean, Jefe?"

"The true goal of all religions, and the true goal of all living things for that matter, is the innate desire to make contact with our primary energy source. A tree, for instance, grows towards the sun for a reason. It grows towards the source that gives it life, the source that gives *us* life. So, too, are our muscles an example of evolution that allows us to rise from the gravity of the surface of the earth towards the sun. For all living things on earth, the sun is our primary energy source.

"Man, however, has created another world, the world of machines, whose mechanisms all require oil, that grand reliever of friction and prolonger of life, and power, either in the form of electricity, coal, or gas. In the case of the world's mechanical infrastructure, electricity is the primary energy source. Come and I will show you."

We walked up to the ticket window and paid for our admissions. I asked the tour guide if it would be possible to see the turbine rooms as I had on my earlier visit there. She assured me they were still on the list of places the tour covered. I gathered the group together.

"This dam, big as it is, is but a small example of how we have learned to take 'the law of falling' or gravity, as it applies to water to turn a turbine, generating electricity. Electricity powers the mechanized world of man. Think for a moment what would happen if all the electricity in the world should stop at once. What would we be able to do? Nothing, I assure you! We have become slaves to this energy.

"Anyway, my point is that this dam represents a source point on earth that supplies us with the energy whose silence behind our walls and floors has nevertheless become a necessary force of life. When we are in the turbine rooms, touch your hand to the walls of their casings. You will feel a power like no other, and you may also find that your feet don't hurt so much anymore either."

Bruno thought this might be some kind of miraculous moment and decided he would try to enhance the production with Simon giving the play by play.

We arrived in the engine room and everyone began to gather around the turbines. I distracted the guide because if she caught wind that everyone was to be "handling the equipment" as it were, she might think that perhaps we were up to something. I watched each of them lay their hands or bodies against the cold cement turbine housings.

Marian closed her eyes and leaned against the great structure that towered almost two stories above her. A smile came over her face as she shot a look at me from across the room. Jesus and Rusty were immediately rewarded by renewed energy and smiles lit their faces too. Rocco leaned against one, and if nothing else, seemed not to have a negative reaction, which was all I could ask of him at this stage. Simon gave a short intro to set up the shot.

"Simon here. We have made our way to the engine room of Hoover Dam. Dewey has asked each of us to touch the turbine housings in an effort to sense the power being generated by them. I'm going to give you my live impression." He reached his hand out and touched it.

Bruno did a slow zoom-in, to catch the magic of the moment. "Well?" he asked, "What do you feel?"

Simon closed his eyes for a moment before speaking. "Uh, well… I feel the vibration, but I don't feel… wait a minute! I'm beginning to get something. Yes, the energy is starting to flow into me." He brought his hands up to head, as if it was going to explode. "I feel like my mind is blending into the ever-expanding universe of comic oneness. It's beautiful man…. I see lights, lots of colorful lights!"

"Really, Simon?" Bruno questioned, excited that this may be the moment of miraculous glory he has been waiting to capture.

"No, not really," he said, "I didn't feel anything other than the vibration of the motors, but Dewey's right, my feet don't hurt so much anymore."

"You bastard," Bruno replied, quickly shutting the camera off. "That's not funny."

"Sure it is, and you'll thank me later for that moment of comic relief when we edit this whole thing into a show."

Perplexed by the whole event, Bruno gained nothing and as usual, his skeptical nature kept him from benefiting from the many wonders that await an open mind. Simon on the other hand had an open mind, but since you can't show the energy flowing into a person very well on film, it looked more as if he just had a few drinks and was now not quite as grumpy as he had been a few minutes earlier.

"Well I feel something," Rusty said, saving Simon further bashing from Bruno. "I feel something that's not right."

Bruno pulled the camera back up into position. The tour guide became alarmed and immediately contacted security.

"What is it, Rusty?" I asked, walking closer to him.

"I'm trying to understand it, Dewey. I'm trying to use the Mode. Something's wrong here, but I don't know what it is."

I quickly laid my hands where he had. Sure enough, there was a huge irregularity in the pulse of the turbine. "Probably a bent drive shaft," I said, knowing that wasn't the problem, but wanting to lead Rusty to a proper diagnosis.

He put his hands back on the housing and, shutting his eyes, concentrated with all his might. "It's a bearing, Dewey. I just know it."

Just then, two security guards rushed through the door. "What seems to be the problem here?" they asked the tour guide.

"I don't know what these guys are up to, but they're scaring me!" she replied. "They keep touching the turbines and talking about something being wrong!"

"All right, what's going on?" the guard asked us.

I took a step forward. "My name is Dewey Pinkerton, and I am amongst other things, a teacher of mechanics. One of my students here, Rusty, who is also a trained mechanic, noticed something wrong with this turbine. He senses a malfunction about to happen."

"Are you kiddin' me?" the guard said. "What do you think we are, idiots? How did he determine that?"

"He laid his hands on it!" Marian said.

The two men starting laughing, "You're telling me he could sense something about this turbine through fourteen inches of concrete and steel with his bare hands?"

"Look," I said. "I know it sounds crazy, but why don't you have one of your engineers check it out. What have you got to lose?"

The two guards looked at each other and then back at the tour guide. "Why don't you continue on with your tour and I'll hold this pack of loonies down here until I can get engineering to clear this matter up."

"Yes, of course," she said, and the rest of the tour group was escorted out of the room.

"You guys sit tight over here against that wall until I get to the bottom of this," one of the guards said. "And if this turns out to be a joke, I'll make sure each and every one of you spends the night in the county jail."

I was assuring the others that everything was going to be all right, when I walked past a turbine control panel. I quickly glanced down and noticed it registering normal pressure statistics on all turbines in the room. Officials would find these readings in order, and we would almost certainly be detained further. I swiftly ran my hand across the controls and found the one that monitored the turbine where Rusty sensed a problem. A quick rap of my hand on the mechanism jolted the indicator into its correct position, showing that the turbine was indeed exhibiting degradation in its bearing.

I then sat down and the others followed.

“I’m sorry, Dewey,” Rusty said. “What if they don’t find anything wrong? I hope I don’t land us all in jail.”

“Don’t worry, you did great. I would have done the same thing,” I replied.

We were sitting for a few minutes when I noticed Buzz was not with us. “Where’s Buzz, Rusty?” I asked, scanning the room.

“I don’t know. I haven’t seen him since we got down here.”

“I remember seeing him,” Rocco said. “He had this look in his eyes as he leaned against the turbine that was kind of scary.”

“What do you mean, ‘scary’?” Marian asked.

“You know… like a crazy person. I’ve seen it bunches of times in Nam. They call it shell shock. It’s when your reality is completely turned upside down. It can cause post traumatic stress and other psychotic behaviors like nervous tics, loss of speech, inability to integrate with society… you know, the usual stuff!”

“That sounds like Buzz all the time,” Rusty replied.

A look of concern crossed Marian’s face. “You don’t suppose that Buzz drew too much energy from that turbine, do you, Dewey?”

"It's possible," I said. "I didn't think about the fact that Buzz already has more energy than any human should be allowed."

"I'll bet he feels pretty good right now," Jesus said.

"Probably a little too good," I replied. "We may have overdosed him. There's no telling what he might do!"

"Where do you thin' he is now, Jefe?"

"Maybe he left with the tour group," Rusty added. "Buzz has never been one to sit still for very long."

Several minutes later, a group of people entered the room. Two guards stood by the door, while a couple of engineers walked over to the control unit and began analyzing the turbine.

Finally, after what seemed like forever, the engineers approached us.

"Which one of you made this observation?" one asked.

"I did," Rusty said, standing up. "And if I'm wrong I am awfully sorry. You're welcome to take me to jail, but let the others go. They had nothing to do with it."

"Well, thanks, thanks a lot," the man said, putting his hand out to shake Rusty's. "I don't know how we could have missed it before. We had no idea the bearing was about to blow, but indications are, it is. You may have just saved us a lot of headaches, not to mention a lot of money."

The engineers turned towards one of the security guards. "Everything's in order here, Bill. Why don't you take our friends up with the others."

"Wow, Rusty, you're picking this stuff up pretty quickly," Jesus said, patting him on the shoulder as we left the room.

"Yeah, even I'm starting to think there's something to this stuff," Simon said.

Bruno pointed the camera at me. "But we still haven't caught anything on film yet!"

"Doubting Bruno… We're all here for a reason," Marian said, "And I for one, am happy to be a part of it."

We exited the turbine room to meet up with the rest of the group at the top of the dam where the tour had started. As we reached the parking lot, we heard a woman scream. "Look… look over there!" We all turned to where she was pointing.

"Oh, my God, no!" Marian shouted, "Buzz!"

There was an over-charged Buzz, with his motorcycle up on one wheel riding along the dam's edge as he made his way across the one thousand foot span.

"This is what I was afraid of," Rusty shouted, "Buzz not acting rationally, and teetering almost eight hundred feet above the Colorado River."

We all ran to our vehicles in hopes of reaching him before anything bad happened. Several minutes later, we started across the two-lane road that spans the dam.

"For God's sake, don't scare him anyone," Marian pleaded.

"Oh no," Rusty yelled. "Rocco is already ahead of him waiting behind a pillar."

In the confusion, Rocco had passed us all and was waiting for Buzz to get within arms reach.

"We'll never get there in time, Jefe. There are too many cars on this road," Jesus warned.

"There's nothing we can do," I said. "We won't reach him before he reaches Rocco."

We all watched as Buzz's motorcycle approached the point where Rocco was hiding. The other cars had all stopped and the speed of traffic came to a grinding halt. Some people cheered Buzz on, while others yelled obscenities at him. The crowd had grown so large that even security guards could not access the bridge to investigate.

Suddenly Buzz hesitated, as if something was wrong. He looked down the face of the dam and started to loose his balance. He tried to gain control, but began to wobble. We watched in horror as his front wheel went over the edge and then just as quickly, he disappeared along with it.

"Oh my God," Marian cried.

We stood there in shock and disbelief, when all of a sudden the crowd started cheering. Jumping off the bus, we ran to the edge and peered over. There was Rocco hanging over the edge of the dam holding Buzz by one arm. He pulled him back up and let him go onto the sidewalk.

Rocco gave Buzz a big smile and waved to the crowd. "Look you little shit!" he said, out of the corner of his mouth. "If you wanna die, don't do it around us, OK?"

Buzz climbed to his feet and dusted himself off. "I didn't need your help old man, I coulda' made it!" He paused, realizing what had really just happened. "You guys did this to me on purpose."

"Did what, you ungrateful punk?"

"Put doubt in my mind! Made me question my abilities!"

We arrived just in time to witness the two of them about to go to fists.

"Do you believe that?" Rocco shouted. "He says we put doubt in his mind and it messed him up, boo hoo..."

"That's not doubt, Buzz," Marian said. "That's called fear. It's what Dewey was talking about earlier, an inner sense that we may be in danger. It's your intuition telling you to slow things down a bit. Don't be in such a hurry to die. You're still young you know. Maybe this is a sign that you're needed here with us."

"But I've never doubted myself before. I've allowed myself to become weak."

"You're not weak, Buzz. You are stronger for this," Rusty added. "I think Marian's right, slow down a little. You do some crazy shit!"

Buzz turned to Rocco and with hesitation, put out his hand. "Thanks Rocco, I don't think I would be here right now if it weren't for you."

"You don't *think* you would be here? How about, you *wouldn't* be here. I've done some crazy shit in my life too, Buzz. Maybe that's why we both ride bikes… well one of us still rides a bike. We like livin' on the edge. No one's gonna take that away from us. But pushing it too hard doesn't help anybody. That's something that I've learned. You've got to find a balance."

We all looked at Rocco as the two of them shook hands.

"Did I just say that? Without my meds? I don't know what came over me. All right, come on," Rocco shouted to the crowd, "Everybody break it up! The show's over, let's get these cars on the road."

We made our way back to the bus where we were met by security officials.

"Not you guys again," they said. "Haven't we had enough excitement for one day?"

"We're very sorry. At least one in our group has learned a very important lesson here today. We would be happy to pay for any damages."

The two guards looked over the edge of the dam. "Seems the only damages are that twisted pile of 'rice rocket' down there. I'll send maintenance to dispose of that. You could do us a favor and get on your way before I have to fill out my report. I'm already going to have to explain what happened here earlier today. I want to keep my job, you know. I got little ones to feed."

"Of course," I replied. "Thank you so much for you kindness."

We climbed back on the bus and for the first time since we met, Buzz was forced to sit on a bench seat in a vehicle he was neither driving, nor able to do any stunts with, like the rest of us.

Rocco rode his Harley up to the front of the bus and with a smirk pulled his mirrored sunglasses down into position.

"Now that that pesky little Japanese gnat bike is toast, and its rider brought to within inches of humbleness, let's get on with this road trip."

CHAPTER XIX

Devil's Pair O' Dice

Driving thirty-five miles in just under twenty minutes, we arrived in Vegas at "horizon rise," exposing a late afternoon sky of silver and pink. They call New York the city that never sleeps, but this is a mistake. Las Vegas should have this title, since people there *do* almost never sleep. One of the reasons for this is that hotels probably have to stay open twenty-four hours to pay both their electric bills and bulb replacement vendors.

Once inside the casinos, I was taken by the advancements in the slot machine's abilities to taunt you as you pass, trying a variety of verbal enticements. It would not surprise me if before too long these machines identify you directly via your digital room key and will not only taunt you in the usual ways, but will call you by name, knowing already by your traceable habits the kinds of games you like to play.

Most of the group preferred the card tables, delighting in matching wits and faces of stone with others of their kind playing poker. To me, it didn't matter what your game was because "House Odds" guarantee that the great, great-grandchildren of the owners of these magnificent hotels will never have to work an honest day in their lives.

Marian, who was weary of watching grown men parade from table to table like peacocks, testosterone-bathed, and fueled by alcohol, followed me, while I found my usual delight in simply observing the behavior of these gamblers.

While having a bit of fun categorizing various groups of people into types, I happened to notice something very interesting about the random combinations of images that appeared on the faces of these one armed bandits. I found that after nearly an hour of observation I was able to predict with almost consistent certainty the time at which these images would line-up, delivering the gambler a pay out. I did this by counting the number of images on each wheel and multiplying them together, dividing that number by the number of times the handle had been pulled in any given sequence, and then adding… What, do you think I'm nuts? I'm not really going to tell you how I did it.

I must also admit that I a got some help from a feeling in my gut, and from the vibrations of the machines themselves, and had I been a weaker man would have without haste turned a twenty into a king's fortune. However, I resisted, thanks in part to an understanding of a most dangerous law, "That which feels too good, will undoubtedly be done again and again, only with more and more frequency" or addiction, as we have commonly come to call it. In addition, I was not only able to resist the temptation itself, but also to never mention a lick of it to any of the others, even to Marian who was seated right next to me.

"What are you looking at?" Marian asked, somewhat bored with her lack of participation in any of the action that surrounded us.

"I'm reading," I replied.

"Reading what? You don't have anything in your hands."

"People. It's something I learned to do from my teachers."

"How do you read people?"

"You can do it a lot of different ways. One way is to close your eyes. My first teacher was blind, so he taught me to read people by listening. I even learned to drive a train into a roundhouse and park it, all with my eyes closed."

"Sounds dangerous, how did you know when to stop?"

"I didn't, and just like my mentor Mac, I ran it right through the roundhouse the first time. He could have stopped me, but he told me later I never would have learned anything that way. This way I learned plenty. Besides, I think he enjoyed it. He used to say, 'how many times does a man get to run a train through a building and live to tell about it?' After that, he taught me how to tell distance by the sound of the train echoing back off of stationary objects."

"A blind man was the engineer of a train?"

"He was like no blind man you have ever seen. He could *see* more than anyone I know!"

"How has that helped cha' to read people?"

"By their walk, the way they breathe and the many other noises people make. I'll show you. Close your eyes."

"Right now, in front of all these people?"

"Sure, you don't think anyone in this casino has seen someone tired enough to close their eyes?"

Marian smiled and closed her eyes. "OK, now what?"

"Listen!" I said. "Listen to people as they walk by you, and then tell me what you hear."

She was quiet for a moment when a curious smirk crossed her face.

"I just hear noise. Wait, I hear talking, and I hear foot steps, and breathing."

"That's all you need for the basics, tell me what you can about the person coming closer."

She tilted her head and focused. "Their pace is slow and hard," she whispered, "and the breathing is heavy, and I smell a cigarette… Marlboro, Ultra Lights. I know that smell, because a friend of mine used to smoke them."

"Very good, so tell me more."

"They are heavy, and by the pitch of the breathing, I'm going to say it's a man."

"Open your eyes, Marian." She looked at the man, and then at me a bit surprised. "Very good, you were correct."

She clapped her hands like a child learning a new game.

"Everything you have told me is a physical characteristic. Had that man been speaking, even with your eyes shut, his words would betray something about his psychology. But better than that, I learned from one of my teachers, Winger, to hear what is not said."

"What do you mean, mind read?"

"Somewhat, it doesn't always happen and I can't force it, but for the most part, if I rub shoulders or am in very close proximity with someone, I can at least pick up a thought or two."

"But how is that possible? I never did believe in the ability of someone to read another person's mind. If you could, then thoughts would have to be made up of something; something that travels outside their heads!"

"They are and they do," I said. "Even though they are made up of electrical impulses, thoughts are material just like everything else. But being able to read them takes a lot of time and practice."

"Prove it!" she said, crossing her arms and raising an eyebrow as if she was about to catch me in a lie. "Don't forget, I, like Rocco, am from the 'Show Me' state."

I rose to my feet and looked around the room. "I'll be right back." I walked through one of the tight rows of slots, bumping a shoulder here and there, before taking my seat back next to Marian.

"Well," she said.

"That waitress coming towards us is going to ask everyone around us for drinks, but not us!"

The server took the drink orders of several people scattered around nearby, but did not ask us for anything.

"You've got to be kidding me, right?" she said, punching me on the arm. "We're not playing the slots… they never ask people who are loitering for drinks. Come on, Dewey. Show me your stuff!"

"OK, OK, I was just testing you. The man to our left, with the cap on, is about to stand up and go back to his room. He's got a bad headache and will walk over there and ask his wife, the woman with the bad hairdo, tightly clutching her sequined alligator purse, for some aspirin."

We watched as the man rose and just as I had said, walked over to his wife. Holding his head, he asked her for something. He then put what she gave him in his mouth and followed it with a swift gulp from his drink. He kissed her on the forehead, and pointed to the elevators, then walked off.

"You missed the kiss," she said.

"The kiss was an ad lib. He didn't think about it beforehand and like I said, sometimes I don't get everything."

"Wow, you really can do that? Show me some more. What else can you tell me?"

I pointed to a few more people. "The man with the gray hair, a cheater… and the woman next to him, a prostitute. One is dreaming of hitting the big one, and the other wants to make sure they keep enough quarters to do their laundry later. But the most interesting person of all is that young Asian woman over there playing that one slot machine."

It would have been more correct to state the young woman was being played by that slot machine, because she had not moved from her seat in over two hours. Her expressions, as well as a quick brush of her shoulder passing her in these Bandit alleys, revealed to me that she was sure the machine she was sitting at was going to pay off.

"Look, she's feeding in coins so fast she's dropping in one or two more than that spin allows," Marian said.

It was also interesting that she used the traditional handle on the right side. Even though most slot machines have gone to computerized components, some people, mostly right-handed people I would imagine, still believe that somehow it makes a difference.

She continued, almost without stopping, dropping coin after coin. She must have seen me watching her because the look she gave told me plenty.

"Anyway… she's about to tell me off!"

Before Marian could say anything, the woman turned to me and said, "What are you lookin' at?" She assumed that I was only interested in hitting on her and not in scientific observation.

"Don't get me wrong," I replied, "my interest lies in your obsession with playing this one machine, and not with how to lure you away, for God only knows, what perversion that might inhabit me."

She smiled at that, then scowled, unsure if she liked that I *wasn't* checking her out. I had forgotten a law that dictates, "If you pay too much attention to someone they will eventually ignore you, but if you ignore someone sufficiently enough they will be interested in you even more."

"My name is Dewey," I said, "Dewey Pinkerton, and this is Marian Lynn."

"Hi, my name is Nashida Sameeha," she said, without looking up.

"That's an interesting name. What does it mean?" Marian asked.

"It means, 'Student of Generosity'," she replied.

"Nashida Sameeha is a Muslim name. Are you a practicing Muslim?" I asked.

"I'm practicing to be a Muslim, yes. My birth name is 'Sang Lee'."

"Sang Lee, that's a pretty name too," Marian said. "What does that one mean?"

"It means… shit! Cause that's what I'm in now, deep shit. That was my last quarter" she replied. "I'm sorry. I don't mean to be rude. It really means, 'One who behaves like the upper classes,' which is certainly true…even if I am not one."

"Are you in some kind of trouble?" Marian asked.

"Yes, I am," she confessed. "I've gotten myself in quite a mess. I was fired from my job as a hotel accountant at Geezer's Palace for giving some of the winnings back to a customer."

"Why would you do that?"

"They were a middle-aged couple who had lost their nest egg," she continued. "I know better than to give back money, but this couple really needed it. They had a baby who needed a kidney operation and they were desperate because they didn't have the money or much time. They prayed about it and then took drastic measures."

"That sounds very honorable to me, Honey," Marian said, putting her hands on Sang Lee's shoulders to comfort her.

"Well, the irony is that I just made the same mistake they made and have pumped not only the last of my measly paycheck into this machine, but a severance check as well! I guess I was willing to take the chance that I could win enough to pay the money back to the casino and be free from the guilt. The funny thing is… I'm not even a gambler. I've lived here in Vegas for the last four years while getting an accounting degree at UNLV, and worked my way up from a staff accountant to an Assistant VP of finance.

"I don't know what I was thinking. I know what the odds are!"

"Can't you get another job, in a different casino?" Marian asked.

"Not in this town you can't. Once the word is out on the street that you gave money back, you're as good as dead! The only thing I could go back to in this town is…" She stopped, obviously not wanting to expose something.

"What, Darlin'?" Marian asked. "What did you used to do?"

"Dance," she said, embarrassed. "I used to be a stripper. It was the only way I could pay for my education. My parents certainly weren't going to help me. Over all, I was pretty good at it. I earned a Master's Degree in Finance in just three and a half years. In my graduate year, I met a Muslim who helped me rid myself of my past."

"What about your family? Do you have anyone who can help you?" Marian questioned.

"My Father was killed in the Vietnam War, and my Mother moved us to Las Vegas and married an Italian pit boss. They haven't helped me in the past and they won't help me now. Actually, they threw me out of the house when I was seventeen. That's when I started dancing."

"Well, we'll help you!" Marian said, turning to me. "Won't we, Dewey? We can help her… can't we?"

"She doesn't know anything about us," I said.

"Then tell her something. Tell her about the machine. Tell her that she can be on the road to freedom from all of this!"

"Look, Sang Lee. I'm traveling to help a friend in California with a few other people who have left their homes across the United States to travel with me.

"What do you do?" she asked.

"Well, I teach… kind of. I am trying to get the word out on a new teaching. Actually, it's a very old teaching about the science behind the mechanics of the universe. We're nothing formal at this point, just a group of individuals tired of everyday life who are trying to discover something new. You are welcome to travel with us if you want."

"But I hardly know you," she said, "what if I decide I don't like it?"

"You're free to do as ya wish, Darlin'," Marian replied. "If you don't like it, you just hop off the bus and catch another one going the other way."

"A bus?" she questioned.

"Well, yeah..." I said. "Most of us travel on our custom bus, but we have motorcycle riders with us too, as well as a diner that we pull."

"That's my baby," Marian chimed in, "I used to be a waitress and a cook. Then Dewey came through town and before I knew it, I asked him take me away from the hellhole I came from, diner and all."

"So, what are you now?" she asked.

"Why, I'm a chef... and a damn good one too!"

Sang Lee paused and thought for a moment. "I really do need to get out of this town."

"Then it's settled," Marian said. "Where do you live? We'll drop by your house and get some things a packin'."

"I live in an apartment, so there's not much to pack."

Just as we were about to walk away, I gave her a coin from my pocket and said that perhaps just for fun she should try it in the machine to the left of her.

She looked puzzled. "From what I know of how these work, and believe me, I've counted their rewards nightly. The odds are better on the machine I've been playing for the last few hours."

"What do you have to lose?" I asked.

She looked at the slot machine and raising her hand, dropped in the coin. "One coin is even worse odds, you know, since the pay lines are three across and three down and will pay on the center line only."

She pulled the handle and rose from the chair, gathering her belongings, convinced that this spin would be no different from the last several hundred. As she turned around to leave, she heard the third wheel lock into position. Then the bells went off. She swung around to find that she had hit the second largest payout the machine offered. The sound the machine generated is designed to arouse the interest of others and everyone around looked her way while a call was made to the cashier to come award the winnings.

"I don't deserve any of this," she said, looking dazed.

"Your heart is in the right place for having helped others in a time of need. That act alone has freed you somewhat. That's all that matters."

"Thank you, thank you so much. Now I can pay back the casino and leave town with my chin up."

It was at that moment I could tell this young girl's life was about to change for the better. Besides, I knew that the sevens were going to line up, and that a rich older woman with nothing to lose who had been wandering around for over an hour was about to stumble on to that very machine.

We gathered the others and headed back to the bus. Sang Lee offered us a nightcap at her apartment, which also had a large parking area in front allowing us to park the bus and diner for the rest of the night.

On our way out of town the next day, we came upon a limousine stuck at an intersection with smoke billowing out from under the hood. A bald midget stood atop a stepping stool waist deep into the engine from the passenger side. Even though this looked very odd, it would not normally be a problem. However, stuck as it was in the middle of traffic, it left him quite susceptible to the law of accident. About that time, another car in the lane next to him was barreling down the road, weaving from what was almost certainly a high night on the town.

Marian yelled, "Quick, we have to do something."

Jesus pulled the bus up behind the man's broken down car and Marian and I jumped out. Rocco got off his bike and tried to signal to the on-coming drunk driver of the impending danger, while I went to see what was wrong with the disabled car. I pulled the man out of the way just as the oncoming driver swerved by, beeping his horn and flipping us off.

We pushed the man's car to the side of the road, and then moved our vehicles there as well.

"Thanks, I guess. Although, if I had been killed it wouldn't have been any great loss."

"I'm Dewey, what's your name?"

"Lester Van Axel, but almost everyone calls me 'Shorty'!"

"What happened to your limo?" Rocco asked.

"I just dropped off a famous black basketball player and his lily-white escort at one of the local hotels. I can't tell you which celebrity it was 'cause us drivers are sworn to secrecy. Anyway that's when the engine started to sputter, and smoke started coming out from under the hood."

I called everyone together and asked them to gather around the engine. "I would like to know if anyone here besides Rusty, who of course is a mechanic, can help to determine what is wrong with this man's car. Let's start by determining the symptoms.

"The engine started to sputter, and smoke started coming out from under the hood…." I prompted Jesus, who had worked with Johann on cars for many years.

"A demon," he said, smirking. "Naw, just kiddin'. It could be a radiator leak or an oil leak."

"What about you, Marian?"

"Uh, a fire?" she said, softly.

"Do you see a fire, Marian?" Rocco asked.

"No, but I do smell gas."

Rusty scanned the engine and gave Marian a big smile. "It's fuel leaking on to the hot block," he said.

"Good job, Marian. If we hadn't come along when we did it most certainly could have become a fire."

"It *is* going to become a fire," Rusty yelled, "Everybody get back!" We all ran back about twenty feet as car bust into flames.

"That's it," shouted Shorty. "I've had it with this crap. I've been here in this piece of shit town now for four years. I've done the circus act thing, I've worked the concessions, and now I've been a limousine driver for just under a year and they keep giving me all the crap cars. I've had it up to, well… here!" he said, raising his hand to a spot about a foot above his head.

"I am out of here. I'm goin' to California!" He threw up his arms and started walking down the sidewalk.

"We're headed to California, if you want a ride," I yelled. He stopped and turned around. "What'll it cost me?"

"Nothing, we have plenty of room."

"I'll need to pick up a few things from my pad, is that O.K.?"

"Of course, come on." He climbed in the bus with the rest of us and took a seat near the front. Jesus asked Shorty where he lived and signaled Rocco in that direction.

"I'm not used to people being so nice, so excuse me if I don't trust you!" he said.

"Don't you trust anyone?" Sang Lee asked.

"It's a long story. I'm not sure you'll want to hear it."

"So give us the 'short' version," Bruno said, with a shining gold tooth smirk. He pulled his camera up and asked Simon to hold the microphone closer to him. "Could you stand up, I can't see you through the lens." The bus grew quiet. "Oh, I see… you are standing."

"That's not funny, Bruno," Marian said. "Don't mind him, Honey, he's just along for the ride. Of course, we want to hear it. Why *don't* you trust people?"

"You want to hear how hard the life of a midget is? It's friggin' hard! I've been kicked around a lot in my life."

"Let's start with where you're from," Marian continued.

"Well, I was born in Grand Rapids, Michigan, along the Dutch Black River."

"I'm from Michigan, I know that area well. What hospital were you born at?" I asked.

"I was literally born along the banks of the river! When the doctors told my mother she was going to have a midget, she was too embarrassed to go to a hospital. She put me in a hat box and pushed me out in the water and told everyone I was stillborn."

"That's awful," Marian said, "What happened after that?"

"I was found by Dutch farmers downstream and taken in. You'd think my luck would have changed after that, but things only got worse. They were a very religious sect of Dunkards who believed that I was sent from God to do all their shit-work."

"You mean they made you straighten up after everyone?" Sang Lee asked.

"No, they made me clean up their shit! They turned me into a houseboy and everyday I had to clean out the horse stalls and the outhouses for everyone in the commune. They even made me bathe with a hose because I was deemed too dirty in the eyes of the lord to enter the house and like all the other animals slept in a barn. When I was sixteen, I finally left for good. Ever since then I've tried to hold a job in every city I've been in, and even this one has not let me forget that I'm a midget."

"You *are* a midget!" Bruno teased to muster up a good reaction.

"See what I mean!" Shorty replied, glaring at Bruno while shooting him the finger.

"We'll have to blur that out," Simon said.

"What's the camera for?" Shorty asked.

"I've allowed Simon over here and Bruno over there to tape us as we travel. I'm beginning to think that may not have been such a good idea. Try not to let them bother you, were going all the way to the beaches of Santa Monica next. You're welcome along for the ride."

"I don't know how to swim, and I have a good fear of the water, for obvious reasons. But thanks, I really appreciate that."

"You've held a lot of interesting jobs," Marian said, "What is it you would really like to do?"

"If I told you, you would laugh," he replied.

"No we wouldn't, would we?" Marian glared at everyone.

"Well… I have this dream of starting a clothing line for midgets."

Everyone but Marian laughed.

"Wait a minute," Simon said, "I bet you would clean up with that idea. While I can name at least ten fashion designers, I can't name one who designs for the little people."

"Stop the bus!" Sang Lee yelled.

"Here, now?" Jesus questioned.

"Please, I have to do something."

Suddenly it dawned on me. "That's right, you wanted to pay the hotel back before we left town."

"No," she said, "something better than that." Jesus pulled the bus over to the curb and Sang Lee stepped off. She walked about a half a block then turned into a gentlemen's club. She emerged minutes later with a group of young women who followed her out of the front door. They gave her hugs and appeared to be wishing her well. A few minutes later, she entered the bus with a huge smile on her face.

"There, now all is right in the world," she said.

"Saying goodbye to some friends?" Marian asked.

"That and empowering them with the chance to change their lives."

"How's that?" Jesus asked.

"I gave them the money! Now, like me, they can be free and leave this town with their heads held high."

"Wow, that's an amazing act of selflessness," Marian said.

"That's just plain stupid," Bruno, replied. "I would have kept the money."

"'Nashida'," Marian remembered. "'Generous student'! You're Muslim name fits you perfectly."

CHAPTER XX

A Better Route Canal

The final leg of our journey west would land us at the Santa Monica Pier at noon. Buzz, who had never sat still in any vehicle this long, was becoming quite antsy.

"Are we there yet? As much as I like you people, I can't take it in here anymore. I need to get back on a bike!"

"Maybe we ought to get you a car this time," Rusty said.

"A car's not my idea of fun."

"What kind of motorcycle do you want to get?" Sang Lee asked.

"Another Asian toy of course, like a Ninja or an Interceptor."

Bruno smiled and pointed the camera at Sang Lee. "There ain't nothin' like an Asian toy… especially one who can dance!"

"Yeah, why's that Bruno?" she replied. "What do you have against Asian dancers?"

"Nothin', that's the point, I've met a few in my day."

"Asians or dancers?"

"Both."

"Bruno, why do you always have to turn everything into something disgusting?" asked Marian.

"There's nothing disgusting about a stripper who can shake it, Marian. The problem is Asians don't have much to shake! Cute as they are, they're missing the booty."

"You'll have to forgive him," Simon interrupted, "Bruno had a tough life growing up in Harlem. His father split when he was born and his mother worked eighteen-hour days at the Apollo Theater to keep them alive. He couldn't have been any older than six when he became a street-scamming bookie runner."

"And let's not forget hubcap thief," Bruno added proudly, "I once stole the caps off of Donald Trump's limo!"

"What a surprise," said Sang Lee.

"Bookies and strippers were his only friends." Simon continued. "If it weren't for the acts he saw at the Apollo that led him to wanting to become an agent, God only knows what he would be doing now."

"He'd probably be in jail, I'm sure," Marian replied.

"Our pasts are what they are," I said. "No one here is without regret! What's important to realize is that 'we cannot change yesterday until we change tomorrow'."

"What's that from?" asked Jesus.

"It's from the Mode, chapter seven, verse thirteen!"

"What does it mean?"

"I will say it a different way. 'If we do nothing different today, then tomorrow will be no different.' In other words, big changes happen slowly. We must learn how to make small changes every day, and some of those changes need to be how we perceive others. Our minds are full of false beliefs about things, beliefs we did not come to on our own, but have instead acquired by rote from the mindless opinions of others."

Shorty stood up, "You don't have to tell me about how people perceive. I rarely get the chance to show anyone who I really am. When they look at me… all they see is a midget!"

"The Mode has something to teach everyone, Shorty. Be patient, even your time may come."

Sang Lee reached over and put her hand on his shoulder. "Yeah, Shorty, Dewey has already showed me a lot. He helped me overcome what I thought to be a hopeless situation and leave Las Vegas proud of who I am… and I, like you, have only known him for less than two days."

"I don't know," Shorty said, rubbing his baldhead. "I don't think the Mode has anything to help me."

"Look around this bus," Marian interjected, "What a bizarre bunch we are. Do y'all think a mere accident has drawn us together? Something's going to come out of this, I just know it."

"I will have to admit," I said, "that perhaps we have been drawn together for a higher reason."

"That's what I mean, Dewey, it's magical," Marian replied.

"Do you have any magic that can get us to Santa Monica any quicker Dewey?" Buzz asked, "I gotta pee!"

We pulled off at the next off ramp and Buzz took care of his bodily functions. After that, we made good time through the

Southern California desert and after navigating the necessary freeway inter-connectors, we arrived in Los Angeles.

The sun's rays were above us now as we exited the 405 freeway onto the 10 freeway, putting us right on course to dead-end into the pier. We crested a small hill before crossing the Coast Highway and directly above us, seagulls sang their squawking praises for the food left behind by careless tourists.

This was it, the Santa Monica Pier. Several thousand miles and nine people later, we had traveled Route 66 from Chicago, Illinois, to the beaches of Southern California. Jesus pulled the bus up to the nearest head-to-head-to-head-to-head spot with the diner in tow, and as usual, Rocco parked in the handicap zone. We exited the bus and stretched our legs a bit before venturing on to explore the surroundings.

Jesus stopped for a second, a bit confused. "We're taking up eight parking spaces against this curb, which means we will have to pay eight parking meters!" He stepped up to one and examined the fine print. "Twenty-five cents for fifteen minutes? You gotta be kiddin' me..."

"That's eight dollars an hour," Sang Lee said.

"Welcome to California," Simon added.

"What's the big fuss about this place anyway?" Shorty asked, stepping off the bus into a pile of bird excrement. "I've only been here for a couple of minutes and I'm already in shit!"

"For starters," I said, "beaches that face west have the best ingredients for riding the curl of a moon pulled wave,"

"For what?" Shorty asked, wiping his shoe off on the curb.

"For surfing... and secondly, the colder northern winds and the southern hotter winds completely miss this area most of the time. As a result, it is usually neither too warm nor too cool but maintains almost a constant sixty-five to seventy-five degrees all year round."

Rocco pulled his riding gloves off and joined us at the front of the bus. "Boy, I've never seen so many weirdoes all in one place."

"Don't judge so soon, Rocco," Jesus said. "We may be the ones who look out of place!"

Los Angeles is a huge melting pot of culture where quite a variety of people have learned to co-exist. This diversity is magnified in a place slightly to the left of the Santa Monica pier, known as "Venice Beach." Venice gets its name from the Italian city, and although it only has a couple of small water canals giving its name modest credibility, it is interesting nonetheless.

A quick observation of the surroundings revealed several types of people who hang out there. One type was the recreational sports enthusiasts: the skaters, the bike riders, volleyball players and the skateboard riders. Then there were the regulars: the street poets, the muscle builders, the gainfully unemployed, the panhandlers, and the concession vendors. Add a few thousand beach going tourists and "Voilá," Venice Beach.

There is also one other type of sea faring sports enthusiast who would not want to be clumped together with the others due to their truly exceptional love of the most sacred fluid on earth, water. In winter or summer, spring or autumn, they come here almost every day to pay homage to that equally sacred result of the wind and the moon, waves. Surfers do not consider themselves tourists nor do they think themselves locals, but believe they are as much a part of the ocean as the sand, sun, and wind.

We wandered for a while on the boardwalk, overwhelmed with amusements. Mimes and painters entertained us, as children discovered that a dropped frozen banana with sand all over it tasted just as good as the one their parents just handed them… only crunchier.

Rocco and Buzz found a biker bar to hang at, while Marian and Sang Lee shopped for bathing suits. The rest of us shed our excess clothes and headed down to the sand. I wanted to spend some time watching more closely these graceful surfers, dancing in the waves. After a while of observing them, the sun and light breeze on my body, along with the sound of crashing waves, lulled me to sleep.

When I awoke an hour later, Marian and Sang Lee were lying on beach towels next to me browning their skin, and exposing more of it than I had previously seen. The two appeared asleep, so I made no noise to awaken them, but instead, continued my original intention of observation.

I concluded that surfers fall into several distinct visual groups: the longhaired long-boarders and the shorthaired short-boarders. Furthermore, into ones who know what they're doing, and ones that wish they knew what they were doing, called "newbies or wannabees." They almost all had one other noticeable characteristic, that is, not a one of them was fat. Perhaps they may have been at one time, but not now. The physical dynamics necessary to ride waves, day in and day out had chiseled away any unnecessary excess.

Bruno found his way over to us and continued shooting the action around him while Simon interviewed the locals and tourists. Soon there was a group of curious onlookers gathered around us. Simon struck up a conversation with a couple of guys who were waxing their surfboards.

"Hi, I'm Simon, and we're taping a new type of show, called, 'Reality Television,' it's kind of like an ad-lib 'talkumentary.' Do you mind if we ask you a couple of questions?"

"Who are you again, Dude?" the surfer replied, winking at his friends. "Oh, right, a schlokumentary. Sure, go ahead, ask."

"Tell me, what does surfing mean to you?"

"Surfing, huh? Well, I surf to find that elusive state of mind, that connection, that oneness with the wave. It's even harder to do in crowded situations, or on a lousy wave day. It's a feeling you get when everything is going just right. The wave is perfect and you take off from just the right spot, and for a few minutes, you know you are exactly where you should be in the wave and in the world. It's a little piece of heaven, Man."

"That's just great," Simon said. "How long have you been surfing?"

The smiling group of red-eyed punks laughed. "For about two hours, Dude. We just rented these boards and are tryin' it out for the first time." They walked away shaking their heads.

"We'll be editing that out," Simon said, giving Bruno the "cut" sign.

"No we won't. That was priceless," laughed Bruno.

"I know," Simon continued, trying to dust off his ego, "I'll speak to them in their language, you know, their 'lingo'. Then they'll realize I'm for real!"

Bruno, who was still coming down off a good chuckle whispered under his breath, "No stop, don't," and followed Simon like a true director to his next victim.

Simon walked straight up to another surfer. "Dude, next time you're on your stick, hittin' the rip, could ya do a switch stance on the nose, and give me some old school and a slash off the curl for the eye in the sky, man?"

"Sure, mate," the surfer, replied, "That's good oil. I'll get a sweat pozzy on the wave, you squizz, and I'll shows ya some bush oyster and a cactus cane toad's donger, and you can film the little nipper doin an Aussie salute, you drongo seppo!"

"Yeah, man! That'll be great just great," Simon said, waving to him as he picked up his board and ran towards the water. He looked at Bruno, who was now laughing uncontrollably. "What are you laughing at? What'd he say?"

"I don't understand Australian slang, but by the way it sounded, it can't be good."

"Great, that's just great!" Simon complained.

In the meantime, I had been watching a guy next to us who seemed to be unaffected by the rest of the surfers, or by the commotion that was brewing all around him. While Simon and Bruno continued their interviews, I walked over to talk with him.

"Hi, how are you doing? My name's Dewey."

"Dude, you must hate your parents," he replied.

"What do you mean?"

"A name like Dewey must have gotten you beat up quite a bit. My name's Trace."

"Nice to meet you, Trace. Yeah, my name did have its drawbacks," I chuckled. "But I don't hate my parents. They're, you know… parents! You don't seem affected by the tourists or the wannabees or any of the rest of the circus around here."

"Naw, I usually wait until all the amateurs have sufficiently hurt themselves and have retreated back to the beach before I go in."

"Wow, you have great patience."

"I'm in no hurry. I've been surfing since before I could walk. My dad used to take me with him on his long board.

"Your father was a surfer?"

"Both of my parents were surfers, true surfers, some of the lucky ones who were able to do it for a living. They met each other on the beaches of Malibu in the early sixties, about the same time the Beach Boys and Jan and Dean were surfing there. I grew up with all of them, touring the world, following that endless summer from South Africa's Gonubie Reef, Nahoon Corner, Tombstones, Queensberry Bay. Then over to Australia's Phillip Island to Woolamai, and to Bali's, Kuta, Canggu, Balian and Madewi. Those places were my homes growing up. Those oceans have taught me almost everything I know."

"How did you end up here?" I asked.

"A few years back my parents were killed in an accident by a drunk driver while coming home one night. They were gentle, earth-loving people, who would never hurt anything. Anyway, they left me a beach house here in Venice. When they died, I just stopped traveling. I had lost my sense of adventure.

"I feel like I'm missing something though, like there's something I need to do that I still haven't done. You know… I don't feel whole. My folks loved the water more than anyone else I have ever known. They wouldn't have wanted to see me this way. The waves are my parents now.

"What's with you and the others?" he continued. "You don't look like you're from around here."

"We're not," I replied. "Though I did spend some time in the Valley a few years back, my roots are in Detroit, Michigan, and the rest of us are from all across America."

Trace shook his head. "Inlanders huh? What a bummer, dude. I've never known what it's like to not live by the ocean."

"I've traveled a bit too, not around the world as you have, mostly around the U.S., Western Canada, and a tiny bit of Mexico.

"Why those places?" he asked.

"I'm searching for the meaning of life!"

"Have you found it yet?"

"Somewhat. I have learned a thing or two about how things in the universe work."

"Part of the meaning of life is in Mexico? Damn, I've never surfed any of their beaches."

"It wasn't in the places I went, Trace. It was in the people I met, people who still possess ancient knowledge."

"The meaning of life for me is not in people, it's in the perfect wave," he said.

"Have you found it yet?" I asked.

He looked out at the water and stared silently for a moment.

"I've been close. I've come so close. I know it exists, and one day I'll ride it."

He continued. "Out there it's just you and the elements, man. No two waves are exactly the same. It's about you and the balance of the board against the will of the wave. A good ride isn't forced; it's not a fight of you against it. It's more like deliverance, or a cradling. The wave says, 'Stand on my shoulders and I will guide you through the best I have to offer,' and with that you venture through the curl in exactly the best spot. The sea warns you, 'I am powerful and could crush you with one blow.' Nevertheless, you say to it, 'yes, but I am able to feel your pulse and travel your breadth and live to tell of you.' With the wind against the water and the water against my board and my board against my feet, I am connected with the wave in the eternal moment."

"You mean a feeling of continuity, the feeling that there are no jumps in nature, how one thing flows seamlessly into the next and that everything in the universe is connected?" I asked.

"Yeah," he said. "You understand a lot about the sea for a dude raised in Detroit."

"Natural laws are everywhere," I said, "even in Detroit!"

I suddenly became aware that Bruno and Simon were filming. Bruno smiled and gave us a “thumbs up.”

Trace chuckled at Bruno’s signal. “Dude, you know, when I was down in Madewi, Bali, many years ago, I learned that in ancient times there the ‘thumbs up’ was a sign of sexual masculinity. The morning after the wedding of a young couple, the groom would come out of his hut and signal to the rest of the tribe his masculine prowess. If the sign was a ‘thumbs up’ everyone celebrated, but if a ‘thumbs down’ was shown, the father of the groom would be called in to finish the job.”

Simon looked at him a bit surprised. “You’re kidding me, right, the father?”

Trace laughed. “I’m only kidding about the last part. In reality, all the males in the tribe were called in to finish the job.”

“That’s just sick,” Marian said, joining us.

“Trace, I would like you to meet Marian.”

“Pleasure, Darlin’,” she replied, shaking his hand.

“So why are you guys here again?” Trace asked.

“I’m here to help a friend sell a business, and when I’m finished, I’m planning on gathering a group of people together to help me spread the word on a relatively unknown teaching.”

“What kind of teaching?”

“A teaching based on the mechanics of the universe, called the Mode. It’s founded on the principles that our day to day existence is mostly mechanical, in that, our minds are asleep and can only react to life in predetermined meaningless ways.”

“Dude, sounds interesting,” Trace said. “I learned a lot about religion while surfing in the South Pacific. Do you know anything about Buddhism?”

“I remember a story one of my teachers told me that speaks of the true essence of Buddha. There was a monk, who after attaining enlightenment, was asked by his students,

"Are you a God?"
"No," he replied.
"Are you a Saint?"
"No."
"Then what are you?"
"I am awake," he answered.

"Wow, that's powerful. I would love to spend more time talking to you," Trace replied, "Where are you guys staying while you're in town?"

"I have business to attend to in the Valley in a few days. At that time I will be leaving the rest of the group to fend for themselves until my obligations are fulfilled."

"Then you have to come over tonight for a barbeque, and your friends are welcome to stay at my place if they want while you're gone," he said. "It's a huge house and it's only me."

"Thanks, Trace, that would be great. Come on, I'll introduce you to the others."

Just then, we heard screams coming from the water just to the left of the pier. We ran to the water's edge and tried to make out what all the commotion was about. Rusty and Jesus came running towards us from atop the pier.

"Dewey, it's Shorty, he was stepping back to take a picture and he fell off!"

"He can't swim," I yelled back to them, but before I was finished, Trace had jumped into the waves in search of him.

A large crowd had begun to gather, when several minutes later, Trace dragged Shorty to the beach and began resuscitation. The crowd cheered as Shorty came to, and with the exception of being rather embarrassed, he seemed to be all right.

That night we all gathered at Trace's house. We ate great food and drank beer and wine, and the sound of the Pacific Ocean crashing against the shore, and smell of sea salt and of wood burning was particularly vivid. We talked about the Mode and about Buddhism and many other religions that share the common idea of the necessity of 'waking up'.

After dinner, we rested back on the sand, looking up at the stars. "They're spinning again," Rusty said, with his lips perched on his beer and his shoes almost in the fire.

"You're drunk, Rusty," Buzz teased, stumbling near the hot coals himself.

Shorty adjusted the sand behind his shoulders and laid his head back, looking up. "For having such a rough day, I'm feeling pretty good too. One thing's for sure… when I look up at the stars, we all look small."

Marian glanced at me, and then stared up into space.

"They look like ants," she said.

"What does?" Sang Lee asked.

"The stars, there's so many of them. They remind me of ants."

"It's funny you should say that," Rocco added. "In Nam we called ants, 'antchovies,' because when you've been sitting still behind a tree in the jungle for days waiting for an ambush, they were all you could find to eat."

"Gross." Sang Lee said.

"What? That's nothing compared to some of the bugs we ate," Rocco replied. "You'd think the more colorful ones would taste better, but no…"

"Tell us another story, Dewey," Marian interrupted, resting her head on my shoulder. I decided to tell them a story about persistence.

"The moral of this story is two-fold," I said. "On the one hand, it is a story about looking at an old problem in a new way, about trying what was previously thought to be impossible and perhaps coming to a happy compromise somewhere in between. On the other hand, it is a very useful story to those who own a home. It goes like this:"

Ants & Uncools

"Once a man was psychologically beaten down so low, it was thought he would never recover. He was so demoralized that surely something huge, something on a grand scale, must have happened to him in order for him to lose all belief in the world and in himself. The cause of his despair was not the loss of a loved one, or from being fired from his job, or even news that he had been diagnosed with a hideous disease, but that of a very small and very persistent creature, the ant. 'Ant, you say, are you kidding me?' Nevertheless, the truth of the matter is that ants are more persistent and more powerful than you think, especially if you've ever tried to be rid of them.

"Several times a year the ants would travel from their nest underneath the houses and woodpiles and venture to the grand land of cornucopia know as "the human dwelling spots," and one by one would search throughout the walls and surfaces of this dwelling for that which is known to them as the "Golden Nectar", namely, sugar! It is in almost everything we eat and once introduced into our foods finds its way to every nook and cranny of the house. Ants do not care about the path they take as long as it can be traced back to the colony, even if that route is neither the fastest nor the most hidden.

"This man, however, was bound by his religion not to kill anything, even as small and insignificant as an ant. He was a strict vegetarian and gave generously to many worldwide animal rights organizations. However, this did not help his dilemma. The ants were running the house and were on every inch, of every piece, in every room, of everything, he owned.

"One day when the man had reached his wits end, he sat in the middle of the room and meditated on his problem. He did not eat or sleep for days and on the seventh day, while quite weak and tired, a vision came to him.

"He would capture one of the ants and explain to it his plight. He would show the ant what was happening to his life and ask for compassion for his circumstance. In return for his release without harm, the ant would have to negotiate with the colony. In exchange for leaving his dwelling completely the man would agree to have ready for them a food of their liking in a place in the yard where they could always go and know they would never go hungry. The man rose and carefully observed the ants, looking to find one that he thought would be most receptive to his plan.

"After watching the ants for many hours, he selected one and began his plan straight away. After several days, the ant had seen that this man *was* suffering and indeed compassionate. He had already heard on many occasions stories from relatives who lived in other colonies in neighboring houses how their numbers had continued to dwindle while his tribe flourished uninterrupted, for more generations than anyone could count; except of course, for occasional rain sacrifices. This ant became a believer that a man who preserved lives even at the level of an insect deserved consideration, and returned to his colony in not only perfect health, but also beaming with his newfound understanding.

"With his arrival home, the colony threw a party in his honor since the other ants thought for sure he was taken by the rain Gods or some other unforeseen accident. The ant council gathered and asked him where he had been. He replied that the man who lived in the food cornucopia had taken him hostage, and explained to him that he had not so much as accidentally stepped on any of his friends or relatives and furthermore went to great lengths to secure their existence even at the complete loss of his own quality of life. The elders listened with amazement at his story and when he was done, they all agreed to vote on the matter.

"'How do we know we can trust him,' one elder said. 'He is after all, a human.'

"The Queen entered the room and everyone dropped to their knees, which is a lot of knees when you think about it. 'Rise, rise everyone,' she shouted, and with that everyone stood again. 'The fact that our colony's numbers are so great, that we have lived to see our great-grandparents and their great-grandparents times ten, shows me this man is telling the truth. We shall reciprocate the generosity that this being is showing us and not only will we leave his dwelling alone, but shall not require him to hold his end of the bargain and forcefully bring us food to a specific location. Go now, and tell him of our sorrow over his dilemma and of our appreciation of his good gesture.'

"The ant returned to the man and told him what the Queen had said. The man replied, 'Give your Queen my thanks. She is indeed honorable and kind, but the gesture of giving you food not only serves your fine colony but mine as well; come I will show you'.

"The ant rode on the man's hand into the garden. There the men had planted orchards of apples and peaches and oranges and pears, more than the man could ever consume himself or give to his neighbors. 'There is far more here than my people and your colony combined could ever consume,' the man said.

'Now go back to your Queen and tell her of the new cornucopia in the garden and tell her to pass the knowledge of this place on to other colonies in the area as well.' With this act, the man not only saved himself but his neighbors from almost certain insane asylum candidacy.

"You see, ants will never leave you alone unless you are able to strike a bargain with them, which is often a most difficult thing to do."

Marian and a few of the others smiled, while the rest quietly stared at the stars and fire.

Finally, Rocco spoke up. "I would have just squashed the little buggers."

CHAPTER XXI

Tell Tale Tasks

The next morning, I gathered everyone together in Trace's well-shaded back yard to discuss the plan for the coming days. I did indeed have a plan and hoped that it would work out the way I wanted it to.

"I'm going to be gone for the next week taking care of my late friend's airplane business. Since none of you have made any other concrete plans for the future, I'd like to ask you all a favor. I'd like everyone to hang out here at Trace's for the week, and to do something for me while I'm gone."

"Like what?" asked Rocco, cutting to the chase.

"Well, you've all heard me talk about the Mode, and some of you have even seen it in action." Bruno twitched almost imperceptibly. "It was taught to me by some very extraordinary men, and I believe that it can be taught to others. That's exactly what I'm planning to do as soon as I get back. The Mode works for me and I can teach other people how to make it work for them too. In fact, I want you to each do some tasks that will teach you something about the Mode while I am gone."

"Us?" asked a surprised Shorty.

"Yes, you… each one of you, and there's two reasons why I want to do this. First, because the Mode can help each one of you discover something new and wonderful about yourselves and about each other. And second, I'm hoping it will convince you all to come back to Detroit with me and help me teach the Mode."

There was a moment of silence as each one of them took in this last surprise.

"Back to Detroit?" said Bruno, astounded.

"I barely know about the Mode," Buzz said.

"Forget the Mode," Shorty shot back. "I don't know anything about teaching." Trace nodded in agreement.

"I don't need teachers. I can do all the teaching, if it comes to that, but I do need your individual skills to make this happen. You're a unique group of people with an amazing array of talents and backgrounds. You're exactly the kind of people I want to help me do this. It's an invitation to an adventure! Do these tasks to prove to yourselves that the Mode works, and that I can teach it. Then follow me to Detroit and I'll teach you and the world the Mode."

"What kind of tasks?" Trace asked.

"One task will help you begin to see the Mode in your life. The other will help you learn mechanics, which is the metaphor of the Mode. Together, these tasks will help you solve old problems, and open your eyes to new possibilities. I would like you to do them in pairs, like the buddy system. Each person's tasks will be different. They're based on your unique type and situation and are not interchangeable with one another. Some of you will have tasks that only you and I will know about. You won't be able to tell anyone else what it is."

"I don't know. It sounds like work, if you ask me," Shorty said.

"Well, Shorty, you will have to work. But how hard would you be willing to work to get rid of your fear of the ocean?"

"You think you can teach me that?" Shorty asked. "Can you lay hands on me or something? That would be great."

"No, it doesn't work like that, and even if I could, it would teach you nothing," I replied. "These tasks are designed to produce a result equal to the effort, and this effort must come from each of you."

"You're sayin' through working on some kinda task, I'm gonna learn to lose my fear of water?"

"And if learning that cost you some work on the bus…?"

"I suppose it wouldn't be too much to ask."

"What if we don't like it after a few days, then what?" Buzz asked.

"You are always free to go at any time. This is not about doing something for the sake of nothing. It's about learning how to be free from the universal machine, and what that means to each of you will be different."

Sang Lee raised her hand. "What kind of mechanical tasks do you want us to do? I'm not very good with tools. I have awrenchnaphobia!"

"Your mechanical tasks will be suited to your experience. So Sang Lee, you won't be taking apart engines." She smiled as Rocco and Buzz laughed. "I'm going to have everyone do some work on the bus and trailer to get you used to working together. Since we know they're soon bound for the trip back to Detroit, I think this would be the prefect time to take care of any repairs or maintenance, as well as upgrade the accommodations. I know that Shorty would benefit from getting the bus stairs modified, to make it easier for him to get on and off, and Jesus and I have some specific maintenance items that need to be taken care of."

There was a quiet murmur in the room and soon many of them began offering enthusiastic suggestions for things to improve, including the way the bus and trailer looked. They planned to redo the seats and add some wood to the cabin. Maybe even redo the paint and lower the body, give it some new rims and perhaps a pin stripe or two. Jesus called it "pimping our ride". I stopped them after they had run on a bit.

"So people, what do you want to do? While I'm gone, will you try to learn the Mode through the tasks I give you?"

Marian was the first to respond. "I didn't feel like my life was going anywhere back in Missouri and now I feel like I'm a part of something special. I think it's at least worth a try." One by one, they all agreed.

I gave each of them their tasks, one for their life and one for the bus, reminding them for their mechanical tasks that they must not only use the proper tools, but must read the manuals and that the work must be done as a way to practice the teaching.

"I want everyone to think about their tasks and work on them every day. Use what you've learned from me and what you learn from each other, but also add something to it from yourself. When I return we'll talk about how they turned out."

The next morning, Rocco gave me a ride to meet Winger's wife, Anna, at her home in the valley, where I would stay through the week. I had never ridden on the back of a

Harley before and the ride through traffic in Los Angeles' west side was both frightening and invigorating.

It had been a few years since I had seen Anna and she looked tired and frail. After hugs and the exchange of subjective opinions, we settled down to a warm cup of tea on the back patio. Anna was a master at gardening and if she hadn't had such a passion for nurturing life, I think she might have lost it after Winger's death.

"I do miss him," she said, bringing a warm cup of ginseng tea to her lips.

"I know you do. I can't imagine what you have been going through," I replied.

"Things have just gotten so difficult trying to run the business. You're the only one I trust to help me get out of it."

I reached out and held her hand. "Don't worry about it. I'll take care of everything."

"I kept it open just because it seemed like he was still close to me. But I don't have any passion for it," she continued, mostly to herself. "Winger left me with enough to get by quite well. I don't need the headache of having to run a business. I hope he wouldn't mind."

"Of course it's the right thing to do. Let's not worry about it any more tonight. I will go straight to the airport in the morning and start gathering the information we will need to sell it. Now relax for a while and tell me about your garden."

She looked a lot more relieved now that I was there and began to show her ageless Asian beauty once again as she talked about her flowers; how the roses had grown since I last saw them, how the rosemary and thyme and other herbs smelled when the suns rays first hit them in the morning. "*She'll be all right,*" I thought to myself. "*It's good that I came, I'm supposed to be here. I can feel it.*"

We walked for a bit in her garden and as we did, we talked about my journeys over the last few years. I told her a little about the people who had joined me along my way and explained the tasks I had given them during my week away.

"I can see that you are starting to observe this group you've collected in terms of their strong, but different types," she said. "Winger would be very proud to know that you've listened to him. Keep their individual traits in mind as you try to help them. That knowledge will be a strong lever for you."

I spent the next few days going back and forth between the airport and the attorney's offices and all the while, I wondered how the group was doing. I had never been away from them before, and like a father, I wondered how the kids were getting on. Little did I know, they would do just fine. I just had to trust in what I had taught them in order to let go of the fear I had about whether or not they could handle the tasks asked of them. Ultimately they had learned enough.

The Tasks

Rocco and Marian

Rocco maneuvered the bus into a couple of spaces on the outskirts of the parking lot. It would be the last trip the bus would make for a while. Once he'd stocked up on kitchen supplies for the week, the bus would be placed up on blocks and begin its transformation. Rocco and Marian exited the big yellow beast and walked towards the door of the grocery store.

"I don't know what I'm supposed to get out of cooking dinners for everyone," Rocco grunted. "I don't have any interest in cooking. I should be working on the bikes with Rusty, or something."

"He gave us each things that he knew would help us see ourselves in some way. He's turning out to be a very smart fella. I want to learn all I can from him."

"What kind of task did you get?"

"I have to tell one story every night by the fire."

"What is that supposed to do?"

"I don't know, but just like you cooking dinner, it's scaring me a little bit."

As they neared the door, they saw a young man standing by a line of shopping carts, talking on a cell phone. He wore a hooded sweatshirt, with the hood up, and glanced at them briefly as they took a cart and entered the store.

"That guy was weird," Marian said, after they were inside.

"What do you mean?"

"There is something up with him. He's trouble."

"Is this your famous 'women's intuition' talking?" Rocco asked, as they started down the aisles. "What kind of *trouble* do you think he is?"

"I don't know. He was acting funny. And yes, it is intuition, but Dewey's taught me to pay attention to that feeling. I'm telling you, Rocco, that guy was trouble. He was going to rob someone, or do a drug deal," She shrugged. "Something bad is going to happen. I just get these feelings."

"Well, that just sounds like he looked at you, and you didn't like it. I'll bet he's checking out every woman that comes in the store."

They entered the aisle with chips and salsa, and Rocco began loading up in great quantities.

"What do you think you're doing?"

"Buying food! Chips, salsa, beer, some salami maybe."

"That's not food! That's junk. I knew it was a good thing for me to come," she said, putting back half of the stuff. "Listen Rocco, I've done nothing but feed people for most of my life, so trust me when I tell you that just a little bit of effort can go a long way. People love being served something good to eat. It's a chance to do something nice for folks, especially when they're not expecting it. What else did you have in mind for the rest of the week?"

"I dunno… dip?"

Marian smirked. "Rocco, when I tell you I'm making supper, does the picture of chips and dip come into your head?"

"No. You make great dinners. But you know how to cook!"

"And so do you, even if you don't think you do. Now think, what *do* you actually know how to cook?"

"Well, I can grill a steak, and make burgers and hot dogs."

"That just proves you're a man. What else? Lots of people first learned to cook as children. Did you ever cook as a kid?"

"Well, yeah. I went through a phase when I was about seven or eight where I used to help my Mom cook the spaghetti dinner she used to make every Saturday night. And I don't know how to make dough, but once I've got some, I can beat that sucker into a pretty decent pizza."

"Dough we'll buy in a package, and as long as you read the instructions and don't hit it with anything dirty, we should be OK. So it looks like we're havin' steaks, burgers & dogs, spaghetti and pizza. We'll need the fixins for all of that too; buns tomatoes, onions and such, and let's buy some basic salad mixes to go with the sodas, beer, chips and dip you've already loaded the cart up with. What else sounds good?"

"Potato salad, but I don't know how to make it. I've always liked the pre-made kind in the stores better anyway."

She laughed. "OK, I don't think anyone will mind, as long as everything else comes out all right."

While wandering the aisles, Rocco tried to remember the details of what makes a good burger, or his Mom's special sauce, as Marian goaded his memory in helping him choose.

They went through the checkout line and piled their bags back into a cart. Just as they passed through the automatic doors, they heard a woman yelling, "Hey, what are you doing? Stop! Help! Stop that man!"

They turned and saw a woman standing by the cart area with a look of shock on her face and a man running toward the street with a purse clutched in his hand by a broken strap.

Rocco's military training kicked in and grabbing a can of bean dip that was sitting on top of the nearest grocery bag, he ran after him. As the man turned his head to see who was chasing him, Rocco recognized him as the guy Marian said was trouble. Just as the thief was about to dart around a corner, Rocco hurled the can of bean dip at him. It flew hard and straight, hitting him directly in the back of the head with stunning force, causing him to fall to the ground.

Soon, the store manager and assistant manager appeared and approached the man, who was quite dazed. Rocco hurried Marian toward the bus, but not before the woman who had been robbed thanked him in amazement before she ran off to retrieve her purse.

"That was a great shot," Marian said.

"Come on, let's get this stuff loaded, and get out of here," Rocco replied.

"Why are you in such a hurry?"

"'Cause they'll eventually call the cops and I'd just as soon not have to deal with all that."

"Are you in trouble with the law, Rocco?"

"No, no, nothing like that, but I'm not supposed to be off of my meds."

"Where'd ya learn to throw like that?"

"In the Army Rangers, between throwing grenades and knives, I learned an awful lot about how to throw with accuracy. There are actually a fairly large number of weapons that require a good throwing arm; nun chucks, bolos, that kind of stuff."

"Well, it was an awesome move. You could've just let him go and had the store call the police."

Rocco paused for a moment, as if considering this for the first time, then shook his head. "No I couldn't. That just wouldn't have been right. I could stop that lady from being a victim, so I did. Us macho guys are supposed to protect the weaker ones, right?"

"Well, it sure makes a girl feel protected. I'm taking you everywhere I go."

They finished loading the balance of the groceries into the bus. "So I guess I have to believe in 'women's intuition' after all," Rocco said, "because you had that guy nailed the minute you saw him."

Marian knew it was an effort for Rocco to admit that he recognized her ability. "Its part of what Dewey's opened my eyes to. He's teaching me to use those feelings to read people."

He smiled, "Well it sure makes a guy feel protected. I'm taking *you* everywhere *I* go." His face suddenly turned serious. "Listen, if you ever get that twitch about anybody, you tell me, OK? I don't want anybody messing with anybody on the bus, especially Dewey."

"Especially Dewey," she nodded.

"You really like him, don't you?"

Marian's eyes widened a bit. "Yes, Rocco, I really do like Dewey. I don't know if that means anything *special*, if that's what you mean."

Rocco didn't seem to hear the deeper meaning she intended. He just nodded. "I like the kid too. There's something really good about him, you know?"

"Well, between my 'women's intuition' and your 'soldier's protection instincts' we should be able to take good care of him. What do you say, Rocco? Do we promise to look out for Dewey?"

Rocco straightened unconsciously into the 'attention' position. "Yes Ma'am, you bet; it's a deal. I don't want to see anything bad happen. For that matter, I don't want to see anything bad happen to any of the group. Not even that bastard Bruno or that new hippie kid, Trace."

"Rocco, that's the sweetest thing I've ever heard you say," Marian said, smiling at his confession. He frowned. "But don't worry, I won't tell anyone. It's just between you and me."

"Damn women," he said, grumbling, as he settled himself into the driver's seat. "Always gotta have a secret in their pockets."

Rusty and Sang Lee

Rusty angrily tossed a wrench into the toolbox. "Dewey knows I'd be more useful working on the bus. This little dirt bike of Trace's is just something new for Buzz to play with until he gets a real bike, but it's not important. It's like he's giving me busy work."

"I don't understand it either," Sang Lee answered, calmly. "But I trust his intentions. I'm not sure what my task is meant to do either. I'll try it anyway, just to see what happens."

"What are you supposed to do?"

"He said I had to find a way to do something nice for everyone in the group, but it had to be something that they couldn't do for themselves and it had to be the same thing for everyone. You know... a group something."

"But he didn't tell you what that thing might be?"

"No, but I remember him saying there was a way to find out what that thing is." She closed her eyes, trying to recall the moment. "He said to open my eyes in a new way, to try to see everyone as if for the first time, every time." She shrugged. "Marian has already started practicing this. He says women are slightly better at it than men."

Rusty thought about how each task was suited to the person performing it. His mechanical task was to fix the bike, which Trace had donated without a second thought, so that Buzz would have something to ride. Buzz without a bike was beginning to get on everyone's nerves.

His other task was to study some of the science of the Mode and to try to perform a small bit of molecule re-arranging. Dewey had given Rusty some notes to read and some visualization exercises to perform, and had fired up his desire by telling him, "You're going to come along faster than the rest of the group, and I think you're going to surprise yourself with what you can learn to do." Still, the busy-work with the bike wasn't nearly as galling as being shut off from the repairs on the bus. He couldn't help, couldn't watch, couldn't even talk to anyone about what was going on. He just didn't understand what Dewey thought he was going to get out of that. He looked at Sang Lee.

"Well, at least your task sounds like it means something. Any ideas yet?"

"No, of course not, it's just the first day. I don't expect it to come to me right away. But I do have work to do back at the bus," she said, as she stood up.

Rusty looked up from the bike. "Well come back every once in a while, or send someone, just to check that I'm still breathing and stuff, OK?"

She laughed. "I'll come back to keep you company in a while. I could even help with the bike, if you want. Sooner or later I have to get over my fear of wrenches!"

Rusty smiled in disbelief. "Help me, what, sweep up? Organize the tools by size? Dust the bike? What can you do?"

She gave him a hard stare, and pointed at some of the tools around him, "Socket wrench, screwdriver, compression gauge, torque wrench," she pointed her finger at him. "Jerk. You know that old saying about 'assuming' and 'ass'? Well I think we know which one of us is the 'ass'. I once had a boyfriend who was into cars, who tried his best to teach me, when he wasn't busy screwing my friends behind my back. He was a jerk too. Just because I don't know how to use those tools, doesn't mean I don't know what they're called!" And with that she stormed out.

Trace and Shorty

"OK, so remember, no matter what happens, I've got you covered. I won't let the ocean take you. Are you ready dude? Are you sure you still want to do this?"

Shorty looked at Trace a bit unsure, "I hate being afraid of the water. I've gotta do this, but I have to tell ya... I'm still pretty scared."

They worked their way into the water until it was up to Shorty's knees, and then after a bit to his waist, where he had to deal with the ebb and flow of some fair-sized waves, which sometimes came up to his neck. Trace kept a hand on Shorty at all times and kept telling him what the next swell would be like, as he could read the waves the way I read cars.

Eventually, Shorty was comfortable enough to allow his feet to leave the sand and let a wave lift him up and over its crest. He smiled as his feet touched back gently on the sand. Soon, Shorty was hooked on that moment of weightlessness when the waves lifted him.

One time, he floundered a bit as a large wave broke just before it reached him. Trace had prepped him for what to do if he was caught by a wave, and could hear in his head Trace telling him, "Hold your breath!" just before the wave slammed into him.

Holding his breath, he tumbled for what seemed like an eternity before suddenly feeling a hand close around his arm. He found Trace pulling him back up to the surface where he could breathe again.

"Thanks, man. I thought I was shark bait."

"No problem. I told you, don't worry, I'll be right here. The more you relax, the easier it will be. In fact, it's best if you learn how to take a few tumbles and not have it ruffle up your manhood," he said grinning.

On one of the swells, Shorty found himself at the peak and looked down on Trace in the valley between waves. "Hey, I'm taller than you!" he chuckled.

Trace showed him the dog paddle, then the backstroke, which by its nature keeps the face clear of the water. Within a few days, Trace had not only taught Shorty how to swim, but also introduced him to body surfing, the most primeval form of wave mastery. Done right, your head is always clear of the water, and ultimately the wave pushes you onto the safety of the beach. Shorty loved it.

"You're totally getting the hang of it, little man. Let's surf some waves in tandem." Trace told Shorty when to take off on a wave and together they body surfed the same wave, about five feet apart. Shorty was caught by a few waves in the process, but he gained confidence after surviving each one. After an afternoon of surfing on some decent sized waves, Trace and Shorty climbed out of the water onto the beach.

"Well, what do think? Could you handle a wave that caught you by surprise now?"

"Yeah, I think I could," Shorty replied. "The big waves still give me that sinking feeling in the pit of my stomach when I see them coming, but I could go back in the water right now."

"Whoa, Shorts, you'll have plenty of time tomorrow. Let's de-prune for a few minutes. Besides, don't you want to reap the rewards of your new-found talent?"

"Huh?" Shorty said.

Trace nodded in the direction of two young girls sitting on blankets several yards away that were looking at them and giggling between themselves.

"They're probably telling short jokes," Shorty said.

"I don't think so, my man. That's the 'you're cute, come talk to us' look. I've seen it before. For all you know, they may both want the short guy."

"Well I guess it wouldn't hurt to see what's up."

After the girls nibbled but didn't bite, they walked back down the boardwalk towards Trace's house. They were just passing a basketball court, with three guys shooting hoops on one of the half-courts, when one of them called out, "Hey Trace, come help us out on a two-on-two for a few minutes."

Trace looked at Shorty, "Mind if I join 'em for a bit?"

"Not at all, man. I'll just sit here and ogle some more girls while I soak up the sun."

"Better put some more sunscreen on that head, Shorts, you're starting to look a little over-toned on the chrome dome."

Shorty felt the heat coming from his head. "I will, thanks, Trace. I don't need to shed any more brains than I already have."

Trace joined the others on the court. They played a fast game to twenty-one, based on a lot of shots from the perimeter and quick drives to the basket. Trace moved well and had a good jump shot, but he and his partner lost in the end by six. After the game was finished, Trace came back over to Shorty and sat down to catch his breath and drink some water.

"You put up a good game."

"Yeah, but that doesn't help when the other side scores more hoops. That guy was killing me on drives to the basket."

"Yeah, I know. I saw that."

Trace looked surprised. "Do you watch much basketball?"

"I've seen a fair share."

"That's not something I'd expect from, you know… a person of your stature."

"You mean a midget. It's OK to say it."

Trace paused for a moment. "Ok, it's not something I'd expect from a midget."

"Yeah well, people aren't always what you expect, are they?"

Trace turned towards the other guys on the court and could hear them joshing each other about the game. "Ok, so what do I do to stop a guy like that?"

Shorty smiled up at Trace, a bit surprised. "You're asking me?"

"Yeah, you say you know some basketball, tell me what you saw."

Shorty shrugged his shoulders. "Well, for starters, your footwork is all wrong for stopping a drive. You're always a step too far forward when the guy starts his move; he's looking for it. When he sees you in that situation, he goes for it, and then you're toast. You've gotta stay one step closer to the basket until he starts his drive. Then you can close up on him and try to stop him."

Trace looked at Shorty in amazement. "Are you kidding me? You saw all that from just this one game?"

Shorty shrugged again. "That's the part you asked me about."

"What else did you see?" Trace asked, in shock.

Shorty paused for a brief moment, deciding whether to give it all to him at once. "You're slow switching on defense. Hey, I know defense is not a big part of a two-on-two game, but when the other guy blows by your partner, it's up to you to stop him."

Trace glanced back at the court for a few moments as he processed this new perspective. "You know, I think you're right." He quickly stood up and called out to the guys for another game. Walking on to the court, he winked at Shorty as he stepped into the face of his opponent.

They played virtually the same kind of game as the first one, only this time, every time his opponent drove towards the basket, he found Trace solidly in his way with his hands up in the air. On two occasions, Trace's partner fell for a head-fake and the shooter ran past him, only to find Trace standing there like a wall. This time, Trace and his partner won by six points.

He walked back to Shorty, shaking his head. "You, my man, may be a midget, but you knoooooow basketball."

Shorty laughed. "I guess we both taught each other something, huh?"

Trace thought for a moment. "I guess we all have something to share. Dewey's putting us in situations that bring those things out in us." All of a sudden, it seemed as if anything was possible; that he would be able to conquer everything he put his mind to. Trace hadn't felt this good since before the death of his parents. He became anxious to return from the beach and share his experiences with the others. "Let's get back to the house and see what's up with everyone else," he said, looking at Shorty with a new fondness.

He and Shorty walked down the beach towards his house. Trace thought about the basketball game, and how all of a sudden after Shorty's analysis, the ball had seemed huge to him, as if it was twice its normal size. He'd been aware of where it was at every moment. He also thought back to Dewey's explanation of how the Mode helps you see old patterns in new ways.

As these thoughts bounced back and forth in Trace's mind, he looked at the spume of a wave that had just crashed on shore. As gravity swept it back towards the sea, for just the briefest moment, the pattern of the basketball he kept seeing in his mind outlined itself on the sand, before it too returned to the sea.

Did I do that? he thought, to himself.

Trace looked at Shorty smiling, but he was looking inland, completely unaware of the vision that had just transpired. "You know, Shorts that Dewey really knows something."

"Yeah, I get that feeling too," Shorty said. "But the question is… what does he know?"

"Something we are already on the road to learning..." Trace answered. I for one am someone who is going to think about that."

Buzz and Simon

"You moved."

"No I didn't."

"Yes you did. I saw you. You're doing it now; twitching your foot," said Simon.

"Yeah, well you talked and you're supposed to not speak," Buzz answered, indignantly.

"I only have to do that when I'm on camera, which I can't figure out how to do without looking stupid."

They both brooded in silence for a moment.

"You're doing it again."

"What?"

"Twitching your foot!"

"This sucks!"

"Why, because you can't do it? Maybe that's the point."

"What? That there's something I can't do? I don't need that."

"Haven't you ever failed at something before? Because I sure have. That's one of the reasons I'm here! My last plan didn't work out so well."

"Well sure, I've tried some things that didn't work out, but nothing that was, you know, crucial. I've never failed at something that I've set my mind to."

"Oh yeah? What about the Hoover Dam incident?"

"That wasn't my fault! You guys planted doubt in my mind. Before I met you all, I never doubted anything!"

"Listen Buzz, I've failed more times than I can count, and you know what? It doesn't mean a thing. It only makes the time when you finally get it right all the sweeter. You just get up from whatever knocks you down and you do whatever is next. I know that sounds simplistic, but it's the truth. So here's what you do. You do your task, try to stay still for ten minutes, and if you can't do it, you tell Dewey and try to do the next thing he dreams up for you. And that's all."

Buzz was shocked. "You mean... just like that, admit defeat and then move on to the next task? I'm not sure I want to do that."

Simon was adamant. "You've got get past the stuff that makes you stumble. Yeah, OK, I blew it in New York, but you know what? I've still got someone who wants to know what I'm doing next and I'm not blowing that; and just because I'm talking doesn't mean you can move around. Are you going to give this a shot or what?"

Buzz tried to settle down, which for him took an already amazing amount of concentration. "OK, so I try, and if I can't, then I can't, so what, big deal. I bet I'm not the only one who can't do their task."

"That's the attitude!" Simon said, smiling, "And it's very possible that I'll be one of those that can't do their task either."

Buzz jumped up and walked around the small room in Trace's house that they were using as his "quiet spot".

"Listen, you're worried that you won't be able to communicate without talking. I always have to do that in a race, when the sound of engines drowns out everything else. I use what I call 'finger Zen'."

"'Finger Zen'?"

"Yeah, you could do it. Everyone can. It's all about the fingers and eyes. It's charades, gone simple. Here, I'll show you. If I point at you, what do you think?"

"Me?"

"Right; and if I point at me?

"You!"

"If I put my finger to my lips?"

"Be quiet."

"Thumbs up?"

"OK."

"Point at my head and twirl my finger?"

"You're crazy."

"Yeah, that may be true. Anyway, you can see that you already know a little bit of finger language. You can also do numbers easily. You can point… I think you'll be surprised at how much you can say."

"Well I hope it's enough for anyone watching to understand. Now, try to be still again."

They sat in silence. After a few moments, Simon raised his finger, catching Buzz's eye, and pointed to Buzz's fingers which were drumming quietly, but fiercely, on his thighs.

"This is never going to work."

"Try working up to it gradually. Start with fifteen seconds then move up to thirty. Before you know it, you're at ten minutes. Keep at it for a little longer and then we'll go work on the bus. My suggestion? Try twitching only on the inside."

Bruno and Jesus

"Well?"

"Well, what?"

"Well, aren't you going to light it?" Bruno asked, gesturing towards the pile of firewood and kindling.

"Yes, I am," answered Jesus.

"Sometime this year? The D-man said for you to have the fire-ring lit every night by the time the sun went down, and he told me always be there to make sure that it was done. By the look of the sun on the horizon I'm thinking you've got about ten minutes."

"I will wait until the last minute."

"Why? Just take the matches and light the damn thing!"

"Shhhh, be quiet, I can't concentrate."

After another minute, Bruno's impatience forced him to speak up again. "You're trying to light it with your mind, or something, aren't you?"

"You're not making this any easier. Aren't you supposed to be doing something?"

"Other than watching you light the fire, no, not at this moment."

They sat for another minute.

"Jesus, can I ask you something?"

"Right now?"

"Yeah, I need to know the truth. Can Dewey really, you know... do miracles?"

Jesus didn't answer.

"Well, can he?"

"God, he does miracles. Mr. Dewey, he just does things most people don't know how to do. When you don't understand what someone is doing, it looks like a miracle, or magic. But it's still possible to learn; even for you and me."

"Well it doesn't look like you're learning it very well. The sun's gonna hit the horizon any minute now."

"Yes, but it is important that you understand this distinction. You *can* learn to do it. Simon can learn. Sang Lee and Shorty can learn. But it takes a good teacher and Mr. Dewey will be a very good teacher. You will see."

"Well I've missed all the action so far. All I have to go on is hearsay."

"Maybe your time hasn't come yet. Don't worry, it will."

"Well, even without any miracles on tape, I think we're getting footage that's gonna pay off big."

"Pay off for who, Mister Bigshot?"

"Well, everyone. You, Dewey, everyone on the bus."

Jesus laughed. "Do you think Mr. Dewey cares about the money? Oh no, it's you and Simon he wants. You're here for a reason, though I can't imagine what that might be. Now hand me some matches so I can light this."

Bruno pulled a new book of matches from his pocket and tossed them to Jesus as he stood up and walked away saying, "I'm going to see if Rocco needs help with dinner. See you back at Trace's."

He hadn't taken three steps when he heard the sound of the fire lighting. "Catch," Jesus said, tossing the book of matches at him. Bruno caught them with one hand and stuffed them back into his pocket. It wasn't until he got back to Trace's that he looked more closely at them. Not a one of the matches had been used.

By Friday, I had given the lawyers the proper identifying serial numbers and licenses of each of Winger's planes as well as a list of his other business assets and the process was begun that would put them on the market. The lawyers would take care of the sales and I would sell or dispose of any other personal artifacts that were still located in the hangers, as well as make arrangements for the termination of the leases.

Anna and I said our fond goodbyes just as Rocco arrived late that afternoon to take me back to Trace's house. It took me a second to realize that both Rocco and his bike had a new look. He was still in boots, jeans, t-shirt and vest, but the boots were shiny, the jeans weren't ratty, the t-shirt was clean, and the vest was new. He was actually kind of color coordinated, and he had an interesting symbol sewed on the back of the vest that looked like a gear. His much-loved hog had gotten a new paintjob. It was a deep, warm yellow with black highlights and an intricate set of patterns flowing across it, one of which I recognized as the same gear symbol that was on his vest. He stood next to the bike with a huge grin.

"What happened?"

"Whaddya mean?" he said, attempting innocence.

"You and the bike! Don't tell me you both dressed up just to come get me!"

"How do you like it?"

"You both look great," I said smiling at his eagerness. "But what brought this on?"

"Hop on and let's get you back to Trace's." He continued in a bad gypsy accent, "All will be made clear to you then." And with that, we were off.

It was great to see everybody again. It helped me realize that I had grown attached to every one of them. Rocco was right; many things became clearer once I got there. As I greeted everyone, I realized they had all gotten a fashion makeover. Everyone was in sharp looking new clothes, but their styles hadn't really changed. Bruno and Simon still dressed up. Buzz still wore his leathers. Trace still wore his Hawaiian shirt and shorts. Marian was in a dress and Sang Lee was in jeans and a shirt; but they all shared a subtle color scheme, and each one had the gear image worked into their clothes in some way or another.

"You guys look great! Whose idea was this?"

"It was me. This is the way I did my task." Sang Lee said, beaming.

"And what made you decide that a fashion upgrade was what this group needed?"

"Because I looked at them with new eyes, like you told me. I realized that everyone's clothes highlighted their individuality, but that we also needed something to show unity. So I helped everyone re-do their wardrobe. Some things we fixed, and some things we bought new. Now we look like we belong together. I even found a design for a kind of badge that I worked into the scheme, based on a gear. You know, to symbolize motors and the Mode."

"Where did you find the design?"

"I found two books open on the table in Trace's house, where I was collecting fashion magazines. One was open to a picture of a beautiful Indian mandala; the other was open to a face-on view of large drive gear. I took it as a sign and worked from there."

"Well I guess I'll need to get the treatment too, if I'm going to keep up with the rest of you." Sang Lee laughed as she brought forward a box and handed it to me. I opened it to find pants and shirts with the new symbol worked into them, along with a priest's robe that had been re-worked to incorporate all of the separate elements that each of the other's clothes had. It was stunning.

"I thought that you could wear that when you teach the Mode in public. It will look great."

"Thank you, Sang Lee".

We sat down to a Rocco-prepared dinner of spaghetti and pizza along with salad and bread. It was great. Everyone wanted to talk about what had transpired over the last week, but I had them hold off while I questioned Rocco on his cooking. Everyone agreed that he'd done pretty well, except for one night when he'd burned the hamburgers he was grilling until they were actually on fire. Rocco was all puffed up with the compliments he was hearing. He admitted that he actually liked to cook now, and that Marian had offered to tutor him on some of the finer points. I asked him about the fresh bread he'd cooked for the evening. He admitted that someone had written out the recipe and taped it to the stove in the trailer. He assumed it was Marian and took the hint. Marian denied it adamantly.

After we finished dinner, we walked to the fire-ring and gathered around it to discuss everyone else's tasks. Rocco and Sang Lee had done well with their tasks. I was optimistic for the rest. I asked Marian to go first.

Marian had attempted her task with all the promise of an athlete on steroids. The first story she told was her own. She revealed to the others that she had lost her mother when she was very young and was raised by her father, who also died when she was eighteen. She talked about him and reminisced about his storytelling, which she remembered most. Now that she was telling the stories, she wanted them to be good ones. She tried that first night to tell some of the stories he used to, but she had to fight her sadness at losing him before he could see her fully grow up. Somehow, each story she told kind of lost its place and sputtered out at the end. Nevertheless, by the next night, she had gotten over that moment, and on that night and each night since, she had told fables, true-life stories, even ghost stories to the great acclaim of the group.

Shorty told me he'd lost his fear of the ocean, and that Trace had taught him the tricks to understanding it. Trace spoke about how great a feeling it was to watch Shorty master the water under his instructions, and then turn right around to receive Shorty's penetrating tutelage in basketball.

Buzz hadn't been able to sit still for ten minutes, but he was now completely committed to attaining that goal. He practiced several times a day, each time advancing his ability to sit still by a second or two. Simon claimed that he'd made it to five minutes once, but based on the comments from the rest of the group, that claim was suspect. They felt that Simon was fudging just so Buzz wouldn't look like a complete failure.

"But he's not a failure!" I admonished them. "Buzz has opened up a capability within himself that he didn't know he had. That's what these tasks have done for all of you."

"I'll tell you something else," added Simon. "Something weird happens when he does get that focused. The air around him gets hot. It's like he's generating energy!"

"He's not generating it, so much as re-directing it," I answered. "All that random energy Buzz normally sends out is being focused like a beam of light through a magnifying glass. It's exciting the molecules around him and causing the air to heat up. It's a great start to being able to actually create energy!" Buzz smiled proudly at this praise, happy to know that he hadn't failed at all.

Simon did pretty well with having to mime when on camera. He showed me the footage later and, despite some very funny moments when his frustration got the better of him, he actually was able to pull off a decent interview with Trace and some of his surfing friends using Buzz's "Finger Zen".

Rusty was just beside himself that he couldn't touch the bus for the whole week, but I'd told them all to let him at it on the last day before I returned. I had secretly told him to check all the work that had been done because I trusted that he, and only he, should have the final say as to the bus's condition. Rusty was quite surprised to find that everything had been done to near perfection. I reminded him that that's exactly the way it should be, if everyone does the work according to the Mode. He had souped up Trace's dirt bike and Buzz was back in his natural element now that he had a set of wheels beneath him.

Later, I pulled Rusty aside for an update on his secret task. He told me, with awe in his voice, that all my assignments had helped him finally unlock some portion of the Mode. It had taken him most of the week, and he had only done the smallest bit of molecular re-arranging by changing 92 octane gas into 87, but he'd done it and had known what he was doing and how.

"It opened up a whole new picture of how the physical things in the world work," he said with amazement.

"It's also going to help you open up the other areas of the Mode faster, now that you've made it over this first hurdle," I assured him. He smiled at this encouragement.

I complimented Jesus on the fire and asked him how he'd done with his task. Bruno spoke up and said, "He didn't always make the sunset deadline."

Jesus shot Bruno a look. "I was never more than a couple of minutes late, and that only happened twice. Besides," his eyes twinkled, "I've learned some very interesting things about how to light fires."

"He's learned some of your magic," Bruno said, letting out an exasperated sigh, "but I've still missed it every time."

"But, Bruno, one of the tasks I gave you was to keep your eyes open for the magic that is happening all around you. Didn't you see anything amazing while watching these people all week?"

"Nope. Oh I heard about this and that, but I was always in the wrong place at the wrong time."

"Don't worry, Bruno. I'll make sure you see some magic before this is all over."

Later, I also pulled Bruno aside to find out about his secret task. I'd told him that he needed to find some way to do something nice for each person without that person knowing who had done it. He had to do something good and get none of the credit.

"Was Rocco's bread recipe and the art books that caught Sang Lee's eye your doing?"

"Yeah," he admitted, looking down and scuffing his feet in the sand.

"Did you find something like that for everyone in the group?"

"Yeah, I think so. Jesus never had to look too hard for firewood. Marian would find little scraps of paper with story titles on them. I tried to do something for everyone. The funny part was watching them ask each other if they did it. I denied it all."

"And that's how it feels? 'Funny'?"

"Well, there is a very cool moment when you see that person put your help to use. It made Rocco's bread taste that much better and Marian's stories sound that much better, knowing that everyone else was digging it too."

"So even though you got no credit for these little kindnesses, there was still a payoff wasn't there?"

He nodded seriously, "Yeah, there was a payoff. It felt good."

I slapped him on the back. "You'll turn out alright, Bruno."

As for the bus, it was almost unrecognizable. The windows had been tinted and the color had been changed to, as Jesus called it, "Ghetto Enhanced School Bus Yellow". They had lowered it, re-chromed the rims and trim, replaced the broken bulbs and painted on the front hood and fenders a stunning flames design. Now the new look of Bruno's bike made complete sense. It had been done up to match the bus. I had to admit that it would look pretty sharp when we traveled out.

All of the mechanical tasks had been completed and everyone had pitched in to help, including the women and the 'non-mechanical' men. An oil change, tune up, wiring repair, brake shoes, and a whole host of maintenance items had been handled to near perfection. Everyone was very proud of their work, and the team approach had made the whole thing enjoyable.

The trailer, by contrast, just looked more like a cross between a small bungalow and a space ship. All kinds of improvements had been made, but that just meant more wires and tubes snaking their way in and out of the trailer at odd places. It now boasted a television and stereo, as well has having been made to sleep four people.

All in all the week of separation had brought us closer together and the group would be thankful later when they would need the very skills they learned, as well as the company of each other.

CHAPTER XXII

Hocus Pocus Focus

Everyone's tasks were very revealing and, much like everything else that has happened since the group came together, we learned a lot about each other. We represented quite a variety of types and for spreading further the wisdom of the Mode, this was both useful and important.

One morning, while gathered around the coffeepot in Trace's kitchen, Sang Lee looked up from behind the entertainment section of the local newspaper.

"I don't believe it," she exclaimed, "One of my favorite artists is performing here in L.A. tonight!"

"Who is it?" Marian asked.

"His name is Crushed Ice. I first saw him when he played

Geezers Palace, while I still had a job there. He's the best rapper I have ever seen. It's rare that you hear one who has a positive message to his lyrics. He raps about the good things in life: respect, family, love. He keeps it real."

"You don't see many Asians at a rap concert, do you?" Bruno asked, sarcastically.

"Funny, Bruno. While most of us may not be able to relate to the negative plights of street blacks, a positive message transcends all races," she replied.

"Very well put, Sang Lee," I said, "Perhaps we should go see this show. I for one have never seen rap live. Maybe there is something we all could learn."

"I'm not sure I want to see a rap concert," Shorty complained. "I usually can't see anything at a concert once everyone stands up."

"Come on, Shorty. I can get us backstage passes," Sang Lee continued. "I know their road manager pretty well. I promise you will be able to see everything."

While some were quite hesitant, I found this to be a unique opportunity to study a very different young culture, a culture that listens to the words, as well as the music, something unheard of in the head banging late 70's and early 80's. Sang Lee was able to obtain tickets with a short phone call to the road manager, Mohammed Bubba, who promised we could meet Ice after the event. We all came to an agreement to check out his show later that evening.

West L.A. at night can be quite a scene and that night was no exception. Rappers and Hip Hoppers attracted a wide cross section of followers from the very white to the very black and all shades in between. There were three or maybe four generations here, and purple hair and pierced lips met butch hair and ballet skirts in this "anything goes" part of town. It made me realize how nice it was to travel with such a diverse bunch, because you often see a wider perspective of cultural influence.

The show was amazing. Rap song language was fast paced and captivating. After the show, we waited backstage to meet Ice. Simon and Bruno continued shooting footage, while Ice sat down with us to talk. He told jokes and spoke in heavy Ebonics, which for us less initiated types led to continuous misinterpretations. After a while of free flowing spirits, Sang Lee, who had not been drinking, noticed that the others had become quite intoxicated, and recognizing the opportunity for uninhibited humor through embarrassment, she asked Ice to start up a round of "spin the tongue."

"What the hell is that?" asked Buzz.

"You know, rappin' off the cuff, making up rhymes on the fly," Sang Lee replied, "Only with middle class white people. It makes for some pretty funny stuff."

"Well I'm not gonna do it. The only rap words I know are 'my nigger'." Suddenly, Buzz remembered he was sitting in front of Ice, a six-foot one, two hundred thirty pound black man.

"Ahhh... Sorry, Mr. Ice!"

"Dats cool. No harm done. 'Ma nigga' is a brutherly term of endearment. 'My nigger' is a white man's black slave. There's a difference, ya dig?"

"It's not as bad as you think, Buzz. Anyone want to give it a try?" Sang Lee asked.

One by one, we all took a stab at this rappin' off the cuff'. One of the more humorous ones was Shorty's Limo Rap, which went something like this:

My name is Shorty and I'm here to say
I used to drive a big ass limo, everyday
It had a twenty-four valve overhead cam

V12 dual exhaust with an oversized fan
With a 62" LCD screen
And 10.1 Dolby, it's a mean machine
Get down, what it is, uh huh, everybody help me wiggle
Limo rap, that's what it is… yeah, limo rap…

Late at night when I went to bed
Visions of movie stars filled my head
Taking a trip to a celebrity ball
Punch the paparazzi if they bug us at all
And when their night of fun was at an end
I'd get some bling and start all over again
Limo rap, that's what it is… yeah limo rap… somebody help me!

"No, I mean really, somebody help me!" Shorty had jumped around so much he had torn the back of his pants. Then there was Marian's.

I'm from the south side, my name is MML
Where sunny side's sup and it's hot as Hell
Ain't got no stunna for a runner, or more of all that
Got a hole in my pocket, but my legs are phat
I tried my hand at the bizz bling bling
But it didn't jive, yo my bird don't sing
And so I'm tellin' you now, cause my word is bond
I really was lost until I met the bomb
That Motoroo,oo,oo, the Motorishi

That's why I'm singin' everyday about the Motee rule
That driving real hard, ain't making you cool
Jus' troubles ahead, they gonna take your purse

And yo gonna end up in a pimped up hearse
So if you're sitting at the root of a rotten tree
That takes apart this land of civil liberty
Remember that I'm telling ya that now's the time
To shut up, or put up, or bust a rhyme
That Motoroo,oo,oo, the Motorishi

Stop y'all… now break it down

So what the man says, the man is true
He gonna tell ya everything that you need ta do
Just confess da sins that ya know you made
And he'll tell what to do to make 'em go away
And your bad ass ride 'ill be thankful too
For cutting it some slack off your heart attack
So you can live free by the golden rule
All ya gotta do is do da Motoroo

That Motoroo,oo,oo, the Motorishi
He's the man, the man who can
The man who can with the wrench in his hand, sing it!
He's the man, the man with the plan
The plan that's gonna free you from the moto jam,
That Motoroo,oo,oo, the Motorishi

We never knew Marian had so much rhythm and poetic talent hidden away behind that southern drawl and porcelain skin. Ice laughed non-stop for what I am sure to him must have appeared to be very bad "Karaoke White Rap Theater."

"That's why I loves ya, Sang Lee, you so right. I ain't laughed dat hard at white people in a mile long. But I really dig da last one. Maybe we can do somin' wid dat in the future," he said. "Listen ya'll, Sang Lee tells me there's something special about yous. I hold her words dear to my ticker, so she must see sumpin' worth keepin' on. So if yo her homeys, than yo my homeys too. I got a few more shows here in L.A., then back to San Francisco to wrap up the tour."

Simon, who had too much to drink, burst into laughter. "Rap up the tour, I get it, that's funny. Rap up… the tour… ha ha." The room was silent.

"Anyway," Ice continued, "if ya'll want to meet me up there, I can introduce ya to a whole new scene."

I told Ice that I still had obligations to fulfill over the next few weeks and that when we were finished, we too would venture north, perhaps taking another famous route, the Coast Highway, and meet up with him there.

Working hard over the next few weeks tending to the affairs of Winger's widow had not only resulting in getting everything sold and transferred in record time, but had also garnered a good price as well. Anna was very grateful and just as I was preparing to leave and say goodbye, she handed me an envelope. I told her that someday she might need every bit of what Winger had left her. Nevertheless, she insisted she was fine and that he would have wanted me to have it. Out of respect and honor for Winger, I could not turn her down. Rocco and I took off back to our camp at Trace's house.

Things were coming together at an accelerated rate and for a week straight, we made plans for the next part of our journey. Everyone felt like a part of the group now and the look of unity within diversity Sang Lee had created, using the symbol of the gear on our clothing, accentuated this point. Knowing it was time to take this to the next level, Bruno expressed how we might accomplish this.

"Look, Dewey. I think it's time we took this thing public and presented ourselves as a commercially viable package. I know when we started out at Simon and I only had dreams of getting enough footage to produce a few television pilots, but it's turned into something more than that. You have what it takes to become a super star, and as much as I've been able to recognize talent when I see it, you have it all: smarts, looks, a dynamic presence, and a message. What better way to promote your teaching than through becoming famous? You don't know what you're sitting on here. This thing could be a huge commercial success!"

The others had been exploring this possibility too and everyone had many ideas about what we should consider the "new and improved" whatever we were going to call this "thingamajig."

"I've got it all worked out," Bruno continued, "We need to start by giving you a name, a catchy name. The others and I agree that 'Dewey', as wonderful as it is, well… let's just call a spade a spade; that name sucks! It's not going to fly in the big leagues. We were thinking you need something that says what you are, like 'the Motorishi' from Marian's rap about you, and we can be your elite inner circle of devoted Motees, called the 'Church of Motor Science'."

"I will have to admit the names do indeed sound fitting to our cause," I said, "But I'm still not sure that the way to expand the teaching is to take the commercial route. I mean, after all, it is what I despise most and continue to fight against, and the cause of much of the 'sleep' and inability of people to be free from the machine. Sleep feeds on the unaware, the herd instinct, the followers of forever changing "in-things" of the day. 'Capitalism begets Commercialism', and produces what Mac called, 'Gottahavititis' disease; a major negative by-product of a free market economy. However, somehow I know in order to spread the word properly it is important for it to reach as many people as possible, using all technology available to us today."

There's nothing like the passage of a millennium or two for the impossible to becomes possible. Technology now makes it possible for an event in one location of the planet to reach almost every major city of the world, via the media, within seconds for an instantaneous global reaction. No longer would a new faith in its infancy need to travel by horseback to the next town, beating its residents into religious submission and forcing on them all kinds of dreadful rules and regulations.

"There is no escaping it, no matter what we do; it is going to be played out in the public's eye. Therefore, we might as well use it to our advantage if possible, helping to deliver the true meaning of the teaching, regardless of the almost certain damage that will be caused by others in the name of the Mode."

"So that's a yes?" Bruno asked, smiling.

Simon jumped in. "Once we generate a strong image, you can prepare lectures or sermons, or whatever you want to call them, and we'll rent small stadiums and halls to deliver them. Both Bruno and I are familiar with contracts and stage production and we already have most of the team we would need to produce a few shows and get the word out here in Los Angeles. Then, with a few road tours and talk circuits, we could have coast to coast exposure of the teaching in no time."

Everyone seemed excited about this prospect and perhaps had already fallen prey to that spoiler of all good ideas, greed, and were not only counting the chickens before they were hatched, but were counting the chickens before the hens had even laid the eggs. I was going to need some level heads on my side if this was indeed the direction we were agreeing on. I would have to rely on Marian and Sang Lee, or perhaps Trace, to help keep things down to earth.

"OK, "I said, "We all agree that we will take the road *more* traveled, in hopes that the added exposure will deliver the Mode to the masses and the masses will deliver us a following of those who have a wish to wake up."

"Agreed," said everyone.

We worked twelve to fourteen hour days making plans and arrangements, and before long, we had put together what would become the framework for our commercial presentation. Bruno and Simon worked together on marketing. Marian would handle meals and makeup, Shorty and Jesus would handle transportation and tickets, while Rusty, Buzz, and Trace handled stage production. That left Rocco as security and Sang Lee as our accountant and image consultant. "Perfect, the only thing we're missing is a lawyer," I said, half kidding.

We continued to develop the logo of the gear symbol, and within it, put a blue sky with a few clouds nicely nested over a barren sand dune. We painted this image on the bus along with our phone number in case any weary roadside victims may be in need of immediate salvation.

Several more months passed and things were beginning to take shape. We had started visiting local auto shops, righting where we could a wrong diagnosis, and helping to show vehicle owners that most of time the failings in their cars were due to *them*, and not due to bad mechanics or defective parts. At first people resisted the idea that a flat tire, a bad alignment, or a worn out clutch could possibly have anything whatsoever to do with them. However, after a while of observing themselves, they slowly came around to the idea that they may in some small way perhaps, unknowingly of course, contributed to that already incorrectly installed and defective piece of crap! Once this idea, that the condition of our cars is a reflection of our personality, is introduced, it will fester like a pimple on a teenagers face, until they cannot help but eventually see that *they* are indeed the root of all their car's evil.

I began to hold lectures at local service centers and occasionally on the beach or at a public park. You know you're making an impact in a big city like Los Angeles, when all of a sudden your name or logo starts showing up in the usual places; telephone poles, posters, bumper stickers and home made t-shirts. Nevertheless, around this metropolis, you are really making an impression when a tagger sprays your name and logo on a nearby bridge.

The day I drove past "The Motorishi" in purple, gold and red, painted across a city block of the Santa Monica freeway overpass, I was… let's just say, shocked!

Bruno and Simon had drawn up a rough business plan that would include a steady agenda of appearances and marketing. We would continue to build a following here in Los Angeles, followed by a road tour that would take us up to San Francisco then east through the Rockies to South Dakota and Nebraska.

There were two places Bruno thought we should capitalize on; one was the traditional anniversary of the famous Sturgis Harley motorcycle ride, an event Rocco was not going to miss with, or without us, and the other was a place called Carhenge, in Alliance, Nebraska. A lot more people have heard of Sturgis than Alliance, but in this small Nebraska town, there is a unique monument called Carhenge. Built as a memorial to a man whose father once lived on the farm where it now stands, it is a replica of Stonehenge in England, except that it's made from cars instead of stones. Of course, it has been adjusted for the astronomical differences of its location from the original. I passed by this area once before but had not even known that such an automotive shrine existed at the time.

With much still to do in L.A., we tried to keep focused on each next step. We continued doing appearances at local shops and public places that would end a few months later at a larger venue, the Wiltern Theater, a beautiful, jade green, art deco style building, built in the early 1930s.

One night, we were holding a planning session at a local Santa Monica pub called, "Ye Old King's Head," a name that everyone always found funny on many levels. Trace mentioned what he had heard from some of his surfing friends.

"Listen, I'm telling ya… the buzz on the street is that 'M', (as the group now called me for short) is making a lot of sense to people around town. A cross section of people too, even the fire department is listening. This movement slices through all age groups, though all financial classes, through all colors and religions, through everything, dude!" Until the "dude", I had almost forgotten a surfer was telling the story.

Simon and Bruno were filming almost continually as the crowds we were attracting began to grow in numbers, and this growth they wanted well documented. I had given more than a couple of handfuls of lectures and our popularity was doing quite well. We continued to attract larger and larger audiences and by the time we were ready to leave Los Angeles, we had become quite well known. One of the highlights of our stay there was being featured on the cover of a local rag, called the L.A. Weekly, whose free circulation guaranteed us a wide variety of readers; even if they were mostly made up of freeloaders, prostitutes and derelicts.

We started our travels north just when the smog season was beginning and not a moment too soon. I had already had enough of living amongst the pollution waste results while growing up in Detroit.

With our new image and a well-defined plan, we installed fax machines and computers in the diner, which now doubled more as an executive suite than a mess hall and bunker. My only regret at this point was that we didn't do too much to improve the look of the outside of it. It had become quite a mutant looking spacecraft, as every kind of antennae and electronic gadget known to man had made its way into an ever-morphing external anatomy.

As we traveled north on Highway 1, Jesus gave us the itinerary. "I will show you places like Santa Barbara and San Luis Obispo, San Simeon and San Jose, and many other cities whose names begin with 'San', which of course means 'Saint', in yes, that most beloved of the romantic languages, Spanish! Those little bastards were all over the place, huh? Just kidding," he said, as everyone laughed.

While traveling through Santa Maria in the early evening, we saw a bus pulled over to the side of the road. It was getting dark but we could still make out the driver, standing at the back of the vehicle along with a few of the passengers, looking along the road for something.

"Jesus, pull over," I requested, and slowing down we stopped a few feet behind them. Also witnessing the potential for roadside salvation, Rocco and Buzz pulled over as well. I swung open the doors and we went to see if they needed any help. "Can we be of any assistance?" I asked, eager to perform my first healing as the Motorishi.

"Well, I dunno," said the bus driver, "We're looking for something leaking. I don't see anything, do you?" I looked at the ground both directly behind the bus and directly behind the diner and could only confirm that I didn't see anything either. "I don't know what happened then," he continued. "I got a light on the dash that the oil pressure was high then I heard a big 'thud' and we lost all power. I was kinda expectin' to see a big splash of something behind us, or at least a drop or two here or there."

I motioned to Rusty and Buzz to come over and look. They crawled under the stranded bus and tried to assess the damage. That's when I noticed the bus was full of elderly people. They must have been on some kind a day retreat or something, because they all looked tired.

"There are people in there who need to get home now," the driver said. "They take medication at regular intervals and even though I've called for a back up, I haven't seen hide nor hair of 'em yet!"

"I don't see a crack in anything," Rusty said, crawling back to his feet.

"Yeah, I don't think it's the oil," Buzz added.

"It has to be the oil," the driver said. "What else could it be?" I laid my hands on the hood and then checked the dipstick. In the dark, I could tell by feel that the oil case was indeed full, but that this was not oil. I smelled and tasted it to confirm my suspicions and called the driver forward.

"Have you put oil in it recently?" I asked.

"Well, let me think. Yeah, a little while ago I pulled 'er into a gas station and asked the pump jockey if he would put some oil in it. I remember telling him to use the oil I had in the back of the bus and I tipped him a few bucks under the board. Then I went to take a piss," he said.

Buzz went to the back of the bus and opened the doors. He rummaged through the odd collection of never used supplies and several cans. There were two cans that did indeed contain oil, but another can contained a substance not known to be effective as a mechanical lubricant... black paint. Seems this unlucky soul was driving a bus full of elderly patients on paint! Of course, the resulting condition would inevitably be a seized block.

There was one small positive aspect to this man's dilemma, and fortunately for him, I knew what it was. The paint was oil base and not water base, which would have thrown out the baby with the bathwater, so to speak, because water molecules are diametrically opposed to that of oil. The difference between synthetic motor oil and synthetic paint's molecular structures are only a few electrons. The trick with paint is, once it dries, the molecules link up to form a thin layer of rubber on the surface to which it is applied. In synthetic motor oil, the opposite is true; when heated up the molecules are designed to resist friction and therefore stay as slippery as possible.

"Buzz, I think we still have a can of thinner from the recent painting in the back of the bus," I said. "Could you get that?"

"Sure, M. But what do you need that for?"

"I'll show you when you get back," I said.

Buzz returned with the turpentine in hand. I asked the others to gather around the engine. I explained to Rusty what had happened to the bus and asked that he assist me in remedying the problem. Even though he grasped more of the science behind the mode than anyone else in the group had, he was still unsure of his abilities.

"You ready, Rusty?"

"I guess so."

We had pulled the oil pan off and had drained what we could of the paint-infused oil into it. I quickly poured in the paint thinner and stirred it around at a slow even pace.

"Wait!" Bruno gasped. "I don't have the camera." He darted back to our bus to retrieve it.

"We can't wait, Rusty, we only have a few seconds to make the transformation before the oil is useless," I said.

"I'm ready," Rusty replied. "Let's do this."

Rusty and I ran our hands deep into the mixture. Having been taught that skin is an organ that absorbs, Rusty quickly rubbed his thumbs and index fingers together, like I was; performing some molecular re-arranging. Then, with the aid of a funnel, we poured the concoction into the block.

"Phew, I'm back," Bruno said, as everyone laughed. "I missed it again, didn't I? You're doing this on purpose!"

We pushed the bus forwards and backwards a few times while out of gear to move the healing solution around a bit. After a few minutes, I asked the driver to try to start the bus. It started once, and then died. It started twice and then died. It started a third time, sputtered, backfired, and then died. However, the next time, I held my hand on the block and the bus started and kept running.

It did not sound very good so my suggestion to the driver was that he take the bus in for a complete overhaul once he had safely returned his precious cargo.

"I sure thank you guys a lot," he said. "I don't know what I would have done without you. Speaking of that, who are you guys anyway?"

"He's the Motorishi," Marian exclaimed, "and we're the Church of Motor Science."

"Well, thanks again, Mister Moto…Motoreezee. I ain't never heard of ya, but I'm sure gonna talk about you now," he said, still unsure of what had really transpired. He hastily returned to the bus and back onto the highway to take his weary travelers home.

"We did good? Huh, M?" Trace asked. "Those folks would have been toast, if we hadn't come along. But how did you get the paint out of the oil with only turpentine?"

"It wasn't just the paint thinner, Trace. He's taught Rusty the molecular magic trick," Buzz explained.

"It's not a trick, Buzz," Marian interjected. "It's the Mode, and I can't think of a better way to live."

CHAPTER XXIII

Saint Frenchman

Long before the city of San Francisco or "Saint Frenchman" was officially established, Spanish mariners used the name "Bahia de San Francisco de Assis" (Bay of St. Francis of Assisi) for the entire coastal area extending from Point Reyes on the North to Pillar Point on the South. It was only logical when Spanish explorers established a mission and army Presidio on the Bay in 1776 that they give it the same name. Interestingly, the city did not adopt the name "San Francisco" until 1847, in honor of a local Mexican general's wife, Francisca. Until then, the little pueblo was known as "Yerba Buena," or

"Good Herb" as a tribute to the wild mint that grew in profusion in the surrounding hills. There was a time in the late 1960's that "Good Herb" would have perhaps been a far more appropriate name, but the city was destined to be known by its Spanish name of "San Francisco".

San Francisco's topology is far from that of the flat mid-western plain states. We would find out that you needed a road map to navigate effectively through the city if one of its more popular landmarks, like the Golden Gate Bridge or Transamerica building could not be seen through the miles of buildings and rolling roads.

For the first few days we behaved like other tourists; admiring the amazing range of architecture and cultural diversity. The group made a list of places to visit: The Golden Gate Bridge, Lombard Street, Alamo Square Park, Alcatraz Island, Chinatown, Fisherman's Warf, and Ghirardelli Square. The food was also quite amazing as a unique cross section of global cultures come together here to call this city by the bay "home".

I especially wanted to see the Cable Car Museum. Cable cars, though still used here for tourist travel, have all but disappeared. One reason was that they used electricity instead of fossil fuel; that diminishing resource made up of centuries of natural processes that we consume within a matter of hours. The argument at the time was that the electrical lines strung above the streets were an offense to the "clear skies" that every American should enjoy as a right.

Cable cars also lacked the flexibility of route that a gas-driven vehicle had. That's what finally pushed the car into the mind of every American (and ultimately, every person in the world); that sense of personal control and personal exploration. Everyone with a car could go where they wanted, by whatever route appealed to them. In the beginning, electric and steam powered cars went the way of the cable car, and we were left with the gas-powered engine.

Now, no one loves the roar of a big well-tuned engine better than I do, but even I can see that the days of the gas engine are numbered. The good days of cheap oil are over and the environmental impacts are becoming noticeable. Sooner rather than later people are going to demand some other way of powering their vehicles. Of course, becoming less dependant on oil would not only ruin the economies of a few states here in the U.S. but also the economy of entire countries in other parts of the world whose sole export is oil. So far, the power of the automotive industry has kept such a transformation from happening, mostly because it wasn't their idea and they can't patent it. Standing in the Cable Car Museum, looking at this old collection of history and kitsch, I felt that it was a shame to see this energy efficient and non-polluting method of transportation be reduced to only a tourist attraction. If Cable cars had survived, we might have moved to electric powered cars far sooner.

Once we had spent a few days sight seeing we settled into a local Motel 3 to get at least half a good night's sleep. I shared a room with Trace, Marian with Sang Lee, Rusty with Buzz, Jesus with Shorty and Simon with Bruno. Rocco preferred as usual to sleep under the stars, even if they were barely visible in the light-flooded sky of this great city.

We spent the better part of the evening discussing how best to spread the oil of the Mode or "The Motee Way" as some people were referring to it.

"I'll call the local papers first thing tomorrow morning and invite them to the lecture at Golden Gate Park this coming weekend," Bruno said.

"Great, I'll prepare flyers and we'll distribute them throughout the city all this week. I'll also call Ice about his show Friday night," Sang Lee said. "He can announce the date to his audience."

"That should help," Bruno said. "I think we can draw a few hundred if not a thousand people. Simon, I want some footage from L.A. to use in the press releases, maybe we could use the 'Elderly Bus Breakdown' or some of the 'Midnight Madness' from Venice Beach. Those crowds were incredible."

All that week we visited repair shops to teach and hand out flyers to anyone who was interested, and by the week's end we had hand delivered over three thousand flyers.

We arrived at Ice's show Friday night a little late, which meant we were lucky enough to miss the crowds coming in, but it also meant we missed the crowds coming in. I would not get the chance until later to observe the variety of types that would be attending the evening's festivities.

Rocco, who was now the newly appointed head of security, walked in front of me, scanning the crowd, first left, then right and back again, like radar, checking for every potential threat. He would always hold his hand back and down when signaling me to wait while he assessed the situation. He was playing his new role more like James Bond protecting her Royal Majesty rather than Rocco Scarbino from Devil's Elbow covering the Motorman of Detroit.

"We're good, M," Rocco announced, pulling his hand into an "All Clear" position as we walked to the security checkpoint backstage.

"Tickets please," the guard, said. We handed him our VIP passes and he led us to an area just to the right of the stage where we could sit and watch the show. There were a lot of people backstage, most of them girlfriends or the newly hand-picked one night "flavors of the day," as well as a host of other professional 'hangers-on' better known as the "Entourage."

Bruno and Simon where allowed to tape as long as they received approval from Ice's lawyer before releasing any content. We conversed for a while with some of the other invited guests and after a few minutes, Ice came by to say hello. He was slow making his way through the sea of monotonous ass kissers who, when you are on top, cannot stop praising you, even going so far as to rank you higher than anything else in their meaningless lives, other than themselves of course. However, when you are at the bottom, they not only despise you and spit on you, but can't even remember your name.

He finally arrived at our group and was greeted with hugs and perhaps a bit of ass kissing as well by some of the group who could from time to time not avoid being pulled into that hypnotic state known as "mass hysteria" anymore than anyone else.

"Sang Lee, Marian, M, Motees, glad ya'll in the house," Ice said. "I want ya to five my legal beater, Mathew Bender." He indicated a thin white man to his left.

"Your what?"asked Shorty.

"My lawyer," Ice said.

"Pl-pl-pleasure M, Ice has t-t-t-t-told me so much about you," Mathew said, shaking my hand the whole time he stuttered. "When the sh-sh-show is over I would like to invite you all to a small p-p-private p-p-p-party over at the Four Seasons."

"Sounds great, thanks," I replied.

Mathew continued, "Ice sa-sa-sa-says he would li-li-li-like me to get to kn-kn-know you a little better. He th-th-th-thinks you're on to something, and is co-co-co-convinced you are going be the n-n-n-next big thing. He says you have s-s-s-substance and not just hype. I can't wait to spend some t-t-t-time talking."

"Thanks, Mathew. We'll definitely talk after the show," I replied.

"Great, see you th-then," Mathew replied and he and Ice continued down the line until they disappeared onto the stage.

The crowd roared as the stage went dark and the sound of drum rhythms and vinyl scratching boomed. Ice performed for almost two hours before the final encore. By that time, most of the group's hands and throats were sore from clapping and screaming, so we rose to assemble our belongings and head back to the bus. Just as we were about to leave we heard Ice announce our show on Sunday in Golden Gate Park. There was a pretty loud cheer from the audience because it seems some of them were already aware of "the Mode" movement in Los Angeles and in San Francisco or had seen us or heard about us around town. Hopefully, there would be a fairly good turnout.

We arrived at the hotel and spent the next few hours with Ice and Mathew talking about the Mode and sharing stories of our lives. Ice told us about being raised by his grandmother in L.A. after his mother had abandoned him there. He talked about his love of language and literature, which hadn't helped him look very cool to his peers, but had occasionally helped him talk his way out of a jam. He'd started out rapping at parties to impress girls, and found that his command of language gave him an advantage in the art. He'd just kept on moving up from there.

Mathew's story was just as interesting as Ice's. Raised in San Francisco by his Jewish parents, both of whom were in show business, his home was like the transplanted salon of a French noblewoman. Many great minds and interesting people had been the guests of the Bender family at one party or another. Of course, some of the ideas expressed at these parties were patently wacky, but that didn't stop his mother and father from embracing them whole-heartedly. In his teens, he rebelled by becoming a conservative, setting his sights on law school. Upon his graduation, his parents were proud to have a lawyer in the family, although they were disappointed at his chosen field. Instead of doing pro-bono work for the environment and the poor, something they could have supported, he had chosen entertainment law. However, a few months later, after he had renegotiated both of their current performing contracts for a bigger percentage of the proceeds, they began gushing about him to their industry friends. His business doubled, then tripled, then he met Ice who had just started moving up the ladder of fame.

Ice was very sharp about the business side of being an entertainer. "So you've been filming this whole gig from the beginning? Man, if this goes anywhere, that old footage will turn into a gold mine." Bruno and Simon high-fived each other. "And now you're gonna take the show back on the road, headed for Detroit?"

"Yes, I want to use Detroit as the base for our operations, but I don't want to miss some of the choice opportunities to teach along the way."

"Well, the Mode sounds like the real McDeal to me. I dig the idea of an allegory. Every time you say 'car', I hear the word 'person' behind lurkin' in the shadows. Right still sounds like right. Wrong still sounds like wrong. I think you're on it, and I want to help."

"Me t-t-too," added Mathew.

"Help how?" I asked.

"Any ways we can," Ice answered. "Between Mathew and me you've got brains and brawn, legal advice, and business know how, plenty of experience taking shows on the mile-long, my semi-famous name to throw around… and oh yeah, I've got a fair chunk of bling to spend these days. So whatda think, white man, does any of that sound like a shoulder you can ride on? Can we join your posse?"

"We'll be on the road for a while. Can you take that long off?"

Ice looked at Mathew. "The San Francisco sh-sh-show was the last one on the t-t-tour. Ice's got the n-n-next few m-m-months off."

Bruno piped up, "They've got some skills to add to our mix."

"And this could open up a whole new avenue for you to get the message of the Mode out there," added Simon.

I could see by the looks on everyone's faces that they were hoping I'd bring Ice and Mathew on board. "OK, it sounds like a winner. Put together your traveling gear and be ready to board the bus by tomorrow noon."

Ice smiled and put out his hand. "We'll be there, ready to flow. What's the initiation for us new guys?"

I looked around at the rest as Ice and I shook hands, and then answered, "Well there isn't one really. We didn't even know we were a team until we got to L.A."

"Well you're a team now, and every team or group or posse has got to have its initiation for the new guys. Come on, what do ya got?"

I thought back to my days with Johann as a teacher, and smiled. "O.K. somebody get me some oil. Everybody gather around…"

With that we were twelve, well, eleven and a half really, with Shorty.

CHAPTER XXIV

Mobster in the Moat

The next few days found us strategizing over Sunday's lecture at Golden Gate Park. We discussed details on how the stage logistics should be carried out, and of the opportunity to promote upcoming events. Bruno believed that the key to properly exposing the teaching through the Media was slow and carefully controlled growth; that we needed to be more than just the "wacky" story you find at the last ten minutes of every news program. Having already generated quite a stir in Los Angeles, we had no trouble convincing journalists to attend our latest endeavor. We needed to use the media and the momentum we had already generated to grow our Motee flock, as well as gain more legitimacy amongst the larger public sector.

Sunday morning was a bit foggy and as the stage team attended to the final preparations of the sound system, Rusty, Marian and I put the finishing touches on the sermon for the day. We were one hour away from show time and though the weather in the park had cleared up somewhat, the fog continued to lie just a few hundred feet above the bay.

Attendance had turned out to be quite good and there were already a couple of thousand people overflowing the park, spilling into the streets and nearby alleys. Crushed Ice was well known in this city and had agreed to warm up the crowd by saying hello and introducing us. He and Mathew fought their way through the crowds to get to the diner that was parked just a block away from the stage.

"Wh-wh-wh, some turnout!" Mathew stuttered.

"Everything looks pimp-tight here!" Ice added. "Lezdothizthang!"

He stepped out on stage to a cheering crowd.

"Yo, yo, yo, how ya'll doin? Ya'll know why ya here today, don'cha? Ya here cuz ya heard there's a new groove happenin' round town. Dez a new Mixmaster in da house who can serve it word up, ya' dig? He can set ya straight when yo lost at the gate. He's da lamb, wiff da plan, ta bring yo' life together, man. So let me introduce ya to *ma* fave peep… the Motorishi." More cheers and applause filled the park. I stepped out on stage and motioned everyone to sit.

"Please, please, be seated.

"Once, a clever smuggler came to the border with a donkey. The donkey's back was heavily laden with straw. The

official at the border was suspicious and pulled apart the man's bundles until there was straw all around, but not a valuable thing in the straw was found. 'I'm certain you're smuggling something,' the official said, as the man crossed the border."

"Now each day for ten years the man came to the border with a donkey. Although the official searched and searched the straw bundles on the donkey's back, he never could find anything valuable hidden in them."

"Many years later, after the official had retired, he happened to meet that same smuggler in a marketplace and said, 'Please tell me, I beg you. Tell me, what were you smuggling?'"

"'Donkeys"' said the man."

The crowd laughed. "I want to thank you all for coming. It's been an incredible journey that has led me here today. This journey has shown me that much like the story I just told, truth does not only lie in hidden places, tucked away in churches, or in hard to reach monasteries of Tibet. Truth can be found right in front of us, even here in the streets of the busiest cities in the world. However, we must learn to recognize it.

"I am sure most, if not all of you, are here today because you too are on a journey of discovery. You might not even know what the purpose of this journey is yet. Nevertheless, you are drawn to this search because something is missing in your life; something that you cannot find in your job or your hobbies or your families and relationships. Something that is nourishing to the soul must by its very nature be elusive. You are all from different backgrounds, different races, different upbringings, and different interests, financial classes, religions and philosophies, yet a common interest has drawn you all here to this same moment in time. This is not an accident, but a calling.

"The Mode teaches us that man is a machine, unable to do even the slightest thing without a push from outside, which always results in a predetermined set of reactions we have built up over the years. We are not free from this machine to do as we wish. You may say, 'that is not possible, look I am able to move my arms and jump up and down, surely this cannot be a predetermined reaction.' However, I am not speaking of this. Of course, we are able to make small and insignificant motions and perhaps even small insignificant thoughts. I speak of 'higher awareness,' not the body.

"Our psyche, which is made up mostly of thoughtless personalities we have learned from others, has by the time we are adolescents, already learned a limited number of responses to all external stimulation. These responses will play out in the same way, over and over again, in every situation, unless they are acted upon by some *extreme* external force, causing shock to our imaginary reality, or by rational and intentional reconditioning. The former event happens by accident, the latter by many years of hard work. Nevertheless, do not lose hope, for we are here today to show you a way out of this dilemma.

"In this teaching, we use as a method of observation, the condition of our machines, our mechanical devices. Machines are good indicators because they are used repeatedly, and over time, record the impressions that expose many years of miss-use and abuse. Our cars can tell us much about ourselves that we cannot learn from books or television.

"If you will look to the right of the stage you can see that we have assembled a variety of cars from the audience. I will use these vehicles to demonstrate my point.

"Bring me a car!" I called.

Rocco drove a randomly selected one up on stage. I looked it over and then laid my hands on the hood to meditate. A few minutes later, I addressed the crowd.

"This car belonged to a man around 6'2", who wore a black hat." The crowd smiled and chuckled. "Who does this car belong to?"

A tall man with a black cap on stood up and turned towards the stage. "That's my car," he shouted. The crowd applauded.

"You may be seated sir. Does saying the man wears a black hat tell us anything about the psychology of the person driving this car?"

A loud "NO" rang out.

"Correct! These observations are merely surface deep. They are physical observations, from noticing that the ceiling of the car is marked with the dye from a black hat, or that the seat is back about the distance of a man slightly over six-foot. These indeed, may all be facts. However, what are some other parts of the car that might tell us something more substantial?"

"The brakes," someone yelled.

"Good, the brakes may tell us whether or not this person is impatient. What else?"

"Fluid levels," another person yelled.

"Yes, that, too, will speak of one's attention to detail or maintenance skills. What else?"

"The tires," a young man shouted from the left of the stage.

"Yes. Tires are very important because they tell the history of every movement the car has made. Many people do not know this but tires can be read much like tea leaves or the tarot. Give me more!"

"The condition of the driver's seat," a man yelled from the back.

"That is a very good one! The driver's seat can tell us a host of things. One thing for instance is the general way in which people carry themselves, whether they are proud or meek."

Rocco and Jesus drove two more cars up on stage and opened the driver's side doors. I asked Rusty to help me observe the seats more closely. He took a moment to examine the first one.

"A timid person molded this one," he said, "Probably a women judging by the size of the impression.

"How can you tell she is timid?" I asked.

"The reason I can tell she's timid is because there are no shoulder marks."

"And what might that imply?"

"She probably held her shoulders forward because she was insecure and perhaps had overpowering parents, or was neglected a lot as a child."

"Hey, that's my car," a frail young woman said, rising to her feet. "I grew up in an orphanage."

There was murmuring from the crowd.

"You see," I continued, "Our bodies seldom change positions when we are in our cars. Once we assume the usual position, so does our psyche, and because of our sleep, our minds fall comfortably back into the passive flow of associations. This thought leads to that thought, which leads to those thoughts, which leads to… 'did I ever put my laundry in the dryer?' Subsequently, we end up thinking the same kinds of thoughts, over and over again. Nowhere is this more obviously than when we are in our cars.

Here is another example: We drive down the expressway with the radio on, a song we loved from our youth starts to play. We turn the music up and sing along. The song reminds us of someone we used to know, someone who broke our heart. Memories flow and flow and before you know it, we are five miles past our off ramp." The crowd laughed.

"And so, what about this next seat, Rusty?"

He ran his hand across the surface of the faded brown leather. "A large man molded this seat. The wear marks are only in the places where his body weight fell."

"So what might that tell us?"

"He eats too much." The crowd chuckled, again.

"Is that all you can tell about this man," I asked.

Rusty looked closer at the seat, moving around it to be sure that he wasn't missing anything. "I don't sense anything else."

"Look at the position of the legs marks," I said. "While the left one appears normal the right one is turned in towards the center."

The audience grew quiet with anticipation.

After a sufficient dramatic pause, I continued. "He drove with his right leg slightly turned towards the left at the point of the upper thigh, but then the shin probably turned right as it approached the peddle. This would be due to a severe sciatic nerve problem in the right rear hip, and this leg position would give some relief to that area."

A man near the front of the stage slowly rose to his feet. "That's my car," he said, almost under his breath. "I've been fat for most of my life. I not only love to eat, but have had a sciatic nerve problem in my right leg since I was a teenager."

The crowd applauded, amazed.

"And so I remind you... the machine does not want you to change. The machine only wishes to force you back into complacency. If you learn to become free, who will feed it? How will it grow? The machine desires your sleep, your obedience. You must learn be free from this mechanical control in order to experience the highest level of being, 'Carvana', that state in which all things exist in the moment, in motion, without resistance."

"Tell us more about Carvana!" I heard from several locations in the crowd.

"In the state of Carvana a man can see what is real, feel what is love, and know what is truth. Though the rest of the world sleeps, we are as an observer, momentarily standing outside all that is happening within us and around us. Our escape, unnoticed by the mechanical forces of life, allows us to exist in the moment, with that which is higher. In a place where conflict is abolished and everything is connected. In the state of Carvana, one already *knows* what will happen next."

"I am a Catholic, and feel guilty about even being here," one woman said. "Will this teaching conflict with my current beliefs?"

"The Mode conflicts with nothing," I replied, "It is a unifying teaching that brings together all religious and philosophical ideas. A Jew may work beside a Christian, and a Muslim beside a Buddhist. This would not be possible in any other faith, but it *is* possible, because the Mode is not about the morality of right and wrong, or the sanctity of religious deity. It is about 'waking up' from the sleep that enslaves us all!

"If anything I have said has made sense to you, if you have ever felt that there is more to life than this mechanical roller coaster we are on. If you have ever wondered about the purpose of your existence or the meaning of life itself; then verily I say… the Mode is here for you." There were a few moments of excited chatter amongst the crowd.

"I would like to conclude today by telling you, we will be handing out flyers in a few minutes to a very important upcoming event. In a few weeks, we are doing a show at a very special place and you are all invited. This place is called Carhenge in Alliance, Nebraska, a tribute to the Stonehenge monument in England, only built out of automobiles. It is there at that shrine, that I will deliver my next sermon. I want to thank you all for coming today and we'll *'see you in Alliance'!"*

Hundreds of people stayed and gathered around the group as they handed out flyers, notifying them of the date and location of Carhenge.

The crowd was slowly dispersing and Bruno and Simon headed back to the diner to edit the latest video footage. They were passed on the way by a Fire Marshall and Police Officer who came to the side of the stage asking to speak to me. I introduced myself and asked how I could help them.

"Well," the Policeman voiced, very quiet, and hesitant, "We don't normally resort to anything outside police procedure in trying to solve cases, but I have heard some of the amazing things you can do. If my Sergeant knew I was here right now, he would probably take me off this case. We've been working on it a couple of weeks already and we aren't any further along then we were when we started. Having said all that, I didn't know where else to turn."

"What is it?" I asked, already aware of what troubled him by his handshake.

"We've been looking for a missing vehicle. We're told there is the body of a Bay Area mobster in the trunk and we haven't been able to find hide nor hair of it."

I thought for a moment whether I would be able to help them at all. "I don't really specialize in that sort of thing," I said, "But because you had the courage to come to me personally, even in the face of possible public ridicule, already shows a great trust and faith in me. Because of this, I will try to help you. Do you happen to have anything that belonged to this mobster?"

The officer reached into a brown lunch bag clutched in his left hand. "I have a few bolts we found in a garage where the car was stored… and a piece of leather upholstery from one of the seats. I'm sorry, it's not very much."

The crowds had not yet fully dispersed, and the media who were left packing up their equipment and wrapping up their local broadcasts, began to sense like Pavlovian dogs that something was about to happen.

It was still very noisy, as I tried to concentrate on the evidence they had brought me. I put the pieces of car parts in my hands and began to meditate. I was getting very strong impressions from them, impressions of deceit and violence. I walked around a bit to see if I received any other information. When I walked towards the street, I felt the energy in the bolts in my hand slow down, so I quickly turned around and began walking towards the bay. First left, then straight, then left again. I traveled through the bushes until my knees rested upon a small wall that separated me from the San Francisco Bay. Then I felt it.

"Directly in front of me," I said, "Less than fifty feet out there." I pointed to a spot just in front of the first pylon of the bridge.

I concentrated hard on the car and an image appeared to me. I started to focus with more intensity on the tires, moving my thoughts willfully down under the water. I forced the flow of energy from my thoughts to the car's tires, agitating the molecules faster and faster until they became hot and expanded the air within them, which had been purposely removed. I then concentrated on the car's cabin. It was completely filled with water. I again agitated the molecules until the cabin too began to be filled with air. In a few minutes, bubbles could be seen careening to the surface of the bay and ever so slowly the car began to rise.

Not only was everyone who was witnessing this captivated by what they were seeing, but I too was amazed that thoughts were lighter in water, easier to move and more powerful.

Finally, the car rose to the surface. The Fire Marshall ran to his truck and with sirens and lights flashing, pulled up to the wall. With the help of many spontaneously converted onlookers, a winch pulled the car to the shore. They pried open the trunk and there, a white bloated mobster, bound and gagged, with a bullet through his head, rolled out and onto the ground.

"He was right here the whole time?" The officer asked, shocked in disbelief. "You have a new devoted follower. Thank you, thank you so much, Mr. Pinker..."

"Motorishi," Marian interrupted. "His name is the 'Motorishi'."

Cameras went off all around us and when I saw the media about to rush us, we had to make our hasty retreat back to the bus. The press was not going to let a story like this go easily and we weren't planning on a public miracle, just yet. We would only have a few minutes as the media questioned the Police Officer and Fire Marshall on what had happened. I had just done something that would seem either miraculous or too unbelievable to be true. Either way, there would certainly be serious repercussions to follow.

We reached the diner and I yelled for everyone to get in the bus, startling Simon and Bruno who were busy editing the latest footage. After Shorty was pulled up the stairs, his feet floating slightly backward, I signaled everyone to hold on while Jesus got us going.

Slowly, we managed to make our way down the street. We were never going to lose the press with the diner in tow and I had to think of a way to escape them.

"Until now, M, all the amazing things you've done, call 'em miracles or whatever, have only happened in front of the group," Marian said. "Nobody but us saw the tornado thing, or the oil multiplying for Angela, or the molecular magic for the bus full of old people."

"Or the slot machine winnings," Sang Lee, said.

"Or your ability to read the minds of the casino patrons," Marian added. "But this mobster thing was public. The media is going be all over us. How can we lose them?"

"What," Bruno blurted! "Wait a minute. I didn't see any of that stuff… what mobster thing?" However, I wasn't listening.

"You've got an idea already, don't you?" Rusty said, smirking at me. "Well Bruno, I think you're about to see what you've been missing."

Bruno quickly pulled the camera up and hit record.

By that time, I was already sitting with my eyes closed, focusing intently on the air molecules around the bus. I began to infuse them with moisture from the bay and agitated the oxygen molecules enough to raise their temperature a few degrees. In just a few seconds, the streets behind us became covered in a thick grey haze.

"Now that's more like it," Marian said, as the herd of paparazzi began to lose our trail, "That shouldn't surprise them at all. Fog in this city is something they expect!"

"This town *is* always foggy," Bruno replied. "You don't expect me to believe you just did that, do you? You know what, I don't even care. All I want to know is what the hell happened back there at Golden Gate Park?"

"M was asked by some local officials to help find a missing vehicle, and he did." Marian explained. "Turned out, there was a mobster in the moat."

"So much for slow and careful media growth," Bruno complained. "I want that footage. Damn, you know what that can do for us?"

"You don't have to worry about that, Bruno," Simon said, "It will be all over the news in a few minutes. When we get to Ice's, we can tape it off the local broadcasts."

A few minutes later, safely within Ice's compound, we turned on the radio and television to assess the damage and plan control.

"This is a breaking story…" the announcer said. "Motor Guru Solves Missing Mobster Mystery at the Golden Gate."

"Here we go, Jefe," Jesus said.

The news reported continued, "Giavonni Bossinni, an Italian mob boss, missing since last Thursday, was discovered today in the trunk of a car, dumped in the San Francisco Bay. Officials tell us that Officer Charles Morgan, who had been unsuccessfully attempting to locate the missing vehicle for several weeks, had asked Dewey Pinkerton, the self proclaimed Mechanical Messiah to assist him on the case. The Motorishi, as his followers call him, was said to identify the exact location of the missing mobster, and the car whose trunk he had been dumped in, by using only a few bits of evidence. Eyewitnesses claim that by holding a few bolts in his hand he led investigators to the edge of Golden Gate Park.

"However, the most amazing part of this story isn't that he found the car, or the mobster, but that he somehow made the car rise from the bottom of the bay to the surface of the water by meditating and speaking a lot of mystic mumbo jumbo."

"Errrr… not again," I thought to myself.

"Stay tuned and we will keep you up to date as details become available," the announcer concluded.

"It doesn't get any better than that unless you're a two headed baby who's found the cure for cancer in Twinkies! That should put us on the map," Shorty said.

"That wasn't so bad," Bruno added, "At least we didn't end up in the 'whacky' news spot. We'll have to see how it all plays out. One thing's for sure, we'll need to prep for a public statement. There's gonna be a wall of reporters knocking down the door tomorrow when they figure out where we are."

We worked late into the night trying to find ways to maximize the effects of the media wave that was sure to follow in the morning, just several hours away.

Dawn came and the first unusual thing I noticed wasn't that everyone was awake at the same time, but that everyone was smiling. Sleeping little without regret had made its way into the very fiber of the group, and there was a sense of urgency in the air now that things were moving at such an accelerated rate.

Busy with the work of a company on the rise, we decided it would be best to split into smaller groups over the next few days. Simon, Bruno, and I, would handle the press about the mobster incident while the rest of the group focused on promotion tasks. We had less than a week to prepare for the next leg of our journey and there was still much to be done. Promotion packages still needed to be sent out, flyers mailed, local radio and press junkets done, all to insure the largest audience yet at the Carhenge event.

Bruno had arranged for us to meet the local press for an interview later that morning, but one young female reporter had already tracked us down and was waiting in front of Ice's compound gates.

"I can get rid of her, M," Rocco said, trying to cover me so the reporter couldn't get a good look.

"It's OK, Rocco, I will talk to her." I walked down the long stone driveway and met her at the gate. "So, you found me, very good. I was wondering where you've been."

She turned and looked around her, as if I were talking to someone else. "Me?" she asked, cautiously. As I would find out later, she was new to reporting, a journalist just out of the local city college, working freelance to try to earn a position on the San Francisco Chronicle.

"Yes, you," I replied. "You were the one standing to the left of me yesterday, at the edge of the bay.

"And you remember that? With all that was going on?"

"Of course. You were wearing a white blouse and had green earrings on."

"That's amazing," she replied, smiling. "I took a chance and came here because I am a big fan of Ice's. He's been talking you up pretty good since he met you in L.A."

"Do you know Ice?"

"Not personally. I attend all his shows, when I'm not studying, of course. Listen, do you mind if I ask you a few questions? This is my first scoop."

"Well, then let's make it a good one. Rocco," I called up the driveway. "Open the gates."

"Please, come in and ask me whatever you want." We made our way to the foyer and into Ice's library.

"Wow, look at all these books," she said, running her fingers along the titles as she walked. "Shakespeare, Plato, Thoreau, Dickens… and Twain; he's one of my favorites. *'Always do the right thing. It will gratify some people and astonish the rest'*. I never knew Ice was so well read. There are many things I don't know… like how you found the missing mobster yesterday." She stopped, and smiled. "How did you find him?"

"He was never lost," I said.

"What?" she asked puzzled.

"Sometimes, we cannot find things because we forget where we put them, but what we cannot find is not lost. I will give you an example. You come home after a long day of work and open your front door, the phone rings and you enter the kitchen to answer it. Your keys, which are in your left hand, are usually dropped at the foyer, but because the phone rang, you have carried them into another room. When you answered the phone, you set them down next to the receiver. Later that day, you get ready to leave and running your hand along the edge of the table in the entryway, you notice the keys are not there. You are sure you put them there, you always put them there."

"I have done that a million times," she laughed.

"The point is… are the keys lost? No, your attention was on something else when you set them down."

"Wow, I never thought of that before. Nevertheless, what does that have to do with finding the mobster? He didn't put himself there."

"No, but someone else did. I simply traced the vibrations of matter from a few bolts that belonged to the car and they led me to the place of their origin."

"What about raising the car from the bottom of the bay? I have never seen anything like that before."

"Using the same principles, I agitated the air molecules within the tires and car cabin until there was sufficient buoyancy."

"You make it sound easy," she said, snapping a picture of me. "I suppose next you'll be telling me anyone can learn it!"

"Well, I have had many years of practice… and a few good teachers. Would you like to hear about them?" I asked.

"I would be honored," she said sitting down next to me. "Thank you for seeing me. I wouldn't have stood a chance against all the other reporters in this town. You have done me a great favor."

"You are here because you followed the trail of vibrations. Use this gift in everything you do. You said it yourself, '*Do the right thing. It will gratify some people and astonish the rest*'."

We talked for over an hour and by the time she left, she had a story that would change her life. We spent much of the rest of the day meeting with the press, but we'd given her the story first, and were much briefer when speaking to the national affiliates.

When the last of the camera crews left the diner, we gathered to discuss the interviews.

"I still can't believe it," Bruno said, smiling, "NBC, CBS, ABC, all the local papers… Now we'll have the legitimacy I was hoping for. We are gonna be huge!"

"I want the sermon in Alliance to be special, Bruno," I said. "I want it to be pure, and as much about the teaching as possible. National exposure like *60 Minutes* is bound to draw a wave of whackos as well as legitimate followers. There will be plenty of media attention on this one. We need to make sure the Mode is the message people leave with."

CHAPTER XXV

Planet Alliance

Having finished tying up the many loose ends that always seem to accompany being in one place for too long, we finally pulled the bus back out onto Highway 80 that would take us eastward towards Alliance, Nebraska. The morning was hot and we were hoping we wouldn't find ourselves in a heat wave over the next week as we traveled through the Pacific Midwest.

We drove through Reno, Nevada, before heading east on Highway 80 through west Utah and up to Salt Lake. We thought the Mormon capital of the world would be a good place to spend a few days lecturing, preparing, and promoting the upcoming event. The "Sermon on the Mound" as we now called it, was only two weeks away, and would coincide with the five-planet alignment of Saturn, Uranus, and the Moon, squared off by Mars and opposed by Mercury.

We arrived in Salt Lake by mid-morning. I will have to say and I think everybody there would agree that it would have been better if this great lake did not have so much salt in it. Not only has it become its chief feature, giving it its name, but also the physical results of all this salt itself when the lake is not completely full of water is something quite un-attractive. Never mind this small oversight in God's otherwise blemishless perfection, because those that call themselves Mormons are more than compensated for it by the greatest law to ever have accidentally been given to man and sanctioned by God himself! That is, "the ability of a man to have more than one wife".

Spending the next few days in Salt Lake was good for the group. It gave us time to prepare some of the staging platforms that we would use at the "Mound." Rusty and Buzz were able to weld enough pieces of stage together that it only needed to be assembled at the center to be fully functional. Marian, Sang Lee, and Buzz kicked in by preparing signs and getting the word out on the show.

A week and a half later we set off from Salt Lake and traveled east on Highway 80 through the southern part of Wyoming. I think this state was originally named "Oming" and when people would come there, they would question the oddity of the name and ask "Why Oming?" Then it must have stuck and they eventually called it "Wyoming," but I'm only guessing.

As we headed east to our next destination, the sleepy little town of Alliance, everyone noticed at some point or another that there seemed to be an increasingly enormous traffic problem developing on Highway 80.

"Perhaps we should listen to the radio for an accident report or other warning," Sang Lee asked. "Why else at this time of year, in this remote a place, would there be so many vehicles on the road?"

The funny part was, almost everyone who passed us, without fail, smiled and cheered as they went by. Anyway, it seemed that perhaps Mount Rushmore was having a special event and we had just missed the announcement. It wasn't very much later that Bruno drew the conclusion that these motorists were indeed coming to the Sermon on the Mound and not some further destination as we had imagined.

By the time we turned from Highway 80 north to the 385, we were in a sea of cars that were to become the earliest arrivers to the event. These people would have to camp out another three days before the show, and the line behind us was approaching twenty miles of attendees.

The day before the show, our camp was surrounded by cars as far as the eye could see, and many people who had already been there for a few days helped us to set up the stage and other equipment necessary to produce our little miracle in the field. Carhenge itself is a pretty interesting place. It seems so bizarre to see cars arranged in unnatural positions yet somehow the totality of the whole thing did not seem out of place in the flat open fields of Nebraska.

I did not sleep much that night, and it had been quite a while since I needed to. However, tonight was the eve of something special, a pivotal moment for the teaching and I wished that my mother, father, and even Johann could be there to witness it.

CHAPTER XXVI

The Sermon on the Mound

This was it, Carhenge, in Alliance Nebraska, the big show. Since the public incident in San Francisco with the mobster and the subsequent media attention that followed, momentum had begun to carry us along quite nicely. We were drawing the attention of many types of people now: some followers, some curious onlookers, and a variety of journalist and press agencies.

I wanted this sermon to be something special, something more than just another public spectacle. I wanted our new followers to experience a unique ritual, which would solidify their faith and foster their alliance. I wanted this event to be an initiation so transforming that afterwards the Mode would spread like wildfire by the Motees themselves. I wanted for one short night, for them to experience a little miracle in the open fields of Western Nebraska.

Rusty and Buzz assembled the stage they had created in Salt Lake that formed an artificial mound in the center of Carhenge, tall enough for those near the back to see. Marian and Sang Lee worked on wardrobes, while the rest directed traffic and solicited volunteers from the thousands of early arrivers to help with the public seating logistics.

Cars surrounded our camp with just less than twenty-four hours to go before the show. Many people who had already been there for a few days helped us finish setting up the stage and other necessary equipment. Dozens of portable restrooms were delivered and car seats were brought in from three local county junkyards. We arranged the seats in rows, creating colorful pews that radiated outward like spokes from the center stage. It was obvious that there was not going to be enough seating for everyone.

As the horizon rose to meet the sun that night, fires burned in small handmade pits and people played music and sang songs in anticipation of the big event. When all our work was completed, we gathered around a fire, staring up at the stars, as we had so many times before, when I noticed that Marian looked troubled.

"What's on your mind, Marian?" I asked.

"Nothing. Why?"

"When a woman replies 'nothing' with a face that says everything, you can be sure that it's something!" I said. Everyone laughed.

"Then why do I have to tell you? You could just read my mind, right?"

"Do you want me to read your mind, Marian?"

"No, I don't! Not right now anyway. I'm OK… really. Let's talk about it later."

"I'll read her mind," Shorty blurted, putting his hands to his temples and closing his eyes. "You gotta problem with the lunch menu tomorrow, huh?"

"Of course not," she blasted, "It's not that at all."

Rocco, who sensed the true nature of her dilemma, steered the conversation in another direction. "Look, you knuckleheads, tomorrow is a big day for all of us; let's not ruin it with petty bickering. We should be discussing details, like crowd control and public safety."

"What's to discuss?" Shorty said, "There's already so many people here, there's no way we will be able to control anything. "

"Let's just hope nothing gets out of hand," Rusty added.

"We have to be careful that nothing bad happens," I warned, "or the Mode will be tarnished before it has a chance to really shine."

Later that night after everyone else was sleeping, Marian came and sat down next to me while I read over the sermon one last time. Her face had not changed much since earlier that day and I could tell there was something she wanted to get off her chest.

"Dewey," she said, softly, "I need to tell you something. I'm sure ya've already read my thoughts and are secretly laughing at me."

"No, I haven't, not this time. I can tell you needed to work something out and I wanted to give you the privacy to do that on your own."

"Well, that's pretty good mind readin' already. I've tried to ignore it, but somehow it always ends up finding its way back into my thoughts."

"What is it?"

"I can't tell you... That's not what I mean. I mean... I don't know how to tell you."

"Marian, when I first met you, you spilled water on my lap and didn't even say you were sorry. Now I generally expect the normal reaction to mechanical life, an 'excuse me', when we bump someone, a 'bless you' when someone sneezes, or a 'sorry' when someone spills something on you. But you didn't do that."

"You know why?" she asked, with a smirk on her face "It wasn't an accident. I did it on purpose. I didn't even think about it first; something just made me do it to you. You stood out in that room like no one I had ever seen before. I didn't even know you, but I trusted you right away. I couldn't have helped myself if I wanted to."

"That's what I mean," I replied. "If you had just said you were sorry, like every other mechanical reaction in life we have all become accustomed to, then that moment may have passed us by. You created a pause in the flow of associations that caused me to look at you, to be drawn to you, to see you. You stirred up feelings in me I had put aside for many years in order to fulfill the needs of this teaching. I knew you were special."

"But I am not worthy of being special. I am nowhere near the level of understanding that Rusty is. I'm not a good match for you."

"Are you suggesting I should be romantically interested in Rusty?" I asked. She laughed, releasing some pent up energy. "Maybe you are a match, someone who counterbalances my type."

"I know I believe in you. I listen to your stories and the teaching of the Mode. I watch the way people respond to you. I try to help you with the sermons and such, but I never feel like it's enough to pay you back for what you have given me."

"You don't owe me anything," I replied.

"What I'm saying, Dewey is… I think I'm falling in love with you… no, I know I am. I'm just not sure it's the best thing for you right now. The line of teacher is blurring for me. I won't be able to separate wanting to be with you from the teaching."

"For now, that's not a problem. Don't worry about it, things will work out fine. In this moment, I am the teaching, but later on, the Mode will take on a life of its own. I will no longer be important to it."

"Don't say that!" she scolded, "You will always be important to it. You are the one who found it. You will always be remembered for bringing it to the world."

"I am the road the Mode has followed. I am insignificant in the overall picture. It is not the teachers, but the teaching of truth that matters. Don't worry about it anymore tonight, Marian. You should try to get some sleep. You can stay here under the stars with me if you want, I would like that."

"Thanks, Dewey… I mean, M. You've made my troubles vanish, just like you always do."

"'Dewey' is fine. Now get some rest, Mare."

She laid her soft brown hair across my arm and snuggled her head up under my shoulder. I looked up at the stars and asked the angels for guidance once more before finally shutting my eyes. *"It's time,"* I heard Mac saying in my thoughts, *"It's time to give it everything, no matter what the cost."*

The next morning we gathered in the diner to go over the last minute details of the day's events. Cars lined every road and parking lot for miles and even the Alliance authorities had to call other local cities to send over additional fire and police forces to help with crowd control. Rocco's tattoos and muscle-t clashed with the authority's uniforms in both color and design, but nevertheless, they worked together on public safety. Rusty, Buzz, and Shorty prepared fresh oil for baptizing, and Sang Lee and Marian pressed white robes with gear symbols that the others and I would wear.

By noon, the crowds had almost doubled again. I had been laying hands on cars of believers all day when my attention was drawn to the stage by Rocco and a few Fire Marshals. They were worried that if this day was as hot as the day before, there may not being enough water to keep everyone hydrated.

I asked Marian how much water we still had. She went to trailer, came back, and announced we had seven five-gallon bottles and about twelve cases of bottled water.

The heat had already climbed to ninety-five degrees and I could see that people were becoming uncomfortable. Rocco and his team, who had done their best to act as parking attendants for those who arrived after us, were unable to do anything about the thousands of cars that arrived before us. This caused sections of the population to be car-locked until the event was over. Because of this and other safety concerns, the fire department requested that we immediately begin passing out the water we had until more could be brought in.

We formed a line, each of us about six feet apart, and with the help of many others began to pass the water down the line to the front of the stage.

"This is going to be useless," Shorty snorted. "It's like giving a pig a bath in a cup of water. We're never going to have enough."

"Have you still so little faith, Shorty?" I asked.

"It's just not possible," he retorted.

We each started passing water out like a fire drill to the people closest to us, and asked them to pass them back. From the stage, you could see the hands of the people in front turning and passing back the bottles like a great, choreographed movement. When all the of water was passed out, we stood to watch when we would see the last of the bottles handed back and at what point the crowd would not have any to pass along. We watched for over thirty minutes but never saw the point at which the water ran out.

Everyone was amazed and could not stop talking about it for the next few hours. Bruno, who filmed the distribution, was still a bit perplexed.

"So what do you think now?" Marian asked him, knowing he could not possibly deny what had just happened.

"What, that?" he replied, "That was pretty cool, but it's like the fog thing; I never really saw anything happen! I'll have to watch the footage in slow motion and I'll get back to ya later."

As the time drew nearer, television helicopters started buzzing overhead, each looking for some footage for the evening news. Ice would play for an hour, warming up the crowd with his mix of rap, hip-hop and esoteric lyrics. I would follow with the sermon, and then a pivotal moment in the evening where I would baptize the crowd with the oil of Carvana.

There was the sound of people cheering everywhere as Ice stepped onto the darkened stage. Hundreds of fires could be seen in small pits and the smoke trails filled the starry sky. Suddenly, the lights started to pulse and the crowd rose to its feet with a thunderous roar. A loud heavy bass guitar and kick drum pounded out a one-hundred-forty beats per minute dance mix beat as everyone started to move in a rhythmic wave.

Fifty-five minutes later the music reached a fevered pitch and the stage grew dark and silent. The crowd roared for several more minutes, and as I approached the mound, everyone rose once again to their feet and cheered my name. "Motorishi, Motorishi, Motorishi."

I gestured for the crowd to sit and settle down before speaking a word.

"Thank You! Thank you all for coming. Let those who have heard the call of the Mode rejoice, for the Mode is at hand!" Amen and cheers rang out from everywhere. "It has been a long journey that has led me here. However, it is by no mistake that I am here. Just as it is no mistake that you are here.

"'Where does your awareness stop?' a wise man once asked me. Today that is what I am asking you. You may have many useless facts in your head. You may read many books and boast that you are very smart; but you may not be aware of anything! You may not know that you are impatient, or ignorant, or arrogant, or any other word that ends in 'nt'. You may think you have all the answers, until you are asked this question: Where does your awareness stop? Does it stop when you are asleep, or when you are sitting at your desk at work? Does it stop when you daydream or desire something with lust in your heart? The problem is we believe we are aware all of the time, which could not be further from the truth.

"Perhaps it is best to talk about a time in which awareness cannot be present. Awareness does not exist when we are angry, or selfish, ignorant or bored. It is not possible to forget something, or misplace something when awareness is present. So why is it that we believe we are aware just because we are not sleeping? You'll notice I did not say 'when we are awake', because to be awake is something entirely different from the state of non-sleep. Do not lose faith, for the answer is near.

The answer is in the Mode and the mechanics of nature. Your machines will show you the Mode. Your car will show you the Mode. Learn from them because they are the mirror of who you *really* are.

"How many of you replace your brakes before the recommended time?"

A loud roar and show of hands ensued.

"You are the impatient ones. How many of you drive so slow and careful you don't have even one scratch on your car?"

Another roar from the crowd and a show of hands ensued.

"You are the cautious ones and miss much of the passion of life. How many of you haven't read your car's manual?"

Almost everyone raised their hands.

"You drive a chariot of the Gods; but know it only as a horse cart!" The crowd went crazy and the roar was so loud it was almost deafening.

"Can you give us an example of mechanical abuse?" someone yelled, from the crowd.

"I have just given you three and yet you do not see. Here, I will answer your question, yet again."

"Never run your machine out of its primary energy source. If it's a car we are speaking about, never run it out of gas, oil, or water. If it's a man, we are speaking of, then it's food, air and impressions. Running out of a primary energy source shows a lack of foresight, and lack of foresight leads to damage to the machine. People who wait until the last minute for everything are constantly damaging their machines."

"What is the essential purpose of a machine?" yelled someone else.

"In its most basic form, a machine is nothing more than a clever lever. All machines are attempts to make something bigger or heavier move with the least amount of effort. In this respect, an ant is a very effective machine. He is capable of moving up to fifty times his own weight. The reason that ants can lift so much is because their body size increases as a cube of their length, while the cross sectional area of muscles increases as the square of their length."

"I don't understand," said an elderly man, "Cars are much heavier than the load they carry,"

"This is true," I said. "But surely a car can carry enough gas to take not only the weight of itself, but the weight of its cargo for hundreds of miles without stopping. The distance traveled, say four-hundred miles divided by the total weight of the vehicle, say, twenty-five-hundred pounds is equal to about six and a quarter pounds per mile; extremely efficient. A man would be lucky to carry his own body weight plus six pounds for ten miles without a need to rest."

"Tell us more, for I am a sinner against the machine," someone yelled.

"Yes, tell us what we must do to wake up!" shouted another.

"Every motor has its Mantra… and we can learn to hear it. The next time you are sitting in your car, try to be relaxed and at the very center of the vehicle… not physically, but with your awareness. Wait before you start the engine, and absorb all that is around you. Next, start the car, put it into reverse, and back out of your driveway or garage. Make sure you come to a complete stop before shifting into drive. Accelerate slowly. Let you and the car find a balance; tire against road, foot against pedal, hand against wheel, a proper speed for its weight and form. When all these things are in order, both the car and driver have reached Carvana; that is, the moment in which a car can perform the best with the least amount of effort, and the driver is aware and in harmony with his surroundings. All systems are running at an optimum performance level, including the driver. A car in this state can last forever; a man in this state will never die.

"To keep a car in this state of bliss is a difficult task at best. To keep a man in this state is much harder still. However, to obtain this state consistently requires harmony between what happens to us on the outside and how we react to it on the inside! We are the 'x' factor that is always changing. We are the ones always moving the target.

"One day we are pleased with the sights and smells of spring and drive quite slowly, sunroof open, and are patient as a homeless man hobbles across the street. The next day we are cut off, and pound the steering wheel and floor the accelerator with a feverish craze in our eyes, cursing and wishing hideous plagues upon our assailants! Anger can never heal anything, and this behavior brings breakdown to the machine. Only a car, and a man in the state of Carvana, is truly whole, healthy, and safe.

"Look to your actions and recognize them as re-actions. See that being awake is different from not being asleep. Let your mind ponder the existence of something higher than itself. Search for truth that will help change you, for we are broken machines in need of many repairs. Though we cannot always be true to the laws of Universal Mechanics, we must strive to achieve what we can. Highways cannot be built in a day. Have faith and be patient, and listen when you can to what you car has to say, and remember to *be* your car's Mantra and thus experience Carvana."

The crowd began to rush the stage, and for a moment I was concerned for everyone's safety.

"Tell us, what are the rules that we should live by, so that we too may be in harmony with the universe?" they cried, dropping to their knees and clasping their hands together.

Ice began to play, while Rocco and Shorty guided people into single file lines, where Rusty and I began anointing them with oil.

"Come, come, everyone, and speak of your automotive sins as I anoint you with oil and tell you what you must do." I continued with the eight automotive beatitudes:

Blessed are those who wait at the red light,
For they shall develop patience.

Blessed are those who use the right tools,
For they shall have no scars on their knuckles.

Blessed are those who perform regular tune-ups,
For they shall inherit no breakdowns.

Blessed are the junkyards,
For they giveth us spare parts.

Blessed are the car washes,
For they giveth cleanliness.

Blessed is the purest oil,
For it is the blood of Carvana.

Blessed are the mechanics,
For they shall be called the Sons of Chilton.

Blessed are those persecuted for owning an old Clunker,
For the kingdom of renewal awaits them.

Night had turned to early morning by the time the last of the crowds had made their way to the front of the stage for their anointment and penance. Fires were burned out and so was everyone else. Things were winding down. The police and fire departments again helped in getting the crowds on their way. I sat still for a long time staring into the fire as the last of the ashes rose to meet the cool morning sky. The sermon was a huge success. Estimates were that over ten thousand people attended. I had a feeling of calm come over me, even though I was quite drained, both physically and emotionally. I watched the group move slowly, with purpose and intent, as they began to gather around me. They were all riding on a cosmic high that had elevated them to a level they had never experienced before. If I didn't know any better, I would say that their feet weren't even touching the ground.

CHAPTER XXVII

Rally Alley

The drive east on Highway 90 out of the Black Hills of South Dakota was one of the prettiest parts of the country we had seen, and the long curving road leaving the mountains was lined with pine trees whose protected meadows bore the fruits of the most wonderful types of flowers and wildlife.

We headed east and soon it became more and more obvious that Rocco was getting exited about our next stop, Sturgis, South Dakota. He would repeatedly run way ahead of us then circle back to our rear, pop wheelies and weave wildly across the road. This was not Rocco's normal behavior.

Yearly in August, riders from all over the globe come to this tiny little town in the lower plains of this most noble state to revel in the splendor and the wonder that has become the Sturgis Ride, where Harley Davidson motorcycles reign supreme as the center of everyone's attention. Rocco had attended Sturgis rides in years past, but had missed some of the most recent ones, and he was due. I was happy he would finally get the chance to be in his element, hanging with those of his kind.

Sturgis is a place most bikers, especially Harley riders, hold as one of the required sacred yearly pilgrimages if you call yourself a "rider," but unlike the pilgrimages of Muslims to the city of Mecca or the Jews to Jerusalem, bikers make this journey almost every year and not just once or twice in a lifetime.

We were within fifty miles of Sturgis when we started to be flanked on both sides of the bus, as well as the front and rear, by motorcycle riders. Nothing else sounds like a Harley and every minute brought more and more riders until the procession reached a thunderous roar that could be heard for miles and miles. While some were riders who had attended the Carhenge event, others were riders who must have heard of us through the news and had come from many other parts of the country. I saw homemade versions of Sang Lee's symbol of the gear repeated on motorcycle jackets, saddlebags, and bandannas.

Bruno and Simon were busy riding back and forth in the sidecars of a few of Rocco's friends, filming the grand arrival from all sides. A news helicopter flew back and forth above us for a while, and as we entered town the local police cycles joined in, helping to keep the caravan moving through suburban neighborhood traffic stops.

We finally pulled into town to a crowd of thousands, whose cheers and whistles made Rocco smile from ear to ear, because even though he had many biker friends, he had suddenly become somewhat of a folk hero amongst his fellow riders.

There was no mistaking his bike in the crowd since it was painted like the bus; bright yellow with orange and red flames that made it stand out even amongst some of the most unique and creative paintjobs we had ever seen.

We noticed three things immediately as we drove down the streets, besides the motorcycles of course, which were throttle to throttle for as far as the eye could see. The first was half-dressed or, depending on how you looked at it, half-naked women. Second only to having a hotter "hog" than everyone else was having a hotter "babe" than everyone else and there was more pink showing that day then at a swine convention. The other two things were tattoos and leather! Leather accessories were sold everywhere, from saddlebags to sandals, and just in case there was one small area of your body not already covered by your favorite symbol or a master work of art, there were tattoo parlors every fifteen steps, insuring no matter what shape you were in you could stumble in for a rest on a pincushion.

Pulling into downtown Sturgis, were waved into a section on the main drag specifically set up for our arrival. On our way here, Bruno and Ice had made some phone calls to the Sturgis sponsors, and because of their efforts, we were greeted with the finest hospitality this town had to offer, beginning from the moment the wheels of the bus came to rest.

We spent the day visiting the local landmarks and hanging out in some of the biker bars. It was great to hear so much about the love and devotion most of these bikers have for the rides. Besides Sturgis, two other big rallies happen throughout the year: the Daytona and the Laconia. Those three make up the big ones, the ones that are fifty years old or older. Then there are the tours. They don't happen on a specific date but are pilgrimages that you can make any time during the year, like Four Corners or Three Flags. These events have been around ten to twenty years. The only requirement is that you have three weeks, start to finish, in order to get your status for completing the event. Three Flags is a touring rally that is limited to about three hundred people a year. The world's toughest riders are the "Iron Butt Riders", but again, they have to complete several other "thousand miles in twenty-four hours" days to help qualify for the Iron Butt Rally that is held every other year.

Later in the evening, some of the gang went out to sample the nightlife, while Marian, Simon, Mathew, Buzz and Rusty and I all stayed with the bus to catch up on chores, sleep and all of the little things that you want to do after having been on the road for a few days.

Ice found a bar with a dance floor and dragged the group in to see them get their moves on. Rocco watched Shorty, Jesus and Trace taking turns dancing with Sang Lee and Ice and Bruno dancing with some other adventurous women who had also taken the floor. An older biker that Rocco knew from previous rides and wild times came and stood next to him, also watching the dancers.

"So how did these losers end up on your new gravy train?"

Rocco turned to look at the guy, astonished. "Who, these guys?"

"Yeah, man, two blacks, a hippie, a wetback, an oriental, and the short feeb. It sounds like the setup for a joke, or the attractions at a circus sideshow."

"Hey, man, these are all good people."

"Oh, come on, I've hung around with you some. You hate hippies, you're no friend to the blacks or Muslims, you laugh at wetbacks and freaks, and you spent a fair amount of time trying to kill all the *Charlies* you could. You can't tell me that hanging with this Motorishi dude has changed you that much."

Rocco stood silent as the accusation rolled around in his mind. It was true; he had a whole set of patterned responses that got triggered by the mention of a particular racial type, but he somehow always got past that when he was dealing with the group. M had put him in direct contact with the people he was most likely to have issues with, and there had been issues. There still were, but Rocco felt like that was all behind him. His issues used to be like, "Hey, you're a Mexican." Now they were more like, "Hey, you ate all the cheese doodles." All of a sudden, he could feel the gulf between him and the biker in front of him. This guy was still reacting to the machine, the mechanical forces that acted within him without his recognition. M had pushed Rocco well beyond that state, and Rocco hadn't really noticed it until now. He also realized how dangerous this guy's ignorance was.

He looked around the room and took in all the immediate details of the scene. He felt like he could hear Marian's alarm bells ringing. Although bikers were a diverse lot these days, there wasn't a non-white face visible in the room, with the glaring exception of those in the group. Most of the bikers in this crowd were older, and Rocco didn't think that he would find many dentists, lawyers, or software designers amongst them.

Rocco made a threat assessment, noted the available paths of egress, and settled on an extraction plan. He excused himself to the biker and began walking onto the dance floor to gather up his friends. Just before Rocco got there, another tough looking biker stepped up to Ice, who was dancing enthusiastically with one of the women, and said, "Hey man, she's with me, so beat it." Ice turned to face him, his intent visible in his eyes, and Rocco moved in just in time to place himself between Ice and this lunatic.

"Sorry, man. We didn't know," Rocco said, "She didn't tell us."

"Hey, you're Rocco Scarbino!" Rocco nodded. "And this guy's with you?" Rocco nodded again. "Well then I won't kick his ass, just get him outta here. Is he a friend of yours? You got sub-humans as friends?"

Rocco held Ice back from leaping at the guy. "Yeah, he's a friend; one of the best. But I can take a hint, so we'll be hittin' the road now." He turned and looked around at the rest of the group who had gathered around, taking a quick headcount. "Let's go, Ice. We'll find a bar with good music."

Outside, Ice confronted Rocco. "Hey man, what was that about? I had the dude cold. I can stand up for myself."

"Look, Ice. You just didn't realize the size of the problem." Rocco explained, "It wasn't just *that* guy that hated you, it was everyone in the bar except us. They hated all of you guys. Those were classic, piece-carrying racists and once you got started with one of them, well, the rest would have just had to join in, and everyone in the group would have become a target. While I coulda saved one or two of you in that situation, I probably woulda lost one or two as well. My way, we all get out uninjured." He paused, and then stood up straight. "Protection… it's my job!"

Ice looked at Rocco with a dawning respect. "Straight up, my man. Good move on yo' vet ass."

That night, as was always the case at this event, there was to be a concert by one of the legendary biker bands. I was given the honor of introducing the band and was made the ceremonial "Hog Meister" for the evening.

I was led up onstage by Rocco who surprised me with this introduction, "Most of you don't know that I first met the Motorishi in a dark, stinky, nothing of a bar called The Devil's Elbow Saloon in Western Missouri. I shared shots with this man and, at first, I thought the feds had sent him to spy on me. You know, to see if I was still taken my meds and holding down a steady job... I wasn't of course!" He paused for the crowd laughter to fade a bit. "I later found out he was smart, and funny, and sympathetic, and not *too* much of a weenie!"

The crowd laughed.

"My first impression of him was completely opposite from the truth. It took time to see it. And just when I realized that I'd found a truly good human, he was hassled by one of the few mean-spirited bikers left in this world."

The crowed booed, enthusiastically.

"His famous words to this thug are forever etched in my mind and heart and I would like to share them with you now. When asked if he had ever ridden a hog, he replied, 'I don't have to ride one to know when I've seen one!'"

Everyone laughed and cheered Rocco on. "I had some time to think about his remark. It wasn't until the bikers in the bar had kicked his ass into the street and we were riding out of town that I finally replied... 'I would rather be one, than to have never ridden one!'" The crowd erupted in cheers.

"I think today he may not feel the same way about it. Let's ask him. Fellow Hogs, I give you... the Motorishi!" I could barely hear over the cheers as I addressed the leather-clad assembly.

"Thanks for that, Rocco. Yes, there was a time when I slipped up and spouted off something that I would later truly regret. Never before have I met a more loyal friend than Rocco, and I know that that remark, while not aimed at him, still cut.

So I have this to add to my now infamous and often regrettable line; 'it takes one to know one, and once you've known one like Rocco, you never go back'!"

The crowd chanted Rocco's name and I had never seen him more proud than he was at that moment. Nevertheless, I could see that there was something else still on his mind. I stepped back, and he returned to the microphone.

"And let me tell you something else. There are a lot of bikers who would still kick the Motorishi's ass if he said that today." The crowd booed again. "As a matter of fact, I met some like that this afternoon, right here in Sturgis." The crowd booed, even louder. Rocco was staring right at the two thugs he'd run into in the bar.

"Those bikers I ran into today reminded me of me… back when I was a stupid. The Mode changed all that. The day of the stupid biker is over. Those kinda folks are gonna find out the hard way that they're on the wrong side of the tracks."

The crowd cheered wildly. Rocco brought out all of the rest of the group onstage and made a point of touching each one as he did, a hug, a handshake, a pat on the elbow. He returned to the microphone.

"These folks here," he said, pointing at us. "When I look at them now, I don't see color, I see friends. Motees, you might call us. Treat us well, and reap the rewards. Give us grief and you'll have to answer to me. I may know something about the Mode, but that doesn't make me a weenie. I still know how to kick a little ass!"

The crowd went wild and Rocco took a place with the rest of the group. I stepped up to the microphone. "And now, ladies and gentlemen, babes and hogs, Motees and Methodists, I give you… The Doobie Brothers." With that, we were escorted off the stage.

Three days later, we finally set the wheels of the bus back in motion and left Sturgis to the cheers of thousands of our newest friends. An entourage of several hundred bikes led us out of town. Most of the folks leaving with us lived in the northeastern part of the country and we were honored that they would escort us back to Detroit.

CHAPTER XXVIII

Detroit Madness

"Mode Messiah's Message to the World," newspapers across the country were printing. By the time we were within fifty miles of Detroit, journalist and news agencies' helicopters and trucks were surrounding us on nearly every side. Bruno, Simon, Ice and Mathew were addressing a demanding press, while the rest of us discussed the business of Motor Science. The message in the media's eyes was that this new, actually, very old, way of looking at ourselves and the world was changing the very fabric of society. Using our machines as a metaphor for our mechanical reactionary behavior to the world had caught on. People were becoming more interested in waking up.

We arrived in Detroit just before horizon-rise and by the looks of things, would not see downtime anytime soon. Interviews went late into the night and by one in the morning, we all needed to get some sleep. We set up camp at a hotel downtown and settled in for a night's rest.

The following morning, we received a call from the news program 60 Minutes, asking me if I would do an interview. Though we were prepared to meet them at a local NBC affiliate, they insisted they fly in to meet with us in the diner, to bring home our image as a grass roots movement with a fresh new message. The interview went like this:

> **60 Minutes:** As a self-proclaimed mechanical Messiah, you've been making quite a stir in the media lately. What would you like people to know about you?
>
> **Motorishi:** I am a humble man and do not proclaim divinity. Others, who have seen my work, have given me this title. I preach an ancient teaching, perhaps as old as religion itself called the Mode. That I have been chosen to deliver it to the world is beyond my will.
>
> **60 Minutes:** Where did this teaching come from?
>
> **Motorishi:** From men who struggled for decades to discover it. It came from a hidden place where a long line of protective descendants called "The Librarians" have guarded it.
>
> **60 Minutes:** Where is this place? Surely, the rest of the world would like to know.
>
> **Motorishi:** It is not for the rest of the world to find. The knowledge necessary for us to free ourselves is already all around us.

60 Minutes: Do you mean in the forms of religious teaching?

Motorishi: Yes, there and in many other places as well.

60 Minutes: Who else besides your teachers have been to this secret hiding place of knowledge?

Motorishi: It is said that all those who have risen to the level of Prophet have been there.

60 Minutes: Prophets? Like who? Jesus, Mohammed, Moses… Al Sharpton?

Motorishi: What is important is not who has been there, but what they were taught. The Mode teaches us that man is not as in control of his destiny as he believes he is.

60 Minutes: But why cars? What is the connection with mechanics?"

Motorishi: Mechanics is what I know. I use it as a metaphor for the Mode.

60 Minutes: You travel with a group of followers, twelve of them, I believe. Is there a reason there are only twelve?

Motorishi: There are eleven and a half, really; Shorty is a midget. Nevertheless, twelve has significance in relation to the root number of types of people in the world. Everyone is either a pure or combination of one of these root types.

60 Minutes: What about the mobster incident in the San Francisco Bay? Did you raise that car from the bottom of the bay as a publicity stunt, like Jesus raising Lazarus from the dead?

Motorishi: Many things can be done once one has an understanding of the laws that govern the universe. What may be perceived as magic may in fact be quite possible in the real world. What is most important is that we learn to see that we are not free. As we are now, our lives are determined by the mechanical forces, and not by our own will. Once we understand this, we may begin to have the possibility of change.

60 Minutes: But how did you know where the car was? Were you tipped?

Motorishi: I followed the vibrations. Everything in the universe vibrates, and for every series of vibrations, there is a trail that can be followed.

60 Minutes: Your followers are called, 'Motees', sounds a bit like Star Trek's 'Trekkies'; Are you concerned that your movement may become too commercial?

Motorishi: Yes. That is always a possibility with mass exposure. There is a law that states 'anything which gets too big shall be crushed by its own weight'.

60 Minutes: How do you plan to avoid that?

Motorishi: I don't. In fact, it is a necessary step in the evolution of the universe. In the Mode it is called, 'Pranata', from the Sanskrit word 'Prana', meaning balance. It is nature's way of shaking off the moss, so to speak. That which is not true to the teaching will be eliminated.

60 Minutes: What do you foresee as the future of the Mode? Do you think it will rival other world religions?

Motorishi: To rival is to be in conflict. The Mode does not rival, but unifies all religions.

60 Minutes: The world has been moving into a religious factionary state for the last few millennia. A change in that direction would be very refreshing. I want to thank you for meeting with us. We will be sure to have you back regularly to follow your movement as it continues to grow.

Motorishi: My pleasure, I assure you.

With all this momentum behind us, we sought to set up our operations somewhere in downtown Detroit, perhaps even in the old Fred Motor's facility. Rusty and Buzz wanted to see us produce a line of "green cars", limited production models that would run on a combination of battery and solar power. Jesus and Ice insisted the cars come with a top-notch eight speaker sound system with lots of extra bass and were quick to draft a well "pimped" version as well.

Over the next few months, we located and moved into our new offices. Our "World Headquarters" as Bruno called them would be just off Interstate 75 on Mack Avenue right next to the Grand Trunk Western Rail lines. On a clear day, we could just see the northwest corner of Fred Motors Field and the shimmering water's edge of Lake Tacoma, which sits between Lake St. Clair and Lake Erie. The sounds of trains running behind the complex all day was quite soothing to me. It gave me such fond memories of my time with Mr. MacGregor. Every time I heard a whistle blow the image of Mac's face laughing at me filled my mind, and it felt good that his memory as well as his teaching was alive and thriving in me.

We established the framework and business ventures of our newly organized company. Bruno had secured numerous endorsements from companies like MotorZone and Earl Schleb. We were courted by major car companies, and were even seen as the revolutionary new deliverers of marketing messages to the fashion industry, and companies like Levi and Nike all wanted to do advertising campaigns.

We started traveling in small groups instead of one large one, in order to cover more ground. It wasn't uncommon for us to travel from Detroit to New York to Miami to San Francisco to LA promoting the teaching and meeting with as many of our new Motee followers as possible.

There were two major events currently on our agenda. One was a concert and sermon planned for Central Park and the other was the grand opening of our first "Tune-Up Temple." The Temple grand opening ceremonies would bring most, if not all, 11 ½ of us together again and would be taped as a two hour MTV special.

Our latest major endeavor was finally coming to fruition and soon the first of our "Tune-up Temples", auto repair stores that have an in-house confessional, would open its doors in just a few weeks time. The temples would have highly trained mechanics that would diagnose and heal troubled cars while teaching the Mode. Rusty and Buzz were in charge of this venture and were busy training enough certified Mode technicians, to handle a chain of twenty of these "Tune-up Temples" along the eastern coast. If all went well, they had hopes of taking them nationwide the following year.

Bruno and Mathew spent most of their time reading and writing contracts. Because there was a lot of legal business to attend to, they would sit for hours on end, dotting all the "i"s and crossing all the "t"s. Oddly enough, even though Mathew could type much faster than he could speak, he also had his stuttering affliction in his hands, but still was able to keep his mistakes to a minimum with the help of spell check,

Sang Lee was now Vice Guru in charge of accounting and had a staff that filled most of the office's second floor. She was in her element again. She often told me how complete she felt, and how giving back the money to the couple in Vegas put her on the road to her true destiny of finding the group which gave meaning and purpose to her life.

I had found quite a companion in Marian and she and I moved in together later that same year. The press referred to her as my personal assistant, but she was much more that. She was the heart and soul of our operation, and without her, we would not have reached as many people with the Mode. Besides her many administrative tasks, she was asked to write a cookbook, based on her Indian named recipes that she had fed us throughout our journeys. She appeared on the Tonight Show and there was even talk of a cooking show of her own in the fall.

Ice and Shorty designed and promoted "Motee Rags," a line of organic hemp clothing colored with all natural dyes. This had been a longtime dream of Shorty's and the clothing market for dwarfs and midgets had been completely missed by the major garment industry. Ice gave the line credibility and added a modern hip-hop fashion sense that was comfortably fitting. Needless to say, the little people loved it and the rap community took to hemp clothing like vinyl does to scratching; it was a natural.

Rocco felt at the top of his game. He started a motorcycle chapter called "The Mode Warriors" to promote the teaching, and had thousands of members join up for his newly touted "The Impossible Rally".

The rally would be held in June and start in Detroit. It would travel the path I took to meet my teachers across the Pacific Northwest, up through Canada to Anchorage Alaska, then back down the coast through Washington, Oregon, California and into Mexico to the village I stayed at with the great Captain O'Connell. From there it would travel north to Los Angeles and all the way back to Michigan via the route I took the first time home and finally down Route 66 to Los Angeles, once more. Then up to San Francisco, over to Alliance, Mt. Rushmore, Sturgis and finally, back to Detroit.

This Rally was to be of the "Iron Butt" category which would require the riders to do over a thousand miles a day for three weeks straight classifying it not only as the longest and hardest ride ever, but earning the title of "Super Mega-Titanium Butt" Ride.

Jesus started up a truck and bus driver's school, lecturing on long distance driving using the Mode principles. Trucking and bus companies from all over the world sent their drivers to learn how to become safer, more conscientious drivers.

Simon was offered the dream show he'd been waiting for when MTV picked up twenty-six weeks of the show he and Bruno had labored over, while the group was forming and traveling the country. The show was so popular they decided to run it twenty-four hours a day, on a newly released MTV3 channel. The show used a MTV3 logo with the words "Motorishi Television" and Simon's big mug and usual smirk, with what was now our standard visual background, a cloudy blue sky over sand dunes. Bruno and Simon finally had the bona fide hit they'd been waiting for.

Even the Smithsonian Institute in Washington, D.C. called and wanted to discuss an upcoming exhibit they were planning, which would feature the bus, the diner, and Rocco's Harley. The curators also asked if they could gather some other historical artifacts for display as well. Some of those items included our "Dust Bowl Museum" souvenirs and even a few of my earliest repairs, like the princess phone I first took apart at the tender age of four. They had even dug up the car I mysteriously started at the rest stop while traveling home during the years I spent with my teachers.

Everything was moving along quite nicely, according to the mechanical flow of associations. We were becoming world famous. We now had cell phones and the Internet, and news of the effects of the Mode spread rapidly around the globe.

Marian documented through photography much of the flavor of the group forming and was now knee deep in gathering press on us. Seven out of every ten magazines in any store you walked into had one, or a combination of all of us, on its cover.

She gathered newspaper articles as well and soon a whole room of our offices was devoted to the Mode archives. After a while, I noticed she was only collecting good press. I asked her not to ignore the negative side of life; it is as important as the positive to balance perspective.

Overall, I felt satisfied that the path we had chosen was the right one. We live in the age of global communications and that alone propelled us to success. The Mode was out there in the world, gathering momentum. However, I was beginning to feel the weight of my own breath.

CHAPTER XXIX

True Tune-Up Confessions

The skies were clear the morning of the grand opening of the first Tune-Up Temple, which was a good thing because rain clouds had been looming around for days. Simon's crew was there exceptionally early setting up for the production, and the smell of fresh brewed coffee drew me towards its place of origin. *Strong and sweet*, I thought, remembering for a moment the ways of Master Swami. However, I could never really take it that way. At least I was able to drink it without sugar these days, but was never able to go cold turkey. I still liked a touch of half-and-half to cut the black.

Just then, Simon walked through the door, slightly disheveled and eyes red. "Morning, M," he said, yawning.

"Late one last night, Simon?"

"You bet. Where's the coffee?" He began following his nose. "I've flown between LA and New York five times in the last week and a half alone. Have you seen the ratings for our channel?"

"No, I didn't think they were out yet."

"34 share, baby… a 34 share! Ouch," he yelped, touching the coffeepot with his knuckles. "I would have been happy with a 10 share! You *are* the man! What time do we open?"

"Ten o'clock and the line's already a half-mile long. I imagine it will be four times that by noon," I said.

"This is a big day for you. You and Rusty have been working hard to make this happen."

"I know, thanks," I replied.

"I'm gonna go see how the crew's doing. I'll see you in a few," Simon muttered and he walked away.

I walked through the Temple and inspected its readiness, all the time wishing my parents, who had died a few years ago, could have been here to see it. My father would have liked this concept, but most importantly, it would have given him cause to hand out his famous Cuban cigars. While my mother, well, she would have been proud as usual, as long as she had her cell phone with her and the ceremony didn't run into her favorite soap.

At a minute to ten-o'clock, I opened the front door to a warm local welcome. Simon finished the opening monologue and turned the microphone over to me.

"Hello, everyone. I want to thank you for coming to the grand opening of the Tune-Up Temples. Please be patient and we will try to get to all of you."

Simon stood nearby adjusting his hair to maximize his best side on camera and began taping an introduction. "'Tune

Up Temples' are a retail chain of tune-up and repair centers aimed at the proper diagnosis and healing of the machine. Each location has its own confessional bays where you can confess your automotive sins and repent for your mechanical abuses. Their certified Mode mechanics have studied at our Mode University and have shown they have what it takes to properly read and heal your cars, and are fully qualified to administer penance. They have adopted as their very foundation Chilton's 9½ commandments, which are written on the walls of every center."

Simon walked inside and pointed to the wall where the commandments had been painted. The camera panned back to show the facility in all its glory.

CHILTON'S 9½ COMANDMENTS

1. *Always read the manuals.*
2. *Always use the right tools for the job at hand.*
3. *Be where your tools are.*
4. *You shall not covet your neighbor's tools.*
5. *Acknowledge the tune-up day and keep it holy.*
6. *You shall not exceed the limits of the car.*
7. *You shall not be in a hurry.*
8. *You shall not bear false witness against thy car.*
9. *Never use third party parts.*

½. *Most important, always remember…*

"No one knows what happened to the last commandment. Perhaps the page was torn out of the original book or the author died before finishing it, however, it is now used as a reminder that there is always more to learn."

Simon traveled outside to get a shot of the Service Menu and explained a little of what each service was about before turning the cameras to me in the confessional-bay ready to receive customers, perform readings, recommend types of healing, and administer penance for abuses.

TUNE-UP TEMPLE SERVICE MENU

#1	Confession and Penance	$ 25.00
#2	Confession and Oil Change	$ 45.00
#3	Confession, Reading, Penance, Oil Change	$ 85.00
#4	Confession, Reading, Penance, Brakes	$ 120.00
#5	Confession, Reading, Penance, Tires	$ 150.00
#6	Confession, Reading, Penance, Healing	$ 250.00
#7	Reading, and Oil Change	$ 45.00
#8	Reading, Alignment	$ 65.00
#9	Reading, Temporary Demon Removal	$ 250.00
#10	Reading, Permanent Demon Removal	$1250.00

VALUE MENU

#11	Reading Only	$ 25.00
#12	Directions	$ FREE

I began with the first customer, a man who looked slightly nervous about all the cameras and commotion.

"How may we help you today?" I asked politely.

"Yes, I'll have the number three with twenty-fifty weight oil please," the customer requested.

"Of course," I replied, and rolled my hand to prompt him to continue.

"Forgive me, er... your Motorness, for I have sinned," he said.

"What is the nature of your sin?" I asked.

"I have missed my scheduled tune-ups for so long that now my 'check engine' light is on, and I fear that I have broken something serious."

"What are the symptoms that support this fear?" I questioned further.

"Loss of power, an almost failing idle, a slow clicking noise," he replied.

"Does the transmission shift normally?"

"Yes."

"When did you first notice the results of your neglect?" I asked, moving my hand across the hood of his car, feeling everything it had to tell me.

"Last night, as I pulled up to a stop light, just before I got home."

A read on his car started to come to me. "How many miles over your scheduled tune up are you?" I continued.

"About 35,000 over," he said, and hung his head down in shame.

I paused. "You know you must be punished for this? Not by me... but by the intensity of your repairs. You deserve big problems, you realize that?"

"Yes, of course, your Mystic Gearness," he apologized.

I laid my hands on the car for a moment. "You have a bad coil and this is causing your engine to misfire."

"Phew" he said, wiping his forehead.

"However, that is not all," I responded, "You also have bad shocks and are in desperate need of an oil change and a major tune-up, along with windshield wiper blades and new front brakes."

"It's that bad, your Spocketness?"

I looked at the man for a moment. "Your clothes show that you are a procrastinator, since you have stains on your shirt that are older than a day. Nevertheless, worse than that you wait too long to fix your health, your teeth and your back, and your gut sticks out like an overstuffed pillow. You are an exact mirror of the way you treat your car. You have always waited too long for everything.

"Your repair costs are $1500.00, and for your penance, you shall drive around with a sign that we will place in your window for one full week announcing to the world that you are a 'tune-up avoider', also stating your repair costs; to be followed by 'Don't let this happen to you!'"

"Yes, thank you, Motorishi, thank you," he said, getting out of his car and falling to his knees.

I gave him the sign of the gear (fingers closed in a fist with the knuckles slightly separated) and anointed him with oil. "Go now, and let the spirit of Chilton be with you."

The man left bowing his head as he was led to the waiting room, while an assigned mechanic took his car to the repair bay. The next car pulled forward.

"And what will you have, sir?" I asked.

"I'll take the #5 'Rhino Style' (extra tread), tires," he said.

"Do you want P205s or P220s on that," I asked.

"P205s please," he replied. I motioned him to continue.

"Forgive me, Motorishi, for I have sinned."

"Tell about your dilemma."

"I have been driving on bad brakes and bald tires," he replied.

"This is most dangerous," I said, scorning him.

"Yes, I have risked the lives of both me and my family. I have been meaning to get them replaced, but I never can seem to find the time."

"How bad are they?" I asked.

"Very bad. A couple of tires are worn through to what I am sure is all but one of the belts. And the sound of grinding brakes must mean I am into the drums," he confessed.

"You can make the time to take care of this, but you choose other distractions and desires instead." I laid my hands on the hood. "Like baseball games and strip clubs and drives to the local bar with your buddies for a couple of quick ones before heading home to your wife and kids."

The man became nervous and started to fidget. I looked him straight in the eye.

"You can do this. You can change this in yourself if you want to bad enough."

He dropped to his knees weeping like a child, realizing he had done a great injustice to himself and his family, and was beyond forgiveness. "Please tell me what I must do!" he cried.

"You must put new tires on your car right now," I responded.

"Yes, I will. Take it from me this instant," he said pleading.

"But not only this."

"I was afraid of that, your Motorness."

"You must put new tires on your life. You will not visit a bar or strip club for as long as your new tires last and you will hug your wife and kids every day and be thankful for their existence in your life." I paused for a second. "As for the baseball games, you can still go to those, but take your wife and kids with you. Do you hear me?"

"Yes, sir. Thank you, sir…" he blubbered. He too moved to the waiting room while his car was taken to the repair bays.

I turned around to address everyone else in line. "Let this be a lesson to all seeking forgiveness for your motor sins, that recognition of the errors of mistreatment of the machine is the beginning of freedom from that same mistreatment of ourselves and others. Look at your cars now as you wait. What will you see? You will see yourself in everything."

Next, I stepped up to the car of a very rich and beautiful woman. "What will you have?"

"I would just like a wash," she said, quite unaware of everything else going on around her.

"A wash? Do you know where you are?" I asked her.

"Why, I'm at the new Motoruski Car Wash, right?"

"Take for example this car," I said, shouting it so everyone could hear. "It is driven by a beautiful woman!" Her ego fed, she smiles a huge face-stretching smile. "Its paint is in perfect shape, the tires are good, and the chrome shines like a thousand suns." Beside herself from the attention, she gives small hand waves to everyone. "This car is obviously cared for by someone who enjoys things that look good." I laid my hands on the hood and closed my eyes for a moment.

"But wait!" I said, as the others looked on anxiously. "She is here because she has heard that this is the newest 'craze' and not because she desires the truth about herself." I opened the hood and looked inside. "Something is not right on the inside! There is corrosion and rust on almost everything in here. The seals are all worn through and the engine misfires. This car, while looking young on the outside, has been neglected inside for far too long."

The woman was embarrassed and insulted at my accusations and drove off calling me a charlatan as she sped away.

I smiled. "What is hidden by glamour on the outside will eventually surface from the neglect of the inside. That woman only cared about her looks and nothing more. It was reflected in the appearance of her car and in everything around her. She does all she can to buy herself time, because to her without beauty she feels worthless and has nothing but emptiness inside. However, this is a great mistake. What matters first is the inside, then the outside. A shell may be very beautiful object, but it is still just a shell unless a life lives inside. Rust never sleeps. This is true in many ways. Once the inside goes bad, eventually the outside will begin to reflect it."

"Come, come everyone, who is next?" A great number of people shouted and crowded forward, even more anxious than before to unburden themselves after this demonstration. The few that attended only because of the "herd instinct" moved quietly to their cars and eventually drove away.

Over the course of the next half-year, according to our original plan, we opened Temples all over the country. They gave people easy drive-up access to the ideas of the Mode along with a basic service that they needed. The Temples were a big financial success too, which eased the worries of Ice, who'd provided the initial seed money, and Bruno, who was concerned about every detail of how we marketed my image and the Mode. In fact, everything was going so well that I could almost physically feel the weight building up on the other side of the karma-scale. While I was sure that weight would come down against us at some point, I just wasn't sure how the universe was going to deliver that package.

CHAPTER XXX

Fred Motors – Buy our Cars or Die!

Just a mile away from our offices in Detroit, Mitch Murphy sat behind his desk staring at the snow on the TV screen and tried to still the anger that was pounding his head into an instant migraine. He had to maintain his composure. More than that, he had to quiet his mind enough to think clearly.

He was in danger, and part of his rage was the result of his feeling of being threatened. His career was at stake, along with the lifestyle that it allowed him. Too many sacrifices had already been made at the alter of conscience for him to give everything up now without a fight. Nevertheless, he knew he couldn't just lash out in the mindless fury that tempted him. He knew people who could arrange an accident for me. He'd never had to ask that favor before, and knew that he probably shouldn't now, but it helped just to know that the option was open to him. He almost smiled at the thought, but could only muster a grim satisfaction that helped to calm his nerves and bring reality into a little clearer focus.

He pressed the button that killed the TV and thought about what he'd just seen, trying to find some angle he could use to turn this into something other than a complete disaster. The tape was made only an hour earlier, from one of the morning shows based in Detroit. The piece was a feature, with a reporter on location at the first of the "Tune-Up Temples". The Temple was a big hit with the locals and was soon doing most of the automotive work in the area. "How did this city compare, in things automotive, with others that didn't have a Temple?"

The answer to that question, according to the reporter, was nothing but positive for the city and its citizens: lower car repair and maintenance costs, longer periods before repairs were needed, in some cases lower auto insurance costs, and gas mileage almost doubled. Accidents and automotive infractions both went down by almost half. An EPA team had concluded in a recent study that the air purity within a fifty-mile radius of the town had improved by a significant amount.

All this good news pissed Mitch off. However, it was the next segment that scared him enough to bring his anger to a level that had thankfully left him speechless.

The reporter had stopped a local who was coming out of the Temple and briefly explained some of the benefits and statistics that the viewers had just seen. Then he asked, "What is your response to the impact that the Temple seems to have had on your community?"

The man uncrossed his arms, "Well, all I know is my car is gonna last a lot longer now than it was before I started coming here, and that will probably help the environment, *and* my wallet! I won't be buying a new one as soon as I would have before, either. When I do, I'll be listening to the Motorishi and his bunch about which cars are good or not. In fact, if he made a car, I wouldn't look at anything else. I'd take it... on faith, you might say." He smiled at the reporter then quickly shook his hand and moved off to his car.

The very thought of me getting involved in the making cars made Mitch's blood run cold.

He looked at the two people who had brought him this tape and had just watched his reaction to it. Jeremy Bowen was Mitch's personal secretary. He was seated in a chair across from Mitch and, though Mitch had taken plenty of flack for having a male assistant (mostly of the "he's gay" variety), Mitch had to admit that Jeremy had become so essential to the way he operated that he couldn't imagine finding another person with the same frame of mind. Jeremy was as ruthless as Mitch was. Mitch liked that. Jeremy just didn't have the experience that Mitch had and showed it in his eagerness and lack of subtlety, otherwise he would have been an opponent.

Standing besides the television screen, Joanna Walters was the picture of big-business feminine cool. As Vice-President of Sales & Marketing for Fred Motors, she was attractive, but not flashy, fashionable, but not too cutting edge, in control, but not aggressively "alpha". She had blond hair and a curvy shape, and if the rumors about her love life were true, included both genders. Mitch only knew that she had the most cunning mind he had ever met, besides his own, and that she was the only other person besides Jeremy that he could count on to follow his lead in difficult matters like this one. He turned towards them.

"He's got to go down." They looked back at him quizzically. "The Motorishi! Dewey Pinkerton! I've given him enough chances. We have to take him down, now! We can't afford to let this guy's voice get stronger. We have to start diluting his message and ultimately, we've got to take him down!

"Joanna, I want a wave of negative publicity to start rolling out about this guy, and I want it to get worse and worse. I want disinformation. I want cranks. I want wacky theories and foolish witnesses. I want exposés of his charlatan ways! You need to get this going through every channel we can possibly solicit, influence or outright buy. Do you get what I'm looking for, here?"

"What am I supposed to blame on him? Cleaner air?" Joanna asked.

"No, you'll need something more than that. That's where Jeremy comes in." He turned to Jeremy. "You have two important tasks. First, you must somehow infiltrate his group. We need to get a spy in their midst. I want investigators on his trail and a team of people examining every aspect of their past and present to see if there's something we can use to get a grip on their privates. Second is to place a call to Senator Charles. Remind him that he owes us. I want a hearing scheduled to investigate certain aspects of the faltering automotive industry, and the Senator needs to know that the Motorishi is the sacrificial lamb on the alter of the media, in the name of keeping our economy healthy."

Mitch smirked at them both, just barely under control. "I want the Motorishi dead, but I'll have to settle for seeing him ruined. I want something on him and I want it yesterday! Move, people!"

CHAPTER XXXI

Digging in the Dirt

Within a week, Jeremy had two private investigators trailing me and the other members of the group. He used additional PIs for surveillance when members of the group went off on various errands and trips. He also created a research team that included a half dozen auditors and information specialists. This team collected and analyzed everything they could get their hands on from the group, including new intelligence coming in from Jeremy's operators in the field. They gathered an incredible collection of material from my past and the past of my disciples, including copies of birth certificates, school records, and legal records. There were photographs from a variety of sources, a large pile of the spotty media documentation during my rise to fame, and even the occasional artifact like some of my old clothes.

The group became used to seeing the two PIs around, although we thought they were from the press working on a story. We didn't have any reason to be suspicious, which is exactly what Jeremy was hoping. It meant he stood a good chance of getting someone deep inside our organization without us knowing it.

Within the same week, Joanna started to create a buzz she hoped to expand into a headline grabbing set of stories. She took what little filth Jeremy could give her, put a spin on it, and spread it through the journalistic community; the Motorishi was a fraud, he was a joke, but worse than that, he was taking advantage of people and in the end, they were going to look foolish. She planted seeds in the minds of some of the journalists she talked to; that no one was perfect and that they might want to start looking for the "dark side of the Motorishi story."

At the end of the week, Joanna and Jeremy met again in Mitch's office to assess their progress. Joanna walked in with a copy of the tabloid newspaper, *The World*, and unfolded it to show the huge headline, "I Had the Motorishi's Baby," over a picture that showed a heavily pregnant woman standing next to me at a street corner. The caption to the picture said, "Baby Already Demonstrates Amazing Powers!"

Mitch laughed and asked, "How did you get that arranged?"

"There's never a shortage of people who want to be famous, even for just a few minutes," Joanna replied. "We approached the 'mother' with a suggestion of how she might get her moment of fame and a handful of cash. She jumped aboard instantly."

"That's just the right tone for this campaign. It's going to start harmless, but it's going to turn nasty very quick. What has the research team come up with?"

Jeremy cleared his throat, "We've found out some interesting items from the background checks. The surfer, Trace, was busted once for drug use. The old biker spent a night in jail for drunk and disorderly. Bits and pieces like that, but nothing juicy and none of it current. All this stuff is well in their past.

"We have two of our guys in the general circle of media hangers-on that always seem to be with the Motorishi and his bunch," he went on more enthusiastically. "They've made some kind of contact with each member of the group, but so far, on my direction, haven't pushed any further. They are still primarily observers, and I think their observations will give us the key to pulling this guy down.

"One thing we know for sure is there's an amazing amount of money coming through their door right now. I think that might be their weak spot. None of them are really prepared to handle money on that kind of scale. The girl, Sang Lee, is the only one with any financial experience, but it's different now, this is not Casino money, it's their money! The money trail may have a weak spot we can exploit."

Mitch sat back and mused about that for a minute, "A financial faux pas… he loses his money and his credibility… trouble with the law and possible jail time. I must admit, I'm liking this!"

He sat up in his chair, animated. "But why wait for them to make a mistake. Let's help them a little! Let's craft an 'offer' of some kind that they are likely to bite on, something that looks like the smart and upstanding thing to do. Once they cross the line, we get them busted for it, embezzling, or tax evasion, something along those lines! Jeremy, did you call the Senator?"

"Yes, I did, and he thought it was quite a coincidence that he was just thinking of starting an investigation of his own. It seems he has already received half a dozen calls from other constituents in the oil and auto industries with grave concerns about spiraling financial losses."

"Good. Call him again in another week and let him know that we'll be giving him a prime piece of theater, if he's up to the lead role."

Jeremy nodded. "What about the deal, for the Motees?"

Mitch stood up. "Start looking into what kind of embezzling scenario will get this guy strung up, Jeremy. And Joanna, you do the same for the tax angle. You have forty-eight hours. I want bait they can't resist. Now move!"

CHAPTER XXXII

30 Pieces of Bling

Bruno and a few of the others were in the habit of going to an Irish bar on Poplar Street most Wednesday nights as a place to meet informally and blow off some of the week's steam. Paddy's was an unpretentious place, but Irish to the core and besides the disciples, some of the regular staff as well as the ever-present press contingent had also become Wednesday night regulars. Everyone understood that this time was "off the record" and it appeared news people had just as much steam to blow off as the Motees. Therefore, Bruno wasn't too surprised one Wednesday when Chet and Will, two news guys that had been hanging around for the last few weeks, stopped by and began shooting the breeze with him. While they bantered back and forth about the weather over a beer, Bruno tried to remember what organization they were with. Some wire service, he seemed to recall, but he couldn't put his finger on it. They had asked a few questions at press briefings, but hadn't published anything yet, as far as he knew. He'd asked them about it before and they'd answered with something about "waiting for the story line to develop", so he figured they must be on assignment for a feature of some sort.

The conversation turned to how well the Temples and the shows were doing; that each achievement seemed to out-do the one before it. Selling was Bruno's world, and he couldn't help but strut a bit. When they asked just how much money the organization was bringing in, Bruno replied, "Now you guys know I can't answer that, even unofficially. However, let me just say between you and me that this has gone way beyond anything I had ever envisioned. It's just huger than huge!"

They all chuckled in response, when Will spoke up. "I'll bet the IRS hates you guys." Bruno's face tightened up at the mention of the IRS.

"Are you kidding me?" Bruno answered. "I think those bastards love us. They're taking their cut, and let me tell you it's no small amount."

Chet appeared puzzled. "Don't you have a tax exempt status? I covered the church circuit in the south for a while, and all of the churches had applied for, and received, tax exempt status."

"But don't you have to be, you know… a real church to get that kind of a break?" Bruno asked.

"Well, I'm no expert," Chet replied, "but the way I remember it is, it didn't really matter what kind of church you were, and believe me, I saw some weird ones. The important part was that you had to have someone who was recognized as a 'bishop' or 'overseer' of the church and that this person could hold in trust all of the assets of the church. Once you've jumped through the legal and paperwork hoops, it's a done deal and your tax paying days are over."

Bruno thought about how much money that would put back in their hands. "Do you think we could meet whatever the requirements are for this? It sounds too good to be true."

Will glanced at Bruno and Chet and then shrugged his shoulders. "I don't see any down-side to trying it. The worst that can happen is that you are turned down somewhere along the way. Besides, it says 'Church' right there in your name; 'Church of Motor Science'! They'll have to give you the nod!" All three men laughed.

Chet said, "You know, I did make a good connection down south with a real sharp lawyer who was working for a few of the bigger church organizations. He'd be a good one to walk you through it. I can give you his number, if you like."

Bruno smiled. "Sure that would be great. Thanks for the tip and the connection. If I'm gonna do this, then the sooner the better. If this guy can get us in the door quicker, then we'll make it worth his while."

"Sure thing," said Chet. "I'll get his number to you tomorrow."

Chet, Will, and Bruno all smiled. "If this works out, then you guys can ask for any interview you want, in the time and place of your choosing," Bruno said. "It's the least I can do for you."

"Thanks," Chet replied.

"Yeah, thanks, Bruno. We'll keep that in mind." Chet and Will turned and moved deeper into the room "I'd say that fish is hooked," Chet whispered once they were out of earshot. "Now let's see if they can be reeled in," said Will.

The lawyer's name was Richard C. Tripton, and as Bruno sat in his office, he marveled at the speed with which this idea was moving. From bar-side conversation to this meeting had taken only two days. He hadn't even mentioned it to anyone else in the group, because he wasn't taking it completely seriously himself, until now.

"You have no idea the number of organizations that apply for this exemption," Tripton told him. "It's quite popular. For most organizations, it's just a way to stay alive because they are so small that paying taxes on what little assets they have would kill them. But for the more successful groups, your Catholic Church, your Baptists, your Scientologists, it's a considerable piece of change back on the bottom line."

Tripton pulled forms from file drawers and shuffled papers around as he spoke. He pulled one of the sheets from before him and handed it to Bruno. "The person you designate as overseer will have to sign this form. It acknowledges the role they play in the organization and it promises to keep things on the up and up. The rest of the application is strictly filling out forms and paying fees."

Bruno said, "Well, I could be the overseer. I'm high up in the organization and I play a big role in the day to day operation."

Tripton shook his head and answered, "The IRS won't buy that. They want to see the name of the most prominent guy in the organization. For your bunch, that's Mr. Pinkerton. Have him sign that, send it back to me, and I'll have the rest of the paperwork completed and ready to go. You'll be tax-exempt within a month."

Bruno thought about it for a moment. He wasn't sure how I would react to this idea. He had run the numbers the night before, and this exemption would potentially save almost a couple of million dollars we would normally have to pay to the IRS. I hadn't really expressed much interest in how the money side of things was run, as long as everything was legal and fair. "*This was legal, wasn't it?*" he wondered. *"After all, a lawyer was telling him he could do it!"*

Bruno voiced the one doubt that he couldn't seem to get rid of, "I'm still worried that this kind of exemption is only for religious organizations and that somehow, we won't measure up in the eyes of the IRS."

Tripton smiled. "Mr. Goldblum. The definition of a church, according to the IRS, is very loose and general, as it should be, considering the number of odd and real religions in the world. Tell me, does your group ever hold some kind of meeting or congregation?"

"Yes."

"And do the participants in your events perform any rituals, say prayers, or meditate on an agreed or shared vision of some kind?"

"Yes, they do."

Tripton rose from his seat and straightened his jacket, "Then I tell you now, sir, you have nothing to worry about." Bruno stood also. "Besides," said Tripton, reminding him again, "It says 'Church' right there in your name, right?" He smiled and laughed.

Bruno put the form in his briefcase and shook Tripton's hand. "I'll get this signed and back to you within forty-eight hours. I'm in a hurry to make this happen and I'll pay additional fees or expenses to help that along. Please keep that in mind as you make the preparations."

"I assure you, Mr. Goldblum, it will be slicker than... well, let's just say, it will be handled very quickly."

Bruno left and Tripton looked out the window. He picked up the phone and dialed as he watched Bruno's car move towards the exit of the parking lot. After a moment he spoke. "I've given him the paperwork and if my instincts are to be trusted, I'd bet that we'll see a signature soon." He listened for a moment and said, "I'll keep someone here at all times, in case he has it hand delivered or something. There's nothing else I can do until we have it. Let me know if anything changes." Jeremy hung up the phone and pulled off his fake mustache and wig, massaging his lips and scratching his scalp.

"I hate waiting."

CHAPTER XXXIII

The Last Oil Change

“Dewey, I want you to see something,” the voice said. I rubbed my eyes and pinched the skin on my arm once to verify I was awake. I felt nothing. I looked around but could not tell where I was. I rose from my bed and followed the voice.

“Have you forgotten already what I have taught you?” the voice continued. “Maybe this will ring a bell.” There was the loud sound of a train whistle.

“Mac, is that you? Where are you?” He appeared in the form of an angel, only with a blind man’s cane.

“I am where I have always been, only without all the dead weight of course.”

“Mac, it’s so good to… kind of see you,” I rubbed my eyes once more, hoping it would clear things up.

He laughed. "Don't you remember a thing that Captain O'Connell taught you regarding the food chain and feeding the angels? Sean, that pompous, drunken ol' goat, I knew he'd never make a good teacher!"

"That sounds pretty funny coming from a bagpipe totin' blind Scotsman," said, Captain O'Connell, coming up from behind him.

Just then, Isaac appeared. "Did you hear the one about the Irishman and Scot who bet an Englishman a hundred pounds on who could stay under water the longest?" he asked.

"No," the others replied.

"Well, you poor bastards," he laughed, "they both drowned."

"Sean, Isaac!" I yelled. "I can't believe this. Have any of you seen Winger?"

"Of course," Isaac whistled. "Winger, come out, you apple pie-eating, flag-waving, young pup." Winger began to materialize.

"Did I hit my head on something last night?" I wondered. "The Seekers of Wisdom," together again at last. However, before I could say anything more, they signaled me to stay quiet.

"I'm afraid this is not a happy reunion for us, Dewey. We are here to warn you," Isaac said.

"Warn me about what?" I asked.

"That you are coming to the crossroad. The place where all that you have worked for and all that the universe has worked on you will intersect the all that is working against you."

"What should I do?" I asked.

"Until the crossroad, you still have a choice," Mac said. You can see this thing through to its end. Or you can get out now, before the weight of the world comes down on you."

"Am I going… to die?"

"Of course you are, silly," Mac replied, "You're still human, aren't you? The body is really, truly overrated you know. But, it's not your time, quite yet."

"Remember that everything is material," Sean interrupted, "It is all connected to the food chain. You're job here is nearing completion. You have fulfilled the prophecy and delivered the seed of the Mode to all the tribes of mankind. You have built your church upon the 'block'. You can stop it all now, or continue on. The Mode will continue to stand on its own now, with or without you."

"One day your soul will dwell in the skies with ours." Winger said.

"Speak for yourselves," Isaac rebutted. "I may be the oldest but, I'm not dead, yet! Do what you must, Dewey. But, first let me show you something." He raised his hands and everything around me came into focus.

The skies darkened again and the air was hot and thick. I saw a small boy digging in a dumpster, perhaps for something to eat. He reached down deep and surfaced with a small tube in his hands. He desperately squeezed it in his palms and began to rub it all over his face and arms. He was searching for something to shield his skin from the sun. I suddenly looked around and noticed everyone was covered from head to toe in protective clothing. They sky was black with ash and smoke and people coughed as they hobbled slowly down the streets. The horizon was lined with high-rise luxury penthouses, whose windows were dark and tinted. Large purifiers lined the rooftops, and guards stood at every door. "*Was this the sign of things to come?*" I wondered.

"This is the sign of all that opposes the Mode," Isaac continued. "This is hell on earth. However, there is another version. Let me show you," he said, raising his hands again. Suddenly, a beautiful white light began to glow.

I could see an intersection, where a man in luxury car was just cut off by a woman in a sports car. "I'm sorry," the woman said, coming up along side him.

"That's OK," he replied. "I was probably sticking out to far anyway. Have a great day."

I looked out at the roads beyond us and noticed that all of the drivers looked peaceful and happy. Very unlike the way I remembered them as a child in Detroit. There wasn't any traffic and the skies were clear and deep blue.

At that moment, I saw the prophecy both past and future pass before me all at once. I knew what I must do. I would make the right choice when the crossroad came.

"We are counting on you," the Seekers said. They drifted from view and I woke up.

It was the day before our next big show at Central Park and Bruno had come to me to sign some legal documents that would set us up as a Church. I didn't know at the time what that all meant, but it did mean that we were now officially called, "The Church of Motor Science". Bruno mentioned something about us being a "Prophet organization that was non-profit, as opposed to being a non-Prophet organization, which would profit." I laughed at his explanation and signed the papers.

Gathering us all together again in one place proved to be somewhat of a challenge, since promoting our various business ventures took us from coast to coast. We gathered in the shop that night as we usually did, around the lift, where we would work on our tour bus, just a day before it was to be delivered to the Smithsonian.

Working together as a group had always produced the best results and I often used "group maintenance" as a way to introduce new ideas whose concepts are more easily absorbed while one is performing a task that involves working with others. I wanted to make sure the vehicles were in their best possible shape before giving them up to the Smithsonian and the world, since they represented the very essence of our journey and were the results of what the teaching was about. These mechanical specimens had been our home, our kitchen and bedrooms, our living rooms. We had collectively traveled over one hundred and eighty thousand miles in them over the course of a five-year period and had improved just about every square inch of each of them.

Tonight was no ordinary gathering and I wanted to use this occasion to remind the group not only of the journey that was now behind us, but also of the one that lay ahead. I had been thinking for months now about the level of our success and about the teaching itself, contemplating the path I had chosen. Johann had told me the road would be difficult to travel and that even though I had chosen the commercial path lined with the wallets of demons, it nevertheless gave me chills remembering how he warned me that the results of this path are not likely to end well.

"The teaching is all that matters." I had weighed this repeatedly in my mind and had decided a long time ago that this may lead to an end for me, but I had never weighed what the cost would be to the others. They were not as strong as I was and perhaps could not withstand the pressure should something happen to me and everything came crashing down on them.

Is the Mode strong enough to survive without me? Can the group help it grow on their own, without my impetus? I wanted to find a way to show them something, something that would help to remind them if I were gone how they should continue, how they should carry on the teaching without me. I decided I would use this last bit of work we needed to do on the transmission of the bus as an allegory for my fate.

There was a solemnness in the air and everyone seemed to feel it. We were all a little more in focus and did not succumb to the usual chatter and flow of subjective opinions. The only home we had known for the last few years was about to become an exhibit at the Smithsonian, and we would never again be able to return to those simpler times. Not that life had become harder, but it had become much more complicated.

Rusty and Buzz finished an assessment of the engine. The transmission had at least one leaking seal and there was a tooth or two in the flywheel, which needed some machine re-tooling.

"Dinner will be ready in a few minutes," Marian announced. Even though we had a full cafeteria in the office itself, this would be the last dinner prepared in the diner. Sang Lee poured us some wine and we all toasted.

"I would like to say a few words before we all embark on our last night together with our soon to be preserved 'Smithsonian Exhibit' and also, because tonight is the eve of the concert in Central Park. I feel very thankful to have met each and every one of you. You have all enriched my life more than words could ever express. However, your greatest adventure is only about to begin.

"I have mentioned before and wish to mention again now, that as foretold in the Great Book of the Mode, someday a student of mechanics would come to free the world from the slavery of the sleeping machines in ourselves, and would help the world awake to the laws of the Mode.

"It was my destiny once somewhat free from this sleep and control of the law of accident, to deliver it to you. It has also happened by fate that each of you represents the twelve types of man, well eleven and a half types. Anyway, the point is that between all of you, there is the ability to pass on parts of the teaching that correspond to the many different types of people there are in the world."

"Come, let us sit down at the worktable everyone, and I will speak to you about something that weighs heavy on my heart." Everyone gathered around the table. I grabbed a bag of small gaskets and handed them out to Bruno on my right and Marian on my left and asked that they be passed down the line.

"Everyone, take one." They all looked a bit puzzled, but because this was such a solemn occasion, they did not question me.

As the gaskets were being passed down the line, I told this story:

"Once, a scholar asked a boatman to row him across the river. The journey was long and slow. The scholar was bored. 'Boatman,' he called out, 'Let's have a conversation.' Suggesting a topic of special interest only to himself, he asked, 'Have you ever studied mathematics or grammar?'

'No,' said the boatman, 'I've no use for those tools.'

'Too bad,' said the scholar, 'You have wasted half your life. It's useful to know the rules.'

Later, as the rickety boat crashed into a rock in the middle of the river, the boatman turned to the scholar and said, 'Pardon my humble mind that to you must seem dim, but, wise man, tell me, have you ever learned to swim?'

'No,' said the scholar, 'I've never learned. I've immersed myself only in thinking.'

'In that case,' said the boatman, 'you've wasted all your life. Alas, the boat is sinking.'

"Are we more like the boatman or the scholar?" I asked.

"The boatman," Rocco said.

"N-n-no the s-scholar," said Mathew.

"It is a trick question," I answered. "I have told this story, because we must learn to be both. We must be wise, but also know how to keep this wisdom alive in time of peril. The wisdom of the scholar represents the 'teaching' itself, and the boatman's practical ability to swim, represents the 'survival' of the teaching. And I... represent the boat. In other words, to save the teaching, it must learn to swim, to survive without me." I raised the gasket in front of me in the air.

"Everyone, take this gasket, it is my body. Whenever you replace that which is worn out, do this in remembrance of me. Let this memory remind you that all things eventually wear out and need to be replaced by something new."

"Does this mean you're comparing yourself to a seal meant to stop liquids from leaking out and ruining your driveway?" Shorty asked.

"No, Shorty, this means, do not let old thoughts or old ways of doing things prevent you from growing and learning something new. Remember that our ultimate goal is freedom from what binds us here."

"More fiber in our diets, huh?" Shorty interrupted.

"No, Shorty. Freedom from the machine in order to live more under the laws of fate and not the laws of accident."

I poured some 20/50 weight oil in a large pan and held it up. "All of you, use this in your work tonight, this is my blood. Whenever you do an oil change or a communion, do so in remembrance of me. Let it remind you that oil is the blood of Carvana, giving longevity of life to all machines!"

Shorty raised his hand. "Yes, Shorty," I responded cautiously.

"This gasket doesn't taste very good and I'm havin' some trouble getten' it down with only oil!" he said, holding his throat.

"No, Shorty, you're not supposed to eat it, it's symbolic! It's allegorical. It's an analogy for crying out loud!"

"Oh," he said, spitting it out on the floor, "I must have missed that part!"

"You're starting to creep me out," Rocco said. "What's this all about?"

"Soon you will all have to be strong. You will have to make a stand for the Mode."

"What are you saying?" Marian asked.

"I'm saying that the end of my time is near and soon you will all have to act on what you have been taught."

"I don't understand what you're getting at," said Sang Lee.

"Yeah, Waz up?" chimed Ice.

"Look, it's all very complicated," I said. "All I know is something might take me away for a while."

"No," everyone shouted. "Are you leaving us?"

"I don't know yet," I replied.

I looked at Bruno and sensed he was a bit nervous.

"We won't let anything happen to you! We will all stand by your side," Rusty shouted.

"Before the horn beeps three times, Rusty, you will deny me."

"What are you talking about, M? I would never deny you!"

"Look everyone, calm down, I am trying to explain. I may not be with you much longer."

"No," Marian said, hugging me. "Why haven't you told me this?"

"Because, even I wasn't sure until tonight. Someone will betray me in order to fulfill that which is written, that the one who will come will be persecuted in the name of the Mode."

"No way," Rocco said, standing up and moving into a defense stance to protect me.

"Look, everyone. There's nothing you can do about it. Just remember what I have taught you. Remember what the teaching is about, and use what you know to help the teaching survive. Help the teaching swim."

We talked late into the night as the wine flowed. By three in the morning, everyone had fallen asleep, either from exhaustion, or from too much to drink.

Marian, Rocco, and I were left sitting alone by the fire. No one said a word for a long time, while we all tried to get a handle on the excessive flow of thoughts and emotions.

"Look, you guys. Things are going to be all right. It is destiny that will I suffer at the hands of my enemy before the work is completed. In this case, the enemy is success. While having it has succeeded in spreading the word of the teaching, it has also left us with a heavy burden. I have said before, it's a law of nature that a tower built too tall will eventually fall from its own weight. We have come a long way. We have grown the teaching to an enormous size. There must be an adjustment to the teaching, a cleansing. If I have to take the fall for it, then so be it. It will be better in the end, you will see.

"Now get some sleep, tomorrow is a big day for us. We will be spreading the teaching to hundreds of thousands of people live in Central Park, and millions of viewers worldwide via satellite. This is a big opportunity for the Mode. We must make the best use of it we possibly can."

Rocco lay down to sleep and Marian and I walked back to my office to read over the sermon for Central Park one more time. I sat down in my office chair and leaned back. Marian came over to me, lying down across my lap, she put her arms around my neck and kissed me. Together we sat quietly, looking around the room at the pictures and keepsakes we had gathered from our journeys. There were pictures of everything from Buzz jumping the bus to magazine covers of Marian in Rolling Stone and Cosmopolitan. How beautiful she had become. Every magazine on the planet wanted her on their cover. However, that's not the only beauty she radiated. She lit up a room from the glow of a growing soul.

"Look at all this stuff?" she mused. "It's as if you were a rock star; a Leroy Neiman, an Andy Warhol, you and the Dali Llama on the cover of Time, for God's sake. It has all happened so fast."

"I know, it has, hasn't it? These are my favorites," I said, reaching over to the corner of the desk. They were toy models, released in limited editions, of the bus, diner, and Rocco's Harley.

"Don't die on me," Marian whispered. "I don't know what I would ever do without you."

CHAPTER XXXIV

Den of Thieves

I arose a little later than usual with a kink in my neck from sleeping in my office chair the night before. Putting my hands on my head, I pushed from side to side, cracking every vertebra as I walked to the kitchen for a cup of coffee before heading off to the showers. I was met around the ceremonial "coffee bean altar" by most of the group, with the exception of Simon and Bruno, who were at the MTV3 production trailer out at Central Park. The rest of us however, were busy preparing java to our liking, or grabbing the favorite part of the paper. All hands seemed to be scrambling for one thing or another, when Marian came through the door.

Everyone had forgotten for the moment, due to pounding heads and bloodshot eyes, the magnitude and ramifications of what I had told them just the night before... everyone except Rocco and Marian that is. They appeared to be distraught by the realization that things may not always be as they have been and that the Mode may need to survive on its own, without me. I looked both of them straight in the eyes as I passed by.

"Everything is as it should be," I whispered. "Give me all you have today and we'll make this show the biggest and best ever." Marian gave me a hug and Rocco pulled down his mirrored sunglasses, just far enough to expose his blood red eyes. He smiled and gave me the thumbs up.

We arrived at Central Park in the late morning and took up refuge at our production trailer just behind the stage. Summer storm clouds had been moving across the eastern coastline since early morning, and even though the concert wasn't set to start until six-o'clock that evening, well after the peak heat of the day, the chance of rain was becoming more and more threatening as time passed.

Early arrivers to the event had been camping out for days and police from all five boroughs were called in to assist in crowd control. By mid-day, attendance numbers were estimated at two hundred thousand, and because this event was not ticketed like some of our earlier events, the park needed to be closely monitored to make sure there was as little trouble as possible. A short time later, we met up with Simon and Bruno at the MTV3 production trailer and watched on their monitors the pre-production gyrations the crew had to go through to coordinate a show of this magnitude.

The production schedule had Ice set to be the opening act and Marian and Shorty to join him for the opening number. Then, I would take the stage with Simon and Rusty, while Buzz and Trace brought cars behind a huge curtain. Baptisms and confessions would follow, before wrapping up with the Sermon of the day.

This crowd at Central Park looked quite a bit different from the one we attracted at Carhenge, or any of our earlier events for that matter. For one thing, they were much younger and a lot more culturally diverse. There were the usual Motee followers of course, but quite a large number of people were there because of the herd instinct, because it was the hottest show in town and not because they had thirsty spirits. This element always bothered me. They were decent people, but they weren't seeking inner unity. They were after outer sensationalism.

To make matter worse, because we had allowed the city of New York certain marketing rights, in exchange for allowing us to use the park free, it seemed greed had gotten the better of them. There was Motorishi merchandise everywhere, bumper stickers and T-shirts being sold from every corner of the parking lots and walkways. Countless caravans of people consumed hot dogs, popcorn, and peanuts, while street vendors called out to the crowd, like baseball games, riding three-wheeled bicycles stuffed with overpriced concessions. There were many biker clubs, as well as car clubs, bearing Motee symbols and slogans on leather jackets, headbands, and antennae balls.

Of course, the "lunatic fringe" were there in all their psychopathic glory. Charlatans mimicking me were dressed in wild costumes and pretended to perform miracles on people and their cars. One man in particular took spark plugs, and putting them in his mouth, they lit up. They were nothing more than lasers, which had become huge selling items in grocery and convenience stores.

New estimates touted three-hundred-fifty thousand people had arrived and by the looks of it, were getting quite restless. As six-o'clock approached, the crowd began to chant.

"Motorishi, Motorishi, Motorishi," they yelled, and the wave made its way from the front to the rear of the park and back again several times. In the final seconds, the image of an old film countdown beamed onto the stage. Lasers shot through the clouds and Simon stepped out to the roar of endorphin-induced hysteria and cheers from the crowd.

"Heeeeeeeeeeeeeello New York! I'm Simon, from MTV3, the Motorishi Television Network, where it's *all* Motorishi, *all* the time. Today we have a great show planned for you. You've heard him on the radio. You've seen him on TV, in magazines and books, and you are about to see him in person!

"Once again, he has come to bring us deliverance…" he paused. "From what?" he asked, the crowd, putting his hand to his ear, awaiting their reply.

"From the machine!" they yelled in unison.

"As well as teach us how to be free from its influence!" Simon added. "It's all about living more in harmony with the larger plan of Universal Mechanics."

The crowd resumed their chant.

"Motorishi, Motorishi, Motorishi."

The lights went out and the roar of the crowd blended into the sound of rhythmic drumming.

"Ladies and Gentlemen, Crushed Ice!"

Ice's music filled the park and the crowd went crazy as he went into his number one hit, "The Motorishi". Marian and Shorty joined him for the song, and for a moment, everyone had forgotten the troubles that loomed just overhead. When Ice completed his set, Simon re-took the stage.

"Ladies and Gentlemen, the moment you've all been waiting for… The Mooooooootorrrrrrrrrrrrrrrishi!"

I walked out to deafening cheers and waited a few moments before raising my arms, in an attempt to bring the sound down a bit. After a few more minutes the cheers subsided.

"Hello, everyone. Thank you all for coming. I would like to start by telling you an old Sufi story about the value of truth;

'If you want truth,' a Sage once told a group of Seekers, who had come to hear his teachings, 'if you want to hear what I have to teach you, then will have to pay for it.'

'But why should I have to pay for something like truth, when we can surely get that for free?' asked one of the company.

'Haven't you noticed,' said the Sage, 'that it is the scarcity of a thing which determines its value?'

"Ah, you may say… This show is free! The reason I told you that story is this: Truth is only for those who are willing to pay, not with dollars, but with 'sense', with the suffering caused by the realization that we are not free. While I have allowed this show tonight to be delivered to you free, it will not come without a price. What that price is only you will know and will have to decide for yourself if it is worth paying.

"Could I have some assistance, please?" I asked as light flooded the stage and a large curtain was lifted revealing a row of vehicles for me to diagnose. They were arranged in a long slightly curved row, engines towards the crowd with their hoods already open. Simon joined me onstage to reveal the make and models as well as each car's symptoms.

"This first car," Simon announced, "is a 1986 Chevy Tahoe Truck. It has a rattle coming from underneath it as well as a squeaking noise and pulse feeling when coming to a stop."

I walked up to the car, laid one hand on the raised hood and the other hand on the right front side fender and meditated. I then walked around to the driver's side door to get a better look inside the cabin. A camera followed every move I made and the audience was able to view it on two one-hundred foot television screens to either side of the stage.

"Who can make a diagnoses from what little we have just seen and heard?" I asked the audience.

"I can, I can," yelled out someone from the right. Rusty and Buzz helped the man up on stage.

"What's your name, sir?" Simon asked.

"Jimmy Delgado," the man replied.

"And what is your diagnosis, Mr. Delgado?"

"You got a bad tranny and brakes!" he blurted out, and waving, jumping headfirst back into the crowd.

"Close," I said, "but not quite. How about anyone else?" Another man was frantically waving his hands and jumping up and down. He too was assisted onto the stage. He looked the car over and stuck his head inside the driver's side window to examine the interior.

"You have a loose muffler and bad brake shoes, as well as at least one bad rotor."

"Very good," I replied, "you are generally correct. However, let's be a little more specific. What brake shoes or rotors need replacing?"

The audience cheered the man on. He looked perplexed as he thought for a moment.

Finally, he said, "I can't tell from the little bit of information you gave me, or by looking at the car. I don't think anyone can," he replied. That was all that Simon needed to taunt the audience for some support.

"Mmmmmm" began to be hummed by those closest to the stage. Within seconds, the sound could be heard a mile away, "Mmmmmmmmmm," like a great beehive, louder and louder, until it sounded like one huge massive wall of sound.

The stage went dark and a single spotlight shone down on the car and me. I looked up and gave my reading.

"This car does indeed have a loose muffler and is in need of brake and rotor work, but the key to which ones lies in an observation of the car cabin." The camera followed my head inside from the opposite front passenger window.

"Notice that both the channel selector on the radio and the volume knob on this model are not digital. The wear marks rest on a frequency, which confirmed by the state license plate is known to be serviced by a Hard Rock radio station. The volume control is worn at such a level, and by the size of the speakers mounted on the backseat deck, that it would make it impossible to hear the rear wheels at the time of slowing down or stopping. That leaves the front brakes, or more specifically, the front right rotor, which has been worn clean through." The crowd cheered and applauded as Rusty pulled off the wheels and both he and the camera inspected the brakes. "Indeed," Simon yelled. "The front right rotor is the only one worn through." Simon continued to describe the next vehicle as I moved from one to another, dispelling common miss-diagnoses.

The clouds had been drawing closer and the sky darkened as they billowed tighter and tighter together, forming a thick black blanket. I feared that heavy rain now might endanger both the crowd and our crew, as electrical wiring was everywhere.

Ice continued to perform while baptisms were given and the whole crowd began swaying and chanting as if they all were in a daze. I slipped away from the spotlight to just off stage and began to focus my thoughts on the air around me. This wasn't much different from the tornado winds I had encountered earlier in my travels, and I wondered if I could affect them in any way. I meditated on the air touching my body until it became warm and dry. I exerted more and more energy until the wave of warm vibration moved upward into the sky. The music blared as I pushed out more of this calm warm space until a small portion of the clouds just above the stage slowly began to open.

I continued until the results of this energy began to push outward the size of the exposed hole. The stars above the opening were glowing brightly and the overall effect of the clouds in every direction but right above us was very beautiful.

When the music came to a stop many people began to look up, and noticing the stars just above us, led them to chant and cheer more and more. The moon was full and shone brightly down on the park as we continued to heal and administer penance to these perpetual sinners of the machine. Once the confessions were completed, and I was again alone on the stage, I began to address the masses.

"The Mode speaks of all and everything," I said. "It tells us that things are not as they seem. That we are not who we think we are, and that we are not awake. Nevertheless, it does not leave us there, helplessly alone with the realization that we cannot act, but only react. It tells us what must be done, so we too may exist outside the laws of accident and experience true Carvana.

"Man believes himself a God, able to do great things and influence many. However, this is not true. Man's God is his ego, and as long as it is fed, he believes all is well with himself and the world. He will even go to church on Sunday to thank only himself for all of his good fortune. To enter the kingdom of the Mode, you must be able to shed this illusion. You must break free from the belief that the world revolves around us. As we are, we are nothing but transmitters, processing energy for an unknown purpose. However, through the Mode, we can feed the angels."

"What does this teaching have for women?" a small elderly woman shouted, from the left of the stage. "I don't give a crap about cars!"

"I teach the Mode through cars because I am a mechanic, but this teaching is not only about cars, it is about the laws of the universe. It's about waking up and can be taught through any trade. What kind of work do you do?" I asked.

"Oh, I don't work anymore, but I used to be a trial lawyer."

"Then you may be right, for it is easier for water to flow uphill than it is for a lawyer to be free from the law of accident."

"What the hell do you mean by that, sonny?"

"Waking up! Being free from the laws of accident. Lawyers, like many of the intelligent elite, believe themselves already awake. This is a great mistake and makes it more difficult for them to grasp the concepts of this teaching. Regardless of what you do, the point is that many things can be learned by simple observation. Cars do not get into accidents, people do. So we must look at ourselves, whether it is through our machines or through our many other possessions. These observations taken over time can help us truly see we are not free from the machine."

"I can find that out in any book!" another man protested.

"As I said in the beginning, all that is worth knowing costs something. The cost may not necessarily be calculated in dollars, but in effort. Here on earth we value rocks called diamonds and metals called gold and platinum because they are rare. If everybody had some, their value would be null. Esoteric knowledge, or truth, is of this category. Just like diamonds found in the ground, bits of truth can be found in all religions, but you must first sift through mountains of dirt.

"Once, I found a book in the bargain bin at a famous book store written by a Guru I studied. The windows of the store were lined with the latest murder mysteries and various affairs of the rich, political and famous. Yet there in the bargain bin, was a book I already knew held many of the world's greatest secrets for only three dollars. Though my purchase was small that day, I knew that I had found something greater than all the world's diamonds and gold combined.

"But we are here today to talk about machines. The benefits we gain from machines are not without a price, the price is the spending of precious time and resources. Machines cannot run by themselves, they need fuel and need to be maintained or they will stop working completely. Oil is the blood of all mechanisms. Oil was once the flora and fauna of the earth. It is interesting that all mechanical devices man has every built, require something that was once living to feed and lube them. Without oil, there would have been no technological advancements in our world. We may continue to invent ways to synthesize oil, but we can never avoid the fact that all machines encounter resistance and friction in order to function."

I began to sense a general uneasiness from the crowd. There were far more curious onlookers than devoted followers and their energy was becoming negative.

Just then, merchandise began to be thrown on the stage, a Motee cup here, a bobblehead there. I noticed everyone had become so hypnotized by the event; they were more under the influence of the machine than ever before. I stopped speaking and listened to the sounds around me.

I could hear, "T-shirts, get your Motee t-shirts. Bobbleheads, Motorishi bobbleheads here. Tattoos, get your Motee tattoos."

In an effort to commercialize and capitalize on the movement, this marketing blitz had gotten way out of control. Even though many would benefit from the sales of all these items, the extreme volume of products being sold in the name of the teaching did not sit well with me. I was about to go on speaking, but could not shake this feeling of growing frustration that was beginning to build up in me. I just could not contain it any longer.

"Why have you all come?" I shouted. "Are you here because it is fashionable? Are you here because you have heard this is the new cool thing? Are you here because you have nowhere else to go? Here you are in a place of worship and yet you treat it like a den of thieves!

"How many of you checked your oil this morning, or your tire pressure, or your gas gauge? This teaching is about freedom from the machine! If we don't pay attention to our cars, then we can learn nothing about ourselves!" I walked over to a bobblehead, which had been thrown up on stage and picked it up.

"Is this what I have taught you? Is this what all my efforts have been for… a bobblehead for God's sake?"

The crowd became silent. As I looked out at them, I calmly spoke these last words.

"The Mode is not a piece of merchandise. It cannot be bought or sold. It is not a symbol, a word, or even a thought. The Mode is a state of being and it can *never* share the same space in you with greed or envy or ego or hate. Those of you who in your hearts know that what I have said is true, let your hearts guide you. Follow that which you have verified in your life. Listen to your car and practice your mantras. The path to the Mode will only blossom in you if you have properly watered it with the efforts of your own sweat and blood.

"To know the machine is to be free from being one! Live by the Mode and be free my friends." I dropped the microphone and walked off stage. The audience was stunned.

"What's up with him," someone from the crowd shouted.

"Yeah, I thought he was supposed to do more magic tricks," another blurted.

"When do you raise a car from the dead?" shouted another.

I was led backstage by Marian and as I passed Bruno, I said, "Et tu Brute, Et tu..."

"What do you mean, M? My name's Bruno!" he replied, confused. He did not yet fully realize that what he had done had set into motion the fulfillment of the prophecy.

Rocco, sensing my displeasure, stayed behind to have a few words with Bruno, since he had warned him early on not to ever mess with me, while I was whisked away by Jesus and Marian in the limo.

We drove up to our office compound, where we were met by a flood of reporters. Light bulbs flashed as the herd instinct once again led the crowd of pushing and shoving parasites to surround the limo. Rocco pulled up behind us and started to make his way toward the door of our car. After a sufficient amount of muscle, it opened and he led me through the back door of our office building.

Reporters yelled questions over each other, so that no one sentence was ever clearly heard. I did hear bits that when blended sounded quite surreal. Things were becoming blurry and I had to sit down. Once we were free from the mob, I walked to my office to rest.

Rocco remained at the building entrance to make sure no one got in unless they were a part of the group and for a minute there was more or less silence as I sat back in my chair. I wasn't there two minutes, when there was a knock at my office door.

Who is it?" I asked.

"It's Rocco, M, there's someone here who needs to see you."

"Come in then."

Rocco stood there with two men in dark gray suits with ties so straight you could tell they were not a part of the media posse.

"My name is Eli Williams," said the tall black man with a shaved head. "I'm with the FBI. This is my assistant, Kent Dungwiler." They both shook my hand. "We are doing an investigation for the Justice Department of your company's involvement in a few legal matters. I have here a subpoena issued by the Senate Committee on Economic Stability."

He handed me the subpoena and a business card. "If you have any questions call me. Otherwise, we'll see you at the hearings," he said, and walked out the door.

The next few days were a nightmare. Reaction to my meltdown, mixed with the disillusionment of the fans seeing me go off like that caused a snowballing effect in the media. None of it was good. Fans publicly denounced me and the rag magazines had a field day.

The Enquirer and the Sun Times were the most brutal. They produced pictures and stories that didn't even resemble the truth and made a mockery of the Mode and of many of the group.

One cover showed Marian pregnant with the caption, "Cult Love Slave, Carrying Satan's Demon Seed". Another magazine ran a story titled, "Disciple Admits Motorishi Was a Hoax". Then there were the Newspaper headlines, "Motorishi Loses it in Central Park", "Guru Goes Cuckoo", and, "Motorishi Blows Head Gasket".

I didn't mind the bad press so much as I could separate myself from it, but I am sure it hurt the others. We decided to lay low over the next few weeks until things settled down a bit. That would give Mathew and I time to figure out what this Senate hearing was about and how we could best defend ourselves.

CHAPTER XXXV

The Motorishi Goes to Washington

As we drove towards the U.S. Capitol building, I thought about how the whole mood of our journey had turned tense and troubled over the last few weeks. Negative stories showed up in the press on an almost daily basis. The core believers felt like I'd sold out. The ones who jumped on our bandwagon were just as quick to jump off (thus jumping onto a new bandwagon) and declare me a fraud.

Fraudulent versions of the Mode were popping up, but they were either quick-buck scam artists ("Mechanical Enlightenment while you sleep!") or crazies getting in on the act ("The Mode proves that Flying Saucers are real!"). The media lumped them together with us as part of a general movement and the public wasn't inclined to make much of a distinction. My credibility was going down the tubes, and this call for questioning wasn't helping to make it any better.

We'd all heard about the Senate Investigation into Economic Stability. It had started a couple weeks ago and covered a wide range of industries, but spent a lot of time on the automobile, steel, oil and energy segments. It was no secret that some sectors of the economy had taken a downward turn over the last couple of years. However, there was a fair amount of debate as to what the actual causes of that decline might be.

Most of that debate was along party lines and had played itself out in the Senate hearings, where much of the discussion was about differing ideologies. Nevertheless, one thing had come though loud and clear as the hearing progressed. Short-circuiting the economy in any way, whether intentional or not, was tantamount to being a traitor to America. A good economy was American. A bad economy was anti-American. That was a simple line that all politicians could see, regardless of their beliefs. If the American public thought you were supporting an anti-American business policy, then your career as a politician was at an end. Our stance in all of the areas under investigation was going to rub some of the politicos the wrong way.

When they handed me the subpoena after the Central Park show, I was stunned. I never thought of the investigation as anything connected to the Mode at all. Nevertheless, apparently our influence was being felt in higher places than even I had imagined. Someone wanted to know what we were really up to.

We arrived at the Senate entrance on the north side of the Capitol building and gathered before climbing the imposing steps to the entrance of the Senate chambers. I was surrounded by the group, as well as four Federal agents who had been with us since I'd been served, to ensure I would make good on the appearance. I was suddenly glad that they were there, because the scene on the Capitol steps was chaotic. A large number of reporters and demonstrators surrounded us and the agents had to close around me and push their way through the crowd. While the reporters called out questions, demonstrators from various economic factions yelled their slogans and protests. The Federal agents were joined by Capitol Police who dispersed the crowd enough to let our group pass.

As we began climbing the steps, another party began to descend on the opposite side. I looked closer and recognized Mitch Murphy in the center of the group. At that same instant, he looked up and saw me. We both came to a stop at the halfway point on the stairs. A lot of the past and even some of the potential future came very clear to me at that moment.

"Doing a little business with the Senate today, Mitch?" I asked.

"Just making my views known to a few folks on the hill, as is the right of any American citizen," he answered with a smirk. "Are you sure that you don't want to take a last minute stand under the Fred banner? We could probably make a lot of this annoyance go away, you know."

"Mitch, we both know that you'd rather see me go down than to have me working for you. I think you're looking forward to my time under the microscope. Didn't I promise before, 'that which you wanted most?' Well, maybe that day has come."

He smiled uncomfortably. "How do you know what I want? You'd better save up all your 'special energies' for what's ahead of you. You smell like fresh meat to me, and these Senate boys are hungry."

I smiled at him. "I hope your tracks are covered."

"Well, gotta go oppress the masses!" His walk faltered a moment. "Have a nice day!"

With that, he and his entourage moved down the steps. The group stood around me stunned, uncomprehending, not knowing who Mitch was or what had just transpired between us. However, I could feel it. I was walking into a trap, and Mitch had his hand in setting it.

Mathew and I had talked before about how to handle the questioning. We both agreed that I had nothing to hide and while the Mode was bound to have an impact on a variety of industries, it was inevitable that in the end these industries would benefit from the change. We could stand our ground knowing that we weren't doing anything wrong or illegal. I had a sinking feeling as we entered the Senate chambers that none of that was going to make a difference anyway.

The rest of the group was led to seats behind one of the long tables set up for those who've been called to testify. The floor was full of Senators and other political assistants, as well as a selection of Congressional members, here for the media exposure, and the "assistants" accompanying others called to testify. Most of them were lawyers, but there were a smattering of wives and girlfriends as well as family members and industry bigwigs.

Mathew and I were led to seats at the long table which supported microphones, pitchers filled with ice water, empty glasses, legal notepads, #2 pencils, and (incongruously enough) boxes of Kleenex tissues. As we began to get situated, there was a rise of murmurs from the public gallery, above and behind us. Mathew and I turned to look and a large group of our Sturgis biker friends, now part of a bike club called "The Mode Warriors", entered the gallery and found seats amongst the commoners, news people, demonstrators, and a sprinkling of eighth graders on field trips. I wasn't sure that their appearance was going to help me, but it sure felt good to see them there in support. Then an even bigger murmur washed through the gallery as I saw Johann enter, looking as usual like a crazy man. He shooed one of the bikers out of a seat and took a moment to look around in challenge before he sat down.

Another man and his lawyer were already sitting at a table, speaking to each other as we sat. He appeared to be wrapping up a final statement and after a few brief "thank you's" to various friendly Senators and some of his advisory staff, he rose and left the table.

They called my name and the show began. The transcripts tell the story.

Senator Armbruster: Mr. Pinkerton, we have asked you here today because there is some concern going around that your endeavors are harmful to the automotive industry, among others, and at a time when our economic well-being is of primary concern to the people of this country. How would you respond to that characterization?

Dewey Pinkerton: I'm not sure how I should answer such a subjective question. Define "harmful", "well-being" and "the people". Is it "harmful" when nature and evolution, and even 'the people', favor one path and discourage another? One might argue that the well-being of the American automotive industry is in need of a rather massive shake-up in order to survive.

Senator Brunswick: Mr. Pinkerton, when you say that, it sounds to me like you are advocating the ruin of the auto industry. Surely, that's not what you intend?

Dewey Pinkerton: (mutters; Don't call me Shirley) I'm not the one to say that it should or shouldn't succeed. Nevertheless, for the industry to remain stagnant is to invite irrelevance. "The People" won't be frustrated in their choices for transportation, any more than they will be frustrated in their choices of a toaster, or a TV, or a politician.

The crowd tittered at this, and Senator Armbruster frowned in response.

Dewey Pinkerton: As the times advance, all of these must change to meet those new demands. Out of many of the most significant industries, the auto industry is one of the most backwards.

Senator Armbruster: Mr. Pinkerton, we are trying to determine if you are a threat to a significant portion of the economy of this great nation. I would advise you to take the questions seriously. Now, it certainly appears on the surface that your, uh, movement has had an adverse affect on a variety of industry and service segments related to the auto industry.

Dewey Pinkerton: I can tell you Senator that my intention has always been to have an affect on people, not industries.

Senator Armbruster: But you wouldn't argue that, intentionally or unintentionally, you have affected these industries?

Dewey Pinkerton: Everything is connected, and for every action there is an equal and opposite reaction. However, it would be ludicrous to say that the current state of the automotive industry was brought on entirely by my actions.

Senator Brunswick: I'd like to look at the impact of one particular piece of your organization, these Tune-up Temples. Now, recent surveys in the regions where you have opened these stores indicate that the number of automobile repairs, overall, has decreased by almost fifty percent. Ancillary numbers show that the cost of what few repairs are performed has also decreased by a similar percentage.

Dewey Pinkerton: So, people's cars are lasting longer between repairs, and the cost of repairs has come down. I'd say that those are positive affects, wouldn't you?

Senator Brunswick: But the other side of that coin is that workers in factories making replacement parts are being let go because demand is down. Other commercial repair outlets are going out of business, and many now unemployed mechanics are being counseled by government re-training experts to seek another line of work.

Dewey Pinkerton: But the customer is saving money and driving a healthier, safer car!

Senator Brunswick: And I'd believe that, if I thought it was actually the case. But isn't it possible that instead of performing superior repairs, the religious mumbo-jumbo you push on your customers is lulling them into *thinking* that their cars are being treated to a higher level of service than normal?

A noise began to register up in the gallery. It sounded like lots of people sneezing. I turned to look and saw that the Mode Warriors were hiding their faces behind their hands and making fake sneezing noises that sounded an awful lot like the word "Bullshit". I turned back to the Senators.

Dewey Pinkerton: But my approach *is* superior to the common previous methods!

I saw Mathew wince. Telling people that you are superior doesn't sound very good, even when it's true.

Senator Brunswick: But, Mr. Pinkerton, your crusade has all the look of an attack on the automotive industry, and this body cannot stand by while you or someone like you strikes out at a symbol of the American Way of Life. You can point to the success of your organization and claim that you are just doing business, but when your business starts costing your fellow Americans their jobs and their security, then you step into our territory.

Senator Charles: Mr. Pinkerton, I'm still a little fuzzy on the whole religious angle of your campaign. The name of your organization is "The Church of Motor Science", isn't it? Is this really a church? Or just a business presented as a religion? A smart, hip, marketing campaign?

Dewey Pinkerton: While it is true that money has flowed to my cause, much of that has flowed back out to support the teaching. A business? A religion? Does it matter?

Senator Charles: Mr. Pinkerton, I'm just trying to get a simple answer to what I hope is a very simple question. Is this church... a church? Or a business?

Dewey Pinkerton: I'm at a loss to choose, Senator. I... I guess I'd have to say that we were a business. It's no secret that, financially, our efforts have been very successful.

Senator Charles: That's true, Mr. Pinkerton. And as an American I applaud your entrepreneur's spirit. However, the Internal Revenue Service and the Justice Department do not applaud the creative way that you have conducted this business.

He began pulling out a series of official looking documents from his briefcase and handed them around to the committee.

Senator Charles: Through those two august bodies, it has come to my attention that your organization has in fact filed a claim for exemption from taxes on the basis that your organization is a religion. At the same time, your organization has made millions of dollars from the good people of this country and paid yourselves handsomely, from the evidence of your personal accounts, and lived well from the evidence of your corporate accounts. You have taken advantage of the system, sir. Moreover, I suspect that you have taken advantage of your clientele as well. I submit to the members of this committee, that you are in fact a criminal and should be taken into custody this very instant in order to be arraigned for your offenses.

Dewey Pinkerton: There must be some mistake, Senator!

Senator Charles: The only mistake is yours, sir, in thinking that you would get away with this. I'm looking at a copy of the request for tax exemption and it has your signature right here at the bottom!

The Senators looked over the various documents as the room erupted into cacophony. The bikers were yelling at the floor. Others in the gallery were yelling at the bikers. Democrats were yelling at Republicans. Finally, Senator Armbruster made himself heard and the room quieted down a bit.

Senator Armbruster: We have a representative from the Justice Department with us today. Mr. Johnson, these documents appear to have been researched and gathered by your organization.

Mr. Johnson: Yes, Senator. We've been compiling a case against this... church... ever since we found out about the possibility of tax fraud. The department has taken the opportunity of today's hearing to have a signed warrant for the arrest of Mr. Pinkerton approved by a judge and ready for immediate use.

The Senator looked around at his colleagues, who were a bit stunned. There was a thundering silence from the dais.

Senator Armbruster: Well, gentlemen. Do we have anything more to ask Mr. Pinkerton? Then Mr. Johnson, I guess you are free to take Mr. Pinkerton into custody. Will the House Guards please assist Mr. Johnson?

Four guards closest to the front of the floor all turned and came towards me. One pulled out his handcuffs and fixed them behind my back. As they walked me off the floor, I turned to Mathew who shouted as they led me away, "d-d-d-Don't w-w-worry, there has ga-ga-ga-got to be some mis-mis-mis-mis-mistake!"

I shook my head and said just before they led me out, "I don't think so, Mathew. Bruno sold us down the river. Not intentionally, but nevertheless he's given them the ammunition they needed to get at us." I was then led to a police van, placed inside and taken off to jail.

The group was stunned as they left the Senate chambers, scared and confused that they too may be arrested. Fearing the worst, they retreated to the hotel trying desperately to avoid the media blitz that would surely follow. Just as they reached the front doors of the hotel lobby, a man jumped from behind a tree with a camera and a microphone in his hand startling everyone.

"Are you with the Motorishi?" the man asked.

Rusty, fearing for his own life, as well as the life of the others replied, "You must be mistaken. We don't know him!" Just then, a car that had been waiting for a dog to cross the road beeped its horn three times.

CHAPTER XXXVI

Punchless Pilot

Mathew came to see me in jail the next day, just before the scheduled arraignment hearing.

"Y-y-you were right, it was b-b-Bruno! I c-c-confronted him and he t-t-told me the whole story. What a sm-sm-sm-sm-sm-schmuck!" Mathew explained to me how Bruno had been suckered into the tax exemption deal, and how he had me sign the document without my really knowing what it meant.

"Don't be so hard on Bruno. If it hadn't been him, it would have been someone else. Maybe even you!"

"N-n-no way! I could n-n-never do something like that to you!"

"But it wasn't intentional, Mathew. Bruno just got carried away, and the circumstances were stacked against him anyway."

"Well, everyone in the group is m-m-mad at him, and their talking about sh-sh-sh-shutting him out completely. Hardly anyone will t-t-talk to him now."

"Tell them that I said to share kindness, not anger. We've been though too much together to go at each other. We're going to need to be even stronger now!"

"Well, Rocco is the one that will have to w-w-work hardest. Especially after he br-br-broke Bruno's nose when he heard what he had done."

"Tell Rocco and Bruno both that I said, for my sake, they will have to come to terms with each other. I need all of you on the same side. Now tell me, have you tried to find the people that suckered Bruno?"

"Yeah, we followed every lead Bruno gave us and they all came up dr-dr-dry. The p-p-press guys that sold him in the f-f-first place, the l-l-lawyer that d-d-d-did the d-d-d-deal. All of them have c-c-completely disappeared like they n-n-never existed in the first place."

"I'll bet they didn't exist. It looks like Mitch may have covered his tracks pretty well."

"I w-w-wish you had told me about m-m-Mitch and how much trouble he could cause. We m-m-might have done something to p-p-prevent this!"

"You can't stop this, Mathew. No one can. It's moving according to a higher plan that neither Mitch nor I have control over. Now, tell me about the case. What do you think will happen at the arraignment?"

"Well, the case against you l-l-looks pretty s-s-solid, since we can't prove that we were c-c-conned. It looks like the p-p-prosecution is going to start looking for enough reasons to in-in-indict the entire group. If that happens, I won't be y-y-your lawyer for very l-l-long. I'll be in the cell n-n-n-next to you."

"Then we need to see if we can cut a deal. They can have me if they let all of you go."

"N-n-no! I won't do that! You du-du-du-didn't do anything wrong and we're entitled to try to pr-pr-pr-prove it in a court of law."

"Look, Mathew, I appreciate your passion, but they are going to take me down one way or another."

"No. I w-w-won't listen. We'll get you off! I swa-swa-swa-swear it!"

I could see that Mathew was very agitated by my offer of a plea bargain. On the surface, it ran against the grain of much of the teaching. Nevertheless, I had deep reasons for wanting to spare the rest of the group. It was the only way for the teaching to survive me. I could only hope that the trial would be quick and we could find some way to get the focus off me and onto the teaching itself.

Later that day, the guards led me to the courtroom with my hands in cuffs and wearing my prison yellows. They used to be called "prison blues" but too many escaped prisoners were found wearing them without being noticed, so they changed the outfit to a bright yellow jumper. I sat with Mathew at one table and the prosecution attorneys sat at another. We had just a few moments before the bailiff called out, "All rise, the court is now in session! The Honorable Shane T. Lockmiller presiding in the case of the Federal government of the United States of America verses Mr. Dewey H. Pinkerton. You may be seated."

The Judge, an old man with a very weathered look and an unsmiling countenance, took his seat and arranged himself.

He looked at our table. "How does the Defense plead?" he asked in a serious tone.

Mathew, glancing at me for a split second, rose to his feet. "Innocent, y-y-Your Honor," and then sat back down. The Judge appeared puzzled for a moment and then just as quickly stiffened up his brow.

"Prosecution will present their opening arguments. You have ten minutes." He pointedly looked at his watch, then at the Prosecution's table.

A man rose from the table. He was in his early forties, with salt and pepper hair. He was immaculately attired in the way all successful lawyers are and projected a forceful calm that made it seem like the trial was a forgone conclusion. His name was Michael Wittenstein, and walking over to the jury, he began his case.

"Ladies and gentlemen of the jury, it is my intention to prove to you, beyond the shadow of a doubt, that this man called 'The Motorishi' knowingly evaded his tax obligations, swindled his flock, and with the help of his dozen notorious accomplices, created a phony religion in order to perpetrate this scheme on unknowing citizens like you and me. This man ran a con on the grandest scale and we have all been hurt a little by it. The Government of this great United States will not stand for such an abuse of trust and is committed to seeing justice done!"

He turned and went back to his seat at the table. His fellow prosecutors appeared pleased by his opening, and the jury wasn't immune to his presentation either. They turned to glare at me, this man who had cheated people just like them. The Judge called out, "Defense will present their opening arguments. You also have ten minutes." Again, he looked at his watch.

Mathew swallowed nervously as he stood and faced the jury. "l-l-l-Ladies and g-g-g-gentlemen of the j-j-jury, my client has d-d-done nothing ill-ill-ill-illlilleg… wrong, and has in f-f-f-fact, done much to bu-bu-bu-better the lives of mu-mu-mu-many people just like yu-yu-yu-yourselves. We will pu-pu-pu-prove that the claims of the pra-pra-pra-pra-pra-Prosecution are nothing more than cir-cir-cir-circumstantial and that in f-f-f-fact, there has b-b-b-been a concerted eff-eff-eff-effort to ha-ha-ha-ha-harass my client and pu-pu-pu-pu-put him in the way of the l-l-l-law."

As Mathew spoke, or at least tried to, the looks on the faces of the Judge and the jury, and in fact just about everyone in the courtroom, took on a stunned glaze. The more conscious Mathew became of their astonishment, the more clearly he tried to speak, and of course, the worse his stutter got. When he finished his opening argument there was a hush in the courtroom.

"I'd like to call a short recess and see council and the defendant in my chambers," the Judge finally said, and with that, he rose and left the bench.

The bailiff escorted us into the Judge's chambers, where he sat behind his desk. The Judge glanced around briefly to make sure everyone was present, and then his eyes settled on Mathew. "Counselor, have you participated in a jury trial before?"

Mathew answered, "n-n-No your Honor, my sp-sp-specialty has been cu-cu-cu-corporate and entertainment law. As y-y-your Honor probably knows, its m-m-mostly paperwork and m-m-meetings with other attorneys, and the oc-oc-oc-oco-occasional appearance before a Judge in a h-h-h-hearing or in chambers."

"Well, Counselor, I must be bluntly honest and say that I'm concerned about the effect your speech impediment will have on this trial, and on the perceptions of the jury. I commend you on the success you've had, considering the impact your affliction must have had on you, but I feel deeply that this is not the venue in which you will shine. Besides man, your stuttering will drag this trial out to forever! What am I to do with you, Counselor?"

No one said anything for a moment, but Wittenstein and the other prosecution attorneys were whispering amongst themselves. I realized that I had a way to cut this Gordian Knot.

"Your Honor?"

"Yes, Mister Pinkerton. Have you an answer?"

"What if I agreed to change my plea to guilty?"

"Well, that certainly would speed things up. Why would you do that?"

"I would do it exactly for that reason, to speed this up and get it over with. It's me they want, and it's me they can have. The public wants a sacrifice and if the court threw out this charge, then I'm betting that the Justice Department has another charge in its pocket." I looked at Wittenstein.

He cleared his throat. "I'm not at liberty to say at this time. You are right though. There has been a lot of pressure to see you charged."

"So if they don't get me on tax evasion, they'll get me on something else. I'll save everyone a lot of trouble and go easy, but only if it buys the freedom of the rest of the group. The prosecution must drop all of its charges against the members of my group and stop all investigations into their lives."

The Judge thought for a moment, and slowly said, "Mr. Pinkerton, I admire your sentiments, but if the prosecution has any reason to believe that your friends have broken the law, then there's no ethical way we can make that deal."

Wittenstein spoke up suddenly, "Your Honor, the defendant's friends are not at this time under indictment for any criminal activity. They are only being investigated because of their proximity to the defendant. We have no concrete reason to believe that they have broken any laws. I assure the defendant that if he is willing to accept responsibility for all of the charges, the prosecution will cease to investigate his followers."

"You must promise to absolve them of any suspicion," I said, very clearly. "You must discourage any future investigation. I want them left alone so that they can simply live their lives. Can you promise this?"

He weighed the consequences of the deal. He would be able to get me on the charges they had. However, he would only get me. Was that enough? Apparently, it was, because he smiled.

"Mr. Pinkerton, I can assure you that our office will cease and discourage further investigation, and we will make public our feeling that your followers were blindly led into this most unfortunate circumstance and are not responsible for any of the things that you will be convicted of. It's all I can promise. Is it enough?"

He kept staring at me to see how I would react. The Judge divided his attention between us. I nodded. "I'm taking your personal word for an important concession. I trust you. Don't let me down." I looked at the Judge. "I think we have made a deal."

Mathew blurted out, "B-b-but you really are in-in-innocent! You don't ne-ne-nenene… have, to make a deal! If I'm the p-p-problem then let's get su-su-su-someone else to represent you!"

I moved closer to him and nudged him into turning around and taking a couple of steps away from the rest of the room so that I could speak to him in a whisper-quiet voice, "Mathew, don't you see that this is the only way to get something good out of this? Before, they wanted to take us all down! Now, they focus all their punishment on me and the rest of you get to walk away. You'll all be free!"

"B-b-but wouldn't it be b-b-better to have the trial and p-p-p-prove your innocence?" Mathew asked.

"Ah, but Mathew, think about it. We've been set up. We can't defend the accusations because they're fake. There's no way to prove that I'm innocent of something that isn't real. We were bound to lose, trust me. It's prophecy."

Mathew seemed to calm down a bit. "You saw s-s-signs?"

"Well, I saw 'TheGreatest Story Ever Told' and it was pretty much this same situation. So yeah, I guess you could call that a sign."

"But what are we guh-guh-guh-going to do without you? They're going to p-p-p-put you in j-j-jail! What about the gr-gr-group? What about your fu-fu-fu-followers? What about the t-t-teaching?"

"Mathew... Mathew... that's the point. The Motorishi goes down, but the teaching survives! Remember the parable of the boatman and the scholar. The boat sinks but the teaching swims free!" We turned back towards the room and I announced to all, "Let's do it."

Within the hour, I'd changed my plea to "guilty" and had been found such by the court, as well as having been sentenced to five years in prison.

While I was being processed, Wittenstein preened for the press, ensuring that they knew how to spell his name correctly, and made it sound like he'd shamed me into pleading guilty. Some of the journalists caught up to me and my new entourage, the guards, and began shouting questions as I was led to the police van. "I'm very glad that this is all over," I told them. "I'm very sorry to anyone who thinks they have been harmed by me or my actions. I'm off to pay the price. My blessing on you all," and they shut me in the van and locked the door.

CHAPTER XXXVII

Last Ditch Mitch

Three Rivers State Penitentiary, Three Rivers Texas was where I would do my time. Five years gets you three and a half on good behavior and even though technically my offense was criminal, it was not hostile, and I intended to make sure that there was no reason for my behavior to become an issue.

The wind was blowing a thin layer of sand over everything on the morning I arrived. There was sand everywhere you looked. I had always thought sand was beautiful, especially when there was so much of it that only the curves of dunes and the sky could be seen. It has taken millions of years for the combined forces of the moon, water and the wind to grind rock slowly into billions of tiny fragments of silicon glass. Taken on the level of a microbe, these tiny glass fragments could cut you to shreds, but oddly enough, taken on the level of a man, they form a comfortable soft cushion for him to lie on and absorb the sun.

There was a fair amount of press on hand to watch me arrive at the facility in Texas to begin serving my sentence, but all I could think about was the group. I was worried about how they were getting along, and realized that being away from them for so long was going to be a very lonely time for me.

After spending many months in prison, I noticed that inmates tend to fall into two distinct groups; ones who could change but didn't know it and ones who wouldn't change, because they had too much invested in their self-image. I tended to do best with the first group, and often spent time teaching the Mode to any of them who would listen.

One who could change was a boy named Thomas. I say "boy" because he couldn't have been any older than twenty. He was born a farmer's son in Kansas and had been in and out of trouble ever since his father died when he was ten. He was a good kid on the inside, only he didn't know it yet, but with the right training would do just fine in the world. "Is there a teacher in the house?" He stuck to me like gravity and quickly developed a serious appetite for mechanics. He worked beside me on the license plate assembly lines and every day would show signs of improvement.

Visits were the high points of my days. Everything else was drab boredom. Mathew came to see me first. Afterwards I got a chance to see each member of the group over the months of sanctioned visits, everyone except Bruno that is, who no one had seen since my arrest.

The day-to-day routines held little variance. You never really saw anything new. After a while, it became easier to tell the time of day by shadows on the walls and the regimented patterns of daily procedures. As the days dragged on, I fully realized the loneliness I felt being away from Marian and the group. I was too cut off from the outside world to realize the impact we were still having.

In Mitch's eyes, he had won. He had finally rid the world of the dreaded Motorishi, and soon my band of Merry Motormen would surely lose their faith and disappear all together. He had hoped that with me gone the world would forget about waking up; once again lulled back to sleep by the mechanistic hum of life. Returning to earlier rituals of raising their fists and pounding their gas pedals, they would once again destroy their cars more frequently, so he could sell them new ones, just like the good old days. However, Mitch was going to be wrong about this one.

With or without me, people had already begun to change. Even though I wouldn't be around for a while to remind them of the need to break free from abusing their vehicles, they had already become quite unsatisfied with the control big business had on their lives; a control that had been beaten into them since birth through advertising. As if a sleek sports car was the only thing that could get you a beautiful girl, or that a huge gas guzzling utility vehicle will make your family happy and safe.

This control was costing people a fortune in payments and at the pumps. A more conservative approach was ecological, predictable, and inevitable. Therefore, while it was no surprise to me that oil and car sales would continue on a downward spiral after my incarceration, it would most certainly be a surprise to Mitch.

While the Mode and the Motorishi weren't mentioned a lot in the press reporting on these trends, it was attributed to "heightened ecological concerns" and a "budding awareness of the fragility of the Earth's resources" and other general phrases. Nevertheless, Mitch knew who was responsible for focusing the world's lens on that issue. Whether or not they recognized it, people were incorporating the Mode into their lives. Mitch had won the battle but had already lost the war.

Meanwhile, in Detroit, Michigan, Mitch paced the floor of his office at Fred Motors headquarters. He slammed his hand down on the speakerphone. "God damn it, Jeremy. Where are you?" Seconds later the door flew open. "This had better be good," Mitch warned.

"Sorry it took me so long. Here are the numbers you requested. You're not going to like it."

"Let me see that!" Mitch said, grabbing the papers out of his hand. Jeremy stepped back a few feet in case he flew into a rage.

"Damn it, damn it, damn it, this is fifth year in a row new car sales are in decline, and replacement part orders are even worse than before. We have that Motorishi bastard in jail! People are supposed to forget about the Mode. They're supposed to go back to their useless meaningless little drone lives. No one is buying new cars anymore, and the cars we sold five years ago are still running like new. Has he brainwashed the whole world? This 'Motee mentality' has the damn things lasting forever. We have to find a way to stop this bleeding, now! We can't survive like this for much longer. The stockholders are holding *me* responsible. They're crawling up my ass for God's sakes. I told them when a head rolled things would change. I didn't mean *my* head! I'm going to have to go above the Senate now. I can't play that card again. My last chance is Houston!

"Jeremy, get me a meeting with President Houston now or your head's going to roll next!" Mitch snapped.

"Yes, Sir," Jeremy replied, as he flew through the door to get out of the way. As he reached the elevators, he could already hear most if not all of what was on Mitch's desk hit the office door.

President Houston agreed to a one-on-one with Mitch, as the President was still unaware that Mitch had anything to do with the Motorishi's demise and as far as his economic advisors were concerned, Fred Motors was still a leading indicator of the health of the nation. There were times when the President sympathized with the Mode movement's desire to promote a well-informed citizenry and a cleaner healthier environment. However, big business and public opinion, two things which at times are diametrically opposed, still dominated things around Washington.

The two men met for lunch on a Sunday after the President and his wife returned to the White House from church. Both men's postures had been weakened over the years by the stress of their jobs, but Mitch who had not slept in days, looked tired and disheveled.

"Mr. President… Sam, I'm not going to candy coat it. Hell, I'm not even going to try to lie about it, Fred Motors is in desperate trouble!" Mitch said, with a bit of forced humility in his voice. "If Fred Motors is in trouble, then America is in trouble! We had thought that by remov… I mean, we thought with justice being served to that Communist Motorishi bastard's attempt to sabotage our economy, we would once again return the automotive industry to economic prosperity!"

“I think the economy is doing just fine,” the President responded, pouring himself a cup of green ginseng tea. “There was a period of decline, but it was short lived and now most sectors are showing signs of slow but steady growth. That’s what makes everything go around here, Mitch. Growth! The public is spending like never before, they just don’t seem to want what you’re selling!”

“But you have to do something to help us, Sam! It just doesn’t get any more American than Fred Motors! Hell, we’ve been the backbone of manufacturing jobs in this country since the turn of the century, the *last* century for Christ’s sake! Sam, if you don’t help us now, we may lose the entire industry.”

“The auto industry has suffered economic hardships in the past, and some of those hardships were brought on by the industry itself. Remember the 70’s? You couldn’t build ‘em large enough or fast enough, even though there were strong signs the oil industry was about to have a shortage,” the President replied. “That’s a hard lesson to learn, we all know that! Nevertheless, maybe you’re missing the mark on this one, Mitch. Maybe the decline in sales should be telling you something. Maybe this Motorishi fellow was really on to something.”

“Don’t even suggest that that pious kook could possibly be heading the world in a sane direction,” Mitch shouted.

“Don’t raise your voice at me, Mitch. I know we go way back. But this isn’t about us, it’s about the people.”

”The people? What the hell do the people know?” Mitch snapped back. “They only know what we tell them through the press and slick marketing maneuvers. Without us they wouldn’t have a thought in their heads!”

“I think you’re wrong on this one, Mitch. I think the people *do* know what they want, and what they want is change. Moreover, they’re getting it. I would love to help you on this one, but I'm sorry, there's just too big a rip in the consumer tide, and there's not much more I can do if the American people aren't behind it. I have an election coming up to think about, you know! Besides, maybe it's time we really *do* try something new… Hey, that's a great campaign slogan. I'll have to remember that," the President said, writing on a tiny "From the desk of the President of the United States" note pad.

"Mitch it's been great seeing you again, and if there is anything I can do in the near future, I'll be sure to call you."

However, Mitch didn't even hear the President's last words, as the door just barely missed hitting him on the ass on the way out.

After the latest Fred Motors board meeting, Mitch, Jeremy and Joanna were clearing out their desks. Mitch knew that the board was going to cut him loose, but it was still a shock when it actually happened. Jeremy and Joanna were just as lost as he was, and the only thing that made them feel better was when he'd promised them the chance to get back at the board someday. Mitch wanted revenge, but the scope of his target was hard to aim. The board, the President, the public? He wanted to stick it to all of them, somehow. He just needed a better angle before pulling the trigger.

A couple of days later Mitch received an unusual phone call. "Mr. Murphy?" a voice said with a thick mid-eastern accent. "This is… Sheik Mullah."

"Who?"

"Deep Pockets."

"Oh, yes, Senator Charles has mentioned you. What do you want?" asked Mitch.

"I would like to meet with you to discuss our mutual interest in gaining back our rightful piece of the American pie."

"What's that supposed to mean?"

"I mean that you and I have both had a raw deal from your country and that I may have a way to balance the scales. I cannot say any more on the phone right now, it's not safe. Can you meet me tomorrow? I assure you it will be worth your while. I'll be at the Tropyur Tao Deli on the corner of East Grand and Main at 8:00 pm sharp. I just love their food... especially the Asian chopped pickled turnip salad," the Sheik murmured.

Intrigued, Mitch agreed to meet him, but not before he put Jeremy and Joanna on identifying this new acquaintance. Just hours before the meeting, Mitch called on his cronies to reveal what information they were able to find on "Sheik Mullah".

He was indeed an Arab Sheik, from a long line of ruling Sheiks who now control over twenty percent of the oil production and distribution channels coming out of the Middle East. He had six brothers and three sisters, although his parents must have gotten confused at some point because two of his brothers were accidentally named the same name.

The only problem as far as Mitch could see, was this brother was the black sheep of the family, and had a much greedier appetite for money with apparently no scruples. Many times, he'd made money by backing some unsavory plan, usually with questionable legality, and was eventually forced to exist underground. He already had stockpiled plenty of wealth. Some estimated his worth at a whopping six billion dollars, from his share of the family oil business alone.

Mitch decided he would meet this Sheik, in hopes of forming a partnership with just such a financially flush partner in order to pay back for the last time time those bastards who had ruined his life. Mitch was never able to see that he and only he was the cause of his own problems. Nevertheless, deep down in the seats and fluids of his car everything had already been permanently written for anyone who knew how to read it to see.

At 8:00 pm sharp "Rolex" time, Mitch strolled into the Tropyur Tao Deli with Joanna and Jeremy who would lurk around as cover in case something went awry. Mitch stepped up to a table with a man sitting with his back to the door sporting a large white Islamic headdress and a black and gray peppered beard that was visible even from behind.

"Sheik Mullah?" Mitch said, trying not to move his lips in a ventriloquist sort of way, fearing someone noticing him speaking to this stranger. The man nodded and motioned for Mitch to sit down. "I'm Mitch Mur…"

"I know who you are, Mr. Murphy. I have known who you are for quite some time now. It seems you and I have a few things in common right now, hum? That is, nobody seems to like us!" The Sheik smiled and poured three simultaneously torn Sweet'N Lows into a thick black steaming cup of triple espresso.

"Yes, you and I are very much alike," he continued. "We may come from opposite sides of the globe, but both of us have a thirst for power and money. Something we deserve of course, wouldn't you say, Mr. Murphy? Of course, right now, I still have power and money, while you seem to have lost yours."

"Alright, alright!" Mitch blurted. "What do you have in mind?"

"Something that will give you back both power to avenge yourself and money to secure your future. Are you interested?"

With his back to the wall and the bait of revenge dangled in front of him, Mitch had only one answer, "Yes, I'm interested. What do I have to do?"

The Sheik reached under his hooded Moroccan Zaytuna cloak and pulled out a tattered map. The map was of the United

States but the writing was in Arabic. "This is a map," he said looking from side to side to see if anyone was listening, "of all the major nuclear power plants in the United States. What I would like you to do is find someone capable of taking out at least two of them. "

Mitch interrupted, "Are you proposing I have someone blow…" He brought his voice down lower, "…blow up a U.S. nuclear power plant? Are you crazy? As much as I want to hurt somebody right now, that could kill hundreds of thousands of people! I would be put to death for that!"

"I am not proposing anything of the kind," the Sheik snapped back. "What I am proposing is just a temporary shut down. You know, taking them off-line for a while. Just long enough for the price of oil to climb a bit. You will have dealt your enemies a serious blow and I will profit from their discomfort."

"What's in this for me, Huh? I've got to think of my future you know," Mitch protested.

"Of course you do, Mr. Murphy. Of course you do," he said leaning back in his chair relaxing and lighting up a meerschaum pipe carved in the shape of a human skull. "If you can do this, I will deposit five million dollars in a Mexico bank as early as next month. All you have to do is find someone who can pull it off, then I will deposit another five million into that same account when the deed is done. I even have for you a fake passport and identity in order for you to enjoy your early retirement in a magnificent villa on the Mexican Riviera."

"Sounds pretty nice," Mitch said pondering the pitfalls. "I will need two more identities for my assistants and a million dollars each for them."

"Of course, that should not present a problem," the Sheik replied. "It is only just that those loyal to you should also share in your fortune. From this day, you have one year to accomplish this task. I leave it in your hands. Good luck, Mr. Murphy."

"Luck is not a factor, Mr. Mullah, when Mitch Murphy puts his mind to something!"

Nine months later, Mitch gave birth to the final version of his plan. He had made contact with a couple of rebel university students who had been aced out of their nuclear physics scholarships at Princeton University by a couple of Ivy League Senator's kids. "This was perfect, a couple of promising up and coming physicists having their future career dreams crushed by a couple of punks who were merely born political royalty. I couldn't have written it any better myself," Mitch snickered.

Both students had completed internships at several western nuclear fission plants and knew their inner workings and designs with extreme accuracy. The only problem was that all individuals who worked in such places were heavily identified and authorities could easily obtain data to determine who committed these crimes. The job had to be done from the outside and they had to be very careful to make to look like an accident.

They picked two adjacent nuclear power plants to target and would then hack into the Western U.S. power grid system faking a large power demand request. The nearest power plant would respond to that request by stepping up its power output. If the request was too great, the plant would shut down to avoid a system overload. This is exactly what they would simulate only just on the grid's network. The next plant up and down the line would be forwarded the power request, stepping up their production and sending back down the previous grid the requested power. Only the plant downstream would *not* be shutdown, and the resulting collision of power would overload the plant, severely damaging its electrical system, enough they hoped to take months to repair.

The plan was genius because the ensuing electrical surge the plant would take would most certainly damage most if not all the data network systems leaving the investigation to conclude that the only possible explanation was that of electrical malfunction resulting in system failure. There was some risk of course that if the damage went too far and the wrong systems shut down a nuclear fission meltdown could occur.

You see, there seems to be major problems with fission once it breaks containment. Even if its igniting source is no longer present, the reaction itself, which is the splitting of radioactive atom nuclei, continues uninterrupted, burning its way through everything as it burrows down to the center of the earth. Pulled by that ever-present omnipotent force we call gravity.

However, the chance that that would ever happen was very minute, due to fact that the core of the reactor runs on a completely separate system for just that safety reason.

Never wanting to miss a bit of irony, Mitch chose the date of July 4th, because he so desperately wanted to stick it good to President Houston, and everyone else for that matter. But he realized that a large scale event like that on a holiday such as the birth of our nation would surely point to terrorism and much unnecessary probing, so he settled on a date just two weeks later. By spring, everything was ready. The plan would be executed in late July, a season already known to be hot in that part of the U.S. and a predictable time of increased power consumption.

CHAPTER XXXVIII

Free Bird

Two guards stood just inside the door to the complex, speaking in low voices as they exchanged pleasantries, gossip, and news. The smaller one turned and left, and the larger one turned to face the room.

"Alright, ladies," he began, walking slowly down the central aisle, "It's me, Bulldog Miller on watch for the next four hours and as usual I expect everyone to be on their best behavior." He looked to either side of him where two assembly lines were laid out for making license plates. The men working the line were seated at various stations and all wore jumpsuits. He continued talking as he walked down the line. "Pious Johnny Johnson has left to go home to his fat pious wife, his mean-spirited children, and his mangy dog, and has left you in my tender care." He spotted a man down the row on his left and moved towards him. "And I will book no shit during this watch that would reflect badly on Pious Johnny or me. Trouble will be sorely punished."

He stopped at the man and spoke to him directly. "I heard you were trouble last night, Mitchell. Is that true?"

Mitchell looked down at his feet. "It wasn't my fault."

"Are you giving me the 'not guilty' line?" Bulldog responded. "Oh no, that won't cut it, not here. If you're within twenty feet of anything like trouble during my watch, Mitchell, I will beat you for a long time. Do we understand each other?"

Continuing to look down, Mitchell answered, "Yes." Bulldog nodded, turned, and continued strolling down the main aisle.

"As long as we have a nice, quiet shift, then this will be a pleasant little interlude in your otherwise unpleasant lives."

He spotted me sitting further ahead on the right side of the line. "Oh, and we have a short timer with us! Mister Motor Man! Tomorrow is the big day! You're so close to gone that I can barely see you. You're fading out right in front of my eyes!" He affected a blank stare and put out a blind hand. I looked at him from the corner of my eye. Bulldog dropped his hand and laughed at his own joke. "Any last words of wisdom you'd like to share with us, oh Great Prophet?"

Keeping my eyes on my work, I said, "Can I get a witness?" Several men in the room gently murmured "Amen," and "witness" and "tell it." I turned to the kid seated in the line on my right who was jumpy with energy.

"Thomas, you've been a good student. Let Mister Miller see if you've learned anything." The kid glanced briefly at the guard to determine whether he was going to get his ass kicked.

Bulldog looked at me, still seated and smiling, and turned back to the kid. "Go ahead."

I turned to the kid as well. "Thomas, close your eyes and keep them closed until I tell you to open them." He immediately closed his eyes as I took two license plates off the line behind me. I turned to face him and tapped their edges together to make a rhythmic clicking noise. "Your car makes this noise when you accelerate rapidly. It sounds like it's coming from right under the middle of the hood. What have you got?"

Thomas hesitated for the briefest moment and then his face lit up as he answered with assurance, "A bad lifter, or gas with too low an octane rating."

"That's right," I replied, "Very good, Thomas." I changed the sound I made to more of a scraping noise. "Your car makes this noise only when the car is moving. It sounds like it's coming from the left front of the car. It speeds up when the car speeds up. What have you got?"

He hesitated for a longer moment and answered slowly, "A bad wheel bearing?"

I smiled again and said, "That's right, Thomas. Now one more." I held the two plates parallel to each other and smacked them together, in time, against their flat surfaces. "Your car makes this noise only after you reach forty-eight miles an hour. It doesn't speed up or slow down. It sounds like it's coming from the very front of the car. What have you got?"

The kid frowned, "A loose belt?" he answered timidly.

I smiled broader than before. "Open your eyes, Thomas."

He opened his eyes and I turned back to face the guard. "No Thomas, you don't have a loose belt." Bulldog smiled at the kid's failure. "What you have," I continued, "is a front license plate with an out-of-round bolt hole in the lower right corner, courtesy of the Three Rivers State Prison.

"You see, when the owner gets his plates, he'll bolt them on his car, usually starting with the top two and then moving on to the bottom two. When he sees that he can't fit the bolt onto this lower right hole, he'll just leave the plate bolted with three bolts, figuring that that must be secure enough. But at speeds of over 48 miles an hour, the wind whips through the small space between the plate and the car at enough force to cause that corner of the plate to flap against the car, making that noise."

I handed the plates to Bulldog who looked at them carefully, comparing them to each other, holding them up to the light to look at the spacing of the boltholes "I'll be damned. They are out-of-round."

"I told the Warden last week that die number four on the press needed to be re-tooled," I said. "Words of wisdom, Mister Miller? Here's what I have for you. We all have things we must do regardless of whether or not we wish to. But doing these things with care, quality, and pride is a way to increase the number of pleasant little interludes in all of our otherwise unpleasant lives, regardless of whether you are inside or outside these walls."

On the day of my release, inmates out on work duty gathered around and thanked me for making their stay more bearable and for all the mechanical wisdom that I had bestowed on them. Those that were still in their cells shouted out to me as I passed through the chambers, "Way to go, M! See you on the other side," and, "Keep it real, M, don't forget about us."

Finally able to dress in my street clothes, I was taken to the prison checkout where I picked up my personal belongings. I was then escorted through a narrow fenced corridor that led to the front gate.

The guard reached for his belt, lifting the bottom of his overstuffed shirt and pushed back his gut just enough to expose the ring of keys attached there. He fumbled through them looking for the master key.

"Allow me," I said, and raising my hand up, placed it over the lock. With a smile on my face, I chanted a bunch of mystic mumbo jumbo just for fun and then made a motion of all ten fingers flicking. "Hocus Pocus," I said, and the lock opened. The guard stood there for a moment with his mouth open.

"You… you could do that the whole time?" he asked, with a crack in his voice as if at any time now I would strike him dead by just looking at him.

"No, you're lucky," I replied, "It took me until just now to remember the magic words."

The guard let out a nervous chuckle. "Good luck, Motorishi," he said. Until that moment, he had never called me by that name. We exchanged a handshake, then an awkward pause. "No one's comin' huh?" he asked.

"I'll be all right. I've had to make my own way before." The gate closed and I looked up towards the sun, that provider of all life on earth and said, "Thank you."

It was mid-day, the air was thick and hot, and the wind spilled sand over the only visible road that stretched for miles until it disappeared into a sea of heat waves. The group knew I was getting out, but because I didn't know what time that would happen, I told them not to send anyone for me, and that I'd make my own way to them. As I walked down the road, I swung my old suitcase from side to side. The same one I had with me on my travels with Mac and Captain O'Connell and Winger and the old hermit Isaac, and crazy Johann. After all the publicity tours and traveling we did in high-class jets and limousines it felt good to just use my own legs to take me somewhere. Like in the beginning when I traveled as a teen.

I walked for a while and soon the prison was out of sight. The heat was distorting everything, and the road in front of me moved from side to side with such fury it was making me seasick and was beginning to feel as if I was walking on water. A boat, no, I think it's a car appeared in the distance. The image from way up ahead became more visible. Smoke poured out of it from all sides and the brakes screeched as it slowly rolled up to me and stopped. I bent down to look inside, and was surprised to see Bruno's gold tooth shining up at me.

"You didn't think I'd forget, did you? How could I forget?" Bruno got out of the car, opened the trunk, and took my suitcase and threw it in. "How could I *ever* forget?" he repeated, mostly to himself, while slamming the trunk shut. Though the rest of the group was located on a compound within a few miles, Bruno had not been seen nor heard from by any of them for the last three and a half years.

"How did you get here?" I asked, "I thought you would have gone back to New York by now."

"Naw, once you've promoted the 'Motorishi' you can never go back. I've been traveling a little here and there, doing a little of this and that, mostly collecting my thoughts and trying to come to grips with what I've done. You know, I never really did see you perform any of those miracles," he said. "Anyway, you took the fall for me, man. When I heard you were gettin' out, I didn't care how mad you were goin' to be. I just had to come see you. I needed to come. I need to do whatever it takes to make it right. What ever it takes, man. You just name it."

"Faith," I said without hesitation.

"What?" Bruno replied.

"It will take *faith* for you to make things right. Something you have never possessed. Not faith in me, faith in yourself, and if faith for you continually requires proof then you can never obtain it. Besides, what happened to me is history. I brought it on myself. I should have never let it go that far."

"Faith, huh? I don't have much faith left in anything." he said. I didn't respond as I was focused on the sound of the engine. "What is it M? I never could read what you're thinking," he murmured.

"Cylinder number four has a compression leak, and the plugs and wiring harness are shot. You better get them fixed, it sounds serious."

"Fixed? This old thing?" he laughed, "Yeah, I'm going to fix it all right. I'm fixin' to junk it! I never quite had the touch you and some of the others had."

"The condition of this car tells me all I need to know about the current state of your soul, Bruno. Have you fallen so low that you don't even believe in yourself anymore? You *need* to believe in yourself, even without proof of what may happen beforehand. What you need is…"

"Yeah, I know… faith." Bruno interrupted.

"No," I said, "a reground cylinder number four, new plugs and wiring harness!" We laughed and the car let out a loud backfire as we headed down the highway towards the compound.

After a while of silence, Bruno asked, "How about the others? I occasionally see something about them on the news or in the papers. I hear they're still carrying on the Mode. Do you think they'll ever forgive me?"

"I guess we'll see. You represent one of the twelve types and it's just not the same calling ourselves the 'Motorishi and the ten and a half disciples'."

The government had paid themselves back handsomely for what they said we owed them, plus penalties of course, and the group used what little money was left to buy one hundred acres of almost barren desert and built a compound in a little town called "Muertarena". From the Spanish words "muerte" and "arena". Its full name was "El Ciudad de Muerte Por La Arena", which means "the city of death by sand" or "Death City" as it has more commonly become known by the locals in the area.

The group had already restored an old homestead farm, which had been abandoned since the dust bowl era. There are even folk tales that before the original locals were driven away by the sands, the town was called "Oasis Hermoso" or Beautiful Oasis, since it's been said that once water actually flowed from that very spot.

We arrived at the compound as the sun waned, and were greeted by Marian and Sang Lee bringing fresh vegetables back from a garden at the edge of the front gates. Marian cried the second she saw us of course, as Sang Lee ran to tell the others. "He's here, he's here," I heard her yelling as she went from building to building. Before long everyone was hugging, kissing, and talking over each other as we made our way to the main house.

Because I'd been allowed mail and visits in prison, I was fairly up on most of the latest Motee gossip. However, it was completely different from being out of prison and back in the midst of my family. I was greeted by everyone, one by one, as they hugged me and shook my hand. It was an incredible shock of feelings.

Bruno walked a few steps behind. Marian was the first to go to him and give him a long, heartfelt hug. However, no one else moved.

"You think you can cause us all those years of grief and then just waltz back in here like everything's alright?" Rocco said. "You gotta lotta nerve, Bruno!"

"Yeah, selling us up the river, after all we've done for you!" shouted Buzz.

"I didn't know I was being set up," Bruno retorted. "I thought I was doing the right thing."

"It happened like it was supposed to happen," I said. "No one is to blame. We needed to shake off the commercialism. We needed to bring the Mode back to where we started, pure and simple."

"Well, he did that alright," added Shorty. "We lost almost everything we owned."

"You came to us with the shirt on your back, Shorty," I said. "You have a family now and the Mode firmly planted in you. We have only lost what was never ours in the first place."

Ice kicked the dirt with his boot. "Well, either way, he's not one of us anymore. He doesn't belong here!"

Bruno's posture was that of a broken man who could fall no lower. He lifted his head and smiled at me, before turning around and walking back to his car. Reaching the door, he looked back for a moment.

"I'll make it up to you guys, I promise. I'll make it right." He drove away leaving a trail of dust behind him. Though everyone was happy to see me, there was still an uneasy solemness in the air.

The horizon slowly moved up late that afternoon and we built a fire and helped prepare dinner. Everyone was engaged, everyone had a purpose, and everyone's movements formed a continuous flow of rhythmic motion in the room, except for me. They wouldn't let me do a thing but sit and relax.

As time ran on, I got a deeper sense of how big a roller-coaster ride the Mode and the Motees had been on. From the heights we had achieved just before I went to the Senate investigations, the Mode had truly fallen far in the eyes of the public. All of our endorsement deals had been cancelled. They'd closed our office in Detroit and had to let go the staff. Marian's cookbook plummeted. The Motee Rags business that Ice and Shorty had been running went bankrupt after their customers stopped buying the clothes, as did the driving school that Jesus had started. The Mode Warriors, Bruno's bike club, fell apart after repeated harassments by local police and Highway Patrol.

The hardest rejections to take were the cancellation of our MTV show, and the closing of most all of the Tune-Up Temples, with the few remaining being re-named and bought up by Swifty Lube. The popular culture had bought a story about the Mode being a hoax and was moving on from there. Even the Smithsonian Institute had removed their exhibit of Mode-related items. Even at this point in our journey, everyone remained centered, peaceful, and full of hope.

"We have something wonderful to show you tomorrow," Rusty said, like a peacock whose feathers puffed out in full masculine display. "Something big, M," he continued. "We've been pretty busy over the last three years building it, and it's been near impossible to keep a secret from the prying eyes of the locals. We all think we've finally come up with something that expresses the true nature and meaning of the Mode." I prodded for clues but there would be none that night. They had already forgotten that I had hugged each one of them and was somewhat aware of the results of their efforts, but for now was quite content not to spoil their moment.

"We can't let the evening go by without at least one small surprise," Marian said, and after dinner, they led me to a barn-like building and had me close my eyes as I walked through the door.

"Ready?" they shouted, "Okay, open them." I opened my eyes and in front of me was another old bus. This one, I found out later, Jesus had picked up from Rio de Janeiro, Brazil. It was bigger than our first tour bus, much more dilapidated, and painted a fading orange and yellow. "What do you think?" Shorty asked. "Look at the stairs," he continued, showing me how easy risers had already been installed.

"Well, I think it's great, but we can't just go out on the road again can we? Not without some major re-tooling."

"We don't have to do anything soon," Marian said, rubbing my shoulders, "Whenever we're ready… but we may *need* to when you see what we've done," she taunted.

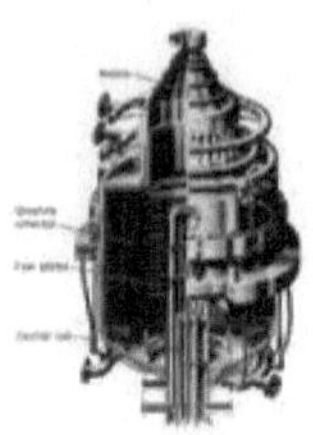

CHAPTER XXXIX

Fishing for Fusion

As we returned to the house, our attention was drawn to the television, which had been on in the corner of the room with the sound turned down. A flashing "Red Alert" banner scrolled across the bottom of the screen. Buzz ran over and turned up the volume as we all gathered around to see what had happened.

"This is a red alert," said the announcer. "A massive power grid failure has resulted in the loss of electricity to large portions of at least eight states. Official early estimates are that two, but possibly as many as three major nuclear power plants have simultaneously gone off-line; causing a snowballing grid failure affecting the Western United States, as well as parts of

Southwestern Canada and Northern Mexico. U.S. officials are not ruling out terrorism, but at this time have no reason to believe that nuclear fission containment has been compromised. Both local law enforcement and the National Guard have been called out to help control and protect these areas. For detailed information, please tune your radio or television signals to local emergency channels. The affected States are California, Nevada, Arizona, Utah, Oregon, Washington, New Mexico and Texas as well as parts of British Columbia and Sonora and Chihuahua, Mexico. Again, this is a red alert."

"What d-d-d-do you think's goin' on M?" Mathew asked. "I'm not sure," I replied, "But I don't have a good feeling about it." I glanced at Rusty for an explanation as to why the compound was not affected.

"We're on generator backup, M," he said, giving me that same look I had given him after the multiplying the oil incident with the young mother stuck by the side of the road outside of Las Vegas many years ago. He knew I wouldn't believe it, but they still didn't want to give up the ghost on their surprise quite yet, even in an emergency such as this one.

For the next few hours, we watched the news reports showing story after story of how cities all up and down Western North America were being affected. Looting and vandalism had broken out in many places and marshal law had to be enacted by the President. The media had their usual feeding frenzy by the light of a full moon and interviewed person after person spouting off "end of the world" prophecy, a habit of almost all people throughout the ages of time, when in peril to proclaim the "Kingdom of God is at hand".

However, what was most interesting about these reports was a news piece filmed in the little town of Puerto Villarreal, Mexico. I had a brief stay there with Captain O'Connell, and being a town run mostly on generators, gas lamps, and fires in the first place, had not even noticed anything was wrong as they partied away like they always did with the "celebraci6n del muerte" or "celebration of the dead".

As the night grew long, we took shifts watching the news while the rest of the group tried to get some sleep. This definitely put a dampener on the tone of the reunion, but everyone did their best not let it affect the fact that no mater what happened, we were all together again. Well, almost all together again.

In the morning, the situation had not improved much, other than the fact that police and National Guard had things somewhat under control. By mid-morning the group could not contain themselves any longer, driven by the extreme relevance of their surprise to the power disaster, they led me to the place where their invention had been kept secret for over three years.

Because I hugged them all when I arrived, it was no secret to me that they had built something special that was creating energy to run the compound. Nevertheless, until I laid my eyes on it, as Mac used to say, "I wouldn't believe it, for having seen it with a blind man's eyes." It *was* an amazing accomplishment, which came from the collective efforts of the group.

They had built a hydropower plant based on a river of perpetual motion. That is, water collected at a dam by steep canyon walls, fed by a man-made river, was forced downward by pressure from the lake above to drive large turbines creating electrical power. Once the water was through the turbines it flowed to one side, then back around an ingeniously designed switchback and lock system that used the tidal pull of the moon to raise the water right back to the lake at the point of the dam. Water that did not flow back by design was pumped up using solar panels and wind driven propeller power. The whole thing was running off virtually all renewable resources, circulating the same water repeatedly through the system. It was indeed ingenious and I was very proud they had come so far in their understanding and practical application of the teaching.

The next few days of news weren't any better. Reports continuously stated that living conditions of these areas were getting worse every minute. No power meant no refrigeration and food began to spoil at an alarming rate. Because waste treatment processing plants were still non-operational, it meant no pumping, and sewage was backing up everywhere causing catastrophic health risks. Thousands of generators were brought in to perform electrical functions and for almost a week, the entire Western portion of North America ran on gas. Gas prices skyrocketed as the oil industry positioned itself to make an outright killing on this unfortunate incident, Sheik Mullah among them.

Just then, the phone rang and Sang Lee answered it. "Please hold for the President."

"Mr. Pinkerton?" a voice said.

Sang Lee handed me the phone, "This call's for you," she said.

"Dewey Pinkerton, ah, Motorishi, this is President Houston. I would like to extend an invitation to meet with you over this power crisis. Well hell, Son, let me just cut to the chase here! What I'm saying is we'd sure feel a whole lot better if you could help us try to solve this thing. Our top experts are unable to give us a definitive reason why this has happened, and well, being an election year and all, we could really use and would appreciate your help on this one."

"Mr. President, while I assure you I am flattered that you would even call and request my help, I am not sure even I could solve such a wide scale problem."

"I assure you too, Mr. Pinkerton that your help would not go un-rewarded," the President continued. "We are prepared to meet almost any request."

"It's not a matter of money," I said. "It's really a matter of scale, not everything can be done by one man. When do you need me there?"

"Yesterday," he insisted. "I will send a plane down there for you in the morning. Will you come?"

So it was settled. In the morning Marian, Rocco, Rusty, and I, would go to Washington D.C. to help the leader of the free world save the power systems we all are slaves to. Wait a minute; something just doesn't seem right about that. This was the same government that put me in jail for the last few years on a technicality. Am I crazy? Nevertheless, I had to do something, even if it meant restoring part of the "machine". Maybe there was an opportunity here to advance the technology of the power system that the group had built, or maybe just an open window for some kind of change.

In the morning, we boarded the private twin-engine Cessna that would take us to Washington. Everything about this plane was familiar to me because I had flown this model's earlier predecessor. I asked to sit up front with the pilot and was exited to see what flight control advancements had been made. The ride took several hours and by the time we landed in Washington, I had secretly been flying the plane for over half the trip. With the permission of the pilot of course, who had always been a devoted Motee follower himself.

We were taken by limousine to the White House. As we drove down Pennsylvania Avenue, I shivered at the sight of the

Senate buildings. We met the President in the Oval Office, accompanied by this security team from the CIA and FBI as well as energy experts and his chiefs of staff.

"Gentlemen, this is Dewey Pinkerton. Better known as 'The Motorishi" to most of us," said the President. "Whether you believe in his teaching or not, you will all have to agree that though he is not that fond of paying taxes, he has a very high reputation in the world of mechanics."

"But this is not a matter of mechanics, Sir. It's a matter of physics," an advisor said.

"It's not physics yet!" the President retorted. "There has been no detection of any kind of nuclear leaks. As far as we know, the system just shut down, and that's what Mr. Pinkerton knows about, mechanics! If we have a broken machine, we need him to examine the mechanics of the system."

"Please, Mr. President, Gentlemen. I know this puts you all in a very unusual position having me here, but what is most important for me is to understand how the system works," I said.

"Very well," said an energy advisor. "Power itself cannot be stored. That means it always has to be moving or it will die, much like a shark. Power distribution systems are based on grids. At any moment, you could have millions of customers consuming megawatts of power. At that same moment you have dozens of power plants producing exactly the right amount of power to satisfy all of the demands as all the transmission and distribution lines send the power from the power plants to the consumers."

"However, there can be times, particularly when there is high demand, that the interconnected nature of the grid makes the entire system vulnerable to sabotage or collapse. When a plant disconnects from the grid, the other plants connected to it have to spin up to meet the demand. If they are all near their maximum capacity, then they cannot handle the extra load. To prevent themselves from overloading and failing, they will disconnect from the grid as well. That only makes the problem worse, and dozens of plants eventually disconnect, leaving millions of people without power."

"Was the system close to an overload?" I asked.

"That's the problem. Power usage *was* high as it normally is this season of the year. Nevertheless, we were nowhere near an overload at the time of the blackout," said the Director of Water and Power.

"That means it has to be sabotage!" shouted another advisor.

"Calm down everyone, we will know soon enough," the President assured the room. "We have a lot of research to do so let's get to it, shall we?"

We labored over the next few days going over failure scenarios and leads from citizens claiming everything from terrorist attacks, to Martians landing and stealing our power in an effort to render humanity extinct. Out of all the rumors, I was most fond of that one since it actually made the most sense. If you want to get rid of humanity, take away their power. People did not know how true this was.

Every night the President updated the country on the situation. Even though the power in the rest of the hemisphere was on, there just wasn't enough of it to reroute out west and if a solution were not found soon, America's economy would be crippled. We would be forced to declare to the world a state of emergency of disastrous proportions.

A week and a half into the blackout the President was desperate. Though some parts of the grid had been restored by power plants that were previously going through maintenance coming back on-line, it was not going to be enough if the nuclear plants were not repaired soon. After much research, I called a special meeting with the President and his energy commission, lead by none other than Senator Charles, who at the congressional hearings was the one to hand me to the gallows. Nevertheless, a decision had to be made and our options, however limited, needed to be discussed.

I stood at the front of the room and addressed the crowd. "Gentlemen, we have been very busy over the last few days researching the condition of the existing nuclear power plants, as well as alternative energy sources, and have these findings to share with you. I think it has been officially stated by the Nuclear Regulatory Agency that at least two of the three affected reactors have electrical damage beyond their ability to be fixed in the near future, perhaps taking several more months to bring back on-line. An alternative to this type of power generation will have to be seriously considered. While my group at a ranch in Texas has succeeded in producing a small amount of hydropower based on a perpetual motion solar and wind system, it is not feasible to build one to the scale necessary in the time required to alleviate this current crises. However, I will leave a copy of the blueprints with the energy commission, and implore you to look at it seriously once this emergency is over."

"In the meantime, there are currently two ways to produce nuclear power. One way is through fission, that is, the splitting of atom nuclei, producing heat that boils water to turn large turbines creating electrical energy. The problem with this method has always been that the fuel required to ignite it and the fuel spent are both radioactive, and stay that way for hundreds of thousands of years. This method has already been in production for decades. The other way to produce nuclear energy is through fusion, like our sun, which fuses atom nuclei together creating heat that can turn water to steam and drive turbines creating electrical energy.

"The problem with fusion is two fold; one issue is ignition, and the other is containment. While fission produces heat, it is only in the thousands of degrees. Fusion, on the other hand, produces heat in the millions of degrees and even though it is not radioactive for long, there is nothing in nature or that can be synthetically produced that could withstand that kind of temperature. Ignition is another issue. It takes an enormous amount of energy to cause fusion ignition, and so far, we don't have anything here on earth powerful enough to cause it. Nevertheless, lasers would seem to be our best direction.

"Theoretically, containment can happen several ways. Gravity is a great container. The only problem is we would need something roughly the size of our sun to create enough gravity to hold a fusion reaction in place. Another alternative is electromagnetic forces. By aligning molecules in a particular way, we can cause elements to stay in place, much as we do in plasma televisions. On the issue of ignition, I have this to suggest. I have found two Universities in the Western United States that are currently working on fusion power alternatives and have facilities already built and ready for testing. Just lighting one of these reactors would generate enough energy to replace the two damaged off-line fission reactors."

"Where could we get a laser so powerful that we could create a fusion reaction in these test sites without having to spend years building or moving one there?" the President asked.

The room was busy with chatter since not only did the possibility of getting the power grid back on line soon loom in the air, many were not even aware we were already this close to creating such a clean form of energy.

"What about using SDI lasers?" I asked.

Just then, Senator Charles stood up. "You're not suggesting we turn our own space based missile defense system on a United States University with the hopes of lighting an untested fusion reactor, are you Mr. Pinkerton?" he shouted.

"Senator, I assure you these reactors are ready to be lit. A few phone calls to the proper officials of these institutions will calm your nerves." The room exploded with talk and disbelief.

"But, that would show the world we have a space based defense system already in place. I'll tell you what that would ignite, a new arms race!" General Gowgem rebutted.

"What could be a greater good than showing the world we can use a weapon of war to create energy?" I replied.

"We will give it some thought and convene in the morning," the President said. "Everybody just try to get some sleep."

Of course, I did not sleep much. I was busy studying the feasibility of just such a maneuver and by morning was convinced more than ever that it would work. We gathered for breakfast, then to the meeting chambers to continue our discussion. A staffer asked me to follow him and led me to the Oval Office. The President came in with only two of his top advisors.

"I want to speak to you very frankly, Dewey," he said in a serious tone.

"Yes sir," I replied, "What's on your mind?"

"Well, this as you know is an election year, and so far my press secretaries tell me I have handled the crisis with favorable results. So far that is. What you are proposing could not only sink me, but my party as well, as those on the other side of the hill are praying for me to slip up, which would most certainly cement my opponent's fat ass tightly into my office chair. So I'm going to ask you again, just how sure are you that this will work? And before you answer I want you to know something." He asked the other two advisors to leave the room for a few minutes.

"I have a five year old daughter that as you know, is dying of leukemia. What you don't know is that I caused her illness. Indirectly of course, but nevertheless, it was me who signed her death warrant. Years ago, when I was a congressional representative, I signed a bill allowing nuclear waste to be stored in my constituency. I was so sure that the waste was secure and harmless that our very home sat only twenty miles from the dumpsite. Chelsea used to play in the fields as a child while I was away in Washington because I told her it was safe. Though there has never been a direct connection by any of the folks who have studied these things, I know in my heart that it was me that let my baby get sick. The reason I know for sure is that her dog is sick too, and the chances that they both would contract such a hideous disease as leukemia together are about twenty billion to one. I've never told anyone this story and the only reason I'm telling you now, is that I more than anyone else want to believe this can be done. I want more than anything for our great nation to forever be rid of this horrific form of energy. I want it so much that I am sure my thinking is clouded. Therefore, I want to ask you one more time. Do you really think this will work?"

I gathered my thoughts for a moment. Never in my life have I been in such an influential position. We have had many opportunities to influence the way people think, but all that paled in comparison with the decision I was about to make.

I never started out on a green platform. My original intention was freedom from the machine, not freedom from fission. Yet somehow, it all seemed connected. If the result was a cleaner safer world, a slowdown of global warming, and the beginning of the cleanest form of energy ever known, then who am I to stop it? Is one kind of mechanical control better than another kind of mechanical control? In this case, the answer was most definitely "Yes."

"Mr. President, the answer is 'yes'. I believe we do have what it takes to make this happen. But be warned. It may be a double-edged sword. It will disrupt the balance of global energy. It will make countries whose whole economies have depended on traditional forms of energy turn against us."

"Thank you, Dewey," he said with a sigh. "Thank you for your time and your wisdom, and of course, your compassionate interest in humanity. That's the answer I wanted to hear. I would like it if you and your friends stayed the night here at the White House. Tomorrow I will have the Secret Service escort you to a chartered jet to take you back home... or anywhere else you would like to go. I meet with the committee tomorrow afternoon. I will bring with me the news that I am all for your plan. Thanks again, Motorishi. You're help in this matter has been greatly appreciated. I'll make sure the perpetual water system your group has worked on gets serious consideration as a future power source as well in the near future."

After dinner, we were escorted to our rooms by guards, when I passed Chelsea's room. I heard coughing and whimpering. As I walked by, I saw peering at me through the slit in the door, a young little girl, and her dog. Turning to them, I was soon stopped by a guard.

"It's okay, Sgt. Randolph," she said, opening the door. "I want to talk to him."

"Hello Chelsea, I'm..."

"I know who you are," she replied. "You're the Motorishi. You've come to help my daddy fix what's wrong with the power. I've heard all about you."

"Well I'm going to try to help," I said. "What's your dog's name?"

"Penny," she said. Her faced saddened. "She's sick too."

"Well you know it just so happens that I had a dog named Penny when I was growing up, and she had to wear diapers just like me."

She laughed and then coughed. "You're funny. Can you teach me something magical? My daddy says you can do magic."

"Do you know what magic is?" I asked.

"Magic is when you do something that no one else can explain," she said.

"Kind of… sometimes it seems like something no one can explain but really…" then I stopped. Who was I to burst a five-year olds bubble about magic? "Look," I said, "I'll show you something."

I reached into my pocket and pulled out a penny. I started to hand it to her, but the guard asked to see it first. After inspecting it, including a hard bite from his teeth, he handed it to Chelsea.

"Do you believe in magic?" I asked her.

"You bet I do," she replied as her face lit up.

"Then hold out your hand and place the penny face up on your palm."

"Ok," she said, and placed it there as I requested.

"Think a thought about moving the penny," I said.

She made a face of squinted eyes and a twisted tongue.

"Now push that thought out of your head and just keep pushing until it reaches the penny."

She stopped for a second and looked up at me. "But that's not magic. That's pushing thoughts."

"Exactly," I said. "That's what magic is. It's really just *knowing* how to do something no one else can explain."

"Watch," I said, making the penny jump up and turn over in her palm.

She clapped her hands and before the guard could respond, hugged me. At that moment, I felt her illness. I knew exactly where it was in her but was helpless. I returned to my room for what would be most certainly be another sleepless night.

CHAPTER XL

Ascension Convention

Unbeknownst to the rest of us, a secret meeting was taking place back in Washington. Senator Charles stormed across the floor of his office. Slamming the door shut, he picked up the phone.

"Damn it, Murphy. Do you know what this could do to us? I didn't just spend the last ten years of my life scaring Congress and the public into believing the instability of oil supplies from the Middle East were real for nothing you know. Steering the Energy Commission into a state of paranoia is the only reason I have been able to keep oil prices as high as they've been. We have stock in that industry. We'll be ruined financially if a clean fusion reactor becomes active. Sheik Mullah and I have a deal, and it goes back a lot longer than my current arrangement with you."

"Look Senator, the Motorishi may be able to do a lot of things, but getting that idiot President Houston to actually follow through on his crazy ideas is a long shot at best," replied Mitch. "What are the chances it'll work? Besides, that bloated Arab moneybag won't do anything. There's nothing to worry about."

"It had better not work, Mr. Murphy," said the Sheik. "It would change the dynamics of the energy world. We do not need, nor do we desire another energy source right now, especially in the United States. Do you understand me, Mitch Murphy?"

"You're Sheikness, I mean, Mr. Mullah, I had no idea you were on the phone as well. Gentlemen, you don't have to worry, nothing will happen. They will never pull it off. You have my word on that."

"Good, because this is serious business. We would not want you to find yourself at the wrong end of your life, now would we, Mr. Murphy?"

"Don't worry. I will make sure nothing happens."

Mitch hung up the phone and pulled on the collar of his shirt. *"Looks like I'm going to need a crash course on fusion,"* he thought.

While Mitch was arrogant, he wasn't completely stupid. After hearing through the political grapevine that President Houston was going to move ahead with the plan to ignite a fusion reactor, he knew he would need an insider to keep an eye on me, and Bruno was his most likely target.

Bruno had made up his mind since he walked away from the camp that day that he was going to make it up to us somehow. Therefore, when Mitch called him with an offer, Bruno jumped at the chance. He would attempt to join Mitch's band of cronies and find out what he was up to and let me know if there was any danger or threat.

Mitch knew Bruno would never betray me, and would only use him as a lure to get me to come to the reactor where he had already planned to fail its ignition and shame fusion for decades to come. More importantly, he would use the opportunity to rid the world of me and the group forever. Letting Bruno in on his secret plan, he had nothing to do but wait for him to tell me of the impending danger. Mitch was tired of failure; everything was going to go his way this time.

The following morning we were escorted to a private jet chartered to take us back to Texas. On the way from the White House to Washington D.C. Airport, I received a very unusual phone call. "Mitch, Mullah, and Charles are all in on it. Reactor containment will fail!" the voice said, and they hung up.

Not wanting to draw attention to the call, I slid the phone back into my pocket.

"Who was that?" Marian asked.

"Wrong number," I replied.

Once at the airport, we said our good-byes to the Secret Service. It was then I let the others know about the call. "Sounds like there's going to be trouble if the President gives the go-ahead to ignite the fusion reactor," I said. "The caller said that Mitch, Mullah, and Charles were involved. It doesn't surprise me that Mitch Murphy would be involved, but who is Mullah and Charles?"

"Senator Charles," blurted Rocco, "The head of the Energy Commission! Wasn't he the dude that got you thrown in jail?"

"Why would he be in on sabotage?" asked Marian. "Who's this Mullah?"

We asked airport security where we could access the internet. We were told in the airport lounge there were several computers, which we were welcome to use while the plane refueled and our luggage was loaded. Upon reaching the lounge, I searched on the name Mullah. It turned up many Arab Muslims, but the most interesting one was a blackballed Sheik, who had been accused but never convicted of energy fraud.

"There's our connection," I said. "Mitch is in on this with a Sheik and the chair of the energy commission. This is bigger than I suspected. They must have been the cause of the fission reactor failures."

"But why?" Marian asked.

"To drive energy costs up," Rusty interrupted.

"Exactly," I added. "Fusion power will further erode oil futures, as a cleaner and safer alternative to fission power."

"But who would tip us off? It sounds like a trap, M," Rocco warned.

"I don't know," I replied, "But we can't take the chance that it's not true. We have to go there and make sure the reactor lights as planned."

"Why not tell the President? Can't they handle it?" asked Marian.

"It will only scare him from trying to light the reactor in the first place, and that's precisely what Mitch wants. If they hear there is the potential for failure, they will never attempt it. This would send America into an energy catastrophe and the economy into a depression. We have to go. We're the only ones who can help." Everything was silent for a moment, each of us grappling with the magnitude of the situation.

"Okay," said Rocco, "we do this the way we've always done things, with the whole group, just like the old days."

"Agreed," I replied. "We'll tell the Captain of the chartered jet we will need to fly to Texas to pick up the others. Then we'll have him take us to an airport that's not too close to the proximity of the fusion reactor site. I don't want anyone putting this together yet."

We didn't really have much time. The first test was set to be carried out a few days later, on Sunday, and we still had many obstacles to overcome. Getting into a fusion reactor site would be hard enough, however with this site about to be lit, security would be next to impossible to thwart. It would take all the "magic" I still had in me, plus what the others had learned, to pull off this miracle.

We secretly text messaged the rest of the group of our intentions and asked that they be ready when the plane arrived just hours later. With everyone on board, we headed to Nevada, telling the pilot we intended to spend a week at a spiritual resort in the desert.

Later that afternoon we arrived at a small landing strip about a half hour outside of Lake Mead. There I surprised everyone by making a phone call… without a phone. I closed my eyes and meditated for several minutes.

While the others questioned me profusely over the next hour, to which I said little, they're questions were about to be answered as an old VW van came barreling down the road in our direction, leaving behind it a trail of dust and a line of cars a mile long. It slowed and suddenly a dirt-covered window came rolling down.

"You still haven't gotten rid of this old thing?" I asked.

"Why should I, it runs like the day it was born. After all, I am a rather well versed mechanic you know," he replied.

"I want you all to meet someone very special," I said. "Sir Isaac Swami, of whom you've heard me speak. Through his knowledge and practice of the Mode, he has lived to be, let me see… I'm guessing somewhere around the age of ninety-five? Am I right, Swami?"

"Dewey, it is good to see you," he replied. "Come everyone get in."

"In that old thing," Rocco protested, "We'll never fit."

"Trust me, my boy, has Dewey taught you nothing?" Isaac replied.

"We call him M," said Sang Lee, "For the Motorishi."

"Of course you do. Hurry, we haven't a moment to use."

"You mean, moment to lose, don't you?" Marian asked.

"No, I mean, *use.* Moments can only be lost when one is psychologically asleep. When one is awake, a moment is never lost, it is used."

"Of course, Sir Isaac," Marian said, apologetically.

"Go easy on them, Isaac," I pleaded. "We're all a little rusty after the last few years."

"I'm just having a little fun," he replied. "It has been quite a while since I have had company."

We traveled to Isaac's camp where we would stay for the evening and get some rest before making the trip by car to Pasadena, California the following morning.

That night as we sat by the fire, the old hermit sought to sharpen our skills. He tested each one of the group for what knowledge and powers they had learned and after many hours of amazing them with the true potential of their gifts, they one by one retired for the evening. It was then he came to me and sat down.

"They are quite a variety of types," he said. "I guess Winger taught you well. It's amazing they even get along."

"Well, there was a time when…"

"But why only eleven?" he interrupted, "Surely that macho punk, American momma's boy Winger, told you there are twelve types?"

"Yes, I know," I replied, "There is one other, the one who betrays me in the scripture. Though I have forgiven him, the group has yet to."

"I see. Where is he now?"

"I don't know. He left when the others rejected him, after my release from prison."

"Well, I am sure things will work out. You have done well with what we have taught you. Though there is a temporary drought of followers now, this too will pass in time. Only next time they will be true followers and not just those who follow the heard instinct.

"Tell me about this Marian, I have already eavesdropped on enough of her and your thoughts to have my mind washed out with soap. She is special to you, hum?"

"Yes, I have never met anyone like her. I fear for her and the others on Sunday. If something were to happen to her or to them, I don't know what I would do."

"You have not learned the power of healing?"

"No, at least I don't think so. None of my teachers covered that one."

Isaac laughed. "Oh, that's right… that was Jesus Christ. The Keepers of the library gave him access to quite a different collection of books. However, I do remember it being covered in the Mode. It can come to you through moments of great compassion, or moments of clarity. Anyway, it would come in handy when attempting what would appear to the ordinary world as impossible tasks. Still, Marian seems special. Protect her as best you are able."

"She means more to me than anything. Of course, I will do my best."

"Then off you go, my boy. You should be with her now, alone in your tent, under the magnificent stars of the western desert. I should get some rest now as well. Though I cannot be of much assistance to your fusion plan physically, I may still be able to help you somewhat. We shall go over things in more detail at horizon fall.

"Goodnight, Dew… I mean, M," he kidded.

"Goodnight, you ol' hermit."

We had only one more day to get ready and the next morning found us debating how to accomplish our goal of breaking into the fusion facility and foiling Mitch's plan to fail containment. Isaac suggested we use the wind and other natural elements to conceal our arrival into the facility and to aid in cover, as we eluded guards and other security checkpoints. Once inside, it would be up to our own abilities to maneuver through the maze of tunnels into the chambers that made up the reactor core. After our plan had been sufficiently outlined, we gathered for a head count.

"We can't drive all the way to Pasadena in the bus," said Isaac. "Surely we would be stopped and ticketed, and at this point we don't want to draw any more attentions to ourselves than necessary.

"Yeah, and I'm not sitting on Ice's lap again," said Shorty.

"Dewey, you and the others go and prepare the other vehicles," said Isaac.

Everyone looked around, but saw nothing except an old rusty car up on blocks under a tattered cover and a pile of motorcycle parts.

"You can't mean that old crap?" Rocco rebutted. "The car doesn't even have wheels and the bike is a pile of scrap metal."

"I'm afraid he does mean that old junk," I replied. "With all our help we can get it running in no time."

Suddenly, Buzz stood up and ran over to the pile of motorcycle parts. "Wait a minute," he said. "Where did you get this?"

"I bought it off a scrap dealer who often travels this way," the Swami replied.

"It's my old bike!" Buzz shouted. "The one I crashed at Hover Dam. I don't believe it."

"Things have a way of finding their way back home," the Swami said.

We worked through the day preparing for the trip and by horizon rise had both vehicles tuned, loaded with supplies and ready to go. Retiring early for the evening, we braced ourselves for what might be the most difficult and important part of our journey together yet.

The next morning we solemnly gathered at the vehicles. Dividing ourselves into two groups, we loaded in the cars and started for California. As we drove, Isaac spoke to us about the physics of a fusion reactor, and of the kind of challenges, we might encounter.

"To light a fusion reactor, precision accuracy is crucial," he said. "Even though space-based defense lasers are in geosynchronous orbits, that is, stationary in relation to the orbit of the earth, igniting the reactors will require precision so accurate it could be equated to hitting an eraser on the head of a pencil from fifty miles away. Or, like throwing a quarter in a parking meeting from four miles away." He chuckled, "I *have* done that once!"

Several hours later, we approached the Nuclear Fusion Power Station in Pasadena. Rocco pulled out a map and we went through the drill one more time.

The first tests to ignite the reactor were set to take place in just a few hours. "I'd better get to work," Isaac said, as the night weather was clear and warm. In order to give us adequate cover, he would need to do a little molecular madness and cause a fog cover to come in. He slowly stroked his fingers together and pointing them in the direction of the ocean began to cause the moisture in the air to thicken. Soon a bank of fog was moving in over the San Fernando Valley.

"We need a way to get over that fence," Rocco said. "It's electric and we won't be able to cut it."

"I'll take care of that," Buzz replied. "This'll be just like the old days."

"But how do you know you can make it?" Rusty asked. "It's higher than anything I've ever seen you jump."

""I'll make it. You just be ready when I turn that power switch off."

"Okay. Good luck everyone," Rocco said, and we positioned boards from a broken wood ladder lying by the side of the road into a ramp. Buzz circled the cars once and without even hesitating, rode the bike up the ramp and over the fence. He landed hard and even though the wheels of the bike bent a bit, he didn't fall off. Raising his hands in victory, he threw the bike to the ground in front of the electric fence power switch.

Into the bushes we went. Rocco and Jesus crouched behind a hedge and cut the fence while the rest of the group strung out behind them. Looking past them to the first guard station, Rocco said, "It looks like just the one guard at this post.

They're probably on a schedule for a check-in with security headquarters and a post relief. I'm guessin' he's been on duty less than an hour and that he has at least another two or three to go. If we can take him out, then we've got a way in that will give us some time before they figure anything out."

Jesus watched the guard by the door. The guard was armed with a rifle, but it was currently slung over his shoulder as he looked around into the night. After several more minutes, he reached into his shirt pocket and pulled out a pack of cigarettes. He fished out a smoke and reached into his pocket again, pulling out a pack of matches to light the cigarette. Jesus smiled. "I know how to do this. Get Ice up here, pronto," he said to Rocco.

Rocco melted away for a moment and returned with Ice. Jesus explained his plan and Ice moved down the hedge to the side of the door. In the dark, his black skin made him very hard to see. Jesus gave him a few moments to get ready and then he concentrated on the guard again.

The guard was halfway through his cigarette and already had the smell of smoke in his nose, so he didn't notice at first when another small wisp of smoke drifted up from the top of his pocket. A few seconds later, the entire pack of matches burst into flames all at once. While he frantically beat at his shirt to try to put out the fire, Ice stepped from the shadows and delivered a quick but hard punch into the guard's stomach, causing him to bend over. He followed up with a deft upper cut that hit him squarely on the chin. The guard fell backwards, unconscious. Ice then motioned for the rest of the group to come follow him into the complex.

"That's how you put a man down in the hood," he said, while fanning his hand back and forth in pain. The rest of the group entered the complex, while Ice and Rocco grabbed the unconscious guard, dragging him inside the door.

Scanning the hallway in both directions, Rocco turned and opened the first two doors on either side of him. He peered briefly into the room and gestured for everyone to follow.

We found ourselves in a storeroom with lockers along one wall. Rocco quickly began rifling through cabinets and lockers and came up with a dozen white lab coats and some security badges for staff members apparently too lazy to keep them in a safe place. We donned the lab coats as Rocco instructed us to tie and gag the guard. Marian and Rusty took on the task with cord and tape found in one of the cabinets.

Just as they were finished tying him, he began to wake up. Marian was securing a makeshift gag around his mouth when she stopped. "There's something funny about this guy." She moved her face to within a few inches of his, as he squirmed, his eyes round in fear and shaking his head back and forth. "He recognizes us. He knows who we are. He's not a guard. I think he works for Mitch!" She continued to watch his every twitch as she spoke. "Mitch's crew has infiltrated the facility already. This guy is proof.

"How big a force does he have?" she asked, "Ten? Twenty? Thirty?" She watched his reaction then turned to Rocco. "They've got about twelve guards including this guy, but Mitch's plan isn't completed yet. They still have to work under the eyes of the real security and Army guards in the complex, just like us." She looked at the rest of the group then back at the guard, who even though roped and tied, was an open book to read. The look on his face told her everything. "I can read him, Dewey," she said excited. "Just like you taught me, I can hear everything he's thinking without him even saying a word."

Rocco squinted. "Well, that's a good thing to know. I'll have to be more careful about what I'm thinking in front of you! It makes sense that there'd be more where this guy came from. It also means that they may not be as slow to shoot as the Army might be. We're not civilians; we're the enemy." Rocco took the guard's handgun.

"Don't you use that, Rocco," Marian said. "I know you know how to shoot, but that's a road we don't want to go down."

Rocco's face became tense with anger, and then he relaxed. "All right, but don't blame me if things get bad" he said, taking out the clip and stuffing the weapon in his waistband. "At least I can scare somebody with it."

He went to a small refrigerator in the corner of the room. Opening it, he looked inside for a few moments before pulling out various jars and stuffing them into his jacket pockets.

"What on earth are you doing?" Marian asked.

He answered without turning, "If I can't have a loaded weapon, I can at least use some alternative ammunition." Rocco signaled us and we followed him out of the room and down the hallway towards the reactor core.

The complex was laid out in concentric circles, similar to the Pentagon, with the control room and fusion core at its center. We had already penetrated the first layer. Rocco instinctively lead us to a spoke-hallway ending in a "T" that made the entry into the next ring. He called Simon and they whispered back and forth a bit heatedly for a moment.

Finally, Rocco laced his hands together and Simon stepped into the human stirrup. He was lifted towards the ceiling, pushed open one of the air vents and made his way into the space between the ceiling and the top of the building. Rocco then herded us back around the corner.

A few moments later, a few fingers made their way out of the vent opening and waved, then pulled back. Rocco turned to the group and held his finger to his lips, indicating silence. A couple of minutes later we could hear the sound of footsteps and some brief words as a guard came towards the hallway.

The fingers appeared again and, using his Finger Zen, Simon relayed that there were two guards, who were armed, walking side by side down the hallway. The first guard was taller than the second one was and they were about two feet apart. He then signaled a countdown until the guards would reach the connecting hallway.

Rocco motioned us back to make sure we weren't seen, then pulled two of the jars out of his pockets and handed them to Ice who was just behind him. He then pulled two more jars out of his pockets, and with one in each hand, studied Simon's counting fingers. When his countdown reached zero, Rocco waited a beat, took a deep breath, and stepped into the center of the connecting hallway, his right arm poised to throw.

While his feat of bringing down the thief at the grocery store years ago was impressive to Marian, it was nothing compared to this studied attack. He launched the first jar, then the second in a blur of motion. Rocco had barely turned when Ice tossed him the next two jars. He caught both and threw one from his right hand without breaking the motion, when he stopped.

"O.K. everybody, let's go." We surged around the corner to see the two guards lying in a small heap, unconscious, with what looked like various jams spattered on the floor. "Mind the glass," said Rocco. He helped Simon back down from the ceiling as Ice checked the pockets of the guards and took their guns, throwing them back up into the air vent.

"Simon and Sang Lee, drag these two losers back to the locker room and tie them up with the other one. Then stay there and guard them. Jesus, clean up this mess so no one can tell that we've been here, then stay here and keep an eye out. If you see trouble, come running."

"Wait a minute. You thin' just because I'm Mexican, I have to clean up?" Rocco shot him the look of death. "Alright, alright, I do it!" Pulling a walkie-talkie off the belt of the shorter guard, Rocco stuffed it into his pocket, and turned and led the rest of us into the next ring.

After scouting ahead a bit, Rocco came back to us. "We're getting close to the control room," he said. "We have to get by one more patrol pair to enter the inner ring. I'm out of ammo *and* ideas. Anybody got anything?" Trace and Rusty, who had been talking to each other in low tones for the last few minutes, came forward and explained their idea to Rocco. After a moment, they brought Mathew into the discussion, and Rocco moved the rest of us back out of sight to the inner hallway.

Rusty and Trace disappeared around the corner and Rocco and Mathew stood where they could see them. After a moment Rocco gave Mathew a hand signal, and Mathew raised the walkie-talkie to his lips and said smooth and stutter-free, "I've got two Motees in the inner ring, send backup!" He and Rocco then moved back towards us, leaving Trace and Rusty in the hallway.

When two guards came down the hallway, they saw Trace and Rusty standing next to each other, both with their hands in the air.

"Hey Dudes, we were hoping to put the sneak on ya, but ya caught us before we tubed," said Trace in his heaviest surfer-patois.

"Yeah," said Rusty in dim-witted agreement, as he and Trace began casually walking towards them.

The guard on the right raised his rifle in Trace's direction. "Stop right there!" His partner finally reacted by taking aim at Rusty, but both of them just kept walking. The guards exchanged a quick glance towards each other. "Stop or we shoot!" They were mystified as Trace and Rusty looked at each other and smiled. Raising their rifles, the guard and his partner pulled the triggers.

The shock to professional shooters of nothing happening was profound. As the guards continued to pull their triggers, examine their safeties, and look at each other in hopeless confusion, Trace and Rusty each grabbed a guard and head-butted them with enough force for us to hear it around the corner. They slid to the floor, unconscious.

Trace looked at Rusty and smiled. "Boy, I'm glad that worked. My life was in your hands. What did you do?"

"I changed the make-up of the gunpowder so that it was an inert compound."

"Wow, that's subtle," Trace replied with admiration. "I would have just melted the firing pin. I twitched pretty good when they pulled the triggers, how about you?"

"Yeah, I still expected to hear a big boom."

Trace re-appeared around the corner and motioned us into the final hallway as Rocco pulled the walkie-talkies from both of the guards. He put one in his pocket and gave the other one to Trace. "Take this back to Sang Lee, Simon, and Ice. If trouble comes, get on the air but remember that they'll be listening too. Mathew, you and Rusty stay here and keep your eyes open. Same drills for you, if you see trouble, shout out."

Looking in both directions, Rocco grinned at Marian and me, the only two left without assignments. "O.K. Boss, next stop is the control room. After that, it's your show."

Marian and I followed right behind him as he moved off down the hallway. He stopped at a door, checked to see that we were still with him, and kicked it down like a superhero in a movie. As we moved inside, we were shocked to find, Mitch, his sidekicks Joanna and Jeremy… and Bruno.

"Well, Pinkerton, I was right all along. I knew you'd show up," said a satisfied-looking Mitch from across a row of computer stations. "I was betting that security wouldn't be able to stop you either. However, it doesn't matter either way because I've just finished cutting all power to the electron alignment emergency backup systems. Containment can't be saved now."

My eyes were glued on Bruno. I couldn't have been more surprised, seeing him there. "Mitch, you are insane. What do you get out of this?"

"Revenge!" he yelled, "For everything… on everyone!"

"They'll find out about your hand in this, you know."

"No they won't! I'll be long gone by the time they finish investigating. All they're going to find are the remains of you and your group of mechanical fanatics! You'll be the one implicated in this terrorist attack. The Mode will finally end like all the other religious whackos: David Koresh in Texas, or Jim Jones in Guiana before him. Even Jesus Christ couldn't save himself!"

Jeremy opened a door just behind them. Joanna hurried through as Mitch turned around to face Bruno. "And Bruno, poor Bruno… He thought all along that he was helping you. But all he's done is nail you to the cross a second time."

Rocco started to move towards the escaping trio when Bruno saw the gun tucked in the back of his pants. He lunged forward and grabbing the weapon, aimed it at Mitch. Rocco looked shocked. "What, you think I didn't know how to handle a gun in the hood?" Bruno bragged.

"Bruno, don't do it. You're not a murderer," said Marian. "He doesn't matter anymore, let him go."

Bruno hesitated a second before raising his arm towards Mitch and pulling the trigger six times, though he only heard the sound of the gun clicking.

Mitch took a breath and checked his body. "See ya, suckers!" He laughed as he went through the door, which Jeremy pulled securely closed after him to meet a waiting helicopter in a field just outside the building.

There was silence in the room. Marian and I were standing next to each other just inside the door. Rocco was stopped in mid-stride as he rounded the computer stations and Bruno was facing us from the other side of the room with the gun still in his hand.

"Now, Rocco, I know that *you* don't know the kinda voodoo that'll stop bullets or melt a gun. So I'm guessing that was you, M," Bruno said, putting the weapon down on the nearest table.

"I could have done that," I replied, "But I didn't need to."

"I made Rocco take the bullets out, Darlin'. And I'm glad I did or you would have been a murderer. Not that he didn't deserve it or nothin'" Marian added.

"I guess I'm glad it wasn't loaded either, but if it came down to it, it would have been worth it. I want you guys to know I only worked with Mitch to get myself into this position, 'cause when I figured out that he had a killing-grudge, I wanted to be sure that I was there to help you. I was the one that tipped you off about Mitch and Senator Charles and the Sheik's plan to sabotage the plant. Now it looks like I'm the reason you're all in this mess again. I was ready to shoot him if I had to, but I'm glad it didn't turn out that way.

He stepped closer to me. "I thought I had finally found a way to make amends for getting you put in jail, to prove to you and the others… I belong."

We were all speechless. I could see Rocco trying to figure out if this was some kind of trick, but it was obvious that Bruno was telling the truth. Marian moved closer to Bruno, hugging him and gave him a gentle kiss on the cheek. "Oh, Bruno darlin', what a noble thing you tried to do."

His eyes began to tear up, but he laughed instead. "Noble? Nobody's ever called me that before. No good, sure, but never noble."

Mitch was probably miles away as an alarm sounded for all personnel to leave the reactor at once. Seconds later a beam of blue light came streaking out of the sky on a path to Pasadena, California. Outside, scientists and security sat protected inside a building of heat retardant rock and glass. There were great sparks at the moment of contact. Every light bulb for miles around lit up momentarily and then everything went dark.

"They've started testing, and that was close," I shouted. "No time to talk about it now, we have work to do. The reactor is still critical. Without repair to the containment shield, the next round of laser ignition will send the reactor into a meltdown.

"Rocco, you take Marian and Bruno back to the others. Gather everyone else as you go along. Give me twenty minutes. If I'm not out by then, get everyone out and on their way back to the compound."

The three of them erupted. "Now, wait a minute…" "I'm not leaving you here without…" "There's no way that I'm just gonna…"

I held my hand up to silence the protests. "I'm kind of in a hurry here, so let me tell you why it's got to be this way. Remember the parable of the boatman and the scholar?"

"Uh, I think so," everyone said mumbling and looking at each other.

"You mean the part about how you represent the boat? That the teaching must learn to survive without you?" Marian asked.

"Yes, Marian," I said.

"But you don't understand, Dewey. I may be…"

"Pregnant with our child?" I replied.

Everyone looked shocked, but no one more than Marian.

"And that's even more reason why I'm not letting you stay in the danger zone. You and the others must carry on with the Mode. There is no other way. You must be like the boatman, able to keep the Mode alive in time of peril. Go now, so that the world may know it was not us who caused this." I pulled her close, hugged, and kissed her. "I want you out of danger. I know what I'm doing. I'll do everything I can to meet you back outside. I want you safe. If you really want to help me, be my incentive to get out of here in time."

I turned to Rocco. "Rocco, you're the only person I trust to make sure that Marian is safe. I'll be worried unless I know that she's in your care, especially now. Do you see that?"

"Yeah, I can see that," he said, dropping his head. "I don't have to like it though!" He looked up, defiantly.

"When was a soldier ever asked to like their job?" I said. He snapped to attention and saluted me.

"Bruno, go with them."

"No way, I'm in for the full ride."

"Listen, I'm running out of time."

"I'm not leaving. I left you once before, I won't do it again."

I looked at Rocco and Marian, who were still standing there.

"Go, go now." I yelled at them.

Rocco took Marian's arm and away they went. I think my heart may have broken just a little bit at that moment.

Outside, the group retreated to an alleyway leading to a storage garage where a very worried old Guru awaited them. Once inside everyone held on as the word was given by loud speaker that another round of testing was about to begin.

With the others safely outside, Bruno and I advanced on the door leading to the center of the reactor. There were two panels on either side of the room, which housed the switches controlling the magnetically aligned plasma electrons surrounding the fusion reactor core. I told Bruno to go to one side of the room, separated by two huge walls of steel. Making his way through the maze of emergency access, he reached the panel on the opposite side.

"OK, I am going to need you to repair that one, while I repair this one," I yelled.

"What? Oh no! Not me. I came along for moral support. I couldn't possibly help you," Bruno said. "What do I know about fusion containment, huh? What if I can't do it?"

"What will happen if you don't try, Bruno?" I replied. He glanced around at the room. "You have to do it. I can't get to where you are in time. I need your help."

"You know, M, I've never even seen you perform a miracle. How could I possibly perform one?"

"It only takes one thing, Bruno, and you can do it."

"What's that?" he asked, knowing he not was going like the answer, no matter what it was.

"Faith…"

"Oh no, not the 'F' word again, that's the one thing I have never had."

"Believe in yourself, Bruno. For once, show me you believe without proof. *Believe* you can do it. We're running out of time. We need to get out of here before the next laser firing."

"Ok, ok… How do I know how far to turn it?"

"Turn until it feels right. Trust yourself."

"I knew you were going to say something like that. Can't you just turn the handle from where you are? You know, do a little of that magic? Look, I'll turn away. That way, I know you can do it."

"Bruno!"

"Alright, Alright." Bruno looked trustingly down at his hand. "Here goes." Closing his eyes, he put his hand gently on the lever. He could feel the powerful vibrations of the reactor start to shake through him as he gave the handle a turn. Steam began to burst out of several nearby ducts, whistling so load I could barely hear him speak. "I think, I…" he yelled.

"Bruno, you did it. We have to go, now." However, he couldn't hear me. I pressed the thought out of my mind as hard as I could in his direction. He suddenly looked up and smiled.

"I heard that," he said. "In my head, I heard that."

"Run," I told him, without moving my lips. *"Run now, I am right behind you."*

Bruno stood up, sprinting as fast as he could towards the vault door. He made it halfway down the long curved corridor before stopping to turn around to check if I was still behind him. Seeing I wasn't there, he ran back to door. It was closed; locked from the inside.

"No, M. you have to get out," he thought to himself. I could read his mind even though I could not see him. He had helped by re-aligning the magnetic protons on half of the reactor. However, that would not be enough. I would need to correct the other half, even though the handle on my side was already broken by Mitch.

Bruno retreated in horror. *"It's alright, Bruno,"* I told him. *"The Mode must now exist without me. Tell the others my work here is through. It will be your time to feed me, for I must now dwell amongst the Angels."* He ran as fast as he could, down the corridors and out of the building.

I raised my hands, and looking up addressed my destiny, *"All that is and ever was or ever will be, blend together in me."*

The second ignition attempt used two laser beams, which hit the building with the same fury and beauty as the first. With my hand on the broken handle, I closed my eyes, meditating harder than I ever had before. My body was electrified, my mind centered and in focus, my will "one" with the universe. I was truly awake, both mentally and psychologically. All that the Mode had taught me came together in the moment.

One by one, the plasma electrons aligned. This time they managed to stay connected for a few seconds longer, long enough to cause a fusion reaction. Suddenly, there was a loud crack, as if a thousand lighting bolts had struck at the same time. The building jerked back and forth and everything around me shook violently, as a great, white, beam of light shot through the center core of the reactor.

Time stood still, and between the stillness I began to feel my being transform. My body became ashes and my being, Carvana.

Bulbs lit up around the test site and down the streets for miles and began popping as the overflow of current reverberated through the area. Ignition had begun, and the birth of this new energy source on earth, as mystical as the sun itself, was finally realized.

Bruno scrambled through the fence outside the compound and made his way to the garage where the Swami and the others awaited him, only to find the rest of the group expecting another arrival as well. As he approached them, they all looked beyond him in disbelief.

"He didn't make it." Bruno cried. "He sacrificed himself so that we may live."

One after another, they each went up to Bruno and made some sort of accepting gesture: a hug, a handshake, a nod of the head. Rocco came last. He stopped in front Bruno and opened his arms. "You have no idea how different it is when you're not here. Now we feel whole again." Bruno stepped into Rocco's embrace. Rocco brought his arms down tightly at Bruno's sides and stepped even closer. Bruno could feel Rocco reach completely around him and lock his hands together behind his back. Then Rocco lifted Bruno just the slightest bit; not much, but enough to get his feet off the ground and make him completely vulnerable. Rocco leaned into Bruno's ear and said quietly, but clear enough for everyone to hear, "You know, I could snap your spine in two right now. It would just take a second. No one could stop me, and you couldn't squirm enough to save yourself."

Bruno smiled slightly, "Part of me would be just fine with that. It would even the scales in a very simple and straight ahead way."

Rocco seemed to stop breathing for just a moment, "And that's why I'm not going to do it, you bastard. You are part of us, part of the Mode, and I just can't bring myself to hurt you."

"Trust me, man. I've beat up on myself enough to satisfy you and the group. Guilt is the heaviest baggage to carry, and I've been toting around a full wardrobe."

Rocco set Bruno down and fussed about him for a moment, straightening his collar and brushing off a spot of dust.

Later that afternoon the President met with a few of his advisors privately. He was elated, spouting off new campaign slogans like a kid with Tourette's syndrome. "We're the party that took the 'Con out of Fusion'" and "'Fusion's no Illusion vote for Houston'." "Damn, I love this job," he shouted.

Gathered at the compound a few days later, the group was still grieving. It never crossed their minds that I might not be with them forever. They were sitting in the house when all of a sudden the television caught their eye.

"Rusty, everyone, you gotta see this," said Marian. They turned up the volume while the news showed a piece about the President's daughter.

"We have some good news to report to you all this evening. The life threatening disease Leukemia seems to be in remission in the first little lady, Chelsea. As a matter of fact," they continued, "Doctors can't seem to find cancer anywhere in her body anymore. When asked how she was feeling, Chelsea had this to say, 'Thank you, Motorishi…"

Later that night, the group lit a fire, as they always did, in a large pit dug for just such a purpose. Lying down on the ground, looking up at the stars, Rusty turned to Marian. "Please," he whispered, "Tell us a story for old time sake."

Marian proudly stood up and addressed the gathering. "How can I resist?"

"What is Karma?" a student was asked by his Master.

"I believe it is cause and effect," said the student.

"That is hardly a satisfactory answer," replied the Master. "Look at that." He pointed to a procession passing in the street.

"That man is being taken to be buried. Is that because he was born with the DNA, which caused him to live a life with which he committed the acts that led him to his ultimate demise? Or was it because nobody stopped him?"

"I am not sure," said the student. "Surely, if he had not been born from those parents, he may have traveled a different path"

"That is true," said the Master. "But would the ending have turned out any different?"

What no one knew in all of this was that Mitch Murphy was already gone with his leeches Jeremy and Joanna for several days now, having fled with their bag of Arab money now safely in a Mexican bank. While they weren't quite on their way to a life of leisure on the Mexican Riviera, having to hide from both U.S. and Arab enemies, they at least had made it safely out of the country.

However, deep in the jungles of Mexico, Mitch and his gang of idiots honked their horn and yelled at the man in front of them who was driving very slow in an old rickety truck overstuffed with chickens on a one-lane dirt road. Furious, Mitch impatiently beeped his horn repeatedly, as chicken feces splattered on the windshield so thick even the wipers only smeared it around.

"It's not supposed to be like this," he yelled. "I'm supposed to be on a beach, with a big umbrella above me and several small ones in my drinks. I've had it!" He shouted, as he jerked the wheel of the car left and hit the gas to try to pass the old truck. This scared the chickens even more and feathers flowed freely, sticking to the already wet car.

"I can't see a damn thing," Mitch blasted and the car flew over a cliff and down into the ravine below.

The driver of the truck, an old Indian smiled and said to his dog, "They expect this truck to go slow and so I do," he chuckled and lit his pipe humming an old ancient song; "Viva buena y consiga lo que usted merece" or "live good or you get what you deserve."

Later that night a special news report showed yet once again the little village of Puerto Villareal, Mexico, and the never-ending parade of the dead as the body of Mitch Murphy along with two other bodies were loaded into the back of the VW hearse.

Rusty turned off the television and asked everyone to gather.

"I know M would have been very proud of all of us," he said, "and perhaps mostly of you, Bruno. We must do what M would have wanted us to do. We must carry on the Mode without him. Besides, if what he tells us is true, then we must struggle to awaken, and with the energy caused by our efforts we will feed him… wherever he is."

"Tell us another story, Marian," the group asked. "Tell us another one for M."

"Let's let Rusty tell one," she replied. "After all, he is our teacher now."

Rusty stood up and raising his hands said, "Speaking of feeding M, I would like to tell you more about the food chain.

The food chain I speak of does not stop at humans on the top, nor the smallest insect or plankton on the bottom of the sea. The food chain encompasses everything from the most distant stars and galaxies to the minutest particles of atoms, both the finer matter of thought and the cold course matter of metal substances.

"Remember, everything vibrates, everything radiates, everything feeds on everything else, and we humans are not at the top, but exist somewhere in the middle. We cannot verify for ourselves, as we currently are, merely sleepwalking through life, what *does* exist at the top. However, we can begin to understand at least one level above and one level below us. Once we thought ourselves at the very center of the universe, a place reserved only for God himself. We are not so special that the chain could not exist without us. Dare to wonder, dare to search for truth no matter where it leads, dare to wake up and feed those above us. Dare to live the Mode. Let me explain with another story.

A boy had climbed a tree. When the wind blew, the tree split, the boy fell, and his leg was broken. "The tree is strong, for it has broken my leg," he said. "It is the wind which is stronger than me," said the tree.

However, the wind said that the hill was stronger, since it could stop the wind. The boy of course, thought that the hill was strongest, to be able to stop the wind, which split the tree, which broke his leg.

"No," said the hill, explaining that the mouse was strong for it could burrow into the hill. However, the mouse denied this: "For I can be killed by the cat." Therefore, the boy thought that the cat must be strongest of all.

"Not so," the cat explained that it could be caught by a rope, and the boy thought that this, then, must be the strongest thing.

The rope, however explained that it could be cut by iron, which was therefore stronger. The iron, in its turn, denied being strongest, since it could be made soft by fire.

The boy now thought that the fire must be strongest, to soften the iron, which cut the rope, which bound the cat, which caught the mouse, which undermined the hill, which stopped the wind, which split the tree, which broke the leg of the boy.

The fire then said that the water was stronger; and the water claimed that the canoe was yet stronger, for it cleft the water. But the canoe was overcome by the rock, and the rock by man, and man by God, so God is the strongest of all.

Then the boy knew that God could overwhelm man, who breaks the rock, which overcomes the canoe, which cleaves the water, which puts out the fire, which softens iron, which severs the rope, which binds the cat, which kills the mouse, which undermines the hill, which stops the wind, which splits the tree, which breaks the leg of the boy.

"Wait a minute, Rusty. I'm having some terrible thoughts," Shorty said, with a squeak in his voice. "Who feeds on us?"

"The Motorishi of course, so be sure to give him something good to eat." Just then, everyone looked at Shorty, who was looking at the size of himself.

"Well at least a tasty appetizer if nothing else..."

www.ingramcontent.com/pod-product-compliance
Lightning Source LLC
Chambersburg PA
CBHW030823310726
48980CB00006B/604/J

9780615264851